Praise for *En*

'The brilliant Emma Cowell ...
laughter, healing and hope in her delicious novels'
Adriana Trigiani

'Beautifully written. Emma Cowell writes with warm
assurance and brings the Greek setting to life'
Sue Moorcroft

'Such an emotive tale of love and loss'
Rosanna Ley'

'A delicious slice of Greek life. A beautiful love story'
Jo Thomas

'A beauty'
Peter Andre

'Breathtaking world building, stunning imagery and genuine
emotion cooked into every page. I adored it'
Helen Fields

'A sweeping novel about sisterhood, courage and new
beginnings that will inspire and delight'
Tessa Harris

'When you look up from your train seat/sofa/garden sun bed
this summer, you'll be genuinely confused you're not in a
taverna knocking back an ouzo'
Caroline Corcoran

Emma Cowell lives in Cornwall with her husband, Tony, and their fur baby, a Russian Blue called Papoushka Gerald Cowell. A former actress and BBC presenter, Emma is currently Head of Philanthropy for national charity Together for Short Lives. Outside of work, Emma is a keen angler and held a Cornish record for over ten years until her crown was toppled. She is yet to get over it but tries to keep calm by practising yoga. Also a keen linguist, Emma is attempting to learn Greek to maintain her love affair with the country where she has set her novels. She is yet to achieve a level of proficiency outside of tavernas and bakeries. *The Island Love Song* is Emma's third novel.

For more info, visit www.emmacowell.com. You can follow Emma on Instagram @emmalloydcowell or Twitter @emmalloydcowell.

THE
Island
Love
Song

EMMA COWELL

Published by AVON
A division of HarperCollins*Publishers* Ltd
1 London Bridge Street
London SE1 9GF

www.harpercollins.co.uk

HarperCollins*Publishers*
Macken House 39/40 Mayor Street Upper
Dublin 1 D01 C9W8
Ireland

A Paperback Original 2024
1
First published in Great Britain by HarperCollins*Publishers* 2024

A catalogue copy of this book is available from the British Library.

ISBN: 978-0-00-862452-1

Set in Sabon LT Std by HarperCollins*Publishers* India

Printed and bound in the UK using 100% renewable electricity at
CPI Group (UK) Ltd

To my twin flame … Greece

A twin flame: It is based on the premise that one soul can be split between two bodies creating the deepest possible spiritual connection; much more than soul mates...

Prologue
Ella

Hydra, November 1997

Ella's eyes fluttered open and the first thing she saw was Harrison. They were finally together on Hydra, and it was perfect. Her childhood holiday memories lived within the rockfaces that hugged the port and lingered beneath the roof of her mother's house where they were staying. Hydra was Ella's birthplace. Being with Harrison on her island was like living in a ten-day fairytale. It felt like she was home; in every sense.

She stretched her arms after slipping out of bed then opened the drapes. The heartbeat of Hydra was already stirring behind the fabric. Bathed in crystal clear light, the Greek island pulsed with romance. The clip-clop sounds of the mules' hooves bounced off the buildings around the harbour. A dawn mist had surrendered to spreading sunbeams, allowing a fishing boat to emerge like a ghost through the dissolving haze. The island began to come to life. Cobbled streets, hidden alleyways ... it was breathtaking.

Ella loved Hydra. It possessed an indescribable magical power and had always answered her pleas. That morning, as Harrison slept, she asked the island to keep their love alive. Even though she was sacrificing everything she'd planned, it was all for him. For Harrison.

'Let us be together for a thousand years and longer,' she whispered.

She smiled as she watched him doze, lightly running her fingers over his chest. He was irresistible; she couldn't help but reach out to touch him. Ella wanted to drink him in, remember every mark, muscle and line on his body. They were going to be parted in January, albeit for only a few weeks. Then she would leave university to join him on tour with his band. She would exchange her dream for his, in the hope it would become theirs. The cost would be her education.

Ella wanted to travel the world as a photographer after university, but she couldn't imagine being apart from Harrison and she knew he felt the same. They'd agreed she would go with him out into their new beyond, breaking through undiscovered horizons together. At least she would still experience other countries; the idea of existing nomadically on the road excited her enormously. It was another version of the life she'd envisioned and one she desperately wanted to share with him.

'Morning, love.' Harrison's deep cockney accent cut through her thoughts. 'I have you for another day, my beautiful El.'

The sound of his deliciously rough voice sent a shiver along her spine. His warm brown eyes sparkled with mischief as he pulled back the sheet, inviting her into his strong arms. Ella was easily enticed into his embrace.

'I love you, Harri,' she said, sinking into his body.

He kissed the side of her head, inhaling her scent, then replied, 'I know you do, love. I know.'

Ella's breath suddenly caught in her throat as she realised he had never said the words 'I love you' in response to her declaration. Or had he? She began to panic and doubt her instincts. As her eyes travelled around her mother's holiday home, the exposed stone walls almost shifted on their foundations and the scent of oregano on a breath of wind drifted through the windows as if Hydra had answered her unspoken question, but she couldn't interpret its response.

Again, she silently begged the island to show her what love was supposed to feel like.

Chapter 1
Ella

Ella looked around at her unpacked boxes in her flat in Camden. The only ornament that indicated someone lived there was a framed photograph of her with Georgia, her sister, and their late mother, Anna. The three of them were washed with golden Greek light as the diminishing embers of the island sun kissed their skins.

It was the sole reminder of Hydra Ella permitted. She had once loved it more than anywhere on earth, but its illusion had expired. It was no longer precious to her. Any stored picture-postcard snapshots were from before she was broken, never to be mended. Before Harrison. She knew – whether awake or in dreams – she'd never love anyone like she'd loved him. He was careless with her heart, but upon reflection, she'd given it away too easily almost twenty years ago. She'd known he would be unable to look after it, and had offered it to him anyway.

Back then, as a love-struck teenager, choosing him was perhaps an unknown urge to cause herself pain, to dwell in that precarious space of feeling almost complete, convincing herself he felt the same as she did. Her stomach would coil in

4

anxious knots; being with him was dangerously thrilling and being without him for even an hour was the sweetest torture she'd ever known. She'd been ill-equipped to process how intensely they had needed each other; they were so young – only eighteen. Her first and, as it transpired, her only love. They'd lived in a dysfunctional loop of creative madness, deeply romantic and passionate, existing on a ledge hovering above insanity, nudging each other, at times, closer to the edge of darkness. He would fold around her, cocooning her in his unpredictable, unsuitable love, writing an exquisite song for her and singing it in her ear. Or they'd pour over her photographs, spreading them out on the threadbare carpet of her student house.

In his embrace, she felt safe, like nobody could hurt her. But he *did* hurt her. And she let it happen for a feeling of security that turned out to be futile, for the sake of a strong arm to sleep beneath or to bask in the compliment of a song dedicated to her. Languishing in anguish under his touch, whispering to him while he slept not to leave her. She'd been afraid he would one day simply disappear, and he had cruelly made her fear that reality. The heap of loss that had once been love found itself with nowhere to disperse. She hadn't been enough for him. But deep down, locked away in the depths of a still bruised heart, against her wishes, Ella still felt an intense love for Harrison.

The scents, sights and sounds of Hydra still lived within her like a disease. Although her birth certificate and passport said she belonged to Greece, she didn't feel it, having been brought up in London. And she'd refused to return to the island since that final trip with Harrison. It had once been the setting for her happiest childhood memories, but she no longer felt that way. He had ruined Hydra for her.

Harrison and Ella once dreamed of living there, growing old together, perhaps having a family, but he had shattered their fantasy and broken her heart. Ella was never going to be ready to confront the ghosts that still haunted Greece and her birthplace, despite the almost irresistible magnetic pull of paradise. It would be like walking in phantom footsteps, so she had deliberately stayed away.

She travelled extensively for work, just as she'd always hoped she would when conjuring up how her life could be as a photographer. The reality far exceeded her manifestations, and she lived a constant adventure, untethered by convention or restrictions. And to think she'd almost foolishly thrown it away for him. Hydra, tainted by Harrison, was the only part of the world she avoided. Until now.

Her sister, Georgia, was insisting they return to scatter their mother's ashes. Ella was trying to dodge her calls and emails, but she could only stave off her relentless and determined sibling for so long.

Hydra was the last place on earth Ella wanted to be.

Chapter 2

Georgia

London, May 2016

'I can't keep Mum on the mantlepiece any longer. It's almost been a whole year, Ella!' Georgia said as she ran her fingers delicately over the urn containing their mother's ashes in her lounge. She was determined to arrive at a conclusion, regardless of what her sister thought. Or didn't think, as was mostly the case. Her sibling had shown little interest in the final ritual of goodbye.

Ella sighed audibly at the end of the phone.

'I don't know … I'm jet-lagged and my brain's not working. I just landed from LA and I'm going to Peru next week. I don't even know what day it is. Just come up with a plan and let me know, or do something closer to home.'

Georgia ground her teeth in frustration. Ella was never close to home because she avoided it. She avoided everything; she hadn't even unpacked her flat. But Georgia was determined to fulfil their mother's last wish, which was to be scattered on Hydra. She straightened her cream dupion curtains, which were never pulled shut. Instead, electric black-out blinds in butterscotch suede set to a timer, descended at dusk. Why was it always left to her to organise everyone else? Ella's lack of planning drove her to absolute distraction. She subconsciously fluffed a cushion, while attempting to impress the importance of committing to an arrangement.

'You only just managed to make time for Mum's funeral and then left me to deal with all her things. And it's starting to creep me out having her above the fireplace, watching me everywhere I go. We *need* to get this done. *I* do.'

'Georgia, she isn't actually in your house. Her spirit lives on the wind, all around, it's just a bunch of dust in a pot, sis.'

Georgia scoffed at Ella's psychobabble and wondered whether she was high. It wouldn't surprise her. Her younger sister dwelt in a world of her own imagination. It certainly wasn't the same one Georgia inhabited. For someone who made a living from capturing reality in photographs, Ella's head was firmly planted in the clouds. Yet somehow she managed to march onwards, winning countless awards for her photography. Given everything that had happened after the Harrison catastrophe, Georgia was quietly pleased her sister spent so much time away. It eased her own considerable guilt.

She tried to press further.

'Delaying any longer feels like we've deserted Mum. Let's go to Hydra at the end of June when you're back from Peru. I'll see if we need a licence. I'm sure you can't go around the world sprinkling dead people in the sea.' A small sob rushed up the inside of her throat, and she disguised it as a laugh before it stifled her voice.

'Just sort it out and let me know, please?' Ella yawned loudly. 'Email me and I'll be there. If I can.'

Ella then said she needed to sleep and ended their call, leaving Georgia no nearer to a definite resolution.

Georgia sighed in exasperation and looked around her

perfectly designed living room which was her favourite project she'd ever completed, because it was personal; her marital nest. But she felt set adrift. Mum had been her sounding board, a stoic voice of reason to anchor her when things felt out of her control – which was increasingly often. Her mother, Anna, had been a midwife, immensely practical and straightforward, traits they shared. Now, there was nobody in the family who understood her; not her sister, and certainly not her husband, Oliver. Despite their monthly therapy sessions that he begrudgingly attended, they didn't seem to make much progress. She'd hoped they could return to their closeness, re-kindle the romance that shone through each moment in the early days. Or had Georgia projected that upon their past through a rose-tinted lens? Her mother had enjoyed how different her girls were and encouraged Ella's wild and feral ways, treating her as extra special, which had pushed on Georgia's nerves. It had led her to lose complete control of her emotions as a child, and she shuddered to think of it now. Those destructive feelings still lurked, though she nudged away the darkness as much as she could.

Instead, she coasted along in her various roles, the most precious of which was mother to her seventeen-year-old daughter, Phoenix. She also supported several charities, sitting on their boards, and Oliver, a property developer, required her to host regular dinner parties to impress potential clients. Occasionally an acquaintance would ask her to cast an eye over their redecoration plans for a room, calling upon her skills as a former interior designer. The exhilaration of feeling useful was fleeting. Her days were filled with people and things, but it wasn't enough. Phoenix was hoping to go to music college in the autumn, and Georgia was beginning to panic about how to fill that void.

Georgia put on a brave face, forcing a stiff upper lip in public and following through on all her commitments before hiding away and weeping in the bathroom or screaming into a pillow when it all became too much. Whereas Ella couldn't give two hoots about responsibility or what people thought and was utterly content to gad around the world taking pictures as she'd long been determined to do. They couldn't be more opposite. Ella lived out of a suitcase, unable to make a home, with no desire to share her life with anyone and was able to control her emotions – apart from when Harrison or Hydra were mentioned. She was self-sufficient and content with her own company, and had been since they were children.

Georgia had felt rejected by her sister when they were little and nothing had really changed over the years, especially since *him*. Harrison. He had ruined everything, but it was unsurprising. Georgia instinctively knew he'd break her sister's heart when she'd first been introduced to him. He was rough, different and although he clearly adored Ella, there was something about him that jarred. Her classist judgement was born of snobbery, she knew. Yes, he was charming and irresistibly exciting, and she understood what her sister saw in him – even Georgia, against her will, found him alluring and intriguing – but she also thought him deeply unsuitable. Though he was studying at the same university as Ella, he was the last person anyone should ever entertain a relationship with. Musicians were the world's ultimate heartbreakers. Of course, Georgia had ultimately been proven right about him. Harrison had turned all their lives upside down, and they were still living with the consequences.

Chapter 3

Georgia

June 2016

'Look at you! You've grown a foot since I last saw you, Phoenie,' Ella exclaimed as Phoenix opened the front door to Georgia's house. Dropping her rucksack to the floor, she pulled her niece into her arms.

'No, I think you've shrunk, Auntie Ella. I haven't seen you for ages! Like a whole year.' Phoenix giggled as she brushed her chestnut curls from her eyes.

'Come on, you two, the reunion can carry on in the car. It's been waiting half an hour because *someone* was late,' Georgia said as she glared at Ella. 'We'll miss our flight at this rate.' She shook her head at them. Their special club of two, which always picked up right where they'd left off, hurt because it displayed a unique bond she shared with neither of them.

'Georgia, we'll be at the airport three hours early as it is,' Ella said, waving to her brother-in-law as she climbed into the backseat. 'Hi, Ollie! Bye, Ollie!'

Ella's nickname for Georgia's husband grated on his nerves. And hers.

But she summoned her brave face, nudging away the ever-present feeling of dejection she had when she was with her sister. Phoenix tenderly hugged her father before turning her attention back to her phone and Georgia chastely pecked Oliver on the cheek. She tried to push aside her feelings about their lack of affection, but it only reinforced how constantly let down she felt by those she loved.

No matter, they were finally on their way to scatter their mother's ashes. She'd achieved something, at least.

In the front passenger seat of the car she'd arranged, she felt the constraints of her carefully crafted life begin to shift as she considered seeing Hydra again. The solemnity of the spirit of their journey to Greece inspired a silent prayer.

Maybe on Hydra, I will find a way back to me and the island will release me from my secrets.

A bubble of giddiness worked its way around the pit of her stomach. She was glad Phoenix was coming with them. Georgia's daughter had never been to the island before, though she'd heard so much about it from her mum and aunt – the good version that was. It was a shame Oliver couldn't get out of work to join them; Georgia could have done with his support, though she wasn't surprised by his absence. He abided by the bare minimum of their therapist's suggestions, which were frequent phone calls to improve their communication. She'd prefer him by her side when she needed him instead of a message to appease her, or merely a brief exchange between his meetings.

Turning to face her sister and daughter in the backseat, she found them swigging from the complimentary bottles of fizz. Her face fell. Nobody had thanked her for organising the car to herald the start of their Grecian odyssey. Instead, they were whispering in earnest, catching up on gossip without her. For once, Phoenix had put her mobile down and her full attention was on Ella. Georgia felt taken for granted and it stung.

The car radio was tuned to a station playing the best of the 1990s. It was inevitable that *that* song would eventually appear. As she caught the opening piano chords to Harrison's most famous composition, she pressed the off switch faster than a lizard's tongue catches a fly. The driver's head turned, and he looked at her quizzically.

'Bad memories of that one.' She smiled tightly.

'Ah ... hatch, match or dispatch? It's on *my* funeral list!' He laughed. Georgia was buoyed to hear someone else other than her had the wherewithal to plan their own funeral music.

'Oh, there certainly was a death ... of sorts...' she said quietly.

Again, she looked to the back seat, but the others didn't appear to have noticed the abrupt lack of music. They were too busy conspiring about something Georgia wasn't party to. Determined to join in, she opened her mini bottle of fizz and, discarding her feelings of isolation, she held it up in a toast.

'Cheers! Or to do it in Greek, *Yiá mas*! Here's to a great girlie time!'

But as soon as the words left her lips, she doubted the sentiment, despite the eager communal clinking of bottles. She'd pressed for so long to make the final voyage on behalf of their mother, it couldn't possibly live up to her lofty expectations. The bleakness of the thought slowly removed any joy she'd started to feel, and her mind returned to that awful day on Hydra she tried not to think about. It still woke her at night, haunting her dreams.

Holding her eyes shut, she tried to dispel the terrible image of the accident as it replayed in her mind. Everyone called it an accident, but it wasn't. Even her mother knew, deep down, what Georgia had done.

She hoped for strength and closure when they got to the island, but despaired if she'd ever find one of those, let alone both.

* * *

After their flight and a quick pit stop at the hotel to freshen up, they had planned to take advantage of their one night in Athens before heading for Hydra on the ferry in the morning.

But Georgia had now been waiting in the lobby for almost half an hour with no sign of Ella or Phoenix. She tapped her foot impatiently. It would soon be dark with no opportunity to take in the sights properly; they'd already missed the last guided tour leaving from the hotel. In the end, she fired off a nagging text to Phoenix and asked the receptionist to call Ella's room. It baffled Georgia as to why her sister refused to carry a phone. She was impossible to get hold of and it was inconceivable how someone could exist without any regular ties to civilisation in this day and age. Ella was unconnected in every way, and it was maddening.

Eventually, after a further fifteen minutes, her sister sheepishly arrived with Phoenix in tow.

'Sorry, I fell asleep. Anyway, it's super early, what's the rush, sis?' asked Ella.

'You might have been here a hundred times before, but Phoenix hasn't. I thought she might like to see the city,' replied Georgia.

'Ummm, hello, would anyone like to ask me what I want to do?' piped up Phoenix. 'There's an amazing bar which has the best view of the sunset, apparently. Let's start there.'

14

Ella agreed but Georgia couldn't help but feel beaten down by the pair of them. But at least they were finally heading out. She hoped they could start to have some fun together.

* * *

'Where are we going now? We really ought to eat,' Georgia shouted as Ella and Phoenix strode off ahead. She was desperate for food and the only pause after the drinks place Phoenix had chosen was to buy beaded bracelets from a toothless woman on the *Plaka*. Georgia had tried to dissuade the others from engaging with the old crone, but, egged on by Ella, Phoenix had shrugged off her concerns. Georgia had beadily fixed her gaze on their wallets and handbags in case any gnarly fingers should try to reach for them during the exchange. At least they'd had that relaxing sunset Aperol together on the roof terrace. It had an unrivalled view of the Athenian skyline and it was stunning to see the way the pinks and golds in the sky had collided with breathtaking clarity across the spectacular city, ancient relics gilded with faded sunbeams. It was the very definition of a 'golden hour', everyone and everything looking glowingly beautiful. Though Georgia had felt uneasy that there wasn't a plan for the remainder of the evening. The bar had felt like a temporary moment of unity, but now the other two were determined to explore every nook and cranny of the tackier tourist spots, darting from place to place.

'I really think we should eat. It's been hours since we had food on the plane and there were only crisps in that bar. Hardly a nutritious dinner.' Georgia's anxiety was increasing as they continued to traipse around the lanes of Athens. She was not having the fun she'd hoped for, and longed for her ylang ylang fragranced hotel room with its sumptuous oversized bed boasting a terrifically high thread-count.

'Come on, sis, relax and live a little. We're in Athens...' Ella said, then made a show of looking at her watch. 'Right, it's officially ouzo time!' She fired off snapshots with the expensive camera slung around her neck as she headed into the nearest bar.

'Don't forget Phoenix is only seventeen and shouldn't really be drinking. And the ferry is at seven tomorrow morning, and we don't want hangovers on the boat...' Georgia couldn't help but scold and she caught Phoenix rolling her eyes. It was wounding and her jealousy intensified, forcing her to stop still.

'Relax! We're on holiday!' shouted Ella as she went on ahead. Georgia looked up at the partially ruined Ionic columns towering within the Hadrian's Library monument. It was a shame they'd been so poorly lit. They would have been showcased so much better had she been the lighting architect charged with the design. Resting her head against the railings protecting the aged site, she tried to summon the courage to endure two weeks with her sister and daughter. Ella's irreverence scraped at Georgia's insides, and she could already feel her emotions bubbling. She wished Oliver was here; at least then she'd have an ally of sorts. But he couldn't make time for it. Couldn't make time for her. She knew they were growing apart despite attending counselling, and wasn't sure what to do about it, other than pretend everything was fine.

The twinkling lights embedded in the far-off hills that surrounded the heart of Athens tried to captivate her with their mystical magic. The view was dominated by the Acropolis. Every carved crevice and cavity in the iconic stone temple was visible like black slashes penetrating the pale rock. It was as stunning at night as it was by day. But yet it didn't quite inspire the feeling of awe she'd expected.

Georgia looked forward to tomorrow when they finally reached Hydra and would abide by the exciting schedule she'd mapped out. That would get them back on track and then she knew she'd begin to enjoy herself.

* * *

'Auntie Ella, what's your favourite place you've travelled to this year?' Phoenix asked as they tucked into gyros – pitta wraps crammed full with chips, charred chicken, tzatziki and salad, making them bulge at the sides. It was a messy thing to eat and Georgia tried desperately to protect her cashmere from a splash of sauce. It wouldn't have been her choice for dinner, but Ella had insisted and, reluctantly, Georgia found herself savouring each bite of the delicious Greek street food. Ella contemplated her answer to Phoenix's question before speaking.

'My last job, Peru, a couple of weeks ago. I was photographing indigenous people around Machu Picchu, and one of them took me to see a shaman doing an Ayahuasca ritual. It was literally mind blowing, like … I left my body. I can't explain it, but it was incredible,' Ella replied dreamily.

'Cool! What's Ayahuasca?' Phoenix's brown eyes widened, keen to hear more about her aunt's exploits.

'I don't think it's appropriate, Ella,' interrupted Georgia. 'People have died from it. You don't want to fill Phoenix's head with such nonsense, do you?'

She shot a pointed look at her sister, but Ella waved off her protests.

'It's not like she's going to run out and score drugs in Athens! Unless she wants to. You can't shield her from everything. She's not a kid anymore.'

'As a mother, you do your best to protect your children...'
Georgia couldn't help but say, though she immediately regretted
her words when she saw Phoenix had spotted the unspoken
message that travelled between the sisters. She frowned as
her daughter's soft brown eyes moved from one sister to
the other, unable to decipher the meaning of the message.

'Fine, I'll tell you about it another time, Phoenie,' said Ella.
Georgia exhaled with a quiet satisfaction.

Phoenix stood up from the table.

'Catch you later, I'm off to explore,' she said, walking away
towards the street which boasted tourist shops, mainly selling
evil eye keyrings, and miniature models of the Parthenon.

'Do you need some Euros?' Georgia shouted after her, but
Phoenix's long legs had taken her quickly out of sight.

Ella turned her head to Georgia.

'Are you letting her loose alone in Athens?'

'It's fine. She likes doing her own thing. Anyway, I've got
her phone tracked on mine, so she won't go far,' she replied.

Ella sipped her ouzo with a wry grin, the ice cubes
clunking against the side of the tall glass. She finished her food
then hoovered up the remains from Georgia's plate before
eventually breaking the awkward silence.

'I know how much you do for everyone and have done for
me. And I'm grateful, I really am. If it wasn't for you, I don't
know where I would be. Where any of us would be.' Her
hand reached across the table for Georgia's. 'The car and the
plane upgrade were a lovely treat. But you really don't need
to impress me. I'm your sister, I already love you. I'm fine
roughing it.'

Tears scratched at Georgia's throat rendering her
speechless. But a quiet guilt snaked around her veins, the
familiar flush of cold that always appeared when they were

18

together. But she reminded herself that Ella didn't remember what happened on Hydra; she was so young at the time.

'And you don't need to protect me,' Ella continued. 'I know you switched off the car radio when Harrison's song came on. I've concluded there's no escaping it, so I let it be.' Ella laughed. 'Now *that's* a great song!'

'"Let It Be"? I should say so. Far superior and not at all schmaltzy.'

'I should be offended at that. You know "Out of the Darkness" is about me and him...'

Georgia tried to keep calm. She picked up her ouzo glass, gripping it tightly, then downed it in one. She coughed as the aniseed liquid burnt. She couldn't believe Ella was talking about *him* again. Harrison. After all these years, he should be nothing more than a distant memory. How long could heartbreak last?

'We have absolutely no idea that's the case, Ella,' Georgia said with a hope the subject could come to a close.

'You started it! I know you were never his biggest fan, but how is this not about me and him...?' She began to recite the lyrics.

'Looking back in time, you are all I see.

'Endless searching for your eyes, I feel you reach for me.

'Our hearts and souls forever joined, living out of sight.

'It's always you; within the darkness you, you will be the light.

'He started writing it when we got together,' Ella explained.

'It proves absolutely nothing,' Georgia quickly dismissed. 'It could be about hundreds of other women – you weren't even with him a whole year. Please, don't obsess. I will never forgive him for what he did, and it took you a very long time to recover. I don't need to remind you...'

She scrutinised her sister carefully, feeling disheartened at the way her face still lit up when she spoke his name. Georgia crossed her fingers under the table. She hoped Ella wouldn't be so stupid as to entertain any notion of revisiting her past. Not with Harrison Sutherland, her supposed greatest love. Georgia was unable to understand the truth in that notion. If they were truly destined to be together, they would be by now. Though she was wholeheartedly relieved they weren't.

And yes, she may have played a part in that, but Ella didn't need to know any of the details.

The one saving grace about being unable to contact Ella easily was she lived mostly 'off grid'. No social media, only a laptop with basic functions and email. It's possible she'd tried to contact him, or he her, but she'd never said as much. Georgia kept tabs on him at all times – at least, as much as she could, given Harrison stayed out of the public eye. He only penned songs for famous singers now and then.

He'd made a success of his life. And he'd made a mess of Ella's. Georgia would never forgive him for that. But she also couldn't forgive herself. Because she was as guilty as Harrison.

The Island

*The island knew they were returning. It had clutched at
their secrets, treasuring them in the depths of its craggy
rocks. Some gods had tried to shatter the stones where their
darkest thoughts dwelt, to release them into the air, but not
even Athos could move their heaviest memories.
The sisters were destined to come back, but only one
would leave.*

Chapter 4

Ella

Saturday

The early morning sea was mirror-flat as the boat left Piraeus port on the mainland, headed for Hydra. The *Flying Cat VI* was crammed with day trippers, holidaymakers and locals.

As they took their seats for the ferry ride, the women all appeared to be in very different headspaces. Phoenix had busied herself on her phone, Georgia was pretending to read a modern re-telling of Greek myths and Ella was desperately seeking distraction. She loathed boats and had done so ever since she could remember. She preferred to be land-locked within a pristine rainforest or viewing the never-ending landscape at the foot of the Saharan Atlas Mountains. The trouble with Hydra was that boats were unavoidable.

She turned her attention to her sister, hoping her uptight, controlling nature wouldn't dominate with militant scheduling. Although this holiday of sorts was to scatter their mother's ashes, it was about so much more for Ella. Returning to Hydra felt like a forced sacred pilgrimage. She hoped that, on the island, she could finally say goodbye to her past for good.

The island had changed her world in more ways than she

could ever admit, and she had almost held it responsible for what happened in her life after she last visited when she was nineteen. Back then, she'd been willing to sacrifice everything she held dear for Harrison. He'd agreed she should leave university, travel with him to Scotland and then explore the world together, going wherever his band took him.

Then Ella discovered she had fallen pregnant. She didn't want to trap him in a relationship, but she hated dishonesty and she owed it to him to let him know. Her future course was shifting too quickly away from her plans, threatening the dream of how she'd mapped her career. And Ella was afraid. She searched for the right time to tell him as the days sped by before he was due to leave for rehearsals. But he abandoned her before she could share her news, disappeared without a goodbye and with no way of contacting him.

All that transpired following his sudden, heartless departure led her to the point of a deepest depression. Ultimately, she'd had no choice. She knew she wasn't fit to be a mother back then.

She leant her head against the ferry window and looked out at the expanse of ocean. What should be the sheer freedom of nothingness had the opposite effect on her; it penned her in. Everyone waxed lyrical about boating on the crystal-clear waters around Hydra, but the idea filled her with terror. The spectacular collision of every imaginable shade of blue – sea and sky and all that lay beyond the horizon – wasn't something Ella enjoyed. She didn't mind swimming, but boats she detested. Yet she couldn't help but be transfixed by the colour palette of the country of her birth, which she had once so loved. As she absorbed the atmosphere of Greece once again through the ferry windows, its arms wrapped her in its ancient romantic embrace. The love for the island she used to have when they visited with their mother began to stir and she allowed it to replace her unease at being afloat.

She turned her head to look at Phoenix, who was still engrossed in her phone.

'Right, put that thing down and prepare to expand your mind, Phoenie. This is the start of your musical education. May I introduce you to Mr Leonard Cohen; my favourite, slightly filthy, but utterly fabulous Canadian who once lived on the island. You're about to tread on musical hallowed ground, my sweet girl. You'll never be the same.'

Ella offered Phoenix a wireless headphone, opened her laptop and selected a favourite album and pressed play. She watched Phoenix smile and her eyes close as she sank into her seat, permitting the music and lyrical poetry to weave their spell.

The ferry coasted over small swells in the ocean, making Ella's tummy leap a little. She focused on the music made of love and lust, despair and regret, like her own personal soundtrack. Despite the distraction, her mind edged towards a place she wished it wouldn't go. But it couldn't be helped. Being with her family inevitably reminded her of Harrison, and she couldn't help but seek out his energy in the atmosphere. They'd always had a magical connection, one that defied explanation, but she didn't wish to ignite that flame again, nor chase him across time. He was like a spectre that haunted her present, but he had no place in it. Yet still, she couldn't rid herself of his memory; it hung like a cloud blighting a clear sky.

There was a Harrison shaped gap in her mind and body. Nobody had been able to fill that space since they'd been separated and she innately knew that nobody ever would. Though it didn't stop her from entertaining the notion of love

24

with another. She owned her pain and was open to someone else in her life, and, as she travelled, she'd harboured a hope to find it one day. It wasn't for want of trying or looking. She had long ago committed to living a rich and full life, and adored the freedom she'd spun for herself. But Harrison had set the benchmark for passion, and she compared every version of love she'd had since to him, which meant she inevitably came away empty-hearted from encounters with any other man. She also suspected it was deliberate on her part. Ella was terrified of being cruelly rejected at her most vulnerable ever again.

When she'd taken part in the ancient ceremony in Peru and succumbed to the hallucinogenic mushrooms and herbs in Ayahuasca, she'd thought she'd found him with her mind. Her body had fizzed with the thought of his touch. If only the ritual had been an exorcism. Instead, it brought forth the opposite effect. He was in the centre of her mind again after having retreated to lurk on the periphery. All because she was returning to the island where they'd been so happy, or so Ella had thought. It was infuriating, and made her want to rip her own heart out and replace it with a boulder. The heaviness would be replicated, but the emotion would be gone. Neither version was preferable to the other.

She didn't want to squander time pointlessly longing for someone she couldn't have and wasn't entirely sure she wanted. She hadn't pined for him like a nun or wasted the years, but she still couldn't clear the corner of her soul that he occupied. Hopefully, returning to Hydra would provide some resolution for their sad chapter. It was about time she found a way to make him leave her heart for good.

As the haunting music lured her into a soporific state, she began to sink downwards to unconsciousness. Against her will, her mind transported her to the day Harrison had entered her life.

* * *

Guildford, March 1997

Ella had been tasked with photographing something 'in the wild' as part of her first year's university course. The ducks were taking part in their mating rituals as the promise of a new season crept across Guildford in Surrey, where she was studying. The River Wey hosted plenty of the birds, and Ella wanted to capture the beautiful brutality of spring, the darker side. It was just after dawn, and as hints of sunlight started to peep through the foliage, she'd paused on the bridge, scanning the water until the peace of early morning was interrupted by the tell-tale quacking, akin to mocking laughter.

There!

Two drakes were pursuing a hen and Ella had sprinted down to the riverbank before stealthily creeping along towards them. Crouching on her haunches, she'd raised the camera to her eye. As one of the males rose up and flapped his wings in a display of prowess and arrogance, his colours glistened. She'd begun to snap as the other took the opportunity to mount the female. It was monstrous to witness and it had made Ella's heart beat faster to see the hen submerged, struggling in the river, almost drowning. She'd had to suppress her panic, knowing better than to intervene with nature, but it took every ounce of her extensive willpower not to wave her arms and scare them away. As she'd shot frame after frame, she'd longed to develop the images immediately, knowing they would be special.

But the morning had been too beautiful to leave, so she'd

gone to sit on a brow above the bank. The sun had warmed her face as she'd tilted her chin upwards, inhaling clean air as far into her lungs as she could manage. Fish were topping in the shallow river, ripples spreading outwards and then disappearing as if they were never there. She'd left her camera and bag on the knoll and carefully navigated the steep slope down to the water, trying not to slip on the dewy grass. Reaching the flat stone edge of the river, she'd observed morning stirring into life; the gentle splashing as the watery surface was breached, the sounds of gliding insects buzzing past and tuneful birdsong enveloped her in a blissful peace.

'Beautiful, isn't it?' a low gravelly voice had suddenly said beside her.

The shock had made her physically jump and she'd whipped around to face the source. In doing so, her foot had snagged on a crack in the concrete, sending her tipping backwards, her arms flailing as she'd hopelessly attempted to prevent her fall. She'd heard her voice scream in anticipation of what was inevitable and her blood had run faster, not just with fear of falling, but also with a thousand other things as she'd caught sight of the person who had startled her. His warm brown eyes had widened in alarm as his hands grabbed for hers.

Ella had felt like she'd been suspended in limbo for minutes rather than seconds before he somehow managed to connect with her waist. But he was unable to get purchase and the momentum of his lunge tipped them both over. They'd crashed into the freezing water together and emerged spluttering and laughing, before locking eyes again. He was almost a foot taller than her, she'd noticed as they'd stood in the river. Where the water circled her ribs, it lapped at the waistband of his sodden jeans. He'd pushed his long hair away from his face, all the while not breaking their gaze. His beard hadn't been thick – perhaps two weeks' worth of dense stubble – but a small piece of weed had become stuck to his chin. It had made Ella smile so hard she'd thought her face would crack open. Every detail was heightened with staggering clarity, like she'd re-focused a grey wash lens and could suddenly see the world in colour for the first time. She hadn't been able to stop her fingers reaching forward to remove the straggly piece of weed and he'd taken her small hand, closing his around it and holding it to his face. It was an intimate gesture between strangers, but somehow it had belonged. Her palm had fitted perfectly against his cheek and they'd stood there shivering with something much more than cold for what seemed like the rest of the morning.

'Hi…' Ella had said softly.

'Hi,' he'd returned in the same deep voice that had caused them to end up in the river. His beautiful brown eyes had crinkled as he smiled, and her breath had caught in her throat. They were the shade of dark treacle, endless pools of the warmest colour. She'd wanted him to kiss her; it felt like the most natural thing for him to do. And as if his heart had heard her plea, he'd leant forward. In that moment she'd known she would always love him.

* * *

From the second her child was born, Ella's heart broke every time she had seen Harrison's eyes looking back at her on their baby's sweet face. It was too painful to endure. Ella knew her mental state at the time wasn't fit for the job at hand. A terrible depression had descended after he left in the early weeks of her pregnancy and nothing could shift the dark storm that had hung above her head, clouding her mind with the bleakest of thoughts. She'd wanted to make the world go away, life felt like it was finished. She didn't have him and having his child would slam the brakes on her career, one that hadn't even started yet. The woman she was in those early days after he left was in stark contrast to the person she'd since shaped herself into, not permitting anything or anyone to distract her from her ambitions. But back then everything had felt hopeless. Becoming a mother wasn't in her plan and giving up her university course and career wasn't an option any longer after he'd left. Though she'd once been prepared to reconsider her plans for Harrison, she wasn't willing to entertain such a thought ever again. Heartbreakingly, that decision had cost her their child.

Giving her baby away had been the most selfless sacrifice she'd ever made, and a self-inflicted punishment she would always have to live with.

But Ella's failure had become Georgia's purpose, and she clung on to the fact that some joy had emerged from the misery, even if her daughter, heartbreakingly, would never know her real identity.

Because no matter how much they loved her, the fact was that Phoenix wasn't Georgia and Oliver's biological daughter.

She was Ella and Harrison's.

Chapter 5
Ella

Chelsea & Westminster Hospital, August 1998

'Ella, she's beautiful,' cooed Georgia as she gently rocked the two-day old bundle in her arms. 'Congratulations! And to you, Mum ... or should I say, "Granny". Your very first grandchild...'

Georgia broke off, sentiment strangling her voice. Ella watched blankly from the hospital bed, her face devoid of emotion. Anna sat down gently beside her, reaching for her hand and taking care not to nudge the cannula that was delivering pain relief. Ella continually pressed the button to administer a constant stream, as if it could prevent the harsh reality from piercing the fog in her mind. Her mother prised the button carefully from her grasp.

'They won't let you have too much, sweetheart. You know why.' Anna was referring to the flag on her records raising concern about her mental health. 'I know you will find your way without the medication. You always have. Come on, my little shining light, talk to me. How are you feeling after the surgery?' her mother asked, tenderly stroking her brow. Ella's brown curls were matted and shrouded her features like she was trying to hide using every available resource.

'Numb,' she croaked as tears spilled silently down her face, the only indication she felt anything. 'I can't look at her, Mum. Please, don't make me look at her.'

'Sweetheart, you need to bond, she needs to feel your skin.' Anna took the baby from Georgia's arms and unfolding her swaddle, lay her on Ella's chest. 'You should try and feed her. I'm here to help you.'

Ella closed her eyes and felt her nightgown being unbuttoned at the neck. Her hand instinctively closed around the tiny body lying across her, feeling warm skin, soft like silk. She heard precious muted snuffles. The urge to love her little one was overwhelming, surging through her body like a tidal wave, but all she could think about was how Harrison should be beside her. But he wasn't.

She hadn't been allowed to hold her daughter in her first moments because of the operation she'd needed immediately after the birth. Ella had lost a lot of blood and didn't quite remember what procedure she'd had to have, but she knew her life and body would never be the same because of whatever had been scraped away or extracted. She wished they could have removed her feelings instead, but there was no such surgery.

Ella looked at her sister. Georgia's face was streaked with the pain of a visible longing as she watched the baby. It wasn't fair for her to see such an unhappy version of parenthood when she was so desperate to experience it for herself. It must be torture, Ella thought, and she felt a flood of shame nudge at the drugs in her bloodstream.

'I'll go and round up some tea,' Georgia finally said, leaving the hospital room.

Ella's gaze reluctantly travelled to her baby and her entire body panged with love, followed by a regret at how alone she felt. The tiny rosebud mouth and unblemished skin were perfect, untouched by the sun, unsullied by pain or heartbreak. But Ella's heart was broken, and she couldn't find a way to unearth the joy she knew she ought to be feeling. Her beautiful daughter who was a product of such immense passion also represented the end of love. She was made on Hydra, where Ella was born, a place she'd treasured, but now every aspect of what used to be cherished had been defiled. Love had been tarnished. She winced with pain as the baby latched onto her breast and she cried not from the agony of yielding milk but from the turn her life had taken.

'You're doing so well, darling,' said Anna, stroking Ella's head and cupping the baby's. 'I know this is hard, Ella. Believe me, I've seen every possible kind of motherhood and there's no right or wrong way to do any of it.'

Ella managed a small smile.

'I want Georgia to have her.'

Anna's face blanched and she frowned.

'What do you mean?'

'I want Georgia to adopt her. It's not fair that she wants a baby more than anything and I didn't and yet here I am...'

'Ella, darling, that's a huge decision you can't take back. You'd have to pretend for the rest of your life that she's not yours. Don't say it if you don't mean it; you'll hurt Georgia terribly, as well as yourself.'

Ella looked down at her daughter again. The shape of her face and placement of her miniature features screamed Harrison, but her olive colouring was Ella's. Even though she looked nothing like Georgia, surely they could explain that away as a quirk of genetics.

'Something positive has to come out of it all, Mum. Now I've seen her, part of me wants to do this, but I also can't let go of what I've always planned to do. I have my whole life ahead and I'm not ready for it to stop before it's started. I'm going back to my course when term starts. Nobody knew I was expecting; she was barely noticeable to anyone but me… And to you both, of course. No, I've made up my mind, I want Georgia to bring up my baby. Can you help start the paperwork? Please, Mum?'

Anna took the little girl from Ella's chest and expertly placed her over her shoulder, patting her back with two fingers. She moved to look out of the window, taking several deep breaths. As she watched her mother, Ella admired how natural she was with babies, whereas everything about this for her felt completely unnatural, it wasn't the way things were supposed to turn out. She saw Anna wipe a tear from her eye and inhale deeply again before turning back with a tense smile.

'Whatever you decide, the most important thing is that she has love.' She mopped the baby's mouth with a muslin square before returning her attention to Ella. 'You know Georgia would do anything for you, but I don't think you should make any decisions just yet.' As her mother fixed her with her bright blue eyes, she looked almost afraid of what Ella was suggesting. 'You've been through a lot – not just physically, but also mentally. She hasn't even got a name yet, so let's just take each day as it comes.'

'Phoenix,' said Ella, closing her eyes and turning onto her side. She pulled the scratchy bedsheet over her shoulder, ignoring the darts of pain from her insides, the agony almost validating her choice.

'What's that, darling?' asked Anna.

'I want her to be called Phoenix. Something beautiful to come from the worst time of my life. I've decided and won't change my mind, Mum. I'm going to ask Georgia.'

'Ask me what?' said Georgia as she re-entered the room.

Chapter 6

Georgia

Hydra, June 2016

It had been years since Georgia had last seen the looming hillsides of Hydra through a ferry window. An overwhelming but surprising sense of connection slotted into place, emerging from where it had slumbered beneath the less pleasant memories. It reaffirmed her decision to honour their mother's wishes to be scattered here, and replaced any trepidation she'd felt about returning. Especially with Ella.

The island slowly filled the panes of glass as they approached the harbour. Painted houses almost became the cliffs, like they were stacked atop one another. Stone bricks, terracotta roofs, and a multicoloured palette of ochre, white and burgundy framed by cobalt sky crowded her view.

She flinched as the ferry honked its horn signalling its intention to dock. In anticipation of arrival, she stood to collect her luggage. Phoenix and Ella were still snoozing in their seats. Georgia's heart suddenly constricted as she saw the identical shape of their slightly open mouths, the way their heads bowed towards one another, crowned with the same shade of curly hair. Although Phoenix resembled her father, her colouring was all Ella. Georgia felt uncomfortable and the trip suddenly seemed like a terrible idea. It may have been preferable to come alone with her sister rather than bring Phoenix, or even better, to have taken a solo voyage. But Phoenix had wanted to see the island she'd heard so much about.

For Georgia, it was a place where her darkest self had emerged. It was a long time ago, but the memories still tortured her. A shiver travelled up her spine as a sense of foreboding knocked against her bones. As if Ella had heard her sister's thoughts, she opened her bright green eyes and smiled at her. She looked out the window, then nudged Phoenix.

'Wake up, sleepyhead, we're here!' she said.

Georgia handed them their bags and acknowledged another similarity. They'd both packed light, whereas she had a full medical kit, five adapters, two phone chargers and three outfit options for each day of the fourteen they were scheduled to be here, just in case the weather shifted dramatically. She clutched her carry-on, which contained their mother's ashes along with a file containing the necessary documents, including several copies of the death certificate, and the undertaker's letter in both English and Greek, the latter translated and stamped by the Greek embassy in London. She didn't want anything to prevent such an important passage of rites. She needed it to go perfectly.

Georgia lugged her large suitcase off the ferry into a wall of island heat. Hordes of people poured from the boat, cases clattering down the metal ramp as excitable noisy chatter became a collective shout. They streamed along the walkway, past harbour tavernas that scented the air with grilled souvlaki meat. The belligerent Hydra cats held their ground as tourists side-stepped their resolute positions in the middle of the cobbles. Georgia's suitcase snagged on the stones, making it tricky to manoeuvre, and she enviously eyed Ella's rucksack perched evenly and neatly over both her shoulders, her camera bag in hand. Her sister was standing still on the edge of the sea wall, looking up at the opposite cliff where their mother's old house sat, and Georgia wondered what she was thinking but was too afraid to ask.

'Are you OK, Phoenix? Do you need some water? Here, put on some sunscreen,' Georgia fussed. Phoenix was craning her neck towards the strip of bars and cafés and Georgia quelled any worries. She couldn't get into too much mischief – it was an island after all.

'I'm fine, Mum, don't nag,' Phoenix replied, and Georgia swallowed a retort, putting on her straw hat and oversized sunglasses. She spotted their transport to the hotel and waved to the driver.

'Ooh look! There's our water taxi!'

She herded the other two towards the boat emblazoned with the hotel name. As they carefully took their seats, she watched her sister grip the handrail and fix her gaze on her feet, breathing deeply. When Ella lifted her head, her olive skin was pale.

'I don't mind staying in town. I'm quite happy in any old studio. I don't think I can do any more boats today...'

Ella tried to stand, and Georgia held her arm, steadying her to try and help prevent a panic attack.

'Relax! You'll love the hotel. They have yoga and reflexology.'

She just caught Ella's underwhelmed response of 'Great!', before it dissolved into the hum of the engine.

Georgia felt hurt that Ella didn't seem enthused by the idea of being together, despite the luxury hotel she'd splashed out on. She'd thought by ensconcing them in a five-star enclave away from town, Ella would be prevented from avoiding her – because she'd have to board a boat to do so – and it also kept her away from their mother's old house, which Georgia knew held painful memories of Harrison.

Yes, the hotel choice was partly out of protection and partly selfishness. But then, there was a chance she'd unintentionally facilitated extra quality time between Ella and Phoenix. There were problems at every turn that Georgia could neither solve nor avoid.

While their boat made its progress, she began to panic about forcing her sister onto Hydra again, confronting their beautiful and grubbier memories. It took all her strength not to grab her own face and claw at her skin, so she sat on her hands instead. As the water taxi sped around the headland, the statue of a boy astride a dolphin was revealed above a white stone windmill. Georgia noticed the sea-creature was more weathered than when she'd last visited, tinged greener by the elements. It had been erected to commemorate the film *Boy on a Dolphin* – a fact she shared with Phoenix, who didn't seem enthralled by the trivia.

'Are there any good bars where we're going, Mum? What's the point of being in Greece if you can't hear live music? It better not be one of your boring spa places,' said Phoenix.

Georgia felt crestfallen before they'd even arrived.

'There are four restaurants on site, and I'm sure they'll have performers in the evenings. You can always get a water taxi into town if it's not lively enough for you. I know you don't want to be stuck with us boring oldies the whole time.' She forced a laugh, but secretly hoped that Phoenix *did* want to spend time with her.

'Speak for yourself, sis. Don't tarnish me with your big beige brush.' Ella's sarcastic barb hit Georgia in the chest and her mouth opened in shock, unable to find a response. Was that how Ella saw her – vanilla and unadventurous? Yes, she enjoyed a conventional life, having married well but forfeited her thriving interior design career to live her dream of parenthood. It was something her sister would do well to remember. Phoenix had given Georgia an unexpected purpose out of the blue, and being gifted the chance to become a mother had been a challenge she'd relished. She wouldn't alter her part in Phoenix's upbringing for all the stars in the clear Greek sky.

By relinquishing her career, she hadn't had to lie to any co-workers about how or why she suddenly had a daughter, concocting a story that may eventually catch her out. She'd also retreated from all her old school friends, unable to create a neat way to present what had happened. Since then, she had made new acquaintances, none of whom knew about their chequered family history. She literally gave up everything she knew and loved to protect her sister and Phoenix and a cluster of resentment towards Ella rumbled deep inside her. She quickly swallowed it away, trying to focus on the beautiful scenery and her exquisite daughter. Phoenix was her daughter in nurture if not by nature.

Georgia's eyes darted from the peninsula to the frothy white wake the boat spurted into the sea, seeking out serenity. It didn't work. As they passed the last headland of Hydra town, she was hit squarely in the chest with the vivid memory that plagued her dreams, which seemed to be increasing in intensity and frequency as time went on. She suppressed the flashes of recollection, and squeezed her eyes shut, only opening them when they were clear of the little bay.

This is what happens when you carry secrets, she thought to herself. *They threaten to erupt when you least expect it.*

Of course, she had no intention of revealing the things she'd hidden from Ella. Georgia fixed things, she didn't destroy them, and the damage the truth would wreak on their family would be catastrophic. They would all fracture irreparably. Forever.

The Island

*The gods listened and waited, wondering who would be
brave and who would crumble under their burden. Who
would emerge as a hero of the piece or, indeed, the villain?
Mortals concealed their true selves from one another, but
occasionally found the courage to step into the light to
be cleansed of the weight they carried. Siblings, whether
immortal or not, harmed each other with words and
violence as they jostled for the upper hand. Gods and
humans weren't so different when it came to family.
But such a competition is never won; there is always a
casualty of war.*

Chapter 7

Ella

The eastern coast of the island was unfamiliar to Ella. She ought to have found the adventure in discovering a new nook of somewhere she loved – or used to love – but couldn't quite muster the enthusiasm.

The pull of the main harbour was like a magnet, the hustle and bustle of real Greek life far more tempting than the pristine cell she was stuck in. She appreciated her sister was trying to make it special, but they could have been anywhere in the world – Mauritius, Corsica, Ibiza... Yet they were on Hydra. To say goodbye to their mother properly they should be in the heart of the town – toasting her at the Pirate Bar and playing Backgammon with the locals. Or drinking in life beneath the awnings, supping a kilo of wine and watching the men tend to the mules and ponies, marvelling at the handler with the white handlebar moustache, which sat like a shelf across his lip. Ella had spotted him in the harbour earlier, and it was comforting to know he was still on the island. It was good to see a familiar face that transported her back to happier times – before Harrison.

As she unpacked her small bag, it struck her how differently she reacted to death compared to her sister. They'd processed their mother's passing as though they'd grieved for different people. Georgia canonised the dead, whereas Ella saw them as the beautifully flawed humans they were. Recollections may vary, she smiled to herself. Her mother was so like Georgia, not just physically with their fair colouring but also in their controlling tendencies. It was why Anna was such a good midwife; she governed the most critical points of life. They hadn't ever known their father; he'd left before Ella was born and Georgia had no memories of him. It had bothered Georgia that he'd wanted nothing to do with them, whereas Ella couldn't care less – it was his loss. Ella didn't seek out what she didn't have, finding contentment with what was in her life rather than dwelling on what was missing. Though she struggled to apply that concept when it came to Harrison and Phoenix.

The sisters had long assumed that Ella took after their absent father, since their complexions were so different. Ella's was more olive in tone, which had been passed on to Phoenix, whereas Georgia had frail English skin that burnt to a crisp after one kiss from the sun. She'd be shrouded in factor fifty from sunrise to dusk in Greece, wafting around in cotton and linen layers with an oversized sunhat. Ella smiled as she dressed Georgia in her mind.

She tossed her much-travelled rucksack to the bottom of the wardrobe and brushed away the dust it had deposited on the pristine bed cover, imagining her sister's outrage if she'd seen it. Her room with its white-washed stone walls and oiled oak floorboards could have graced the pages of a high-end interiors magazine.

Right up Georgia's street, she thought, shaking her head. It looked like Georgia had decorated it herself; it wasn't Ella's vibe at all. She would go along with it for now. Then after they'd scattered Mum's ashes, she'd find somewhere in town to stay. That way she wouldn't need to get on a boat until she left Hydra. And she could part with the island forever.

Ella read the welcome note from the hotel and opened the complimentary bottle of red wine. Georgia had arranged for a printed itinerary to be placed in her room. She took it onto the balcony along with her glass and sat in one of the cream rattan armchairs. Moving the blue scatter cushions to the side, she curled her legs underneath her. She looked out across the expanse of ocean, breathing in the warm, spiced air, and permitted Greece to enter her senses.

Below her room was a lush garden. Magenta bougainvillaea crept along a stone wall, effortlessly clinging to the rocks, its petals wavering in the gentle wind. Ella noticed an immense feeling of peace on this coast. Without the boating activity or animal grunts and snorts, it was tranquil and, of course, incredibly beautiful. Maybe her sister had had the right idea after all. It didn't seem like she was on Hydra at all, though it was unmistakably Greece. With the new perspective, Ella could pretend she was somewhere else. But her heart knew the truth and it was pointless to think any other way.

She unfolded the plan, which was printed on hotel headed paper. Its expensive italic font was the same shade of blue as the cushions.

Saturday: Arrival. Unpack in the afternoon, room service for snacks if needed. Dinner at the hotel sushi restaurant at 7 p.m.

Sunday: Yoga at 8 a.m. Free time until 1 p.m. Lunch at hotel taverna. Afternoon at pool. Dinner at cliffside bar in hotel – informal dining, casual dress.

Monday: Boat to Metochi in the morning if we fancy an excursion - timetable enclosed. Hydra Town for lunch at Anita's Taverna. Agree final preparations for scattering Mum's ashes. Dinner to be decided - room service?

Tuesday: Facials at spa and other treatments in the morning and afternoon (on me!) Boat leaves from Hydra port at 7 p.m. sharp! Scatter Mum's ashes as the sun sets.

Wednesday: Ella's birthday!! 38 years young ... Ella to choose what we do (but I suggest we lounge by the pool then go to town for a drink and take it from there)

On and on it went, each hour accounted for, every moment of the two weeks mapped out, including when they could take 'free time'. Ella knew she'd be unable to stick to the schedule confining her within the glossy resort. She already felt claustrophobic, despite the spectacle of the infinite sea and sky ahead. Her body itched to explore, to photograph island life. This wasn't the Hydra she knew and if she had to be here at all, she'd prefer to be in the port where she could walk to where she wished to be.

Ella folded the paper and placed it beside her. The mainland of Greece was visible in the far-off distance, like a faint pencil line sketched on the horizon. The outline of Dokos island was clearer, being only a short boat ride away. A tiny white chapel perched on its knoll like a gleaming tiara. She didn't remember seeing it before, but most things before Harrison she'd blocked out, especially when it came to Hydra. The trauma of his leaving had shattered her memories along with her heart.

The breeze caught the voluminous folds of her palazzo trousers and goose bumps started to rise on her arms, despite the heat from the sun, as if a ghost had caressed her skin. She took another sip of wine and willed her pulse to slow. Church bells clanged, marking the seconds she closed her eyes to seek out calm. Her mind briefly found it before the crackle of another energy became palpable in the air and Ella felt it grasp her. Her eyes flashed open, looking around as if she was being observed. Again, the breeze coursed through her clothes, like a hand running along her body. It seemed ridiculous, but she wondered whether it was Harrison reaching for her. She let the thought linger then dismissed its absurdity. Why would he?

He'd tried to contact her only once through her agent, a few years after he'd left, purporting to be someone else, pretending to book her for a job. Hearing his voice at the end of the telephone when she'd returned the initial call of enquiry from a payphone was like receiving an electric shock. The fact he'd lied to try and speak to her felt underhanded, almost sordid. Ella hated being deceived. She wanted nothing to do with him, despite what her heart had screamed at the sound of his delicious husky cockney rasp. Ella was terrified of blurting out about Phoenix, angry she gave her up because of how damaged she was by his careless love, furious she almost compromised her career for him. It was now unthinkable that she'd ever entertained the idea for a moment. At the time he'd called, business was flourishing; her photographs graced the front covers and middle pages of respected publications across the globe. None of that success would have happened if she'd been allowed to choose him, but she couldn't be grateful for the cruel twist of fate by his hand. Because of Phoenix. She'd slammed the phone down, unable to have his voice in her life for another second. Ella's agent now screened everyone before connecting them with her and had to meticulously check the details of every job she booked. That way she could evade Harrison and avoid being duped again.

He could have reached out before his single attempt and again since, but he hadn't. Besides, anything he had to say was too little, too late. She doubted he ever gave her a thought as he basked in his musical success she'd heard so much about at every turn – despite trying to avoid it. As the years had passed, she'd toyed with the idea of typing his name into a search engine, torturing herself with the imagined images of him with other women, pressing play on that song and filling her ears with purgatory. But she resisted. Her will was almost unbreakable – she refused to go online other than to check her emails. No good would come of seeing his face again, even if it was only on a laptop. Though he was already there, hidden in folders dating from when they'd first met. She had taken countless portraits of him back then, and had latterly scanned them into her computer, but she didn't plan on opening the ex-files.

* * *

'And for me ... I'll have the edamame beans, miso soup, then dragon rolls and blackened cod for the table,' Georgia ordered, squirming in her chair with excitement. She loved sushi and claimed it helped keep her trim. *Nonsense,* Ella thought to herself. Daily sessions with her personal trainer, minimal carbs, no sugar or salt and no fun – *those* things were responsible for her bony backside. Ella reluctantly selected her supper from the menu, longing for a plate of slow roasted Greek lamb or *kleftiko* with a glass of *retsína* wine instead of Saki. Although she loved Japanese food, she'd rather eat it in

Japan, not in Greece. But as usual, she'd been railroaded by her sister.

Ella enabled Georgia, permitted her to take charge, because one of the things Georgia not only excelled at but also revelled in was controlling everyone. She'd been backed into a corner with this trip, guilted into honouring their mother on the island. Her sister knew it held the most painful memories but Georgia had insisted and Ella had conceded. She'd been avoiding the final ritual of scattering the ashes because it seemed pointless, simply going through the motions of what was expected by convention, and it also in a way marked an ending that she was already too aware of. No matter the age of the child, the death of a parent held a deep significance. It was innately painful, being thrust into adulthood with an empty space above you in the family tree; there was no one left. And what a complex family tree they'd grown. The thought wrapped around her heart as she observed Phoenix across the dinner table, admiring the beautiful young woman she had become in her absence.

There was a man in the corner playing generic background tunes on a piano and Ella continued to look at Phoenix as the tunes washed through her.

'You're doing your staring thing, Auntie Ella,' Phoenix laughed.

'Sorry,' she quickly responded. 'I was just thinking about your music, Phoenie. Which college are you off to in September?'

Her face illuminated in the same way her father's used to when music was the topic of conversation.

'I'm still waiting to hear. I should get provisional offers soon, I think. Trinity or Birmingham would be great, but the Royal Academy would be amazing. It's super hard to

47

get in and I don't know if my auditions were good enough. And then my results need to be what they ask for … so stressy.'

'Don't sell yourself short, Phoenix, you're a wonderful pianist and singer and you had recalls for them all. Oliver and I are ever so proud of her talent,' Georgia interjected a little too enthusiastically. Again, Ella shoved away the regretful stab of guilt she felt for being such a scant presence in Phoenix's life.

'What do you think of "Mr Easy Listening" over there?' Ella asked, grinning mischievously.

Phoenix smirked.

'I don't want to be mean, but—'

'If you don't have anything nice to say, Phoenix…' Georgia interrupted.

'She has a point. The Greek gods will rise up from the sea and spear you with their tridents if you dare to tell the truth, Phoenie!'

Georgia looked away from the table as Phoenix laughed at Ella's stupid jibe. She hadn't meant any harm by it. Then, an awkward silence hung in the air. It was clear that Phoenix didn't understand the sibling dynamic since she looked confused each time there was a tense exchange. Which was often. Their relationship had always been unusual, from the time they were little – which wasn't surprising when they were such opposites – though there were some special memories Ella cherished. On the rare occasions Georgia ceased attempting to control the games they'd played, or stopped prescribing the type of fun she preferred, she would bask in the freedom of Ella's imagination and they would invent characters together, or make houses or castles out of rocks and beach debris. But those moments were now like far off scenes in a film she saw a long time ago. The characters were wisps of recollections, moments out of reach.

Ella was relieved when their first courses arrived, but she could still feel the strain between them simmering like a saucepan threatening to boil. Perhaps Georgia was stressed from organising their break in Greece or maybe she was unhappy at home. Ella thought she should show her sister more grace. She did, in a way, save her life and Phoenix's. As she pushed the slivers of paper-thin sashimi around her plate, she resolved to rescue the moment.

'Why don't you go and give that so-called pianist a run for his money? I dare you!' said Ella, and she could see from the glint in Phoenix's eyes, she relished the challenge.

'I might just do that … but there's something you need to know about me, Auntie Ella. Only one thing comes before music: food!'

Chapter 8

Georgia

After their final course of lychee sorbet, which Georgia resisted, she saw Ella nudge Phoenix, signalling the pianist was taking a break.

She hoped they'd let Phoenix play. Perhaps she could speak to the hotel manager and ask him for a favour given how much she'd spent on the three suites. But Phoenix was already conversing with the musician who nodded and she slid into the seat at the piano. A microphone let out a small squeak of feedback making Georgia wince.

'Hi everyone … I'm Phoenix…' She visibly swallowed away any onset of nerves and Georgia sat up straighter, willing her onwards.

'Um … so my aunt dared me to play for you. I hope you enjoy it.'

She took a deep breath and began. Her fingers ran up and down the keys with a delicate flourish, tinkling high then downwards across the middle register. It wasn't discordant but soothing, elegant, almost hypnotic. Appreciation rumbled across the room. Heads turned and chopsticks were rested on tables, or suspended in motion, as the other patrons gawped at the young woman playing improvised jazz with such astonishing skill. Then, Phoenix segued into a familiar song. The opening chords were held for dramatic effect, followed by the instantly recognisable motif. Diners burst into applause at the iconic beginning as Georgia's gaze whipped around to meet Ella's, their features synchronised in identical horror. Of all the songs to choose… They slowly turned to watch Phoenix once again, and reached for one another's hands, unable to prevent what was happening. Nothing could be done now save for embarking on a feat of endurance. Four minutes and fifteen seconds' worth of a heartbreak marathon.

Phoenix opened her mouth to sing with a delicious huskiness, adding to her bluesy tone. Her face lit up and her contagious electricity infected everybody present. She had the magnetic charisma of a star. It was like hearing the song for the first time, but they were already well-versed in the words.

'Our love won't fade as the years grow old,
'This magic never dies,
'An echo through a memory told,
'On a wind that soars and cries.'
'Oh no…' whispered Ella.

Georgia's body turned rigid, as though rigor mortis had set in.

'Cause you are where I long to be,
'Without you I feel fear,
'I'll carry your love for eternity,
'It's you I'll hold so dear.'

'I can't stand it,' said Ella standing abruptly, her cheek muscle bulging with tension. 'I can't hear his words, not from Phoenix.'

'Don't you move,' Georgia hissed through gritted teeth, which she'd fixed into a smile that had unintentionally morphed into a grimace. She grabbed Ella's arm. 'You encouraged her to do this. It'll be over soon.'

Ella was trembling beneath her hand and Georgia couldn't help the tug of sympathy. There was no way either of them could have foreseen that Phoenix would play Harrison's song. It must have been lurking at the back of her mind since the car ride to the airport; the opening refrain having subliminally crept into her brilliant musical brain. They both inhaled, sucking in painful breaths as the chords crescendoed towards the chorus. Other people around them joined in with the lyrics.

Looking back in time, you are all I see.
Endless searching for your eyes, I feel you reach for me.
Our hearts and souls forever joined, living out of sight.
It's always you, within the darkness you, you will be the light.

The crowds were swaying, some holding their phone torches aloft as if they were at a concert, others recording the moment. Couples rose to dance, overcome by their physical reaction to the romance and pain within the lyrics. Ella sank back down and lifted her wine glass with a shaking hand,

'This is complete torture. Why, why did she pick this to sing?'

'I know,' Georgia said tenderly, holding her hand again. 'It feels like it's been going on for hours.'

Ella smiled sadly and Georgia watched her eyes close as if trying to focus on the sound of Phoenix's voice rather than the words. When the song finally came to an end, almost all the restaurant patrons were on the dance floor, and those who weren't stood and applauded rapturously. Georgia dragged Ella back to her feet, encouraging her to plaster on a brave face. Putting on a front was what they'd both done from the moment Phoenix was born and what Georgia did every single day in her marriage. They'd had a lot of practice.

It took Phoenix a while to make her way back to their table as she received a stream of enthusiastic compliments.

'Darling, you were wonderful.' Georgia beamed proudly, throwing her arms around Phoenix. 'Wasn't she, Ella?'

Phoenix looked to her aunt's face and a shadow of doubt crossed her features. Ella was leaning her hands on the table for support, but she forced a smile.

'Your voice is just stunning, Phoenie, really. You're incredible,' Ella managed before folding her into an embrace. Georgia watched Ella inhale the smell of Phoenix's hair as she buried her face in it. The stab of jealousy for Georgia was excruciating as the song hung between them like an invisible bond, one Phoenix would never know about.

'Your aunt and I were getting all emotional,' said Georgia, pulling Ella away. 'We must be getting sentimental in our old age.'

Phoenix laughed, sitting at the table as the others joined her.

'I don't know about your age, but that song is everything. Not just a crowd pleaser but so much more. I love those lyrics, even though it's probably not very cool, not compared to singing Chet Baker. But I love it. It really speaks to me, here.'

Phoenix gestured to her heart and Georgia trilled a shrill fake laugh. The other two shot her a puzzled look at the bizarre noise she'd made.

'It's a very nice tune, but there's plenty of others that show off your voice much better,' Georgia said.

'Maybe...' started Phoenix. 'But it's like the perfect song. I wish I could write something half as good. The dream...'

Ella stood so quickly that she bumped her thighs against

the table with a jolt making the glassware rattle.

'I need to pop to the bathroom.'

Phoenix watched her leave.

'Is she all right?' she asked as Georgia began to fiddle with her napkin, wishing Ella could control herself as she usually managed to do. But this was too loaded for any modicum of restraint and Georgia was struggling too.

'She's fine, darling ... nothing to worry about.'

Phoenix looked unconvinced. She reached into her small drawstring bag for her lip gloss and applied a sweep before saying, 'Maybe that song reminds her she's single. It's been ages since she had someone. In fact, I've never seen her with anyone. She lives the most amazing, successful life but has nobody to share it with.' She went to pick up her phone from the table, but hesitated and sighed. 'God, imagine loving a person so much you write a song like that about them.'

Georgia couldn't help but snort with the irony.

'Love isn't always the answer to everything, darling. Anyway, she's happy enough in an Ella way.'

Phoenix frowned as she contemplated Georgia's words.

'But she travels all the time, and never stays in one place. No way will she have a proper relationship if she carries on like that.' ·

'Perhaps that's the idea,' Georgia replied before checking herself for fear of revealing too much. 'Don't give it another moment's thought, Phoenix. I promise, she is absolutely fine.'

Ella returned from the bathroom and hovered behind Phoenix uneasily before placing both hands on her shoulders. Her head turned to look up at her aunt.

'I'm a bit done in. I'm going to go to bed. Thank you, Georgia, for the beautiful hotel and you...' She looked down at Phoenix as a choke strangled her voice. 'You ... are exceptional. I know how proud your mother is.'

Georgia squirmed at her words. As Ella left, it looked like her body was laden with lead; she could hardly pick her feet off the ground to take a step.

'See you for yoga at eight!' Georgia cheerily called after her, but she didn't reply.

Phoenix watched Ella trudge away.

'*That* is someone so far from anything that looks like fine. I don't know why you can't see it. The last thing she needs is yoga.'

Georgia took a long, slow sip of water as Phoenix looked at her phone and began to type. She watched the musician resume his position at the piano and wished the whole night away, longing to pretend it hadn't happened. It was a blot on the perfect Hydra night she'd planned. Everything that went wrong – the source of any problem or conflict – seemed to emanate from one source: Harrison. A menacing spirit presiding over their first supper on the island. He was like a demon, holding an unseeable power over them all. Tomorrow, surely, things would look brighter. They had to. Georgia had pinned all her hopes on burying the past in Greece. She knew she had to release herself from all she carried. The burden was becoming too heavy, and she was desperate to set some of it down. But she dared not. She was trapped, unable to command what happened next. Which for Georgia, was absolutely terrifying.

The Island

The island was a seemingly accidental collision of ancient circumstances, regurgitated from the bowels of Hades. But make no mistake, everything was deliberate. The world had challenged humans to exist on this outcrop, but wherever there was light, there would always be darkness.
Love and hatred were the currency of the gods and mortals alike.

Chapter 9

Ella

Ella couldn't settle when she returned to her absurdly tidy hotel room. Being only 9 p.m., it was too early for bed and rest was out of reach. All she could hear were the notes of Harrison's song ricocheting around each part of her brain, piercing every corner like a gust of wind through rice paper.

Despite her earlier resolution not to dwell upon him, she couldn't help it now and it was infuriating. She wanted to scream at him to leave her head. But she knew he would never leave her heart. Phoenix and that love song were at her every turn, an inevitable reminder of what had been lost. How could she ever sever the link without disappearing from Phoenix's life altogether?

Her bedsheets had been turned down, creating a creaseless triangle, and someone from housekeeping had folded her discarded clothes neatly on a chair. There was a box of handmade baklava on the dresser, which she opened, revealing four glistening parcels, oozing with sweet honey syrup glaze. She scoffed the lot. Out on the balcony, the night air was warm, scented with wild herbs. The mainland shimmered on the horizon and the rugged outcrops surrounding Hydra reflected in the water like refracted ghosts. The almost full moon cast a thousand dancing lights onto the sea, as though a pepper pot of glitter had been sprinkled on the surface. Ella imagined mermaids and sea spirits coasting underwater, hiding in the lunar shadows. The opera of night-time Greece was building; cicadas chirruped their overture with increasing persistence, stray cats marked their territory with an aria of caterwauling, and the lapping waves played a recitative. Hydra was as alert as she was. She knew sleep would not come easily, so she decided to go into town and blow off some steam. She hoped to reconnect with the Hydra she used to love and perhaps to erase all thoughts of Harrison with someone else she may meet.

In the mirror, she saw tiredness, visibly worn out not only by tonight but by time. A life spent travelling capturing moments on film. She combed mascara through her long, dark lashes and added a dab of clear gloss on her full lips. With a small swipe of bronzer and, finally, a spritz of citrus perfume, she was ready for the *real* Hydra. The Pirate Bar beckoned.

She called the elevator and when it opened, she found Phoenix inside.

'Auntie Ella. I thought you'd gone to bed.' Her gaze caught on Ella's naturally made-up face. 'Do you have a date?' she asked, raising an eyebrow.

'I have a date with destiny and the authentic island. Coming?' Ella returned her probing look.

'God, yes! Mum's gone to bed with a facemask, and I am bored out of my mind. Everyone here is so proper. Let's go!'

Ella loved how untethered Phoenix was, despite her deeply conventional upbringing. It would have been quite the opposite had she possessed the courage and mental strength to raise her. She would've been slung in a papoose and trekked through all manner of remote, unsuitable places. Much better she'd had a first-class education and stable parents rather than the madness and disarray Ella would have likely inflicted upon her. Yet, for all the trappings of privilege, her spirit shone through. She was a chip off the old block.

This old block, not the other, Ella thought.

'Are we walking to town?' Phoenix said as she looked to her wedges, which added further inches to her impressive height.

'The benefit of a five-star resort is there's no hour too ungodly to call the water taxi.'

'Mum did something right, then.'

Ella turned to her.

'Georgia means well. Her delivery may not always be the best, but her heart and intentions are pure. Cut her some slack. She's very different to you and me. We're wilder, freer, which I know irritates her, but what would we do without her? We wouldn't be here, Phoenie.'

It was true on the surface level and in every other possible way, though Phoenix wouldn't understand Ella's true meaning.

The water taxi was already on standby, and it whisked them around the headland at full throttle. The speed of the vessel did little to dim Ella's hatred of boating. The promise of the port signalled by the inviting lights of the harbour unfortunately couldn't cancel out her irrational fear, though Phoenix's presence was a comfort. Rows of tavernas and bars teemed with people. There was rarely a moment's reprieve from the crowds on the island from Greek Easter until the autumn. Ella remembered the constant flow of tourists and wondered whether many of the local characters remained from her youth. Some had appeared positively ancient when she was little, but then, everyone seems old when you're ten.

'Which one was Granny's house?' asked Phoenix as they neared their destination.

Ella pointed her finger towards the crest of the cliffside to the right as they faced the town. Despite the darkness, the colours of the houses shone through the gloom.

'You see the peachy coloured one, then to the left is a white house with two olive trees in the front? That's it.' No lights were shining through the little windows and Ella felt sad that what was once a vibrant sanctuary for her family seemed to be dormant, slumbering unawares that she was back on the island.

'Such a shame Granny sold it. It would have been so much fun to stay there,' Phoenix said wistfully.

'I know.' Ella nodded, lost in thought as she summoned a stream of childhood recollections. A thousand snapshots flickered in front of her eyes: laughing in the courtyard with Georgia, squirting each other with water pistols to cool off in the sweltering summer heat, climbing the olive trees, seeing who could go higher and then looking down on the garden at the little wooden boat planted with herbs. Georgia had told Ella a monster lived in the boat and they'd made a pact that neither would venture closer than precisely ten footsteps. As she reminisced, Ella suddenly saw fragments of an unfamiliar scene replay, but it was skewed, as if her vision had been clouded. She tried to make sense of it as her chest started to tighten and she gripped onto her seat. It was peculiar, unnerving, but before the memory could crystallise, her thoughts were interrupted by the Greek water-taxi driver who raised his voice to be heard over the engine.

'I thought it was you! I remember your family,' he said. 'Your mother was very kind. She always bought food for the island cats and helped our volunteer vets. You are Ella, yes?'

Ella was taken aback by her strange vision being broken and yet another memory stirred that she couldn't quite grasp.

'Oh ... yes ... I'm Ella. I'm sorry, I'm terrible with faces. Did we know each other?' She stammered the response.

He laughed and shook his head,

'No, not really. I am Vasílis, my father owns the grocery store where your mother used to buy the cat food. I knew she was the English lady who had you and another daughter in the house with the trees. I was too shy to speak to girls back then. But of course, I knew about you. It's a small island.'

Ella smiled at his generous recollections. She felt Phoenix nudge her and Ella turned to look. She seemed to be urging her to do something with her eyes, which widened and gleamed golden in the low light.

'What?' Ella whispered.

'Vasílis, you and my auntie should catch up on old times. Give me your mobile number and I can connect you with Ella. She doesn't have a phone. Total philistine.'

Ella watched on in horror and admiration as Phoenix took charge of the situation, thrusting her phone at the man. Georgia had had more influence on her than Ella realised. He looked bemused and Ella took the moment to look at him. He was handsome and tanned, and his carefully crafted stubble accentuated his jaw. She saw the veins in his muscular forearms when he returned Phoenix's phone, and as he caught her eye, she saw a shyness, which was endearing and more attractive than a simmering gaze of assured sexuality.

'Nice to see you again, Ella, after all this time and so much history. You have come home.'

She smiled at his sentiment. Hydra did in a way feel like home because it was so familiar, and, after all, it was her birthplace, even though she'd been forced to return by

Georgia. She found herself blushing despite the previous horror at Phoenix's match-making attempt. Ella bid him an embarrassed good evening in Greek, '*Kalispéra*', and dragged Phoenix speedily up the harbour steps.

* * *

'*Yiá mas*! Cheers, Phoenie,' Ella said as she raised her ouzo, and they clinked glasses. 'Take it slow, this is Greek rocket fuel – keep adding water when the ice melts. And don't tell your mother!' She didn't want to be on the receiving end of a lecture from Georgia if she brought Phoenix back from town steaming drunk, even though she would be eighteen in August. She wouldn't be the first teenager to sneak an underage drink or two. Ella certainly had.

'So, I have a thousand questions since I hardly ever see you,' Phoenix said as she directed her piercing brown gaze at Ella.

'Fire away, sweetheart. Though I reserve the right not to answer, especially after your thoroughly unsubtle attempt at pairing me off with poor Vasílis. I'd eat him for breakfast.'

Phoenix laughed and threw her head backwards. She was so beautiful; Ella couldn't help the pride that swelled within her. Though, despite her looks being partly down to Ella, Phoenix's demeanour was nothing she was able to claim. Georgia had done that. She was only so glorious because Ella had asked her sister to adopt her, and Georgia was truly an exceptional mother. At least her sister had been able to experience parenthood, even though the cost to Ella's own heart had been immense and always would be.

'What's up with your love life? That's why I'm up to mischief by matching you and the sexy boat man. You've not had a relationship ever, as far as I can remember.'

Ella sipped her drink and crunched the ice cube around her mouth, taking a beat to marvel at Phoenix's directness. As she signalled to the waiter who brought over another round, Ella wondered whether she could share a little, then change the subject.

'I'm happier on my own, Phoenie. I don't have to answer to anyone and I get to experience the world, go where I want, doing what I love. I follow my camera wherever it takes me and that's more than enough. I was hurt badly once, and I don't ever want to feel like that again. I realised a long time ago that relationships and me don't go together. Never have. It's for the best. For everyone.'

Phoenix frowned as she took a sip and Ella poured another slug of water into the glass from a jug on the table.

'Auntie Ella, if you're happy without someone that's great. Though...' She paused to gather a thought. 'It's like you're always holding back. That's not about being alone, it's you. I see it. So does Mum. I feel like I don't know you at all sometimes...' Phoenix's words slurred slightly and again Ella refilled her glass with water, shocked that she was being psycho-analysed so effectively. Phoenix saw Ella as clearly as only one other person had: Harrison. It was deeply unnerving. Ella said nothing, instead turning her head to the sea, watching people mill about on the dock. A cat was sitting on the stone base of the statue on the harbour front and a small boy had climbed up to keep it company.

'What did he do to hurt you?' Phoenix said, pressing for information Ella was unwilling to share, least of all with her.

'It's the past, Phoenie. That's where he should stay.'

'Please, tell me. I haven't seen you for a year and I can't remember the time before that. I only get random emails and those are months apart. Why won't you let me in?'

Ella sighed in hesitation as her mind flashed back to a moment when she'd said the exact same thing to Harrison. The eyes that Phoenix shared with him implored her into submission and the drinks had loosened her tongue. She tentatively began to tell the story of the end.

'He was amazing, beautiful... We were so young. It was 1997 when we met – I was at uni. And God, we were in love, a love you can't even imagine. You never forget your first, I wish I could, believe me. But he...' Ella paused to avoid saying his name. 'He didn't know how to accept love. His childhood was hideous, with terrible abuse that left him feeling abandoned... Despite how much I gave to him, something blocked him from properly committing. To me. I know he loved me, but he never said the words out loud. What happened between us still hurts, even all these years later. Phoenie, please learn from my mistakes. Never give more to someone than they're willing to give to you.'

Her mouth had dried, and she took a gulp of water. Now she'd started, she couldn't stop. It was like beginning a prayer – it felt blasphemous not to complete it. She continued the summary of heartbreak despite feeling as if she was betraying someone by saying it out loud. It was dangerous, but she couldn't help it. Phoenix wouldn't know who she was speaking of, and it was too late to stop.

Phoenix rested her chin in her hand and listened as she unknowingly heard the end of her mother and father's relationship.

'We were at the same university but on different courses and accidentally found each other. It was as though we'd been drawn together by some kind of force. The ancient Greeks would have had a field day with our mystical mad energy, like monsters, gods, demons and curses ... and I do feel like

I've been cursed...' She tailed off on a solo mental tangent as a luxury motor cruiser moored skilfully within the main harbour. Eventually, Ella returned her attention to Phoenix.

'The strange thing is, it seemed like we were together a lifetime but it was actually less than a year. And the end ... it was awful. The worst. He was offered an incredible job opportunity and decided to leave his course early.' She deliberately omitted the fact that he was a musician as it would pique Phoenix's interest too much. 'I don't blame him for taking it. We were only teenagers and so eager to go out into the world...' Picking up a bowl of olives, Ella saw Phoenix was patiently waiting, captivated by the nuggets of her past she was revealing. She usually didn't give so much away, and it damaged her heart dearly to relive such deep-rooted pain, pain which led her to relinquish the only chance of motherhood she'd have. Ella chose a tangy Kalamata black olive from the bowl and it glistened in the candlelight. She put it into her mouth then retrieved the stone.

'I went with him to King's Cross station on the day he was leaving. He was headed first for Scotland and then he'd be off around the world for months. In those days, hardly anyone had phones and there was no social media, so there wasn't really a way for us to keep in touch. Our plan was that I'd leave uni at the end of January and join him so we could travel together. It was going to be an amazing adventure. We came up with the idea on Hydra the November before, while trying to figure out a way to stay together. We'd been back and forth on it for weeks, raking over a hundred versions of our life, but I eventually decided that the only way to make it work was for me to quit my degree. I knew he didn't want me to give up my career for him, and my future was everything to me – I wrestled so hard with it. But ultimately, I couldn't imagine being without him and my decision was firm. I would head to Scotland and find work, then go wherever he went and carve out my career that way. So, that day, we sat on a bench in the train station, and he held me in his arms as I cried, even though I'd see him again in a few weeks. He kissed me a hundred times, but with each touch of his lips, it was like my heart cracked open further. We hardly spoke, all he kept saying was "El, my El, my love" between kisses.' Ella heard his voice echo in her thoughts and she shivered. 'I couldn't walk away. I needed the pain he caused me, like a tattoo on the inside of my heart; a needle dragged through every artery to remind myself how much I loved him. Recalling someone in terms of pain is not healthy, Phoenie … but he was my first love. Memorable for the wrong reasons, for the right ones, and also for those I will never be able to say aloud.'

The silence hung in the air like a storm threatening to break, before Phoenix asked, 'Why did it end if you were going to be with him? What happened?' Her innocence and romantic heart sung through her naïve questions.

'At the station, something profound happened. It was as though our souls fused together, destined to be connected forever as we stared at each other. I can't explain it. It was like an earthquake happened inside me and he felt it in his body too. Phoenie, he was so beautiful, every time I looked into his eyes, I wanted to climb inside him; I couldn't be close enough. He was my absolute, complete torture.' Ella took a fortifying gulp of her drink and continued. 'We had twenty minutes before his train left and I went to get us coffees. I still remember what I said right before I walked to the kiosk – "You'd better give me the address of where you'll be in Scotland, so I know where to find you when I come." I shouldn't have left his side, but our energy was too powerful, and I was overwhelmed by it. I wish I hadn't moved, but...'

Ella paused to muster the strength to bring the story to its conclusion and return to the present. The Pirate Bar was humming with a crowd keen to make their Saturday memorable – music played and people danced, celebrating the moment – and Ella knew she'd never shake off the past until she finished her story.

'Then what...?' Phoenix prompted, noticing Ella's attention had strayed.

The reluctance to journey towards her personal hell was like a physical pain, yet she forged onwards.

'I stood at the café in the queue trying to imagine my life without him, and I couldn't. I felt this bubble in the pit of my stomach, telling me I'd made the right choice to take a different path. It was exciting – a new, unexpected chapter. I returned to the bench to tell him how I couldn't wait to start our lives together and I'd miss him horribly until I could get to Scotland. But he wasn't there. I thought I'd gone to the wrong seat in my haste, so I went to the next row. He wasn't there either. There was no sign of him. I looked around, holding the coffees. I remember they started to scald my palms. I checked the board and saw that his train hadn't started boarding yet. There was still twelve minutes before departure.'

'I looked for him everywhere. On every platform, in every shop, through the crowds of people. But he was nowhere to be seen. Five minutes before the train was due to leave, they announced that the train would depart from platform fifteen, and passengers swarmed to board.

'I rushed up to the barriers, looking at every person as they went through. As the crowd dwindled, I began to cry and panic. I doubted everything, desperately telling myself that he would never do this to me, he must be somewhere close by, I could feel it. Then I heard the whistle of the signalman marking a departure. I saw a late passenger fiddling with their ticket at the turnstile and I dropped the coffees to the floor; they splashed my jeans but I sprinted forward, rushing through the barriers. I raced along the platform, frantically searching each window for his face, but it was starting to accelerate and though I ran as fast as I could, I couldn't keep up. The train exited the station and was gone. He was gone.

'I felt like my insides had been ripped out. He couldn't even find a way to say goodbye with any semblance of love and respect. Instead, he chose to run away like a coward and abandon me without a word, wrecking our plans. I had no way to contact him, no address, nothing.'

She let her words travel upwards into the inky sky to kiss the stars nestled within the constellations before adding,

'And I will never, ever forgive him.'

Chapter 10

Georgia

Sunday

Georgia hadn't expected Phoenix or Ella to join her for yoga, though she wished they'd make some effort to follow her itinerary, or at least have the decency to notify her when they wouldn't. It was disappointing, and only their second day on Hydra.

Zen and calm were precisely what Georgia needed, especially after the tension last night following Phoenix's performance. There hadn't been a peep from her yet. Georgia had pressed her ear to the hotel room door as she'd passed and decided to let her enjoy the extra sleep. Their plan was to lunch together at the traditional hotel taverna with some relaxing pool time scheduled for the afternoon. Perhaps the native food would encourage her sister into a more collaborative mood.

She looked at the clock on the wall, wondering where the instructor was. Everyone seemed to run ten minutes behind 'Georgia time'. She was early for everything.

'Am I late? Did I miss it?' Ella panted as she rushed into the exercise studio, her cheeks flushed in panic. A huge smile spread over Georgia's face.

'You made it! I can't believe you actually came.'

'I am nothing but a walking surprise, evolving every day, sis!'

Georgia frowned at Ella. She seemed lighter, different to yesterday, and certainly vastly altered from last night.

'You're surprisingly cheerful this morning...'

Ella took her place on a mat and straightened out her legs, folding forward with incredible flexibility. Georgia watched with mild irritation as her sister effortlessly rested her head on her knees. She never exercised and yet was blessed with astonishing mobility, highlighting their five year age difference. Ella had no idea how much a woman's body changed past forty, but she was edging ever closer, Georgia thought.

'I've worked a couple of things out,' said Ella, crossing her legs. 'I am officially over the past and now it's all about the future.'

Georgia gasped and clapped her hands in a speedy applause.

'About time! But why the sea-change?'

'Oh, a whole bunch of things,' she said dismissively. 'Do you remember a kid called Vasílis from when we were little?'

'Vasílis ... yes! His dad owned a grocery shop. Why, have you seen him?'

A flicker of excitement sparked in Georgia's tummy at the idea her sister may be about to embark upon a fling, visiting the past in a much healthier way than she had of late.

Ella looked worried and hesitated.

'Last night. He runs one of the hotel shuttle boats. He's incredibly cute and said some really lovely things about Mum. Oh, and I think her house is empty.'

'There's a lot to deal with in that sentence! He's hot, and…?'

'And nothing. Don't get giddy, Georgia. A holiday romance is the last thing I need.'

'Maybe it's *exactly* what you need! Have a fling and get that other person flung from your system once and for all!'

Ella laughed as she assumed the lotus position.

'We're not here long enough for the amount of flinging that would require! But I keep thinking about Mum's house and if anyone lives there. There weren't any lights on yesterday.'

'It's funny. I'd wondered whether I'd want to go and knock on the door when we arrived, but just being on the island again … the memories all around us are enough. I'm not even curious.' Georgia caught Ella's surprised expression and acknowledged her own unusual behaviour. 'I know, it's quite unlike me. But memories of our times on Hydra from before are enough. We're here to say goodbye to Mum and close that part of our lives. The house has probably changed hands several times since she sold it, and I wouldn't want to see it all different. I'm happy with how I remember it.'

Georgia also knew what could still be at the house and it was the last thing she wanted to see. It was already in front of her each time she closed her eyes.

'Wow! I thought you'd barge in there and urge them to redesign the whole kitchen.' Ella laughed, amazed at her sister's intention not to visit.

'I know,' Georgia agreed, pushing the real reason deep down inside. 'But there is something so freeing about being back here again. Like we can all shed what's gone before. It sounds like you're feeling it too. So maybe we can go forward and get rid of all the darkness. Leave it here forever.'

Georgia shivered a little, hoping to rid herself of all her

secrets on the island, wishing Hydra could take her apart and mend her again minus the ever-present guilt. It might help her meet Ella's eye without feeling terrible, even after the significant amount of time that had passed.

Ella was visibly surprised at Georgia's sentiment, and she blinked several times before speaking.

'Well, it sounds like you've already got your guru on, so let's skip class and go for a mimosa or five instead. I dare you!'

'We can't, the teacher will be expecting us,' she said, though Ella's energy was infectious. It tickled at her insides, and she felt giddy about breaking a rule. 'But, I mean, we could, couldn't we?'

'We're not the only ones in the class, the instructor won't notice we're gone. Pull up your expensive leggings and let's get smashed at breakfast!'

They linked arms and slunk, giggling, out of the studio. It was as though the pair of them had been re-baptised by the Greek island air. Cleansed by something in the atmosphere, which had yielded a way to bond that neither of them had expected. Hydra was slowly peeling back their layers.

Georgia always harboured hope they'd find a way to reconnect. Since their mother had died, they'd become even more fractured. The glue that barely held their small family together wasn't there anymore, and they'd drifted; Ella had drifted. The time spent together so far had highlighted their differences, but at the same time, it now seemed to be marking how dissimilar they were in an almost celebratory fashion. And given all Georgia had concealed for so long, she was relieved to rekindle a kind of kinship.

* * *

'This is more like it, proper Greek food!' said Ella as she

scooped up the last dollop of *skordaliá* with a chunk of crusty sourdough. The smell of the garlic pureed potatoes tempted Georgia, but given she'd missed out on her exercise class, she was resisting a heavy lunch as best she could. Her delicious plate of roasted vegetables glistened with golden olive oil and, as the flavours collided around her palate, she'd realised how accustomed she'd become to a dull diet of steamed fish and broccoli. Maybe she'd try something different at supper tonight if she did lengths in the pool later.

The hotel taverna was nestled in a perfectly manicured olive grove and looked like a film set. Cobalt painted tables and chairs sat on a paved patio beneath an overhang coated in pungent white jasmine. The hot air was tinged with sweetness as the flowers baked beneath the afternoon sunshine. Ella appeared happier about the more authentic menu, encouraging Phoenix to try various dips and small plates, and everyone was in good spirits with the promise of a long, languid day stretching out before them. Georgia adjusted her seat further into the shade and spritzed another mist of sunscreen on her arms before hiding her skin again with her favourite cover-up. It was gossamer light and she'd thought it would be useful when she packed it, but the expensive silky fabric was sticking to her sweaty skin. It would be destined for the hotel dry cleaning service after only an hour's wear.

'Mum?' Phoenix began as she fished out a succulent slice of green pepper from the bottom of her salad bowl. 'Could we go into town for dinner? It's so buzzy and busy. I love it. Please...?'

Georgia snapped her head up from her plate.

'When did you see the town in the evening?' she demanded, narrowing her eyes, though she suspected she knew the answer – particularly as they'd only been on Hydra one night.

Ella and Phoenix exchanged a look of panic, and Georgia deduced they'd stolen away without her.

'Don't get mad. I went out for a drink and took Phoenie with me last night. We bumped into each other in the elevator, and you'd gone to bed, so—'

Georgia interrupted. 'Well, we thought *you'd* gone to bed, but the truth is you couldn't wait to ditch me and do your own thing, just as you always do. Thanks for leaving me out.'

She petulantly sat back in her seat, pushing away the remainder of her lunch, then folded her arms trying to contain her hurt. She felt deflated. Her relationship with Ella constantly felt like it took one step forward then twenty backwards. It had always been as such, and she was cross with herself for having hopes they could find a meaningful bond.

They had been close once, but that was born of Georgia's guilt for what had happened when they were children. Thinking back, she'd always been envious of her sister. Ella was more adventurous, amusing, prettier, but Georgia was quite certain they used to have fun together, especially when they were on holiday with their mother. After the accident, that was. Georgia had spent her childhood trying to make amends without ever uttering the reason. Now, things were different, and while Ella's quest for excitement may be admirable to some, she was dragging Phoenix along on her boozy escapades. Georgia intended to keep a closer eye on them both to prevent any adverse influence.

'Mum, don't be upset. Anyway, if we hadn't gone out, we wouldn't have met my future uncle, that heavenly boatman, Vasílis.' She grinned.

'Jumping the gun a bit, Phoenie...' Ella laughed. 'I have much to teach you about men if that's how you think it was going to go.'

'I think you're the last person to give relationship advice, don't you?' Georgia snapped, still smarting at her exclusion from their secret excursion.

'Mum!' said Phoenix.

'It's fine, Phoenie, she's right. Especially after what I told you about my ex,' Ella said in an attempt to defuse the situation, but she had mistakenly ignited her sister's wrath.

Georgia's heart suddenly picked up pace.

'What did you tell her?' she asked sharply.

'She told me how he ended things. I'd like to kill him,' said Phoenix, clenching her fists.

Georgia stood, glaring at her sister.

'What did you say to her? Phoenix, please go to your room.'

'No! You can't tell me what to do. Stop being so horrible to both of us.'

'Do as you're told for once and go to your room this instant. I want to speak to Ella alone.'

Ella stood up to face Georgia.

'You know what, I have absolutely nothing to say to you. I haven't told Phoenix much at all. Don't pick on her, when it's clearly me you're mad at.'

Tears began to prick, stinging Georgia's nostrils and making her head ache. The morning mimosas were beginning to wear off and she felt nauseous. But if she was honest, it wasn't the drinks making her sick. It was the fact that Ella had talked to Phoenix about Harrison. Reckless wasn't even the word. It was downright dangerous. Like she wanted to expose the truth, coaxing it to the surface like a fish lured by a worm.

How dare she, Georgia thought to herself. Ella wouldn't be such a fan of the truth if she knew what Georgia had kept from her all these years.

The Island

Islands, like gods and mortals, had secrets too. Whether it be a hidden cave, a concealed cove or a secret tunnel that led to the underworld. The difference was this island had no care for the sisters' quarrel and wanted to reveal all that had been buried deep for too long. The murky memories still lived on, given life and energy by their dispute. It was only a matter of time before the tide washed them onto the shore.

Chapter 11

Ella

Ella could hardly contain her fury at her sister, but she held it in and managed to endure the remainder of their lunch before swiftly departing for the harbour. Her heart was hammering so hard, her ribcage felt battered. Georgia was unbelievable, trying to control a conversation Ella had had with Phoenix last night when she wasn't even there!

Her angry footsteps pounded along the steep streets of Hydra town as she walked with no clue as to where she was headed. She was utterly fed up with having to get into a boat every time she wanted to put distance between herself and Georgia, which appeared to be a daily occurrence. It was as though her sibling had purposely put Ella in a place to trap her, knowing she'd have to confront her phobia if she wanted to escape.

An elderly woman was making hard work of the steps up a narrow alleyway ahead. The shadows draped over her frame accentuated her tiny figure, which was cloaked in black, and Ella couldn't resist taking a picture. The light was piercingly sharp and she marvelled at its clarity with breathless awe. She would edit the photograph into black and white when she downloaded it later; the contrast would be sensational.

The woman walked towards a shaft of brilliant sunlight, which awaited her at the end of the incline. Her shopping bag appeared to weigh her down and in the other hand she held a stick, which clacked against the ground. Ella rushed towards her and mimed an offer to take her bag. She smiled a gummy grin and nodded as she handed over her burden, stopping to consider her good Samaritan for a moment. They stood opposite one another in the empty alleyway and the woman grasped Ella's wrist with her hand and gave it a squeeze, closing her eyes as she did so. She then continued onwards and Ella walked slowly to match her pace, taking the steps one foot at a time. The old lady's presence was comforting, and the gnarly edge of Ella's fury evaporated into the hot fragranced air.

Rounding the corner into bright sunshine, the side street looked as though they'd stumbled into Marrakech. Towering, spindly cacti were planted in large terracotta urns, reaching their prickly fingers towards the blue sky and casting shadowy angular streaks on the whitewashed stone walls. An orange bell tower glowed brightly against its vibrant surroundings and Ella felt a calm enter her bones as they steadily made their way. Island cats were draped along the kerbs, their paw pads exposed to sunshine like dots of raw pink skin.

Eventually, they arrived at a dark mahogany door and the lady stopped. Her black widow's weeds clung to her stockinged legs.

She must be as drenched as I am, thought Ella. Beaded sweat itched at her hairline as the afternoon sun beat down on their backs.

'*Endáxi*, OK,' she croaked, fishing for a key from the black leather handbag hooked over her elbow. She opened the door to the house and blissfully cool air rushed forth. The tiled hallway was simple and stark, and Ella deposited the shopping bag on the floor while the woman lit a candle on the shrine in the entrance with a match. A photograph of a man and another of a woman sat on the sideboard, accompanied by religious icons. She crossed herself, then moved away and Ella picked up the bag once more, glancing briefly back at the pictures.

'*Bríki*,' the woman shouted from the kitchen. Ella joined her and unpacked the shopping at the table. The simply appointed room had dark brown cabinets, and the stone walls bulged beneath their cream painted coating. The smell of damp rock was soothing – the same mushroomy tang she remembered from her holidays on the island. The old lady boiled a tiny saucepan of water on the stove and stood over it. Ella recognised the art of Greek coffee making and recalled the *bríki* was the pot used in the ritual. Her mother used to do the same and the scent transported Ella back to her old kitchen. The woman spooned in the granules at precisely the right time, so it frothed and boiled giving the 'crema' on the surface, the pleasing liquid separation forming two-tone coffee.

'*Záchari?*' she asked, and Ella knew that meant sugar, retrieving it from her limited Greek vocabulary.

'*Nai, Éna, efharistó*,' Ella replied asking for one with thanks.

The older woman decanted the contents of the saucepan into small porcelain glazed cups without handles. They were cream, rustic and irregular in shape. Ella thought them beautiful and would love a set of her own, if she ever managed to furnish her flat and make it a home.

Home.

She realised she had no idea where she belonged. Vasílis said she'd come home again as he'd ferried her into town with

Phoenix last night, but Ella had no true roots in one place, and didn't possess the urge to settle. She knew instinctively it was because she was stranded in the cracks of a parallel life, running from all she'd lost. Yet once more in Greece after so many years, it was as though she'd remembered what home was supposed to feel like. Reluctantly, she admitted Hydra fitted her and she connected with its energy. Despite her cross words with Georgia at lunch, the conversation she'd had with Phoenix last night – re-telling the gruesome finality of her relationship with Harrison – felt cathartic, like a demon had been exorcised from her body. The island was setting her free.

At the kitchen table, the old woman and Ella smiled at each other. Strangers, yet there was no awkwardness. She scrutinised Ella and nodded in the silence between sips of coffee.

'*Me léne Ella,*' she said, pointing at her chest, hoping her poor rudimentary Greek translated as 'my name is Ella'. The woman's eyes widened in acknowledgement, and she nodded again.

'*Nai, me léne Zina.*' She sipped again at her drink, after replying that her name was Zina. Her eyes were the shade of seaweed green and her thin grey hair was scraped back into a severe bun, but in the afternoon's heat stray tendrils had made a bid for freedom. Her hands shook a little as she held her cup, fingers contorted at the tips by arthritis and age. It was a rare occasion when Ella wished she had a mobile phone to use the translation function.

'Ella,' the old woman said, nodding again.

Zina raised her barely visible eyebrows and looked to the ceiling. She placed her cup on the table, clasping it with crooked hands as a wry smile appeared on her lined lips. Zina gingerly rose from the chair, easing herself upright using the table for leverage, then shuffled to a drawer in the kitchen dresser and returned with a pen and paper. She began to write. When she finished, the note was pushed towards Ella who picked it up. But it was in Greek and she could only recognise the odd character. It looked like hieroglyphics in the woman's spidery scrawl. Ella would ask Vasílis to translate it and she smiled her thanks for the mystery message.

'*Efharistó poli, Zina, ya ton kafé,*' Ella said, thanking her very much for the coffee. Or that's what she thought she'd said.

'*Parakaló,*' she replied, saying Ella was welcome. She grasped at Ella's hands and fixed her with an intense gaze, muttering to herself. She then cupped Ella's cheek in a gesture that took her by surprise. It was the exact same one she had used when she'd first met Harrison. She might have been saying thank you for helping with the shopping, but Ella had no way of knowing. Once again, she smiled and nodded in the universal language of cluelessness.

* * *

After she'd left Zina's house, Ella wandered aimlessly through the streets. Some of the stones underfoot were slippery, polished smooth by the thousands of feet and hooves stamping them into shining submission. As she climbed upwards, glimpses of the harbour appeared briefly through the rooftops, which boasted identical tiles of varying hues: deep russet, burnished auburn or those recently replaced that gleamed a brick orange. The noise from the town became muted like a distant sea-bird's cry. The clanging bustle of the port was almost a memory from up there.

Her thoughts were jumbled, confused by the old woman and the scribble she'd given her, currently nestled in her shorts pocket. Something she couldn't place was pulling at her. Maybe it was her reflective sentimentality about the island, or the idea of scattering her mother's ashes in the coming week. She realised she'd never asked her mum why she'd selected Hydra to buy a bolthole, why she'd chosen to be there on the island for Ella's birth. It was such a specific place. Now, it was too late. She'd never know.

Ella took photographs of the port from above the main drag. Greek flags strapped to the masts of yachts fluttered blue and white in the breeze as the vessels rocked gently in the shifting tide. Rows of awning strings, telephone wires and rope lights created a zig-zag pattern from her bird's-eye view.

Somehow, she had found herself at the bottom of the trail marking the start of the steep steps that would lead to their old house, the place she'd longed to avoid and had vowed never to revisit. But she'd said that about Hydra as well, and here she was. The muscle recall of the climb had long deserted her calves, but they were pinched into reminiscence as she walked towards the setting for the happiest and the saddest memories she owned. The good were all before Harrison and she longed to recapture some of that joy in her heart.

Ella took a breath, summoning her courage, which never lurked too far away, and stood in front of the house. The white stone was freshly painted and the dark blue window frames matched the door's deep navy hue – the same colours her mum had used for the frontage. She raised her knuckles to the front door and rapped three times. Ella waited for the sound of footsteps on flagstones. But there were none. She tried again, repeating her knock before stepping backwards to look at the three top windows. But there was nobody home, perhaps it was empty after all. She felt disappointed, having geared herself up to visit, though Ella supposed it was another connection with the past she could sever.

Re-threading her steps down through the winding streets and stairways, she couldn't help but think about why she was drawn back to the house, when it ought to be Georgia rather than her behaving in such a way. For Ella, it had become a sacred, hallowed place. What happened under that roof changed the course of her life forever, having conceived Phoenix there. Then life had broken her, and she'd been unable to cope. Her thoughts had become as dark and desperate as they could. At times her mind was shrouded in blackness, wanting to make the pain disappear the only way she could think of. She remembered being in London, wishing she could be back on the island to end it where it all began, imagining leaping into the abyss, dashing out her brains on the pointed rocks below. An energy in the air had stopped her doing the very worst, and the responsibility of the little person growing inside her burgeoning belly. The first, and very likely the only, time she would experience the feeling of being an expectant mother. Maybe she'd been sent to the island again at the right time in her life, to make peace with it. The universe was encouraging her to finally release the past and focus on her future. It seemed to be a recurring theme since returning to Greece. Consigning her mother's ashes to the waves would also be a part of that spiritual journey.

Ella hadn't cried about her mum much, even though her death was a shock. Heart attacks tended to be a surprise to everyone involved, especially fatal ones. She had left Georgia to clear out their mother's house in London and arrange for the furniture to be sold. Ella didn't attach sentimentality to material things as it was just stuff to her, but her sister wanted to cling on to clothing and trinkets. Ella's cheeks had remained dry at the funeral; tears only threatened at the sight of Phoenix sobbing. She couldn't protect her from pain then, but she could shield her from their secret history.

Ella sauntered down the final slope towards the port, knowing she needed to find a way to make things right with her sister. Her eyes traced the tips of the hills behind the houses when she reached the harbour. The waves crashed against the seawall as she absorbed the deafening island sounds from the core of the action. The heartbeat of Hydra pulsed around her body and it filled her with renewed determination. She would say goodbye to her mother, relegate all her mistakes to history and leave her broken heart on the island for good.

The Island

The island was a constant reminder of the thin line between life and death. It was like a tightrope stretched between its cliffs; on either side of the precipice was where fate and destiny dwelt, eagerly awaiting the choices made along the precarious route, ready to guide a steady path ahead or orchestrate a deadly turn.

Chapter 12

Ella

There was no need for more coffee after Zina's brew. Happily, the *kafenion* served much stronger fare. Ella ordered a small jug of cool white wine and enjoyed the shade beneath the billowing awning.

The waiter served her drink along with a bowl of olives and some pistachios harvested from the island of Aegina. She sat and people watched, absorbing their movements, allowing the sparkling waves to hypnotise her. A cluster of cats crept forward to the edge of the harbour as a fishing boat docked. She raised her camera, enjoying the varying markings and patches on the feline gathering: tabby, marmalade, glossy black and matte grey. The fisherman gutted his catch and threw the innards to his captive furry audience who took it in turns to feast. Their behaviour was so different to cats on the mainland who had to scrap and scrape for every morsel. On Hydra, they were cared for; bowls of kibble sat on every street corner. Ella's mind travelled to expeditions with Georgia and their mother along with the island's vets to unearth a poorly creature who had been spotted. Anna had been passionate about the care of the animals and always reminded them that the island would be a lesser place without its four-legged furry folks. It was such a beautifully romantic corner of Greece almost from another era, as if time had stood still; no cars only mules or a dreaded boat to provide transport. Once again, Hydra lured Ella into the belly of its soul like a siren call, and she surrendered to its song.

She couldn't help but wonder how life could have been if she'd come here with Harrison to live, as they'd talked of so many times. An idyllic dream they'd shared that had come to nothing. She crushed the pistachio shells between her fingers in anger at her own thoughts, wishing he wouldn't creep into her mind when she sought peace. Taking a sip of wine, she read the menu in the name of distraction, deciding on a mezze of *patátes tiganités*, fried potatoes topped with oregano and crumbled feta, and tzatziki to dip them into. A simple late afternoon snack that would horrify her sister, laden with calories. Guilt snagged at her from their unresolved disagreement. She would make things right at dinner tonight, then start afresh in the morning by obeying Georgia's militant itinerary. They were bound for Metochi across the water tomorrow and Ella intended to be the embodiment of sisterly devotion despite having yet another boat to board. Until then, she'd indulge in Greek food and soak up the sounds of Hydra.

*　*　*

Her stomach was full from the generous portions, and she couldn't be bothered to move, not even when she spotted Phoenix disembarking the shuttle boat. She looked striking in her white sundress. Her long legs already boasted a deep suntan and her curly chestnut mane cascaded down her back. Phoenix spotted her and grinned, striding over, unaware of the admiring glances she received from those she passed.

'Auntie Ella, you've been gone for hours. But I thought I might find you here.'

Ella smiled and received her hug, then emptied the remainder of her second small jug of wine into her tumbler.

'It's deliberate avoidance tactics, Phoenie. But I hope you told Georgia you were coming into town. I don't want to be accused of stealing you away and filling your head with tragic stories of my failed romances.'

Ella's tongue was too loose, but she couldn't help the jibes, despite the earlier resolution to make amends.

'You mean there's more than one failed romance? Do tell!' Phoenix replied playfully.

'I've told you enough and honestly, there's very little else to say on me and men. Is my sister still in a mood?'

She shook her head making her curls ripple around her face.

'Oh, she's fine. Just in one of her huffs. I've tried to talk to her about the perimenopause, but she refuses to discuss it. She doesn't realise how enlightened I am.'

The idea of a teenager schooling their mother on hormones was amusing, especially as Georgia didn't like to be corrected, nor told what to do. Ironic, considering she spent all her time bossing everyone around. Hormones weren't Georgia's problem; she had always been erratic. Ella couldn't ever have imagined having such open conversations with her own mother, who had been quite liberal for her generation, but Phoenix and her contemporaries seemed comfortable talking about anything. Ella realised in the moment that she would never be Phoenix's first port of call for advice as she travelled through her adult years. But she bravely smiled and said, 'You are, my darling one, enlightened and exceptional. Can I order you something?'

Phoenix said no, but Ella beckoned the waiter anyway.

'*Állo éna áspro krassí.*' She held up the jug, ordering another measure of wine in Greek. It was all she knew how to do confidently in the language – order food and drink probably with terrible grammar. She'd learnt such phrases in most languages around the world so she could always feed and water herself wherever she went. She caught Phoenix raising her eyebrows. 'Don't say I've had enough, you'll sound like my sister.'

'Ha! That would be a first. It's so funny, isn't it, how different I am to Mum? And Mum was so similar to Granny. I don't think I'm like my dad *at all*. And no one else is musical. So crazy how genetics work.'

'Hilarious.' Ella snorted, not wishing to indulge the topic of conversation for fear of Georgia's wrath should she uncover it.

Phoenix continued.

'Anyway, I've been thinking about you and your ex. It seems you're unwilling to take any steps to get over this guy. So, in the spirit of my Mum … *I* am taking charge. Maybe I'm more like her than I thought!' she laughed.

'What have you done?' Ella asked as a dull seed of panic crept into her blood.

'Don't be cross … but … someone is meeting us here.'

Ella couldn't deduce what Phoenix was talking about, although at least it had steered her away from talk of her lineage.

Phoenix's brown eyes danced with amusement.

'Don't look, but he's walking over now.'

Ella's mouth suddenly dried in alarm but she exhaled with relief when she spotted it was only Vasílis. The man was handsome but didn't quite ignite a spark for her. But that could be because she'd been so shut off, nobody could get close.

As if she could read Ella's mind, Phoenix said, 'Give him a chance … you never know.'

Ella plastered on a wide smile and through gritted teeth whispered, 'I'll get you for this.'

She turned to greet him. They awkwardly kissed one another on each cheek and he took a seat beside her. Ella's eyes darted between him and Phoenix, giving her the evil eye as best she could without him noticing. There was an uncomfortable silence and Ella took the moment to look at Vasílis as he perused the menu. His tan glowed in the sun's setting beams, accentuated by his black shirt. He had that effortless ease in his body that she recalled from photographing locals here before. It was an unattainable, unmistakable Greek swagger swathed in confidence, stopping just short of arrogance. She was mindful of the sweeping generalisations that ran through her mind, but she found the idea of being near him surprisingly intriguing. She only wished she hadn't already consumed so much wine.

'So.' He leant forward and turned his head towards Ella as his strong forearms rested on the table. 'How is it to be on Hydra once more?'

'It never changes, and I like that. I don't know what I expected, but I'd forgotten how happy it used to make me … a long time ago.'

Vasílis raised his hand for the waiter, then turned back to Ella, his hazel eyes glinting.

'Then perhaps it is time for you to be happy once more…'

She felt a flip in the pit of her tummy as butterfly wings woke from their decades-long slumber. It took her by surprise, and she gulped a glass of water to conceal her sudden nerves and attempt to sober up. Vasílis ordered and exchanged rapid Greek with the waiter, followed by a complicated handshake and a bunch of words she couldn't catch. Ella's mind was swimming and she tore off a chunk from the sesame crusted loaf in a basket on the table. Her mezze hadn't been cleared away yet and she was grateful. It gave her something to do with her hands while she tried to soak up her afternoon drinks with the bread.

'Oh!' said Phoenix, suddenly making a show of looking at her watch. 'I'm such a dummy, I completely forgot. I'm supposed to be somewhere. So sorry, I've got to go.'

Ella gave her a withering look, indicating she could wring her neck for leaving her on such an unsubtly orchestrated date.

'But you only just got off the boat. I'm sure Georgia won't mind if you stayed out...'

But Phoenix was already on her feet and swinging her tan leather saddle bag over her shoulder.

'Oh, I wouldn't dare! You know what she's like if you deign to veer away from her plans. Have fun! Nice to see you again, Vasílis.'

She swanned off with a look of triumph. As she cast a glance behind, her face was beaming with smugness.

'So...' began Vasílis. 'It seems your niece wishes us to spend time alone together.'

'Apparently so.' He returned her smile, revealing perfect white teeth, and any awkwardness appeared to have been dismantled. A waiter arrived with Vasílis' beer and placed a frosted glass beside the bottle. The condensation on its sides immediately turned to trickles of water in the outdoor heat. Ella longed to photograph it and reached for her camera.

'Is this a hobby?' He nodded at the camera in her hands.

'No, my job... my passion. It keeps me out of trouble.' She realised she seemed to be trying to flirt and it felt odd. She raised the camera to her face and took his picture, which made him laugh in embarrassment. The sun had almost disappeared behind the headland, leaving traces of gilded light, highlighting his features. She looked at him through the lens objectively. He was incredibly attractive, and she wondered how many other beautiful men she'd withheld herself from.

'And what trouble could you possibly get into?' he returned her mischief as he coolly sipped his beer.

Ella's heart matched the beat of butterflies' wings as they fluttered in earnest again inside her and she smiled. If her skin weren't so tanned or was more like Georgia's, she'd be the colour of a beetroot. She sat back into her chair and examined the digital display on the camera.

'Will you show me?' He leant to the side and his arm brushed hers. As she reached over to show him the screen, their skin made contact again and she noticed the warmth of it. She caught his cologne, like fresh limes from the West Indies. They looked into each other's eyes, and she brushed a tendril of hair from her face, in a self-conscious gesture. The noise of Hydra seemed to retreat; the animal's hooves became a dull beat on a goat-skin drum rather than their usual staccato snare. The waves were like a caress instead of a thundering crash on the headland and the bubbling hubbub from the bars and tavernas transformed into the distant hum from a lone bee. A strange indecipherable energy seemed to prickle in the atmosphere making her feel uneasy, displaced, almost as if she shouldn't be there. A loud roar from the bar next door shattered the tension and in relief, Ella moved away from him as the moment gently retreated.

Ella permitted the evening air to wrap around her body, which felt like it was being awakened from a lengthy sleep. Something within her had begun to shift.

'Tell me about your family ... your mother, Anna,' Vasílis

said, interrupting her thoughts.

She automatically looked up to the cliff face where her family had spent their happiest times. She sat forward in her chair as she noticed lights were on in the downstairs rooms. As her excitement rose, she managed to stem it. There was somewhere else she was needed now, not basking in the remnants of the past in that house. Her eyes travelled back to Vasílis and she confirmed in her gut there was no spark between them. She trusted her instinct, though it hadn't always done her the greatest service.

'I need to go back to the hotel; I have to meet my sister. But I'd love to go for another drink with you and properly catch up on old times.'

He downed his beer while nodding, and she finished her wine, throwing some notes on the table.

'I have my own speedboat, not just the hotel shuttle. I will take you wherever you wish to go. It is good you are not afraid of the boats,' he said.

She followed him down the steps to the mooring without correcting him.

I can be brave, she told herself, smiling to mask her rising anxiety about inevitably boarding another of the wretched things. She looked around the harbour at the other moored vessels, the Greek letters spelt names she couldn't read. One was called *'Ella'* and she raised her eyebrows at her name ironically being written on the source of her phobia. An echo from the past tugged at her before her mind travelled to turning thirty-eight on Wednesday. Her mother's boat at the bottom of the garden used to be planted each year with fresh herbs on her birthday. It was a funny little ritual, but younger Ella used to love being on Hydra for the celebration each summer, although she didn't join in with the herb planting.

That would have broken her childhood sisterly pact to avoid the boat with the monster living in it, and her mother had humoured her no matter how old she was.

As she sat at the stern next to Vasílis and they motored out to sea, she sought distraction from her fear. Her sister would be pleased that Ella would turn up for dinner, abiding by her plan. Ella looked back over her shoulder to the glow in their old house, but the building was soon swallowed up by the spreading darkness. The twinkling lights of Hydra slowly disappeared, along with her past that lived within the fragments of rocks. She turned and looked forward, leaving her memories to disappear behind her.

Chapter 13
Georgia

'It's going well. I think. Apart from a bit of friction between me and Ella earlier.'

Georgia was catching up with Oliver before she went down to the cliffside bar for dinner. Partly because she needed to hear his voice to ground her and partly out of duty to keep up with their therapy homework while she was away.

She was still smarting from the fact Ella had not only sneaked away with Phoenix without her but had also talked about Harrison. Though leaving anything unresolved niggled at her and she longed to apologise to get things back on course. She felt guilty about having been so mean, but Ella somehow pushed on all her insecurities, which made Georgia's emotions burst forth. Her sister was the only one who inspired such extreme reactions as she kept her tendency towards hysteria mostly under wraps in public. She had mood swings, of course, as Oliver knew all too well, but they were nothing compared to how Ella heightened her feelings like no other could. The horror of what Georgia had done to Ella in the past was inescapable and the secrets she'd concealed since also haunted her, but Georgia liked to keep things perfect. If it looked perfect or at least seemed perfect, then it would be perfect. It had to be. Like her marriage to Oliver. If she ignored their problems and the fact that they hardly found the time for each other anymore in the way they used to, then she could conceal the reality beneath an ideal façade hoping their therapist would fix them.

'Try not to get stressed, Georgia. You barely ever spend time together and when you do, you rub each other the wrong way. Just focus on what you're out there for and keep calm. You know how you get when you're over-wrought.'

Georgia sighed, agreeing with Oliver's summary. She prodded her skin in the mirror, cradling the phone to her ear. Ageing was yet another thing spiralling away from her grasp and she didn't like it one little bit.

'The problem is, she mentioned her ex – *him* – to Phoenix, and—'

'She what?' he interrupted sharply. 'What did she say?'

'Well, that's the worst bit, I don't actually know. She stormed off after lunch without telling me and I don't want to ask Phoenix, so now I'm fearing the worst. Ella can be so rogue; she could blurt out anything. I can see how close she and Phoenix are and it…' A sob squashed her voice, but she managed to gather her emotions by clenching a fist. 'It hurts. I know I didn't give birth to Phoenix, but she is my daughter, Oliver. She's ours. I gladly gave up everything for her and wouldn't change it for the world. But I'm scared of losing my little girl.'

'You know better than I do that Ella won't have a clue she's doing anything wrong. She's not deliberately unkind, just immensely selfish and thoughtless. And I wouldn't worry about her with Phoenix. Your sister can't even unpack a flat let alone try and be a parent. With respect, the girl is a disaster with considerable form for making terrible decisions. The only

96

decent one she made was giving Phoenix to us.'

Georgia exhaled in relief at her husband's pep talk. Oliver was such a rock, able to talk her down when she became highly strung and irrational. He grounded her as she spiralled. When she neared that place, she knew she could be inconsolable. *This is why she could never leave him. She'd be left with nobody.*

She supposed Oliver was, in a way, replacing the role her mother had played. It was one they had shared while Anna was alive, but now it was down to him and she wasn't sure if he was up to the demanding job nor if he wished to be. But the weight of her secrets still pressed on her gullet like acute indigestion. She'd hadn't even told Oliver any of them. If she dared utter them out loud, they'd become real and the ramifications too horrific to contemplate. He'd be appalled, and she didn't want to disappoint him, nor shatter his illusion of her.

Taking the call out onto the balcony, she breathed in the warm night air.

'Thank you, sweetheart, I don't know what I'd do if it wasn't for you,' she said. 'We're so lucky with Phoenix. I couldn't imagine being without either of you, our little family we built against the odds. As for Ella, I have to keep reminding myself how different we are. I'll never understand her. I mean, how she gave up her baby I will never know, but that's her. Though thank goodness that she did.'

'Stay strong. I've got to go and make some calls. Rallying talk time has expired for the evening,' he laughed, and Georgia felt he was being a little unkind, but didn't say anything.

'Love you,' she said automatically.

But he ended the call without responding to her affection. Georgia stared out at the magnificent night-time view, gazing along the dark hills and mountains that loomed in the distance, sweeping around the panoramic vista, before finally landing on the balcony next door. Her body froze and her heart felt like it had dropped into her ankles. Phoenix was sprawled across the rattan sofa on the adjacent terrace, flicking through a magazine. Georgia's skin rippled with a cold flush from being caught out. Her pulse began to thump so hard it shook her whole body. Did Phoenix overhear her call? And she'd been worried Ella would shatter their family smokescreen, when ironically, Georgia might have been the orchestrator of her own destruction.

'Hi, Phoenix!' she called tightly, with a sound more akin to a squawk than a voice. But she didn't answer.

Oh God, she's ignoring me…

'Phoenix,' she said a little louder. 'What you heard was—'

Phoenix's head shot up and she paused for a second before pulling headphones from her ears, which had been concealed by her long hair and the shadows.

'Sorry, Mum, what did you say?'

Relief coursed through Georgia's body, leaving her feeling as though she could faint. Phoenix didn't hear anything after all; she had been plugged into one of her devices. Cursing her carelessness, Georgia resolved to ensure all doors and windows were firmly shut before discussing the sensitive elements of their family dynamic in future.

'Nothing, darling, just saying hello. I'm going to call for Ella, then shall we go to dinner?'

Phoenix nodded.

'How's Dad?'

And just like that, her pounding heartbeat returned, heating her cheeks.

'Wh-what? Fine, of course. Why?' she stumbled.

Phoenix stood and picked up her shoulder bag from the sofa.

'No reason. Just heard you on the phone...'

She looked back at Georgia and smiled again. But her expression was unconvincing. The smile didn't reach her big brown eyes.

* * *

'Coming!' Georgia heard Ella shout from the other side of the door. As it opened, they looked at each other for a moment before Ella flung her arms around her sister.

'I'm sorry, I'm so sorry! I hate it when we fight, sis.' Ella squeezed her tightly before pulling back. 'I didn't mean any harm; you have to believe me. Phoenix asked about my ex and I told her the bare minimum. Not even his name or that he's a musician – I'm not that stupid. Anyway, she's on a mission to pair me off with Vasílis, the little minx.'

Georgia laughed. 'Good luck. Phoenix never takes no for an answer, but I suspect no was the only answer you gave.'

'That's for me to know and for you not to find out.'

'Oh!' Georgia blushed in surprise as her eyes darted around the room over Ella's shoulder. 'I'm not sure you're supposed to have overnight guests at the hotel in case you...'

Ella rolled her eyes.

'For God's sake, Georgia, come in. Nothing happened; he just dropped me back here so I could come to dinner.'

A huge smile spread over Georgia's face, relieved her schedule would remain intact.

'I'm sorry I was unkind to you, Ella. I didn't mean it ... it's just, I suppose when it comes to "H", I'm terribly protective over you.' She looked furtively behind and dropped her voice to a whisper. 'And Phoenix, of course.'

Ella leant forward before checking behind her, mocking Georgia's movements. Lowering her voice she asked playfully, 'Why are we whispering?'

Georgia dismissed her speedily.

'No reason, just being paranoid.'

'Let me grab my camera. Where's Phoenie?'

'Here!' Phoenix said, opening the door, which made Georgia jump. She'd have to be on her guard as Phoenix seemed to be popping up every time she said anything perilous. At least being together meant she could steer conversations away from dangerous topics and keep everything on the right path.

* * *

Dinner was surprisingly relaxed considering the turmoil of the last twenty-four hours. Georgia felt less brittle, and her shoulders had sunk away from her ears.

The far terrace hotel bar was set out on a cliff with the sound of the waves providing the natural soundtrack to supper. They had gorged on grilled shrimp and a wonderful octopus salad sprinkled with capers, all substantially accompanied by two kilos of wine in the Greek measurement. Even Georgia had cast her diet aside and indulged at Ella's encouragement. She also agreed to Phoenix having two glasses of wine. It must be a sign she was finally having fun.

As the evening stretched onwards, the sisters regaled Phoenix with stories of their childhood holidays on Hydra, though Georgia was careful about what they discussed for fear of igniting a memory in Ella.

'We were so carefree back then. We thought we were invincible,' Georgia said.

'And wasn't life more enjoyable?' Ella replied, finishing a tentacle of her charred octopus, which had been cooked to tender perfection on the open coal grill. Georgia couldn't help but agree with her.

'I suppose it was. Days went on forever on the beach, and we'd swim for hours in the sea without a care for our wrinkled skin.' Georgia smiled fondly in reminiscence, forcing her mind to the lighter moments. 'Now there aren't enough hours in the day and my wrinkles are almost all I can think about!'

Phoenix leant forward and grabbed Georgia's hand.

'Well, for what it's worth, I think you're perfect as you are, Mum. Both of you are, my fabulous, slightly weird family.'

Ella and Georgia looked at each other, and Georgia spotted what looked like the beginnings of tears in Ella's eyes. Perhaps Hydra was finally reopening her sister's tethered heart, slackening the binds that had closed it off for so long.

'I do declare Phoenie wiser than the pair of us,' said Ella, wiping her nose with a napkin. 'It's funny, back then we only had each other and Mum. Things seemed different ... and we rarely argued. That's what I remember, anyway. We were too busy finding mischief, fighting invisible monsters or imagining heroes coming to save us. But it was our gang of three with Mum. Kind of like we are now...'

Georgia spotted a genuine sadness on Ella's face in the candlelight. It pulled at her heartstrings, though it was immediately countered by how excluded she'd felt by Ella and her mother. Like she wasn't good enough to join their secret club. Her mind drifted away to an incidental moment on the island when it dawned on her that Ella was their mother's favourite.

It was the summer after the accident and Ella was almost six. She was in the garden and seemed to be counting the paving stones, spinning slowly around, stepping into the middle of each slab, avoiding the cracks. The sun was beating down making Ella's skin glow golden. Georgia was watching from her bedroom window and looked down at her own arm. She pinched it, but only a red mark rose from her pale pallor. She wasn't tanned like her sister.

Georgia saw their mother had come outside and was crouching down beside Ella. Mum stroked her hair so lovingly, teasing out the sun-streaked brunette ringlets between her fingers. Then she stood and joined in with Ella's game. Georgia stared at the pair of them turning around and around with their arms wide. Their laughter penetrated the window and Georgia desperately wanted to be part of it. She rushed downstairs and out into the garden. In her haste, she stumbled on a paving slab and bumped into Ella who went flying into a lavender bush, grazing her knee. Though Ella didn't cry, the game was over and Georgia was made to apologise for hurting her sister.

She had always been horribly jealous of Ella and her reaction to those feelings had manifested in the most disturbing way, exposing the blackest version of herself for a split second. It was horrifying to think she had capacity for such wickedness and cruelty. It made her hate her own skin, wanting to tear it off.

Georgia shook away the shadows of the past, as she had become adept at doing – in public, at least – and returned to the dinner table with her thoughts, trying to ignore the thudding in her chest that had built from her recollection. The night air was stifling, and she felt trickles of sweat tickle the back of her neck.

'Then let's make a pact. To say goodbye to Mum in the way she wanted and to cut out the fighting. Deal, Els Bells?'

She offered out her little finger, deliberately using her childhood nickname for Ella, whose eyebrows rose in surprise. In turn, Ella slowly returned the gesture.

'Pinky swear!' they said at the same time and laughed as they recreated their childhood method of promising; the most serious of oaths when they were little. She saw Phoenix smile, but her eyes lingered on Ella and a small twinge of envy resurfaced in Georgia's throat. She stood up from the table too quickly making her head spin slightly.

'I think that's me for the night, I'm baking hot and desperately need air con. We also have to catch the early ferry in the morning to Metochi and we don't want to miss it.' Georgia picked up her clutch bag before checking herself, attempting to take a leaf out of Ella's book to be more spontaneous. She corrected her instructions. 'Or, we can always get the later one. Or go another day. No big deal, we don't have to stick to the plan. It's more of a guide to have fun, really...'

Ella stood and put her arms around her sister.

'Nice try, sis,' she said, then kissed her cheek. 'Don't change for anyone, keep bossing us all around. And so what if we fight? It's what siblings do. I know you're always just trying to protect me. When we were kids you were the same – don't think I didn't notice what you did.'

Georgia stepped back from Ella, looking for a hidden meaning in her words. The blood suddenly rushed to her head as her knees began to buckle. Dark spots pricked at her vision and the indigo seascape became a swirling mass, merging with the flickering flames from the candles until she felt like she was in a thick black vortex being sucked downwards. She grabbed for the tablecloth, pulling it with her to the ground. Like a muted cry from

103

underwater, she heard Ella shriek along with the sound of glasses smashing and cutlery crashing to the floor. Then complete darkness engulfed her as she crumpled like a ragdoll to the ground.

Chapter 14
Ella

'Are you sure she's going to be all right? She was out cold. People don't just suddenly faint,' Phoenix said to the doctor with concern. Ella could see she wasn't convinced by his diagnosis of heat-stroke and exhaustion. She started frantically typing on her phone as she left Ella with the doctor at Georgia's bedside.

Georgia was under strict instructions to rest. The manager had sent the on-call medic to the bar after her collapse, and Doctor Fotopoulos had brought her out of unconsciousness with some astonishingly pungent smelling salts. He'd checked her vitals and deemed a hospital visit unnecessary before escorting Georgia back to her hotel suite.

It was alarming the way she'd suddenly dropped to the floor. They'd been laughing and joking, nothing heavy, no arguing, but something had set her off. Maybe the wine had made her woozy. She barely ate enough to nourish a gnat, and Georgia was so highly strung with her ideas about how things should run. When things didn't go to plan, she freaked out. But there was no obvious reason Ella could see for her to pass out, and so she agreed with the doctor's conclusion. The night was incredibly humid.

There had always been something about her sister that had unnerved Ella – Georgia's tantrums, overwrought emotions, and outbursts. It was the polar opposite to how she dealt with her own feelings. She couldn't pinpoint it, but occasionally, when they were children, she'd been afraid of what Georgia was capable of in her piques of anger, when her face would turn scarlet and she would stamp her foot, screeching uncontrollably. It had made Ella retreat from her then, and those feelings still endured.

After seeing the doctor out, she went to check on Georgia again, placing a rose quartz beside her bed. It had travelled with her all over the world and was supposed to promote healing. It hadn't done it for her, but maybe it could work its powers on her sister. Georgia's head peeked out from the duvet, a cool compress rested on her brow. She looked so small curled up in a ball, burrowed within the bedclothes. Her blue eyes fluttered open as Ella sat with a jolt, making the bed bounce.

'Els Bells, you're a terrible nurse,' she managed with a small laugh. Ella loved that she was using her childhood nickname. It made her feel their old connection, the one that they'd somehow lost along the way in life.

'Can I do anything?' Ella asked gently.

Georgia considered her offer for several moments.

'Yes.' Her voice rasped, and Ella handed her a glass of water. 'Can we try and focus on moving forward from now on and not speak about *him* anymore?'

Ella frowned. Of all the practical things she could have requested, she was bringing up Harrison?

'Consider it done. There's a bit of an ever-present reminder' – she indicated the other room where Phoenix was – 'but I agree, it's all about the future from now on. I shan't mention him again.'

Georgia smiled weakly.

'Yet, we're still talking about that man.'

'Oh, I'm sorry, I didn't know your new rule began this second!' She pretended to zip her mouth, pressing her palm to her lips she spoke through her fingers, which made Georgia giggle. 'You rest, sis, and we'll hang out in the lounge. Shout if you need me.' She removed her hand from her mouth and stroked her forehead. 'Love you. Get some sleep.'

'Go! You're so annoying. But thank you,' she said to Ella as she left.

The adjoining area of the suite was the size of Ella's London flat. The amount of space was baffling. Perhaps she'd just become accustomed to roughing it. After sleeping in every nook and cranny of the world, she'd long ago realised that a bed and running water were all one needed to get by. A loo that wasn't a hole in the ground was a significant bonus.

Phoenix was sprawled on the sofa glued to her phone.

'Hey. Georgia's having a snooze. That was all a bit scary…'

Ella felt awkward wondering how to console Phoenix who looked so young and frightened.

'I'm searching the internet for why people faint.'

Ella took the phone from her hand.

'Don't! You'll have terminally diagnosed her within the hour if you believe half that rubbish you can read online. It's one of the many reasons I don't have a phone. Georgia is fine, just over-wrought about coming here.' She sunk into the comfy couch beside Phoenix. 'She's always making sure everyone else is happy but that is exhausting, and I think it's bitten her on the backside. We need to be mindful of how fragile my sister is – though she pretends to be anything but – and help her through her process.' She snorted with laughter at her own turn of phrase. 'God, I hate that process word!'

'Me too! So annoying how everyone says, "trust in the process", and "I believe in the process". What freaking process?! It's just life – unpredictable and random. You can't plan for everything.'

She sounded exactly like Ella's younger self, and she smiled fondly.

'What's so funny?' Phoenix looked offended.

'Nothing, I'm agreeing with you. Look, your Mum is...' Ella pulled up short. *Your Mum* were words she rarely used when referring to Georgia in front of Phoenix. She deliberately sidestepped it. But in their tender exchange, she had no option but to use the term.

'...she's wound tighter than us, which means there's more to unravel if things go wrong.'

Phoenix tucked her long legs underneath her and sat upright, winding her hair into a makeshift bun. It was so long and thick, as untameable as Ella's, especially in the hot, salty, Greek air.

'So ... in the spirit of your process, let's talk about your date with Vasílis.'

'Ah, yes. I'd almost forgotten about your little match-making scheme.'

'Well, what happened? I'm dying to know.'

'I fear you'll be disappointed. He took me out on his boat across the waves as the moon rose.'

Phoenix's eyes briefly widened with excitement.

'Then dropped me back here so I could join you guys for dinner. Deeply romantic without any romance.'

Phoenix threw a cushion at Ella.

'You're such a let-down. He's gorgeous. If I was a few years older...'

'Don't you dare! He's too old for you and you're too young

108

for love and all the hideous nonsense that goes with it,' Ella said rapidly, with a sudden realisation that Phoenix was a young woman now. She wasn't the child she'd handed over to Georgia and Oliver almost eighteen years ago, signing her name on the paperwork and entering a lifetime sentence of pretence. Her mind was stuck in that place, but Phoenix had grown, and it was time Ella evolved beyond her pain for good. But the only way to truly heal a wound was with the truth and that was impossible.

Phoenix giggled with amusement at Ella's sudden panic.

'Wow, you have got cynical in your old age, Auntie Ella. But newsflash, I'm not a virgin.'

Ella felt the blood being sucked out of her and felt as faint as Georgia probably did earlier. Phoenix saw the horrified expression on Ella's face and quickly continued.

'Don't tell Mum, please. She'll freak out and it'll be too cringe.'

Ella considered their similarities. If she'd been a model teenager, the exquisite girl in front of her wouldn't exist. And that was unimaginable. No, Ella thanked the fates for her choices – even the ones that brought heartache – because they delivered Phoenix into the world; rising from the ashes of the darkest episode in her life to become a shining beacon of joy.

Within the darkness you, you will be the light.

She nudged the words of Harrison's song away from the chambers of her heart as a glow spread throughout her body despite the underlying feeling that she was betraying Georgia. Phoenix couldn't confide in her mother but the secret irony was she was doing just that.

She chose her words carefully, leaning into the guise of wise old aunt.

'There's nothing wrong with having a physical connection

with someone you care about. But I beg of you, don't offer yourself up to anyone who doesn't deserve you just for the sake of feeling loved or wanted. I wish someone had said that to me when I was your age. Although I'm sure I wouldn't have listened, I'm saying it to you now in the hope that you might. You're nearly eighteen, which is still so young, and there's a world of adventure out there that doesn't have to revolve around another person. Sex is great, more than great in fact, but always look after you first. Don't compromise or lose your heart to someone who doesn't know how to cherish it.'

She tucked a stray string of ringlets behind Phoenix's ear, who looked up at Ella with such love. Her eyes would always be Ella's hidden torture.

'Was that what happened to you? With him?' she asked tenderly.

Ella remembered her promise to Georgia.

'The past is the past. My job is to stop it being in my present and future. There's the adult bit I struggle with. I sound like I'm trying to parent myself, even though I'm about to be the tragic age of thirty-eight next week.' She rolled her eyes in mock horror.

Phoenix picked up the room service menu. The shadows from the muted lighting cast long lines across the room and Ella looked through the balcony windows as a gentle breeze lifted the white muslin curtains.

'I might order pizza. All that drama has made me hungry again,' she said, and Ella smiled at her. Phoenix continued to look at food options. 'It's not too late, you know.'

'I know, room service goes on 'til three a.m.,' Ella responded.

'No.' She hesitated, fixing Ella with her father's penetrating gaze. 'I mean, it's not too late for you to be a mother. You could do it on your own if that's what you want. You can do anything.'

The fear of being uncovered tremored in the marrow of Ella's bones; she was petrified and didn't know how to behave. Phoenix turned on the sofa to face Ella, who brought her knees up as far as they could go, holding them close, like an impenetrable shield between them.

'You'd be such an amazing mum. There's a child somewhere in the world waiting for you whose life you could change. I know how much you love. I feel it.'

The unexpected turn of topic had shocked her, and she had no response. Ella lived with her consequences every single day and it tore her into pieces. But like a moth to a flame, she was drawn to Phoenix's energy time and time again because it was a fusion of her own and Harrison's. Though Ella was aware enough to understand she was no better than him – avoiding love, evading contact and connections – but at least the only person she hurt was herself. Little did Phoenix know that Ella *did* have a child in the world whose life she'd changed for the better. Only because Ella had given her away. And it would probably be the only one she'd have.

The truth was, she was unlikely ever to conceive again. Phoenix's birth was so traumatic that she'd needed emergency surgery leaving substantial scar tissue damaging most of her insides. She had been told at the time that it would be extremely unlikely for her to carry again. It was a physical scar to add to her extensive emotional wounds.

At Ella's silence, Phoenix took her hand and slowly lifted it to her face, holding it against her cheek, leaning into it. Ella's tiny hand cupped Phoenix's beautiful jawline – the gesture that Harrison had made the day they'd met in the river – and the movement pierced Ella's heart with a dagger so sharp, she feared she might never breathe again. Phoenix closed her eyes and Ella watched the dark lashes brush her high cheekbones. She loved her so very much she felt she could burst.

Despite her own longing to shed the past, there was no avoiding it. Being on the island once more had encouraged her to walk in a giant circle, re-living her story with both Hydra and Harrison. She couldn't evade it nor find a way through, though she longed to. She knew Harrison would haunt her until she died, because he was her 'what if'. And the family they could have had together was in front of her in the shape of their beautiful daughter.

She shouldn't have come back to Hydra.

Phoenix opened her beautiful eyes, now filled with tears swimming in the deep brown pools.

'You're already a kind of mother … to me. I wish we were together more often. It's like you see who I really am. Nobody is ever like that with me. Only you, and I love you so much.'

The words Ella longed to shout bubbled up within her and formed on her lips,

I am your mother.

But she mustn't say what her insides were screaming. Ella couldn't tell Phoenix how desperately sorry she was for giving her away, nor how and why she'd arrived at that terrible decision. Instead, Ella leant in to kiss her forehead and inhale her scent. Ella didn't believe in regrets, but Phoenix would be her one persecution until a final breath freed her spirit into the heavens.

The Island

As the sea regurgitated shipwrecks, depositing shards of the dead on the sand, so it would find a way to unearth what has been hidden. Those consigning their secrets and the very worst of deeds to the darkest, deepest pit should be warned; the island knew where all the bodies were buried.

Chapter 15

Georgia

Monday

In comparison to yesterday, Georgia felt quite restored. A good night's sleep had done her the world of good.

This is what secrets do, she thought. *They make you ill and afraid to breathe.*

She made a promise to herself not to drink in the afternoon sun again or overindulge at dinner. But she knew wine wasn't the cause of her fainting fit. It was all she had withheld from Ella and the fear of being laid bare. It had suddenly pressed on her with such force that she'd blacked out, unable to confine her emotions. If she was only concealing the fact that Phoenix was really Ella's daughter, she could deal with it. They'd successfully covered that up for nearly eighteen years. But there was more, another two hidden truths. She didn't consider one a secret as such, merely information she'd withheld out of love and protection for her sister. Although if Ella found out, she might disagree. The other ... that was dangerous and had the power to rip everything to shreds. Georgia shuddered at the thought of Ella's reaction should either secret come to light. She would never be able to forgive one, let alone both. Georgia certainly hadn't been able to forgive herself. Luckily, there was no way Ella could unearth any of it, unless one of the gossipy villagers reminded her if they discovered who she was... It was part of the reason why Georgia had chosen a hotel on the other side of the island, to keep Ella away from the action she was so attracted to, like a pleasure-seeking magnet. Given that she would have to get on a boat to reach the centre of town meant, in theory, she would stay close by. Though it hadn't quite worked out the way she'd planned so far.

Finally, tomorrow, she would say goodbye to her mum. The twelve months since the funeral had been painful, but only for her it seemed, and though the long wait to lay her mother to rest was entirely down to Ella, there was little point dwelling on the reason for the delay. Ella conducted life on her terms because she wouldn't allow any alternative. But having witnessed the growing bond between her and Phoenix, Georgia couldn't wait for the moment that her sister gadded off for work once again, not to be seen nor heard from for months. In fact, she longed for it.

Just before lunchtime, she knocked on Phoenix's hotel room door. There was no answer. Looking at her phone, the tracking app showed her location as the pool. Sure enough, Phoenix was sprawled on a lounger, her long legs oiled to perfection, the tan she'd already engineered was further highlighted by her magenta bathing suit. She was attracting glances from others around the pool but was completely oblivious.

Georgia beamed at her beautiful daughter and was relieved to see that Ella wasn't present, allowing all envious concerns to abate for the moment. She strode over, dodging the blazing patches of sun, and Phoenix's eyes opened in response to the

115

shadow blocking the light and she sat bolt upright.

'Mum! I didn't think you'd be up yet. How are you? Last night was so horrible.'

Georgia perched beside her as Phoenix frantically clutched at her hand.

'I'm sorry for all the worry. I'm honestly feeling great. Too many drinks and too much sun in the day yesterday. Speaking of, I'm off to the shade. Tell me you have SPF on your face? You'll thank me when you're my age, believe me.'

Phoenix sighed wearily.

'I wish you'd be a bit more chilled. Like Auntie Ella. You guys are so different, but I think you could learn a lot from each other.'

Georgia instantly bristled. What on earth could Ella teach her? How to shirk duty and cast loved ones aside, or how to live out of a suitcase despite the perfectly good home she had – if she bothered to make it such.

'I'm glad you and your auntie are getting on so well,' Georgia said tersely. 'But don't be hurt when she disappears, and you don't hear a peep until Christmas. If at all.'

'Whatever. Maybe go easy on her. I know you're hurting after losing Granny, but so is she. She just doesn't show it in the way you do. And clearly her heart is still broken to bits after her ex. I know it's been ages, but maybe you never really get over your first and true love...' she said whimsically.

Georgia chewed the inside of her cheek to prevent herself saying something out of anger, though she was burning like a furnace inside. If Phoenix knew that her favourite aunt had given her away, she might think differently.

Georgia summoned what restraint she had left, wishing they'd only come away for a weekend rather than two weeks. It was going to be the ultimate test of resilience.

* * *

Anita's Taverna was within walking distance of the port. It was set into a square framed with a grove of colourful fruit trees. Stone busts of historical Greek dignitaries sat on plinths in the garden and, unexpectedly, there appeared to be three ducks in residence. They walked in a line, their feathery backsides waddling, chattering together in small bursts of quacks.

'Why can't we sit outside? It's baking in here,' whined Ella, fanning herself with a menu as she slumped in her seat pretending to melt. Phoenix giggled.

'Because the only table available in the garden was in the sunshine. I don't want to risk it after last night,' replied Georgia, mopping her upper lip with a paper napkin.

Ella sat upright.

'Sorry, that was selfish. You look much brighter today, sis.'

Reassured that Ella possessed the emotional intelligence to know she was often self-absorbed, Georgia managed a smile.

'Back to normal and fighting fit! Don't give it another thought,' she said, dismissing any concern. 'Now, I thought we'd go through what each of us want to say in the ceremony tomorrow. I've chosen some readings you might like to consider.' She handed a bundle of pages to Phoenix and Ella. 'We'll each hold some ashes and then after we've said our words, we can release her into the sea. Any thoughts about your speech, Ella?'

Ella thought for a moment.

'How about, have a nice swim…?'

Phoenix dissolved into giggles again, but a thunderous look from Georgia, strong enough to challenge any rain cloud, stopped her laughter short.

117

'This isn't funny, Ella! I've spent ages planning these two weeks and I want everything to be perfect. If you don't care, you don't have to come to scatter Mum's ashes. I'll do it alone, like I do everything.'

Heat prickled at her neck, and she felt her cheeks flush. She knew she was a sweaty blotchy mess.

'Sorry, I was only joking,' said Ella sheepishly. 'I'll just say whatever occurs to me in the moment. And I promise, it won't be silly,' she added quickly after catching Georgia's horrified expression. 'Or maybe you'd prefer for me to stay silent. She was my mother too, you know.'

Her jaw hardened as she glared at Georgia and she, in turn, returned the stare. Her anger was simmering, threatening to boil over. But it was Phoenix who broke their stand-off.

'That's enough. I can't stand it; you two are driving me nuts. You've argued every single day so far, and you don't even seem to actually like each other. I'm having lunch somewhere else. And I'll come up with something of my own to say for Granny. I suggest the pair of you try to get along. Otherwise, I want no part of tomorrow or the rest of this holiday. Both of you, please, grow up!'

Phoenix wafted out of the restaurant, her long lilac dress billowing in her wake. Ella burst into laughter.

'I think we've just been told off by my daughter.' She stopped, realising what she'd said. 'Oh, God ... I ... I didn't mean that. *Your* daughter, of course ... Georgia ... I wasn't thinking,' Ella tried to correct herself, then she swigged so swiftly at the wine that some of it dribbled down her chin. It was the last straw for Georgia, but instead of an outburst of anger, she leant forward, her face like steel, anger piercing the space between them. She gritted her teeth so hard, that a cheek muscle bulged from the tension.

'If you ever, *ever* call her that again, it will be the last you will ever hear from me. And from her. I mean it. I continue to be astounded by your audacity. How *dare* you think you have the right to call her that. You gave that up when you handed her over. If it wasn't for me, she'd be with a stranger, being brought up goodness knows where. Be grateful you get to see her at all because I swear, if you ever call *my* daughter that again...'

Her chair scraped the tiled floor as she rose. Scooping up the papers from the table, she stuffed them in her bag and swept out of the taverna. The beautiful poems and readings she'd lovingly researched and printed out would clearly be of no use to the others. To hell with her sister.

Outside, the chatter of the merry diners enjoying their lunch irked her. Happy families were peacefully sharing food and breaking bread across a table when hers couldn't even have a drink together without a fight. The surge of rage and something akin to hatred flooding her bloodstream was unfamiliar and she suddenly wished Ella had never been born on this stupid island. She and Hydra had ruined everything. As soon as the thought arrived, she rejected it. She wouldn't have Phoenix if that were the case.

But Georgia was trapped – on this island, in her stagnant marriage and in a mess of Ella's making with no way out. The feeling of being completely out of control was a dangerous space for her. Since they'd arrived in Greece, her feelings were running ragged, but until now, she hadn't realised just how triggering she found her sister. They hadn't spent more than a couple of hours together since their mother died and, now she thought of it, since she adopted Phoenix. They didn't know how to be with each other anymore. It was possible they never had. She wished she had the courage and self-possession to keep herself in check around Ella. Coming to the island with her was a dreadful idea and Georgia almost screamed aloud, desperately searching within herself for the strength to navigate their damaged relationship. It could never be what she'd hoped for. She stopped short of falling to her knees to frantically plead with an eavesdropping deity – though she was tempted. It dawned on Georgia that any rose-tinted idyll they'd clung to of their time on Hydra as children was merely another lie to add to the ever-growing pile of destructive deceit.

The Island

The gods heard the plea from the sister for strength. They smiled. The woman should be careful what she wished for. Yes, they would arm her with the courage necessary to endure her time on the island, but there was always a catch when dabbling with the immortal realm. What they requested in return, she had unwittingly agreed to. The consequences of which would alter everything.

Chapter 16

Ella

Ella refused to be the third member of her family to storm out of Anita's Taverna. They must think them mad. The old woman sitting beside the cash register sent her sympathetic smiles between puffs of a cigarette, and Ella heard occasional heated exchanges from the kitchen. She was reassured that family fights weren't solely consigned to her kin.

After paying, she emerged into the sweet scorching air outside and was greeted with a chorus of quacks from the ducks. She raised her camera and began to click. As the mallard flapped its wings, stretching a skinny neck to the sky, it was like looking through a lens to the past, to the day she'd been photographing ducks and met Harrison by the river. She felt the island air vibrate, like an electric shock, and the tremor resonated within her blood. Dropping the camera from her eye, she backed away, and headed for the port.

Sighing in resignation, she knew she'd apologise to Georgia yet again and they'd only been there three days. She wasn't usually one to wish time away, but she longed for this trip to be over so she could be anywhere else but Hydra. It goaded her with its picturesque scenery, which hid a sinister underbelly. It was as though she could strip away its appealing surface and be left with a stinking, putrid marsh, a disgusting bog harbouring mythical ghouls ready to suck out her soul.

Laden with her heavy thoughts, she walked into a shop to buy an apology gift for her sister. Finding a circular piece of turquoise-coloured glass on a simple gold chain, she bought a second matching necklace for herself and put it around her neck. After scribbling a grovelling gift card, she found the shuttle boat and tasked the driver with delivering the token back to the hotel for Georgia.

Lost within her own mind, she found she'd ended up at the other side of the harbour, where a towering statue of a celebrated naval commander dominated that corner of the headland. In his shadow, Ella studied his features. She imagined the ship's wheel he was holding slowly beginning to turn and wondered what action on the open seas would force him to proffer the dagger nestled within his clothing. The monument was testimony to the expert way the Greeks celebrated their past. She wished she could take heed of their example.

Admiring the view of the main town, the colours of the island sang in the sunshine. Hydra was a mound of houses and buildings crowned with barren, rolling hills where little had been built above. She shielded her eyes as she looked to the cliff where her mother used to live. Through her camera, she zoomed in as far as she could and saw the door to the back garden was open.

The owners were home!

Her heart leapt and she glanced up at the admiral and whispered words of thanks. The island had always found a way to respond to her wishes and Ella set off for the house.

* * *

Ella knocked on the door, hoping this time for someone to answer. She didn't want to be disappointed again and there had already been too many letdowns on this trip.

She pressed her ear to the door and was heartened to hear music playing inside, the muted notes barely distinguishable. The idea that people may be living in what was their old holiday home made her tummy feel funny, a mixture of queasiness and excitement. If she stepped inside the house, surely she could cleanse her energy of what was broken and cast it off, never to carry it with her again. Finally, there might be some closure for her fractured heart.

Footsteps sounded along the hallway, and she felt them like an echo within each muscle. She plastered on a smile as her nerves built in anticipation. A prickling rippled across her skin, and she suddenly felt a wave of something akin to nausea. Her legs began to tremble, and she couldn't understand why she was physically reacting this way in expectation of something that hadn't yet happened. A cold wind streaked along the narrow street, lifting the curls from her shoulders. It swirled and circled like it was winding invisible ribbons, binding her to the threshold. Her arms froze, pinned at her sides, and she took an uncertain step back as the door creaked open. A burst of music rushed outwards making her entire body tingle, and her smile fell away as her heartbeat thumped in her throat.

She felt as though she was being pulled downwards into the ground, like she'd become liquid, merging with the dirt underfoot and trickling down the hill to join the sea. She wanted to run but was rooted to the spot. There was nothing to do but absorb the intense gaze that greeted her. The brown eyes that had haunted her sleep for years and taunted her on Phoenix's face.

On *their* daughter's face.

Chapter 17

Ella

Tears stabbed at her eyes making them burn. It wasn't sadness that caused her to cry, it was anger, resentment and, against her will, an overwhelming feeling of love for the other half of her soul, her twin flame. Harrison.

He leant against the doorframe and fixed her with the look she'd seen countless times in dreams.

'El,' he said, exhaling her name in a whisper with what seemed like relief. 'I knew you'd find me one day, love.'

Every nerve ending was alive as the air between them crackled. Ella was unable to verbalise the thousand questions thundering through her mind. Their unexpected, silent stand-off continued, like two predators sizing up their prey, waiting for the other to pounce, not wishing to make the first move. Ella opened her mouth to speak, 'What ... are you ... how...?' was all she could manage.

Harrison ran his fingers through his hair, smiling nervously, reconnecting the direct line from him to her heart. She felt as though someone was bathing her in golden light, adorning her body with love. She saw him anew in the moment. He was thinner, his features more chiselled than before and his dark brown hair was shorter, peppered with a few grey strands, but he was still as breathtakingly beautiful as she recalled. She'd somehow forgotten just how tall he was. His soft brown eyes, now with laughter lines of age, inspired the same spark inside her that they always had. But what had there been to laugh about? He ran. From her, them, and from all they could have been.

He held the door open, but Ella didn't move. He turned and walked back into the hallway. Her mother's hallway. What the hell was he doing in this house? As fury emerged, she stalked in after him, slamming the door, and tried to ignore the assault on her senses caused by stepping into her memories. Her gaze flicked over the furnishings and alighted upon a framed painting of a sailboat called 'Ella'. The one she had seen in the harbour when she was with Vasílis.

'That's my boat I had built. She's moored here, and named for you,' he said, seeing her looking at it.

She wanted to rip it off the wall, and claw it to pieces with her fingernails. As if naming a boat after her vindicated his behaviour. A pity namesake, a moniker of regret, a reminder of what he'd cast asunder. He'd clearly forgotten her terrible fear of boats too. Ella whipped around to glare at him, discovering he'd had the wherewithal to keep a physical distance. She couldn't find the words to begin as he fiddled silently with his hands, running his fingertips over the gnarls and bumps that marked him out as a practised musician. She'd once known every sinew and curve of his body, just as he'd been familiar with hers. But her body was changed, altered inside and out, though regretfully it appeared her love was not, and she resented it. He stepped forward.

'You look amazing, El. I can't believe you're here.'

She folded her arms, suddenly self-conscious in her tattered jean shorts and vest. It was cold, the stone walls shielding them from the sweltering outdoor heat.

Stifled by agony, her voice arrived in a whisper.

'You left me. You left me at the train station and you...'

Ella looked around the room again, anywhere but at him, wishing that wasn't her opening remark. Sunlight streamed through the open patio doors and dust motes danced in the beams. His piano was against the wall where had once been a dresser. The kitchen had the same layout, though the cabinets were different. Harrison didn't belong in this house.

'I can't be here,' she said, turning to leave as hot tears spilled down her cheeks. It took a moment to adjust to the dark hallway. She felt his hand catch hers and she was immediately rendered inert, like a statue. She thought she'd already used up her tears for him, but still they came. Finding him there was ruining the only set of memories of Hydra she still cherished. They belonged to her childhood, to her mother, to a time when her heart was intact. Yet here he was piercing her earliest recollections, tearing them apart, shattering what once was her sweet, innocent bliss, just like he had every moment of her life since he'd left. It reminded her of his betrayal in this very house, where they'd agreed they had a future together. She gave up her daughter because of the havoc he'd wreaked upon her poor heart.

His touch was like holding a burning flame, yet her fingers remained static, refusing to close around his.

'Let me go, Harrison,' she said, gritting her teeth, still facing away from him. His large hand gave the smallest squeeze, and he tenderly ran his thumb over her palm. Resentment began to build, and she turned to defiantly look up at him. 'I said, let me go. You're good at it. You've done it before.' Shaking him off, she cursed her tears, which persisted. A furrow appeared on his brow as his fingers reached out to touch her arm. Then, thinking better of it, he put his hands in his jean pockets instead.

'I'm sorry. I'm so sorry, love.'

Ella almost winced to hear him call her that, his accent as rough and rich as it had always been, hard and yet soft. She felt an angry ripple of desire travel the length of her spine. 'Let me try and explain,' he pleaded.

'Why are you in this house?' she said, her tone dripping with accusation.

He sighed and walked to the sofa, sitting and placing his elbows on his knees. Dropping his head, he held it in his hands. The gesture ignited Ella's wrath. Despite his pitiful stance, he didn't deserve an ounce of sympathy.

'Answer me. What are you doing here in this house, on my island?' she repeated, her jaw clenched so tautly it ached. He lifted his head and his brown eyes bored a hole into her, matching the chasm he'd left in her heart. Again, he played with his hands, his fingers running over themselves, tapping nervously as if he were coaxing music from keys.

'I wanted to be on Hydra again. I felt closer to you here and I could live half the life we'd planned to, almost like I could make amends with us via the island.' His voice cracked, and Ella automatically stepped towards him as he kneaded his knuckles, another familiar gesture. But she pushed away her brief moment of compassion. 'This place was for sale. Of course I didn't want you or Georgia to ever know it was me buying it, so I put it through a company. I s'pose I bought it with us in mind, for the future, so that if you ever came back here like we talked about...' He leant back against the sofa and picked at the calluses on his fingers. 'I fell in love with it when we were here together before, and now, I don't ever want to leave.'

His talking about the broken dream they'd once shared made Ella's blood boil.

'Well at least you're capable of loving something and not abandoning it, even if it is only a *fucking* island,' she shouted.

He stood abruptly and his eyes darkened almost to black. 'Oh, come on, Ella. Are you serious?'

She stepped towards him, jabbing the air with her finger as her voice raised further.

'How dare you buy this house, my family's home, living a half-baked fantasy we had when you didn't even have the courtesy to find out if I was OK, or even alive. And because of you, I very nearly wasn't.'

'Don't,' he said sharply, wounded by her words. His tone softened. 'You have to try to forgive me at some point.'

She was aghast at the thought of absolving him. He was responsible for her being alone, the cause of her inability to settle in case she was rejected by someone she let herself be vulnerable enough to love. But most of all, she blamed him for leaving her so heart-sick that she had no choice but to give up their daughter, forced forever more to pretend Phoenix was her niece, not her beautiful child born of her own body. No, he couldn't have her forgiveness. There was no way to make it right. She stared him down, her face aching with tension as she said, 'I don't *have to* do anything just to ease your conscience, Harrison. You've no idea what you did. And to find you here ... *that's* unforgivable.' She was panting with the effort of containing her emotions, trying to make him understand, but she could never explain it fully. 'You've had years to explain, but you didn't. You ran away from that as well.'

His eyes widened and he gave a small laugh.

'What? I tried to, remember? I called you through your agent, but you slammed the phone down when you realised it was me. And you clearly didn't get my letters. I wanted to find you but you're impossible to track down; you're like a ghost.

129

It was like you were deliberately hiding from me.'

Her resilience faltered briefly. *What letters?*

'It *was* deliberate, Harri.' She could kick herself for using her old term of endearment for him and hated the way his expression relaxed a little hearing it. 'And remember, you're the one who left with no way of me contacting *you*. And no, I didn't get any of your letters and it wouldn't have made any difference if I had. You abandoned me at King's Cross without any explanation, no conclusion, just ... nothing. The love of my life was gone, like I didn't matter. I was willing to give up everything for you. You let me believe you wanted a future with me.'

He closed his eyes briefly, as though in pain.

'Listen to me, love. I couldn't face it. I honestly didn't know how to say goodbye. I couldn't let you give up your degree for me. You'd always hold it against me. But I didn't mean to abandon you. I was trying to protect myself because I loved you so much. Ella, you have to believe me, I didn't mean to hurt you. I was an idiot. I was too young and foolish to process my feelings for you. If it's any consolation, I broke my own heart too.' He paused and ran a hand through his hair. As he stood, his head was only a foot shy of the ceiling. 'I think about you every single day. I do nothing but. I write songs about you, try to reach you with my mind. You're in my dreams and the first thing in my head each morning. I wake up without you in the room where we slept on this island, knowing I lost you and it was all my own fault.' He moved towards her before continuing. 'I prayed you'd come here. I'd say it out loud, like I could conjure you back. Our connection has always been special, more than that, and you know it, El. My feelings haven't changed about you.'

Her automatic response dried on her lips. She couldn't

130

speak, because if she did, she'd plummet down into the depths of them again. It would be too easy to allow the poetry of his words to coax her back to love. But she couldn't forgive him for what he did and the chain of events it inspired.

She shook her head and walked into the garden. The two olive trees were silhouetted against the twinkling sea, the sun behind them. The opposite side of the headland seemed to grow from the tips of their leafy canopy. She enjoyed the welcome heat on her skin, thawing the chill of the interior.

She moved to the tree she used to call 'hers'. Its trunk was rough and gnarly, and she pressed her palm to it. It seemed so huge when she would scramble along its aged branches as a child. There were flecks of delicate olive pollen peppering the bark from the tiny white flowers that would bear fruit later in the year. At the bottom of the garden, the broken carcass of the boat was still planted with every variety of herb, just as it had been when her mother lived there. Wild, faded blooms were beginning to wither and a Hottentot Fig crept its fleshy fingers along the rear wall. The vibrant flowers glowed luminously in the sunshine. It wasn't native to Greece, it was trespassing. It didn't belong here and neither did Harrison. She couldn't look at him directly, so she bravely walked towards the boat, breaking her childhood pact with Georgia never to approach it. It now seemed a pointless promise. Following an urge to torture herself in the name of distraction, she crouched to touch the rotten gunnel and felt a sudden rising panic. She couldn't breathe; it was as though she was being suffocated. The vision she'd had yesterday resurfaced like an apparition. Sunlight was blinding her and the scent of herbs from the flowerbed were accompanied by the flash of a rippling face that appeared in her mind's eye. She squeezed her eyes shut, then felt a tremendous peace envelop her as the image disappeared and her eyes turned to darkness. She dropped her hand from the boat and stood, unsteadily at first, in confusion. Her hand moved to her chest to find her heart pounding. She breathed deeply, letting the peace of the island calm her.

Eventually, Harrison spoke.

'I can't believe your mum sold this house. How is she?' he asked.

'She's dead,' Ella spat cruelly with all the bitterness she could muster. She remained looking at the plants.

'I'm sorry, Ella, I didn't know. When?'

'Last year. Heart attack,' she replied. 'We're scattering her ashes at sea tomorrow. Georgia's here too.'

'Ah.' She heard the amusement in his voice. 'And how is Georgia?'

Bringing up our daughter! She screamed in her head.

'The same. Still married to Oliver, and they have … a daughter. Phoenix.'

Ella turned to look at him, scrutinising his reaction closely, as if he would innately know that she was theirs.

'Phoenix? That's beautiful. Sounds like you chose her name rather than Georgia.'

She shrugged, trying not to delight in his approval of her choice for their daughter's name. She wished she'd never heard the word from his mouth.

Then he asked her the question she dreaded.

'And you… Are you married … kids?'

She dropped her gaze to the ground.

'No and no.'

If he met her eyes, he'd know she was lying about one of those things.

'You?' Ella asked, glancing up briefly, and he shook his head in response. 'Anyway…' she muttered.

132

'So…' he said.

Their heads then turned to look at each other at the same time. The eyes she loved so dearly twinkled at her. It was both a dream and a nightmare come true, to see him again after so long.

'So…' she echoed, kicking her foot into the dirt. She drew a line with her toe, rolling pebbles under her trainers, reverting to the child she used to be in this garden and also the naïve, love-struck eighteen-year-old she had been with him; ill-equipped to understand that pain was inevitably paired with matters of the heart. Like life and death – one wasn't available without the other. Her grief for their loss was woven entirely from threads of their love.

'Have you heard it? The song,' he asked, as an unusual shyness descended over him.

'How could I not?' she began, conjuring grace. 'It's beautiful, Harri.' Her voice snagged in her throat. 'I've only heard it a couple of times. I avoid it. Or try to; it's bloody everywhere.'

He laughed, a rich deep sound she'd always adored, which squeezed her heart further as he said, 'Well, that song bought me this house. It all happened so quickly after … after the station,' he looked embarrassed. It was the least he should feel. 'You haven't changed.'

Ella tilted her head to the side but before she could filter what he'd said, she was suddenly cast in his shadow as he moved to her. She couldn't help but look up, unable to resist what came naturally. She reached out to touch his face and her fingers trembled above his skin, terrified to feel it, yet like a magnet drawing her closer, she made contact. Gently at first, the tips of her fingers feather light as they found his cheek. He brought his hand to hers, and she cupped his face, just as she had the day they met. His tears glistened and hers mirrored his emotion.

'I'm sorry, love,' he whispered. 'I'm so sorry I hurt you.'

Droplets snaked beneath her lashes as she closed her eyes and tracked down her cheeks, refilling the furrows from earlier. As she opened them, she found he was looking at her with such immense love. Like he used to, but with even more power. Ella ought to have known their history was destined to repeat itself. Their souls had joined the day they met and fused more deeply at the train station, she knew it. Their past was almost palpable in the atmosphere. The rockfaces surrounding the harbour already held fragments of their tale, like ancient fossils crystallised deep within their sediment. The island had given them Phoenix and knew Ella's version of what had passed. Since then, Hydra had discovered Harrison's story; separately yielding their accounts of history to the air. But there, together, she felt the island hold its breath as he gently placed his hand on her neck, making her shiver as they danced around their unspoken next move.

'I've missed you, El,' he whispered.

She quickly grasped his forearm to stop him from leaning forward. Every nerve in her body implored him to brush his lips against hers, but she pushed his arm away, summoning every scrap of control she could muster. His face became a question as she slowly inhaled. Her eyes travelled to his mouth, absorbing all of his features, then met his exquisite brown eyes once again.

'I'm sorry, Harri. I can't forgive you.'

Ella turned and walked back through the house.

The Island

The truth was beginning to unfurl and those who watched on were excited. Gods revelled in human misfortune, considering them foolish, unable to conduct themselves skilfully in love or war. What time they wasted not surrendering to their basest desires, whether it was physical love or physical destruction.
The energy of all such encounters gave the island strength; it feasted on the pain of others.

Chapter 18

Georgia

The waitress from the Pirate Bar placed a double espresso in front of Georgia.

'Excuse me, sorry to bother you,' she said to the young girl who slid the bill beneath her coffee cup. 'Do you happen to remember a woman called Anna, an English lady who used to own a house here?'

The waitress looked puzzled.

'I will ask the family who owns this place.' She moved off towards the interior of the infamous harbour bar and Georgia sipped the scalding coffee.

Her eyes flicked up at the cliffside. Ahead of tomorrow, it was like she was searching for an extra connection with her mother, seeking validation or some kind of reassurance that coming to Hydra had been the right thing to do. She could see the seaward door of the house was open and she smiled as a flood of memories washed over her. How different life had been when she and Ella were young, longing to return to the island with the arrival of each school holiday. Who would have thought circumstances would unfurl as they did and ultimately lead them back once more, but this time with Phoenix in tow.

She wondered whether she had the courage to knock on the door and make herself known to whomever lived there. It seemed silly to do so, a fruitless endeavour, like picking at a scab. She would no doubt be disappointed with any changes that had been made that might not be to her taste. There was also a chance that one aspect hadn't been altered and she didn't want to be reminded of what had happened when she was ten and Ella was five. The vignettes of happiness from time spent with her family in the house existed solely in her mind and there they should rest, untarnished. She could organise her memories – the good ones, at least – and the reality might prove too tricky if she was confronted by what haunted her. It might tip her over the edge and that was the truth about why she hadn't gone back, though she couldn't explain that to Ella.

A willowy blonde suddenly appeared in her eyeline.

'Hi, one of my girls said you were asking about someone. I'm Wendy, the owner.'

Georgia gathered herself as social propriety descended and she offered her hand.

'Wendy! I haven't seen you for years. I'm Georgia. My family used to holiday here at the white house there on the hill.' She pointed up to it. 'My late mother, Anna, used to own it. It was always like home to her, and to us.'

Wendy broke into a smile.

'Of course I remember her and you. I'm so sorry to hear about Anna, I didn't know. She always took part in island life, one of those we called *local visitors*. She never missed a party at the bar.'

Georgia beamed, her expression matching Wendy's.

'Oh, goodness, yes. She'd bring us along, dressed up like pirates, then take us up to bed. I think she used to come back down, leaving us in the house. You can't do that anymore.' She shivered at the irresponsibility of leaving two young children alone. Wendy laughed in agreement. Her accent was South London, but her sun-kissed skin indicated the years she had lived on Hydra.

'No social services to call out here. Y'know, I remember your sister as well – you're a similar age as my son, Zeus. *Zephs* in Greek.'

'I always thought he'd made up his name, but he's really called Zeus?'

Wendy gave a throaty laugh.

'Yeah, but what can I tell you? Greece took hold of me – they said marry a Greek god and I married a goddamn Greek! But I love it, especially this island; it never lets you go. Hang on, weren't you and your sister in that awful accident … years ago?'

'Mum!' Georgia heard Phoenix's shout and saw her approaching laden with shopping bags. She was grateful for the interruption so she wouldn't have to answer Wendy's question. And she was glad to see Phoenix after she'd left Anita's Taverna so abruptly before lunch, sick of all the sisterly sniping.

'Phoenix, I'd like you to meet Wendy. She remembers your granny.'

Phoenix smiled and deposited her shopping on a chair. The two women hugged like old friends and Georgia couldn't help but admire her daughter's contagious warmth, how relaxed she was in the company of strangers.

'Another beautiful name,' Wendy said.

Georgia blushed in gratitude but knew she couldn't take credit for it. People were always surprised she had a daughter called something so unconventional. But she'd agreed to keep the name for Ella's sake. She now wished she hadn't.

138

Wendy left to tend to another table and Phoenix showed off her purchases: an olive-green suede shoulder bag with an oversized tassel dangling from the strap, several beaded bracelets, a dress and a chocolate brown, leather-bound photo album.

'I thought Auntie Ella could print some of her pics for me to put in here. I never get to be with the two of you together and I want to remember it, always. Although after the way the pair of you behaved earlier, I could do without the reminder. You really have to stop bickering.'

Georgia ran her fingers over the buttery soft material of the photograph album.

'I know we rub each other up the wrong way, but we always make up. A souvenir of Hydra is a lovely idea, darling,' she said, hoping she and Ella could find accord for the remainder of their time on the island. She only wished she hadn't been reminded of that terrible day by Wendy.

Glancing once more up at the cliff, she saw a figure moving in her mother's garden, masked by the olive trees. Maybe she ought to go there after all. It could be a perfect way to say a final goodbye. If she sought out the more jovial memories of Hydra, they'd override the dreadful recollection that lurked so strongly at the back of her mind.

Phoenix tugged her attention away, unfolding a dress from one of her carrier bags.

'What do you think? I can wear it for Granny's ceremony tomorrow.'

It would look stunning thought Georgia, biting her tongue to stop herself commenting on the length. Instead, she forced a smile.

'Beautiful, Phoenix,' she said, pulling the most convincing grin she could find.

Phoenix dropped the dress in her lap.

'Mum. Be honest. Are you happy?' She tucked her hair behind an ear. 'You don't really seem it.'

Georgia cupped her espresso.

'What makes you say that, sweetheart? I'm absolutely fine.'

Phoenix shook her head.

'I mean in life. Are you actually happy? I know you're upset over Granny, but you seem to be in some kind of battle with everyone. Ella, me, Dad … it's like you're unsatisfied.'

Georgia balked at how intuitive Phoenix was.

'It's just emotional being on the island again. And you' – she pulled the dress from Phoenix's lap to admire it – 'you'll be fighting them off, darling.'

Phoenix frowned.

'Sorry to disappoint, but music is my only love. I'm going to be just like Auntie Ella and be alone, focusing on what makes me happy. If I can't find anyone like you've found Dad, then I'd rather go without.'

At least Phoenix had learnt what a proper relationship was supposed to look like from her and Oliver. Though their marriage was anything but. They'd become strangers under the same roof. From the outside it might seem like the perfect idyll, but love had left home, if indeed it had ever moved in. Georgia hardly dared to think it, but deep down she knew it was true. It was a failure she could hardly stand to admit. And she wished Phoenix wouldn't put Ella on such a pedestal. They were so alike in spirit, which was an immovable, inescapable fact, but she was determined to prevent history repeating itself. Surely that was something she could influence. Because if anyone ever broke Phoenix's heart, she'd kill them. And that included her sister.

The Island

If you fight with darkness, you will only unearth more darkness. The role of the gods was to cleanse mortals of their guilt and confront them with their wrongdoings. Only then could a passage be carved through the rocks to lead them towards the hidden truth of the island and of themselves.

Chapter 19

Ella

Ella couldn't tear herself away from Harrison's house. She sat on the doorstep, unable to leave. She didn't have the strength. It felt as if part of her had died, yet at the same time she had re-awakened.

Leaning her head back against the front door, she knew he was standing behind it. Ella could still feel his energy, the imprint of his touch brandished on her skin. She scolded herself for wishing to cling on to the past by coming to the house. She'd been foolishly drawn to it, as though he'd sent out a smoke signal to entice her. Seeing him again after she'd been determined to let him go seemed to be the inevitable path they were destined to tread. The back and forth of their hearts over the years mirrored the tide as it ebbed and flowed. Their love had retreated occasionally but its flame had never been extinguished. She'd tried to fight it, but their bond had won and Hydra orchestrated their reunion.

'I know you're there.'

She heard his deep voice through the door and longed to sink through it as if she were melting, folding backwards into the house and into him. She felt defeated at the precise time she ought to find the mettle to walk away. But her heart evaded sense just as it always had; he was the other half of her. She wanted to kill him with her love, hurt him as much as he'd hurt her. Even though he said he'd endured his own agony being apart over the years, he knew nothing of what she'd navigated. He'd monetised their pain through his songs, whereas Ella carried it like a millstone, relinquishing motherhood and avoiding emotional intimacy.

'El ... talk to me, even if it's only like this.'

She couldn't help but smile at the absurdity of the situation as she turned to rest the side of her face against the warm wood. She pressed her palm to the door and instinctively knew he was reflecting her precise position. That's what they were, a mirror of the other's soul.

'Harri, I don't know what else to say. We can't go around in circles, which I know we will. I'm still hurt and all I'll want is to punish you for it.'

She could almost hear him breathe and wanted to press her lips to the blue painted surface. It was as close as she dared to get.

'So, punish me. I deserve it, love.'

Tears dropped onto her leg. It was a cruel trick of the universe to toy with her heart this way. She sat upright, then hugged her knees, rocking gently. The handle above her head slowly turned with a creak and the door opened. She felt tiny on the stoop as he towered over her. His expression was warm and tender, though his brown eyes were glassy, streaked with emotion. He sat down beside her, and their thighs brushed. They looked at each other properly for the first time in so many years. The initial shock had diminished slightly, and it finally felt real. Harrison's eyes crinkled at the edges with the beginnings of a smile. They were so close, it was dangerous. Leaning her head onto his shoulder, she breathed in his scent.

He wrapped her in his arms and her palm went to his chest. She could feel his heart as it beat an identical rhythm to hers, echoing the cadence of their history from this life and so many before. Ella urged herself to belong to the moment, not informed by before. He kissed her head, and she heard him inhale. A kiss of love and protection. The feeling of safety resonated throughout her like they were one person: part of the same soul split between two bodies.

'Harri...' she whispered, her lips hovering above his skin, longing for contact. She felt him shiver as her breath flitted across his neck. He held her tighter, then he stood, scooping her into his arms as he rose, cradling her like a child. He walked into the lounge, kicking the door shut behind him, and bent to put her down. It was like trying to stand on a cloud of marshmallow, her legs didn't seem to belong to her body. Eventually she steadied herself, pressing her hands against his torso. Again, the tingling sensation of desire coursed through her veins, compelling her to meet his stare. His eyes sparkled, but she knew he was reluctant to smile in case it provoked her fury.

His heartbeat increased under her palm as her breath became shallow. Snaking his hand behind her head, he pulled her gently towards him. She shouldn't want this, yet she'd never craved anything more. He dipped his head, not breaking their gaze until Ella closed her eyes and yielded her mouth to his. It was soft at first, tantalisingly teasing brushes as their lips found each other's, re-familiarising themselves. Her hands moved to find his face as their kiss deepened. It felt like coming home. Her questions and anger could wait and she let him lead her upstairs.

Their passion was dangerous but undeniable, dominating sense. He kissed her the way she needed to be kissed and her spine prickled with the sensation. Their limbs clung together, tangling, making it impossible to pinpoint where Harrison began, and Ella ended. She was surprised at how nervous she suddenly felt, a re-awakening with each layer of clothing his hands removed, a strap slipped over a shoulder, the scratch of denim on her naked skin, as if his lips were touching virgin territory.

'Trust me, I won't let you go again,' he said, his voice husky with desire.

Any pain was muted, and she teetered on the edge of where their love dwelt. It made her dizzy, the strength of feeling sturdier than the cliffs that surrounded the beautiful island.

'Stop! I can't,' she suddenly shouted, reaching for her clothes. Passion had blindsided her, but she couldn't release their past so easily. 'I'm sorry, I need to go,' she said, pulling on her shorts and retrieving her vest top.

'Ella, don't. Stay. Nothing has to happen, just ... let me hold you.'

She hesitated, biting her lip.

'I can't, Harri. If we ... it's not that simple. I want to, believe me, I do. But I won't make our mistake again. I can't.'

'I understand. It's your choice, of course it is, but you don't have to run away or be afraid. Just stay.'

'Can you hear yourself? Don't run out on me, don't leave ... they're all the things *you* did. Why should I be here another second?'

She stood with her hands on her hips, wishing she didn't long to crash into his body and give herself to him.

'Because it's you and me. It's us, El. We can't hurt each other more than we already have.'

It had been years; she could give him another hour. She made a show of reluctantly sinking into his arms. She silently

145

asked the island to weave a spell of intention around her heart, locking a small piece away to prevent it from breaking again at his hands.

* * *

Ella woke fully clothed, tangled in bedsheets. The hunger pang in her stomach indicated it was close to supper time. Harrison's arm was around her shoulder, and she ran her fingers up and down his forearm, twisting the coating of dark hair. She watched him as he dozed, the smile on his lips ignited her own happiness.

She wasn't foolish enough to consider all was well or fixed. Far from it. A temporary sticking plaster perhaps, but her wounds ran so deep they needed sutures. And she could never let him know about Phoenix, although she was dying to tell him about the glorious creature who'd emerged from their hideous pain.

She was churning with emotion; arousal, fear, guilt ... and unsure which to land upon first. Gently extracting his arm from beneath her, she tiptoed to the windows where the open balcony doors off the bedroom invited in the warm evening air. She could see the opposite side of the headland twinkling with house lights. The rising full moon sent silvery shadows into the cowering crevices of the cliffs, lighting up the dark sky.

Arms crept around her waist making her jump. The heat from Harrison's naked chest connecting with her skin was instant and she held his arms tightly around her. He nuzzled her neck and exposed shoulders, and she turned to him, bathed in moonshine. He stepped back to look at her.

'You are perfect, El.'

She suddenly felt afraid to be in her own body.

146

'Harri, stop. I'm far from perfect. Please, don't...'

She was scared of what else she might say, unsure if she could prevent what might come tumbling from her mouth; accusations, a need to torture him with her misery. He led her back into his bed, and she burrowed within his arms, cocooned in his love. There she slept again.

* * *

She came to once more, but this time she was alone. Wisps of music from downstairs floated up to caress her. The temperature had dipped, cooling her skin. She found a discarded white linen shirt slung across the back of a chair. Slipping it around her, she could smell Harrison and held it to her face, inhaling deeply. The sound of him playing piano was like a balm for her wounds. At university, she'd lie in his bed, listening to him play for hours. His student accommodation had been a mess of overflowing ashtrays and clothes strewn across every surface, yet his keyboard stood pristine and perfect against the wall. To now hear the rich, full sound of an upright piano commanded by his fingers was breathtaking.

Ella crept downstairs to listen. She watched him get lost within the notes as she sat on the bottom stair. The moon lit his profile through the open windows as she stayed silent and still. Then, he began to play the song he wrote for her. Once more disarmed by his love, her body became weak. She cowered behind the wrought iron balustrades as she dared to listen, gnawing at the skin around her nails. The famous lyrics weren't forthcoming from a superstar singer, but from the original architect of those words, as the one he wrote them for watched on. As he reached the final chorus, Ella felt like she hadn't taken a breath, and couldn't quell her tears.

'Looking back in time, you are all I see.

'*Endless searching for your eyes, I feel you reach for me.*

'*Our hearts and souls forever joined, living out of sight.*

'*It's always you, within the darkness you, you will be the light.*'

But he carried on with the song to a part she'd never heard. It wasn't in the released version she'd spent years trying to avoid.

'*If there's no way to love you now.*

'*I have to let you go.*

'*You'll have my heart, you're half my soul.*

'*It's always you, I know.*'

His powerful baritone choked on the last line and Harrison's shoulders moved as his hands dropped away from the piano and he cried.

'Harri…' she began in a whisper, unsure what to say. He didn't turn around, but started to speak.

'I wrote that extra verse on the train, El, when I left you. I sent the finished lyrics of the song with a letter to you, the whole thing.'

She moved over to him and folded her arms around him.

'It's beautiful. Painful, but so beautiful,' she said, sitting next to him on the piano stool.

'I wouldn't let anyone record it. I kept it for me, for us. Silly, really, but I'm a romantic fool like that.'

Ella laughed and wiped away his tears.

'I wouldn't say that, Harri. You wrote the most beautiful love song after callously abandoning me. Which is deeply unromantic in my book.'

Her jest attempted to hide the true meaning behind the statement, but he felt it. His hand reached for hers.

'I know, El. I wish you'd got my letters, I tried to explain it all; why I left. But I s'pose there's no good reason other than I was terrified. I loved you so much, so much it hurt. And I was scared of it being taken away from me. Believe me, I've had years of therapy about us and it makes sense because of how I grew up. It's not an excuse, but it's a reason, love.' Her mind travelled to the first moment when he'd reluctantly opened up a little about his home life.

They walked late at night along the riverbank where they'd first met in the spring. October had ushered in a much-lauded Indian summer and the night was warm and fragrant. They lay on the grass beneath a weeping willow tree and gazed at the stars and moon between the soft, rippling fronds. Ella wanted to delve deeper into his past – he revealed so little about his feelings, always guarded – and they'd drunk enough at the pub to loosen his tongue.

'Is anyone else musical in your family?' Her question was met with silence and they continued to stare up at the night sky. 'Why won't you let me in, Harri?' she whispered, longing to understand him more. The quiet had been peppered by bursts of laughter from bars further along the riverbank. Eventually she tried again. 'What about your love of jazz. How did you find it?' she asked, and she felt his arms tense around her. She knew she'd found the gateway to the hidden Harrison she was desperate to uncover.

'My mum. She'd play Sarah Vaughan or Ella Fitzgerald, and she loved Billie Holiday but that was only when she was really sad. I could tell her moods by which record she played. Some songs meant she was just having a black day or there was one she'd play after my dad...' He stopped speaking and Ella silently urged him onwards. 'After my dad had hit her. It was "Someone to Watch Over Me". I knew if he was home, I needed to be quiet, because he'd find me and do the same to me. Sometimes I wasn't quiet enough...'

Ella sat up to face him as he continued to gaze up at the stars. She put her hand on his chest.

'*Harri, I'm so sorry. I had no idea.*'

He shrugged, still flat on the ground before slowly meeting her eye. She felt the shift in the air between them as he continued to share precious but painful nuggets from his past.

'*He told me I'd amount to nothing, and he wished I'd never been born. That's when he was drunk. Sober, he would take me fishing and behave like a proper dad. He didn't know how to love me. He used to say I was worthless and stupid.*' *He laughed at the spite that had been directed at him as a child. 'When he left Mum, she never really recovered. She had men in and out of the house, desperately searching for the one. But she never found it, all she got was more misery.*'

He sat up to roll a joint.

'*I swear when I win my first Grammy, I will hunt him down and tell him what a useless piece of shit of a father he was.*'

Ella's mind returned to the present Harrison, sitting beside her on the piano stool in her mother's old house.

'Harri, I know your upbringing was horrible. The way you respond to love makes sense. But I wanted to be the one to swoop in and save you, to give you permission to love. Yet you repeated your parents' pattern and my poor heart never recovered. It still hasn't. You played out your pain on us, on me.'

Her heartache was her own truth, but she needed to be released from it. He couldn't do that for her, but he could help her on her way to be free of their past.

'You will never know how sorry I am. Y'know, I looked for you in every woman to try and make up for it, but I couldn't accept someone caring for me, and anyways, nobody did it like you. Not a single person showed me love like you did.' He cracked his knuckles, making Ella wince with each clunk. 'After you, the few girlfriends I had were all quite similar. One even looked a bit like you. They were well spoken, creative, brunette… I've been chasing you across the years and I didn't know it until I started therapy. What an idiot.'

She lay her head on his shoulder.

'You're not an idiot for wanting a bit of posh totty like me!'

'Hey, you're not that posh!' he retorted, nudging her with his elbow, but there was a smile in his voice.

'I've done the same, looked for you in everyone. I broke their hearts before they could break mine. I was terribly callous with some of those men, and I feel horrible. That was your fault as well, just in case I wasn't being clear.'

His hands begin to play again, adding a melancholy soundtrack to their scene with a jazz standard she recognised from his repertoire of old.

'More than clear. But at some point you have to let go of something that happened a long time ago, even though it still hurts. Otherwise, you said yourself, we'll go around in circles. Again.'

Ella stood and walked into the kitchen. She filled a glass with water, her mouth suddenly dry from panic. Was this something that could be construed as an 'again'? She wasn't sure she had the fortitude to forgive him or to enter into whatever this was. The advice she'd given to Phoenix about never giving your heart to someone if they couldn't look after it was moot when it came to Harrison. And how could they genuinely be with each other when she was hiding the truth about their daughter? She sipped her water while wondering why love with him in the moment seemed so easy, yet when she tried to picture it in the real world, it felt nigh on impossible? If she ignored reality, they could peel away layers of their past and pretend none of it mattered. But there would always be a gaping hole in her history, and she'd be duping herself if she thought he wouldn't uncover it. He'd find it in her eyes.

She heard him hesitate on the piano, then make a mistake with a chord. He tried to repeat the phrase, groaning in frustration as he again attempted the refrain. But the same thing happened.

'Are you all right?' Ella asked and he turned his head to her in the kitchen. She could see in his eyes he was unnerved. But it was a brief glimpse of something she couldn't pinpoint before he recovered.

'Yeah, fine. Just a tricky chord I can't...' His hands left the keys, and he closed the piano lid. 'You know I've still got all the letters I wrote to you if you want them. They all came back marked "return to sender", though I could see they'd been opened and probably read. I didn't know if you'd gone back to uni or not so I sent them to the only address I could remember – Georgia's.'

Ella was unable to contain her shock and dropped the glass of water, but didn't flinch at the sound of crystal shattering on slate. She had been afraid of her anger bursting out at Harrison, but it suddenly paled in comparison to the red rage that descended, like a sea-fog coating her eyes. And the blind fury was entirely directed at her lying, cheating, control freak of a sister.

Chapter 20

Georgia

'I think we might finally have plain sailing, and I'm so relieved, especially ahead of tomorrow.'

Georgia was bringing Oliver up to speed on yet another eventful day on Hydra.

'I'm so glad for you. It's like trying to follow a soap opera with you and your sister.'

'You're telling me! It's been quite exhausting. I'm about to get into bed, but hopefully things are headed in the right direction. Ella actually bought me a gift, a lovely necklace that she sent to the hotel with a sweet note. It said *"Truce? Love Els Bells"*. I was quite taken aback. I mean, there's lots to work through and she needs to apologise ... again ... but I'm sure we can find a way to be proper sisters. For Mum, if not each other.'

She cradled the phone under her chin so she could close the doors and windows, straightening the curtains as she drew them shut. She hoped to avoid any accidental eavesdropping on her conversation.

'I must say, I'm enjoying our chats. They're more meaningful somehow with you being away, it's much easier like this.' Georgia closed her eyes. It was what she was afraid

153

of; he was enjoying being apart. 'Oh, and I spoke to Phoenix earlier. She said she had a nice time with you this afternoon,' Oliver continued.

A large grin spread over Georgia's face at the change of topic and she re-entered the conversation. 'She did quite a bit of shopping and it was so good to be together, just the two of us.'

Oliver groaned.

'My credit card is wincing at the damage.' She heard him hesitate and began to worry. 'She also said she's concerned about you. Said your emotions were a little extreme of late and that you fainted. Why on earth didn't you say anything?'

Georgia felt embarrassed that her daughter had told tales and alerted Oliver to her overly wrought reactions on Hydra. He always sniped at her emotional responses, which is why she hadn't mentioned it to him. She tried to assuage her husband.

'I'm absolutely fine, it's just ever so hot out here. And I'm a bit tense, I suppose, with Phoenix leaving for college soon.' She hoped that was an adequate response to appease him.

'I can't believe she'll be off in a few months,' he said.

'Don't! The thought is horrifying. Although if she's accepted by one of the London ones, she could maybe still live with us.' She almost pleaded with the air; she wasn't ready to let Phoenix go yet.

Oliver took a deep breath and she knew what was coming.

'Georgia, you have to let her be independent. Goodness knows we've done everything to set her up to succeed. What happens next is out of our control. Out of *your* control,' he added pointedly.

She sank into one of the armchairs in the lounge of her hotel suite, picking at the juicy green grapes nestled in the fruit bowl then straightening the cushions behind her. She was skipping supper and Phoenix had said she'd eat in her room and watch a movie – which Georgia had confirmed via the tracking app. Oliver was right, but the time for their daughter to leave home seemed to have arrived so quickly. She could still remember the feeling of Phoenix as a tiny, wriggling bundle in her arms. The sleepless nights that had stretched forever … which she didn't resent for a moment, though she had begrudged the updates Ella demanded in those early days. She would call on a crackling line from university, tearfully asking about 'my Phoenie'. Oliver eventually had to intervene and sit Ella down for a serious chat when she next came to visit. Georgia remembered pressing her ear so hard against the door to listen that her skull went numb. It had been heartbreaking, but necessary.

'Ella, I know this must be impossible for you,' Oliver began. 'But you can't keep calling for news or referring to Phoenix as yours. We kept the name you chose out of respect, but now it's time you start respecting your sister and all she's sacrificed. All we have sacrificed to help you. Especially when things, you know … got rather tricky for you. Mentally, I mean.'

'But…'Ella started to interrupt, and Georgia felt the pain in her voice even through the door.

'No, Ella. You need to listen very carefully. Georgia is doing her best to adjust to motherhood, but your continued demands are pushing her to the limit. You simply cannot hold this over her forever. You made a choice, and you need to stick by it. It's too late. We're her parents. We legally adopted Phoenix, which is what you asked of us, and that's that. You need to learn to let this go.'

Georgia knew Oliver was trying to be kind, but without the context of his facial expression, she winced at the *harshness of his words. Yes, she was being tested, but Ella had been in a terrible state, in the fug of the darkest depression, even suicidal, after Harrison abandoned her shortly after she'd discovered she was pregnant. So much so, Georgia had begged Oliver to send her to a private clinic to get help. It had been where Ella spent the Easter break that year. Instead of chocolate eggs and roast lamb, she'd received intensive counselling, and medication, which thankfully hadn't harmed the baby.*

'But you mustn't hold this over me either, Oliver, saying how you've given up this and that. You're lucky, you can buy solutions to your problems. I can't, I'm a student with nothing,' Ella responded. 'And yes, I know I have to live with my decision, and I am grateful to you both; you're much better parents than I could ever have been. But it's harder than I thought having Phoenie near. Maybe I should have given her to strangers to bring up, that way she wouldn't keep breaking my heart.'

Ella's noisy sobs pulled at Georgia so hard, she felt like she could burst, almost wanting to hand Phoenix back to her and make it all go away.

When she'd agreed to the adoption, she'd known their relationship would never be the same. The threat of one of them revealing the truth would always be lurking like an invisible shadow. But Phoenix was everything to Georgia and she would always be grateful to her sister for giving her that chance. It had just become so terribly complicated. She'd willingly given up everything she knew and loved to protect her sister and provide Phoenix with the stability she deserved. But such was the trickiness of deceit; the truth could spring up and catch you unaware.

Though there was no way Ella could find out about any of

the other things Georgia had bottled up. It felt liberating in a way, knowing her sister would never uncover the lies she'd fed her, though they troubled Georgia constantly. After they scattered the ashes tomorrow evening, her path forward could then continue unblemished by Hydra, and the threat of her terrible secrets being unmasked could rest at the bottom of the seabed with the remains of her mother.

* * *

After a long hot shower before she headed to bed, Georgia slathered cocoa butter on her arms and legs. The smell reminded her of a holiday to Barbados with Oliver just before they married. It had been a time when her focus had been her interior design career, pleasing Oliver in the bedroom and pleasing herself by overseeing the refurbishment of their Chiswick home. It struck her as a simple existence. Now she had little interest in those pursuits and her career she'd gladly relinquished for motherhood would be hard to pick up again if she felt so inclined. With a ring on her finger, any professional ambition was swallowed up with her determination to be a parent. But she'd failed to conceive, and Georgia didn't enjoy the mass disappointment that inspired; the sympathetic hand squeezes from her mother, the gentle pat on the back from Oliver at the monthly evidence they weren't pregnant yet again and the jolly pep talk from her sister encouraging her to believe in fate. None of those did anything to ease her shame at her own body letting her down. Oliver didn't want to be an 'old' father given he was fifteen years her senior, so they had agreed to proceed to parenthood as soon as they were married. But those years of fruitless trying had driven an unspoken wedge between them. She'd refused to accept fertility treatment, believing it would happen unaided; she was convinced she could do it. But she'd blamed herself and he did little to persuade her otherwise. And then she began to blame him. But suddenly Phoenix changed their world and gave them what they'd longed for. She wondered whether Oliver would be open to a more intensive style of counselling to try and repair the damage that had blighted their marriage, like a creeping poison ivy, strangling what was left of love. She innately knew he'd deride the suggestion. He already felt he was doing enough.

Georgia focused on the only positive thought she could unearth – that the fighting with Ella may have finally abated. Fingering the pretty necklace her sister had sent her, she linked the stereo in the living room to her phone and selected a random playlist. Disco classics began to boom from the speakers, and she wrapped her towel tighter and started to dance. She was self-conscious at first, but eventually the infectious driving rhythms took over, and she flung her arms aloft, spinning around with abandon. Her towel fell away to a pool on the floor making her giggle. She felt wild, free from clothing and any constraints. It was so out of character and for a moment, old worries and anxieties dissolved into the music.

A loud thumping, out of time with the bassline, jolted her senses back to reality. She bashed the off button as she realised the banging was coming from the front door. She braced to be remonstrated by the manager, although it wasn't that late, surely nobody would be asleep yet. Pulling on a robe, she tied it firmly as the incessant beating continued.

'Just a sec!' she trilled, briefly checking in the mirror before opening the door. Ella was revealed as the culprit, and Georgia exhaled in relief. She wasn't in trouble after all.

'Thank God it's only you! Look, I'm wearing the necklace

you…' She trailed off as she absorbed the sight of fury on her sister's tear-stained face. She stormed into the suite, her back heaving from rapid breathing, as the bright moonshine penetrating the muslin drapes enhanced her silhouette.

'Ella, what on earth's going on?' Georgia asked in concern. Outbursts of extreme emotions were much more her realm than her sister's.

Ella rounded, visibly seething, and strode over until they were nose to nose.

'How … could … you?'

She spoke through gritted teeth, like she was unable to open her mouth fully, for fear of what would emerge. A droplet of her spittle landed on Georgia's lip, but she was too afraid to wipe it away, as grotesque as she found it. She started to tremble, searching for what could have possibly happened as her eyes travelled in confusion to the bundle of papers Ella was holding. Her sister suddenly grabbed her arm with fingers that pinched through her fluffy hotel robe.

'Ella … I … don't…'

Ella's hold tightened, squeezing Georgia's skin.

'How could you hide these from me?' she spat.

Georgia was too afraid to speak, but Ella shook her, having grabbed both her arms, the crunch of the paper bundle made her wince.

'Answer me!'

Georgia's voice was strained as she tried to reply with a smile, which instantly betrayed her fear and discomfort.

'Hide wh-what, Els Bells?' Georgia was desperately reaching for something to soften Ella's tone.

'Don't you dare call me that. You're not my sister.'

Her knees began to shake.

'I … I don't know what you mean.' Georgia found a little

composure and managed to shake her off, attempting to put some distance between them. But Ella was intent on invading her space and Georgia felt trapped in the confrontation.

'Harrison's letters. You hid them from me, you lied to me. All this time. How could you?'

The wind was knocked out of Georgia's lungs, but she somehow found the energy to slink to the other side of the coffee table, searching for some breathing room. She pulled at her dressing gown, gathering the collar close to her neck.

'What are you talking about? I haven't lied about anything. And I don't know anything about *him*—'

'You're lying again!' Ella roared, making Georgia physically jump. 'He wrote letters for you to pass on to me. For years. Ever since he left. You were the only person in the family whose address he had. He wanted to stay in touch … and you stopped him! You let me believe he didn't care, that he didn't love me. You watched me struggle. Because of this, because of *you*, I gave up my baby!'

She screamed her last sentence, so much so, Georgia was concerned someone might call the police, or worse, that Phoenix may overhear. Ella's face suddenly crumpled, and she sank into the sofa, her head in her hands. She cried in a way Georgia hadn't heard since she'd returned from King's Cross having been abandoned. That was the day she'd confessed she was pregnant.

It was a feral, angry wail. Georgia took one step towards her, then thought better of it.

'It … it wouldn't have changed anything, Ella.'

Ella's angry face shot up from her hands.

'You don't know that, and I didn't get the chance to know because of *you*. I could have understood why he left; I wouldn't have been as broken. I wanted to kill myself and

Phoenix because of him. Don't you get that? Oh, but you do because you paid to make that problem disappear at that expensive treatment centre you sent me to. But it didn't all magically go away.' She stood again, angrily wiping her tears away with her fists. 'I might have been able to look at my baby and not regret ever having met Harrison. But I couldn't. This is your fault, Georgia. All you do is control everyone and everything around you. You've manipulated me and my life enough. You kept these from me because you thought you'd lose Phoenix. Admit it!' she shouted. 'I gave you the chance to be a mother, which I will now never get to experience for myself, and you've engineered every single thing that's ever happened to me. But it ends now.'

Ella stared with a look of pure hatred.

'How did you…?'

'How did I find out?' Ella interrupted, her mouth snarling in disgust. 'Because Harrison is here. On Hydra.'

Georgia blanched whiter than the pristine hotel bedsheets. She felt panic flush through her.

'Ella … I … I thought Harrison … that you'd never see him—'

Ella cut her off.

'Well, you know it all don't you, my sweet, caring *sister*? Except you don't. Because here's what's going to happen.' She moved to Georgia, still gripping Harrison's letters. 'I will scatter the ashes tomorrow with you, for Mum and for Phoenix's sake, and then I am leaving this place. I never, ever want to see you again. Because if I do, I will tell *your daughter* exactly who her biological parents are. I have absolutely nothing to lose but you … you will lose *everything*. I will never forgive you for this.'

She brandished the pages at Georgia's face, making her

161

recoil before storming across the room. Georgia followed, frantically trying to catch Ella's arm.

'Ella, wait!'

She reached the door and depressed the handle, her voice icy as she said, 'Go and see Harrison for yourself and explain what you've done. There aren't enough words to apologise for your actions. It's over, Georgia. You and me. We're finished.'

'No, Ella, please listen. I was trying to protect you from him, from being hurt any more, you have to believe me,' she said, her voice shrill with desperation. But ... wh-why is he... where is he?'

Ella slowly turned, then started to walk towards her as Georgia retreated until the back of her calves hit the table with a thud. She had nowhere else to go. Ella's voice was taunting, coated with a deliberate faux sweetness as she said, 'You walk up the hill to the right of the harbour, where you'll find a white house with two olive trees in the garden.'

Georgia covered her mouth in horror.

'What's wrong, *sis*? Did the Hydra cats steal your tongue? Yes, that's right. You've tried to keep us apart for years, but this island has pulled us all back together. Me, him ... you and Phoenix. Because Harrison now owns Mum's house.'

Chapter 21

Ella

Ella paced around her hotel room, pounding the floorboards repeatedly. She wanted to scream, to hurt something or someone. What shocked her the most was the blistering outrage she felt towards Georgia. Her sister was her puppeteer, shaping the path her life had taken. And Ella had been oblivious.

She searched for calm and an objective view. Harrison's letters sat tauntingly on the coffee table. She was desperate to read them, but also terribly afraid. He said he'd finished writing *that* song on the train after he left her at the station, sending the completed lyrics along with the first note. And it was in front of her now, along with his explanation. It could have been enough to appease her back then, but she'd been so angry and hurt. If she'd received consolation or an acknowledgement of their love, would it have been sufficient to have shed her heartache immediately? She would have had a means of contacting him, preventing her descent into the destructive misery of her own mind. She could perhaps have found the strength to be a mother. Now, Ella would never know.

She shook her head in disgust at Georgia. Hydra had unmasked her sister and brought Harrison back into her life.

Yet what she feared the most – though wanted more than anything – was to forgive him. She'd dwelt in a dark space of resentment and bitterness for so long, she didn't know how to step into the light. She was wrung out by him, her sister and the island. And being with Phoenix was almost impossible. She'd hoped it would become easier with time, that the raw feelings would mend enough for it to sting less. But it hadn't. Whoever suggested that the passing of years heals was a liar.

Despite what she had threatened Georgia with, Ella would never reveal Phoenix's true parentage. She might wish to punish her sister, but Phoenix would be a casualty of that war and it would be unforgivable. More unforgivable than anything Harrison did.

Outside, the evening was balmy, and Ella looked at the stars. Thousands of lights twinkled in the deep sapphire sky and her eyes traced familiar constellations. The milky way was like an artist's streaking silver thumb print blended into a perfect canvas. She'd always wondered which stars Harrison could see wherever he was in the world. That evening, she knew they shared the same sky. Looking to the navigators of the ancients sparkling above, she called to the island for guidance.

She felt Harrison's energy reach for her, like a fingertip running along each vertebra. But her head was marred by a fog of confusion, and she suppressed the urge to yield to her basest desires. It wouldn't solve anything, it would only create reams of other problems.

Her anger had retreated and what remained was a naked, base pain from her sister's actions, like an open laceration across her skin. Ella went inside and picked up Harrison's first letter, which might yet prove to be vinegar on that wound. Resting her head on the arm of the sofa, she turned onto her back, looking at the ceiling. The rotating fan began to hypnotise her as she cradled the paper to her chest, and her eyelids became heavy to the point that she could hardly hold them open. The hidden verse he wrote for her that he'd kept private from the world drifted across her mind...

If there's no way to love you now.
I have to let you go.
You'll have my heart, you're half my soul.
It's always you, I know.

Ella sank into a semi-conscious state as she replayed their meeting today without words, just sensation and feelings laced with regret and pleasure. She envisaged lying beside him so vividly that she could sense the warmth from his body. His arm underneath her shoulder, holding her close. She felt him kiss the side of her head and pull her nearer as she conjured words from him, unsure if they were real, but she heard them as if he were next to her.

I will love you 'til the day I die. And then forever, and longer, love.

The imagined sound of his voice uttering words he'd never said and the make-believe safety of his arms engulfed her with protection. A hand on his chest, his heartbeat beneath her palm. It was like he was in the room. She didn't know if she was awake or asleep, here or elsewhere, suspended in the atmosphere, in their own private universe where only their love existed.

You'll have my heart, you're half my soul,
It's always you, I know.

Her Harrison, the other part of her, the only real love she'd known. After years apart, he was now merely a brief boat ride away. It was an additional torment to have to journey to him via her most hated method of transport. But they were finally back in the same place, the island where their history lived, and his story of when they were separated was beneath her fingertips within the letters.

And Ella was somewhere in between, unsure where to turn.

* * *

```
                     c/o The Bonham Hotel
                  35 Drumsheugh Gardens
                   Edinburgh EH3 7RN
                    January 20th 1998
My El.
   I've broken your heart, I know I have.
But there was no other way, love. I don't
know how I can make you understand why
I've done this to us. I've told you about
how I grew up, the way my parents behaved.
I was determined not to be like them, but
I know I've failed. I am as guilty as my
father. I hurt you for loving me just as
he did to me, although my crime was worse
in a way. Because I know how it feels to
be abandoned, and yet here I am, doing it
to you.
   The thought of you still at the station
kills me. I had to run, I couldn't look at
you anymore and I didn't know how to say
goodbye or tell you that you had to stay at
university, not leave it all just for me.
We have to be separated by circumstance,
but I know it isn't the end. It's the
start of our lives. I will be in Scotland
rehearsing and then who knows where, away
for months on tour. We can't give up our
ambition for each other, even though the
temptation to do that consumes me. We've
```

166

both worked too hard to stop life before it begins and there's no way for us to be together right now without you sacrificing so much and that's not how it should be. Love should be equal.

I will send this to your sister as I don't know where you'll be and how long this will take to reach you, though I hope and pray you return to your course. It's what you are destined to do, and I can't take that away from you. I shouldn't have agreed on Hydra that you should come with me. I was caught up in the romance of us. I blame the island, it stopped me revealing the truth, but I'm not good with saying how I feel, you already know that.

I know this isn't enough, but if we'd continued, we would have hurt each other more than this. I don't want that, even though in this moment my pain is unlike anything I've felt. And I'm sure yours is worse. You'll probably hate me and that's maybe easier. So, hate me, tear up our memories and despise us.

You will always have my heart even though I couldn't give it to you. Not now. Maybe not ever. I don't know how to risk my love and I doubt I ever will. That's the damage I will live with. Though it won't feel like it, I'm protecting you, protecting us.

You are going to change the world with your photographs; you're so talented, and I am so proud. If you want to reach me, if only to shout and rant at me, I am at this

hotel for a while. I'll continue to write
to you from wherever I am in the hope that
one day, when you're ready, you will know
where to find me.

   I finished that song I wrote for you, for
us, and the lyrics are on the other page.
It may not come to anything, but if it finds
its way out into the world and should you
ever hear it, know it's about you. Because
it's always been you and always will be.
You are the other half of my heart and
soul. I know you will never forgive me but
we will always have Hydra. I will always
think of it as our island.

   I'm sorry,
   Harri xxx

Ella tried to imagine how she'd have felt reading the
letter back then, in the throes of raw, unbridled heartbreak,
pregnant with Phoenix. He'd let her know where he was and
if Georgia hadn't hidden his letters away from her, she could
have gone to him and told him about Phoenix and their lives
could have turned out so differently.

But he also could have been right. They might have drifted
apart, hurt each other in a far more destructive way, spun
around in a toxic circle until it dissolved into nothing but
animosity. And Phoenix could have been a victim of their
heartbreak, more so than she already unknowingly was. Ella
would have resented him if it had unfolded that way, if she
had foolishly given up her studies to be with him. In some
ways she was glad she hadn't done that, because it had given
her an incredible life, but it had been a life without him and
their daughter.

Leafing through the countless envelopes, the postmarks indicated the regularity with which he'd tried to stay in touch over the years. The missives came from all over the UK, Europe, Asia and America.

She read the lyrics to Harrison's song and couldn't help but smile at his words in the letter about the song he'd written – *'it may not come to anything'*. At least he had something incredible to show for their heartache, a song beloved and adored by millions, plaudits, awards and a beautiful testament to their love, which he could never have predicted when he wrote it. Ella had Phoenix, but she didn't – she was their secret legacy. A permanent bruise lived inside her heart, with a wall built to protect herself and yet still, the impact of their ill-fated relationship persisted. Like ripples from a pebble dropped into water that lingered on the surface even though the stone had disappeared from sight.

Ella stared at the papers in front of her, edges lifted from the night breeze wafting through the open doors. She knew what she wanted to do and the energy of her decision fizzed throughout her body, leaning firmly into destiny. She'd encouraged everyone over the years to trust in the universe's plan and it was time she took her own advice. The island had presented an opportunity for closure, for a beginning and an ending.

Tomorrow at sunset, out of duty, she'd scatter her mother's ashes and say goodbye, but tonight, there was only one place she wanted to be. And she'd been kept away from it long enough without resolution or satisfaction. It was time for her to stop running and yield to what was inevitable. It had been written in the stars, but they might yet still be able to rewrite their future. Harrison had been placed within reach and Ella intended to accept whatever fate had determined.

Chapter 22

Ella

The island during the witching hour was eerily silent. The mules and ponies that frequented the front of the harbour were safely tucked away in their stables and the cats which crowded the walkways in the day were nowhere to be seen. The only sounds were the occasional creak of yacht masts and the splash of a wave against the sea wall. The hum of the engine from the water taxi receded as it headed back to the hotel and Ella felt sympathy for the bleary-eyed boy who'd dutifully shuttled her around the headland at such an ungodly hour. She was so steadfast on her course that even the familiar panic she usually endured on a boat was somewhat dulled.

Beside the deserted bars, she paused and looked upwards to Harrison's house. It seemed bizarre to call it that. A warm glow was coming from the lounge doors. She knew he would be awake; she'd felt it. The other windows along the cliffside were shrouded in darkness; his was the only light. Again, his song echoed through her mind.

Within the darkness, you, you will be the light.

It was their song and was out in the world, sustaining the force of the love affair that had inspired it.

She felt each strike of her knuckles against the front door

170

throughout her body and allowed the rush of energy to touch each neglected corner. The muted piano music from within stopped. Harrison's proximity resonated deep inside her, every footstep reverberated in her bones. The squeak of the handle made her stomach dance in anticipation as the night wrapped around her while she waited. Then, as the door opened, light flooded forward, illuminating her face. Harrison looked at her and Ella's intention rushed through the air between them. She stood on tiptoes to reach his lips with hers. It was the gentlest of touches, like a butterfly's kiss, and their mouths remained pressed together for an inhale and an exhale as their twin flames began to merge into one again. She lingered in the sensation of expectation, a honeyed, teasing agony. Her hand reached for his face to hold his cheek as she pulled back to look at him.

Joining the words from his letter with the man in front of her she took a sharp breath. Their love might be the death of them both, but she knew she couldn't exist in regrets. He was half of her, and Phoenix was the whole of them. He wouldn't hurt her as before; she wouldn't let him.

She kissed him again, now with a greater longing as they fitted back together into their perfect physical union. One of complete familiarity. There was no need for words as they both knew their bodies would say what their mouths were too afraid to voice.

They moved like phantoms through the house and upstairs. Her feet barely touched the floor, not registering textures or fabric, only his touch. He re-took the space within her soul that had lain vacant since they last made love. His arms, his breath, and the shape of his mouth that she'd seen and felt in her dreams was real again, though his face seemed brand new as he moved above her. Tears escaped her eyes as Harrison

171

owned what he'd always possessed, and she was engulfed in his love, brought back to life with each wave of passion deeper than the previous. Her whole being tensed in anticipation as their hearts reunited and flashes of golden lights darted across her eyes as she climbed upwards beyond her understanding of possibility. Their power was greater than ever. Their bodies were altered by time, but they were as they'd always been beneath their surfaces. Just as a vine will coil around a pillar to ground it for growth, so too they clung to one another, entwined in every fathomable way. There was no other place she would wish to be, where she fitted perfectly around him, body and soul. Ella offered herself entirely to the sensation of re-discovering what it felt like to give and this time receive true and complete love in return.

*   *   *

Tuesday

Music roused her senses as she woke the next morning alone in Harrison's bed. It was the day she would scatter her mother's ashes; the reason for travelling back to the island.

It was a ritual she hadn't considered important before, adopting a more spiritual doctrine to the rite of human frailty. But at that early hour, when the light was crisper than ever, she realised it *was* significant. It signified the ending of a part of her life she needed to say goodbye to. But that would all come later; she wasn't ready to think about it yet.

She turned her face down into the crumpled pillows, then stretched every limb. Resisting rational thoughts or logic invading her mind, she bathed in the noise of Hydra waking as her muscles recalled the night before. Through the open bedroom doors in the early morning sunshine, the island was alert. Boat engines blasted then subsided to a hum, hooves clopped along the lanes below the house and church bells clanged their metallic, pious reminders. Those island sounds had once punctuated times between school terms, but today, they were once again the soundtrack to love. All of Hydra's quavers represented a diminished chord of sadness and a triad of joy; the past, the present and the possibility of the future.

The smell of coffee garnished with the heady scent of cinnamon sent a waft of perfume through the bedroom. It felt perfect, though she was under no illusion that the scenario was anything but. She pushed away reality and dwelt in the moment among the sheets that were wrapped around her legs like cotton pythons, helping to constrict the thud of guilt in her mind to silence.

She smiled as she recognised the music drifting up the stairs. The blissful crackle of Bill Evans playing on vinyl took her straight back to Harrison's bedroom in his student house the first night they were together…

*   *   *

March 1997

Ella bashfully covered herself with the duvet as Harrison faced her. His hair was stuck with sweat to his forehead, and she smoothed it away as he did the same to her. It made them both laugh, giggling at nothing and everything. They couldn't stop staring, unable to pause their connection, which had only just begun but felt like it had always been there.

'How did I find you, El?' he said as his hand travelled to her face.

She smiled.

'You pushed me in the river this morning.'

173

His laugh was a gloriously rich sound as his fingers began to mime the record revolving on the battered stereo in the corner. Her shoulder became a piano made of skin and she couldn't look away from him. She wanted to climb inside his brown eyes, warm like the colour of darkest honey. He was so different to any other boy she'd met. He spoke with such eloquence, which in his rough accent was alluring and seductive. She enjoyed his duality, how unexpected he was. It was thrilling.

'If you close your eyes, El, and imagine where you are in twenty years, what do you see?'

She took a deep breath and felt her long eyelashes brush her cheekbones, as his exquisite fingers continued to play on her body.

'God ... I'll be nearly forty ... but I will have taken pictures on every continent in the world, photographed people that live in the farthest flung places, travelled wherever I wanted and whenever I wanted. That's my plan and nothing will stop me.'

Her eyelids opened and their gazes reconnected. Her fingers reached for his chin, brushing over his soft beard, tracing his lips as he kissed her fingertips. He ran his hand through his hair and propped himself up on his elbow.

'I don't doubt it for a second. There's nothing that could hold you back, El, I can feel it,' he said.

She shivered somewhere deep inside of her.

'And you?' Ella asked.

'I'll be earning a living from playing piano, but most of all, I want to write songs that change people's lives. To one day write the perfect love song that gets played at weddings, funerals and every event you could ever have ... that's the dream.'

Ella looked at him with an almost anticipatory pride.

'I know you will, Harri, I can feel it too.'

The awkwardness of a first night encounter was absent, as his gaze remained fixed on hers. Whether it was a minute or an hour that passed, it made no difference. This was something beyond the realms of a casual fling.

'Will you play something for me, now?' she asked.

He kissed her tenderly then sat at his keyboard, the muscles in his naked back tensing and moving as they sent his hands across the keys. It was a song she didn't recognise and the piece seemed incomplete, as if he was making it up, but it was the most beautiful music she'd ever heard. She reached for her camera that she always had with her and photographed his shoulders, his hands and fingers.

* * *

In Harrison's bed on Hydra in the present, she found it hard to join those young people with who they were now, back in one another's orbit once again. The way they were when they'd met was made of such an innocence, oblivious of the pain they could cause one another; singing, loving and smoking endless joints – but getting high on each other more than the contents of their tatty roll-ups. The memory made her giggle, because for the first time in so long, the stab of abandonment that she associated with the memory of Harrison past had started to retreat.

'And what are you laughing at, love? *Kaliméra*.'

His husky voice took Ella by surprise as he wished her good morning. She suddenly wondered if he knew any other Greek phrases and longed to hear the words in his accent more than anything. As she turned to take him in, the morning light kissed his contours, defining his body. Her fingers itched to trace the sunbeam's wake. He placed a delicious smelling cup of coffee on the bedside table and leant over to kiss her. She traced his taut arms as he hovered above, his naked chest inviting her to taste his skin.

'Coffee first, you in a minute,' she said, grinning as she sipped her drink then humming her appreciation as it hit its mark.

'Is it OK? I … I couldn't remember how you took it,' he said, perching on the edge of the bed.

'Really? After the thousands of cups you've made me?' She took another delicious sip. 'Perfect – cinnamon and no sugar – you didn't forget.'

He looked out of the windows briefly before turning back to her.

'We're really here, again.' He half smiled lazily.

Ella cradled the cup in her hands and sat up, pulling the sheet to cover her nakedness. It felt like their very first time again. She looked at him in the clear morning light. His features – forever seared on the inside of her eyes – were unchanged, and there was no part of him she didn't know. Loving all of him was not a choice, it was what lived within her, out of her charge.

'Look at you,' he said, his grin widening. 'It's like a dream.'

Her cheeks ached, not having smiled in such a way for longer than she cared to remember. It felt like old times, but as the caffeine coursed through her bloodstream, she checked herself. It could never be the same. A sentiment which could also be applied to her relationship with Georgia. Ella's face fell at the thought.

'Talk to me, El. What are you thinking?'

El… Nobody else had ever called her that. Only him. She took another blast of coffee; the cinnamon tang garnered her the necessary strength to speak.

'I'm thinking … a lot of things. I don't know where to start, Harri. I read your first letter. The one you wrote with the lyrics after the station.'

He ran his fingers through his hair. A gesture she knew of old, one that meant he was nervous. Though his hair was shorter now, it was still thick and dark. Her fingers prickled with the urge to mirror his gesture as a flashback from the early hours streaked across her mind – her fingers wrapped in his hair holding him impossibly close, yet not near enough. His exhale was pointed, and he nodded as if awaiting a painful reaction. She continued in the most rational fashion she could conjure.

'It… The letter made some sense, but I find it hard to detach the person it was meant for from the person I am now. I don't know if it would have been adequate. You broke me, Harri; you didn't just break my heart, you smashed it to pieces. I wanted to be the one, be *your* one. And you wouldn't let me. I felt like I wasn't enough to change your world. Everything we talked about here on Hydra… We'd agreed together that I would leave uni and be with you. But now I think about it, you didn't say no, but you didn't really say yes either.' She looked down at her cup. 'I would have given up everything for us. And I gave up so much of myself because *you* chose not to be with me.' He had no idea she meant Phoenix, but she finished her thought anyway. 'You didn't ever want me to come, did you? You were just too gutless to say it out loud.'

He went to interrupt and disagree, but she persisted.

'No. You wanted to go out and be a rockstar on tour, write your songs, play other people's music until you could make your own. Enjoy the groupies, no doubt, and be that guy. You didn't want me to hold you back. So, you can blame your shitty parents, but I don't. I blame you. I blame you for being a coward, for being unable to tell me that you didn't love me enough to fight for us. In fact, I don't ever recall you saying those words to me either. In my mind I cannot hear you saying *"El, I love you"*. I mean, I felt love, but maybe that was only when you were inside me.'

'What?' he said, outraged by her sudden spite.

'So what was I left with? A feeling that I wasn't good enough for your heart to open. Can you imagine, given how much I adored you, how horrible that felt?'

In the recesses of her mind, the frustration she was accustomed to when it came to her unshakable feelings of love for him sprang forward. She felt like she had betrayed her family by returning to his bed, and worst of all, she had let herself down. Because what had it all been for? She had mourned a spirit, a ghost of a reminiscence that was as destructive as it was magnificent.

Ella avoided his gaze; she couldn't look at him. If she did, she knew what would happen. She curled her legs in front of her, hugging her knees, trying to create a barrier between them.

'El, look at me. Look at me, love.'

He placed a hand on her shoulder but she turned her head to the side, wishing his touch didn't send shocks through her skin.

'El, I did love you. I still do. I don't know if I said it, I'm sure I did. But if I didn't, I'm saying it now. I love you.' He was still trying to catch her eye to make her understand. 'What more do you need? I'm sorry. I don't know how many times you need me to apologise. I won't do it forever. After all these years, isn't it enough? If it's not, it will break us apart.'

'Apart?!' she shouted. 'We aren't even together. I don't

know what this is.'

A slurp of dark liquid spilled from her coffee onto the white sheet and she caught a second drip on the rim of the cup with her finger.

'You spoiled what we had,' she said, watching the spreading dark liquid blemishing the linen. 'It wasn't perfect, but it wasn't ruined either. You did that by running away, repeating everything you'd learnt from your parents. You can blame as many people as you want, but at some point, you need to blame yourself. Take responsibility. Because whenever I've thought about us, I've punished myself. Wondered what I could have done differently, or how I should have made it better for you. And all that wasted, pointless energy sucked the life out of me, and I almost forgot to live. But believe me, I won't let you or any other man ever stop me from living the fabulous life I have now. Because even if I could forgive you, Harri, how can I ever trust you after what you did?'

She lifted her head and boldly met his stare. As their gazes joined, her heart contracted at the emotion in his beautiful brown eyes, the same eyes their daughter had inherited. He looked at her with a knowing that transcended earthly understanding and the tragic knowledge that inherently dwelt in the pit of her soul surfaced; she would never know a love like theirs again. But she needed space, to gather her thoughts, not swayed by love and lust. She needed to reacquaint herself with rational thinking to consider whether she could take a leap of faith and ever trust him with her heart again. Her sister had no influence in her decision, but Phoenix did. She had concealed that she was her birth mother for so long, surely she could do the same with Harrison.

The thought made her uneasy. If he found out, she

would be as guilty as him ... if not worse. She already was, in part.

Ella found a smile and kissed him tenderly, caressing his face with her fingertips as she did so. She dressed, and they exchanged a look, both comprehending the power of their joining and the equal strength it would require separating once more. Whether it was a permanent farewell or not was entirely up to her to decide; she would not be guided by any other voice but her own.

Chapter 23
Georgia

The day had finally arrived to scatter her mother's ashes. But Georgia could barely apply a sweep of nude lip gloss, her hand was shaking so much. She managed to smooth the sides of her hair, cursing the morning's humidity as fly-aways poked out of her chignon at every conceivable angle.

Her reflection in the bathroom mirror showed electric blue eyes – the result of a whole night spent crying. Red rims made them gleam almost turquoise, like the sea surrounding the stupid island. It felt like she'd had another bereavement, but she was determined to abide by her schedule, despite what had happened with Ella.

Phoenix had joined her for a bedtime cuppa in her room last night and Georgia had managed to see off her incessant questioning regarding Ella's whereabouts before retiring tearfully with a 'migraine'. Another lie, more untruths.

She and Ella were once again at loggerheads. Worse than that, this might be a fight they couldn't recover from. Georgia admitted to herself that she'd likely have reacted in the same way if she were in Ella's shoes and threatened all manner of hellfire to rain down upon the perpetrator of her misery. Georgia crouched on the cool, marble bathroom floor and hugged her knees. How did it get to this? She blamed Harrison for the world of pain that had afflicted their lives ever since he'd deserted Ella. Knowing he was on the island tempted her to march up to the house and give him a piece of her mind. But how could she do that without revealing the fact that he'd fathered a baby? A child who was now *her* daughter in name and in the eyes of the law, even if her musical talent and spirit firmly belonged to Harrison and Ella. There was no piece of paper Georgia could sign to remove those facts.

Her entire adult life had been about fixing Ella's mistakes or trying to prevent her from making more by protecting her. Her intentions had always been good, though it wouldn't seem like it to her sister. Georgia couldn't have foreseen that Ella would have her baby adopted. When she'd concealed Harrison's first letter, she'd meant to hand it over eventually. But the right time never presented itself. Ella had been so depressed and Georgia hadn't known what to do for the best. And then it was too late to admit what she'd done. Despite all her efforts, the elaborate curtain she'd woven to conceal the darkest doings within their family could now be thrown open. She needed to gather herself and press on with the day's purpose.

She reached for the printed itinerary she'd created for the holiday, squinting at the ink with blurred vision. Saturday, when they'd arrived, felt like a year ago, and each carefully arranged day had been marred by increasingly severe arguments. She scrunched up the paper in her hand. They were supposed to go to the spa that morning. She didn't expect Ella to attend and the prospect of fielding Phoenix's endless enquiries about her weighed Georgia down like a piece of lead sewn into the lining of her stomach. But she'd slap

182

on a smile and elegantly nudge questions aside. It was what she did in the countless social situations she was thrust into when entertaining Oliver's clients; mostly odious types who had money but no manners. Removing their clammy, wine-emboldened hands from her backside, not making a scene, no fuss, just grinning and bearing it… That was the strength she needed to draw upon to endure the day ahead until sunset when the ceremony would take place.

She picked up her phone to call Oliver. Still hunched on the floor, she dialled his number, feeling the rising knot of emotion in her throat. It was like a blood clot threatening to haemorrhage. Everything had become so intense, as if another power was orchestrating her breakdown. Hydra was a grubby reminder of all the guilt she held deep within.

Oliver's voice interrupted her thought.

'Morning Georgia,' he answered hurriedly. 'I'm about to go into a meeting, can you be quick?'

'Hi … I…' Her voice was strangled, and any attempt to be breezy had disappeared. She burst into noisy sobs, trying to concoct a sentence between gasps.

'Georgia, you're scaring me. What's happened, is Phoenix OK?'

'No … I mean, yes, she's fine … it's … it's *him*.' She gulped.

'Him who? You'll need to be much clearer if you want my help.'

Georgia momentarily managed to dam her tears, but she was afraid of Oliver's furious reaction. She located a slice of poise.

'Harrison. He's here. On the island.'

'What? How in God's name is he there?' said Oliver. His tone betrayed his underlying anger, just as she'd feared.

'He lives in Mum's house. He bought it. And now, he and

183

Ella … I don't know. But I'm scared, Oliver. I'm so scared.' Her voice rose in pitch and volume as the horror of this unexpected turn became truer with each word. She longed to find her stiff upper lip and sweep the latest drama under the carpet, but the rug had been pulled from underneath her feet.

'Tell me the facts and for goodness' sake calm down, would you? This is not the time for an emotional outburst. Now, what does he know about Phoenix?' His questions arrived in quick succession, like bullets.

'I don't know. Nothing, but I can't be sure. Ella found him and then she and I had a huge fight. He told her about his letters I kept from her.'

'What letters?' His voice became cold. 'Georgia, what have you done?'

'What have I done?!' She was immediately incensed. 'I only wanted to keep our family safe. I was trying to protect my sister and *our* daughter from him. He wrote to her all the time after he left her, but he only had our address, so they arrived marked to me. After reading the first one, I didn't want her to have any more to deal with or any way to contact him. She was so unwell, and I was worried for her baby. But they kept coming, so I sent them back to him … after I read them. And they didn't stop even after we'd adopted Phoenix, and I thought that…' She inhaled deeply, choosing a rare honesty no matter how painful. 'I thought that if Ella saw the letters, they'd get back together again and Phoenix would be taken away from us. And I'd never get the chance to be a mother again.'

Oliver's voice softened a little.

'I know Georgia, but … this might be the worst thing you've ever done.'

184

It wasn't the worst thing, but Oliver didn't know that. She shut her eyes, flushed with disgrace at his judgement as he continued.

'You know how she feels about him. And she'll blame you for keeping them apart. Which, essentially, you did. I can write the script. She'll go on about destiny and her so-called bloody soul mate or twin something or other – whatever she thinks they are. I'm not sure how you can come back from this. Especially with him there on that island too.'

Georgia's jaw clenched and she began to grind her teeth. She'd called Oliver for reassurance or sage advice. But instead, he had fed her insecurities, her guilt and darkest fears.

'Well, you've been very helpful,' she said sarcastically. 'God, I do everything for you and Phoenix and never ask for anything in return. And for once when I need you, this is the thanks I get.'

'Georgia, wait…' Oliver tried to interrupt. But she continued, standing from the floor. She started to rearrange her cosmetics on the vanity, which were already in neat rows.

'No! I can't depend on any of you – my so-called family. And now, when I should be preparing to say goodbye to my mother, instead I've got to protect that child from finding out who her father is!' Her voice was now as high as it had ever been. 'All I've ever done was try to shield everyone I love from pain and now I've got *him* to deal with. He's the reason we're all in this mess in the first place, and now it could ruin our family forever. Why did Ella have to have *his* baby?'

She abruptly hung up, and placed her hands on the stone countertop, wondering how such a carefully crafted world had suddenly descended into complete chaos, teetering on a knife edge threatening to plunge from perfection to ruin. She slowly raised her head, daring to look at herself in the glass … and nearly jumped out of her skin. She whipped around to face the figure behind her reflected in the mirror.

Phoenix had a look of absolute horror etched into her beautiful features.

Chapter 24

Georgia

Georgia's heart was pounding so loudly, she feared she would faint again. Her brain raced frantically, trying to retrace her words to recall what Phoenix could have overheard. It was like trying to wade through tar.

Phoenix remained in the doorway of the bathroom with folded arms, waiting for Georgia to speak.

'Oh, Phoenix, I was just chatting to your dad about someone from his work…'

'Don't lie to me, Mum. I'm not an idiot. Auntie Ella has a baby? If you don't tell me, then I'll have no choice but to put the pieces together or go and ask her myself.'

'No!' Georgia shouted, then swiftly dialled down her volume. 'I mean no, it'll upset her too much. Look, come and sit down.'

She guided Phoenix to the sofa in the lounge. Taking the opportunity to scroll through her options, she knew she mustn't allow herself to be steered towards any questions about fathers. She also knew she had no choice but to admit that Ella had had a baby. Georgia steeled herself to tell a part-truth and yet another part-lie. She'd been backed into a dead end and there was no way out of it with complete honesty.

Not if she wanted to keep the remains of her family intact.

'We don't talk about it because it's too painful for Ella. Yes, there was a baby, but she had it adopted when it was born.' She took great care to ensure not to reveal the gender. 'Your auntie was very young and at university, only a bit older than you and in a terrible state at the time. There was nothing else she could have done. I know it's hard to understand but please don't quiz her about it. She'll just get upset and today is going to be difficult enough for us all.'

Phoenix frowned as she digested what she'd heard.

'But I don't get why you were talking about it now. Have you been fighting with her again?'

Georgia's patience began to fray.

'I am asking you not to say anything, Phoenix. Please, stop asking questions.'

'Why do I get the feeling you're lying to me?'

'I have no idea, darling. I've told you the truth. My sister had a baby and it was adopted. That's all there is to say, and you will break your auntie's heart if you mention it.'

'Was it with him, that guy who left her at the station?'

'Right, you've used up your last question on the subject and it's not my place to talk about it.' Georgia deliberately softened her tone, desperately wishing Phoenix would be placated. 'You overheard a private conversation, and some things are for grown-up ears only.'

Phoenix visibly bristled, but Georgia continued.

'Look, I know you're not a child, but there are reasons adults do things that are hard to understand.'

Phoenix nodded, her expression pained. She looked at her fingers and seemed to be counting.

'I think it's sad. If it was with that guy, then the baby must be about my age,' she said, but Georgia couldn't reply, her body frozen with tension. 'I've got a cousin who has no idea I exist.'

Georgia wrapped her arms around Phoenix, not only to distract her but in the hope some relief might arrive, and the subject would be over.

'Phoenix, it's what Ella wanted, and we have to support her choice. Now, let's get to that spa to be made beautiful so we can say goodbye to your granny later.'

Georgia's heartbeat was thumping at an almost unsustainable rate. A series of dreadful events could have slowly unravelled if she'd opted to tell the truth. It would have been like pulling at a stray thread on a delicate silk jumper; it would eventually be ruined, there was no way to repair it. How on earth would they get through the ceremony that evening without an awkward question or a slip-up? It was already going to be tense with the stand-off between her and Ella. She could only pray for divine intervention and that Phoenix would choose not to pry.

As they looked at each other, Georgia almost flinched at how much her daughter's eyes were a match to her memory of Harrison's. It was haunting. There seemed little way to avoid what appeared to confront Georgia at every turn on Hydra. It was like the island was taking revenge on her for what she'd done there. Georgia was caged in lies.

Or was she?

One secret had already arisen from the past in the letters, and Phoenix's adoption was also threatening to surface. Should Georgia just confess to Ella her other burden? She suspected the harm would be immeasurable if she told Ella the truth about the accident, which she thankfully didn't seem to remember. But Georgia simply couldn't carry it around with her any longer. Perhaps judgement was already approaching, and there was a way for her to get ahead of it.

'I'll get my bag,' Phoenix said, moving to the door. But she stopped short and turned around. 'You would tell me if there's something important I don't know, wouldn't you? It's just … when I heard you on the phone, it sounded like you were talking about me.'

Chapter 25

Ella

It was a sticky, humid afternoon and cooling off in the tide was a relief. Ella also had no wish to return to the hotel and risk bumping into her sister. She needed to find somewhere else to stay after Mum's ashes were scattered.

As she swam through the water, Ella yielded to the salty current, permitting it to take her where it wished. She wanted to stay suspended in the warm sea, cleansed of Harrison's touch, but though his fingerprints could be washed from her body, his soul had wrapped around her heart years ago and hadn't let go.

Ella deliberately sank downwards, imploring the tide to remove her memories, to make her forget everything so she could begin again. She remained under water for as long as she could stand and then screamed. Bubbles streamed from her mouth, tickling her skin as they spewed forth while she forced out any remaining breath from her body.

She hung in the aquamarine world until her lungs began to beg for air. As she broke through the surface, she felt an anxiety surging through her, like she'd never been so frightened. She couldn't catch a breath, nor calm her body enough to swim. She started to splash about and her head submerged once more. She gazed upwards and willed her heart to slow. The strange vision she'd had the past couple of days returned as a rippling face appeared above her. She kicked towards the sunlight and the face dissolved. Coughing and spluttering, she managed to swim to the dive platform and hauled her body from the water.

Propped against a rock, panting, the hot afternoon sunshine dried her skin while she tried to make sense of what had happened. The recurring daytime mirage was baffling, and it had only started when she'd set foot on Hydra again. Was it a memory from a past life, or the island playing tricks on her?

She looked at her pile of clothes. She'd make do with what she had for the ceremony, as if it mattered anyway. Her mother was already gone and throwing some dust in the sea wasn't relevant in her own version of grief. She already felt her mother's presence if she needed to call upon her, in the air, on the wind, all around.

The sparkling sea seemed to stretch for an eternity, invisibly joining the sky. In a few hours, Mum's remains would drift and merge with the current, living forever within the clear blue water. Ella tried to focus on the spirit of the impending ritual, rather than the multi-layered horror of being cornered in a boat with Georgia.

Ella mulled over her sister's motivation for preventing her from reading Harrison's letters. It was obvious, but deeply cruel of her. Since arriving on Hydra, events were urging her to find forgiveness for those who had wronged her, but she was yet to locate the necessary compassion.

She lifted her camera and photographed the cliffside to calm her mind, the beautiful ripples in the rock formations moulded and shaped by the elements, the frothy patterns in the sea. She captured swimmers, their bodies distorted in the swell as refracted light coated their skin with an otherworldly glow. Through her lens she saw a boat rounding the headland, and she zoomed in. It was Georgia and Phoenix. She watched them close-up through the camera like a voyeur. Her sister's jaw was set firm beneath her sunhat. Phoenix was holding her hair back as the wind whipped her curls. She tipped her face to the sun and Ella took her picture. She looked like a goddess, or a nautical figurehead. After a few days of sun, her skin shone.

Ella started to dress, bracing to face her sibling and the looming service. She put the turquoise stone necklace around her neck, identical to the one she'd bought for Georgia, but it felt like an empty gesture now she knew how she'd been betrayed. Ella's T-shirt clung to her slightly damp skin, and it was a struggle to pull on her scruffy shorts. Her fingers brushed a piece of paper in her pocket and she saw it was the note from the old woman, Zina. The ink smudged a little as droplets from her long, wet hair plopped onto the paper. She still hadn't found out what it said since distractions had loomed at every turn. She looked around to see if there was anyone nearby who could help translate. She spotted a rotund man sunbathing who was also on his phone and craned her neck to eavesdrop. She confirmed his nationality as Greek from the odd word she could catch and waited patiently until he ended his call. The way he was enthusiastically chattering, it could be ages. But more time spent on the rock waiting for him was time away from Georgia.

Eventually there was a window for an approach.

'*Parakaló* ... please,' she began. '*Yiá sas*, hello, do you speak English?'

He turned his head and smiled. His body was slathered in so much tanning oil, he shimmered like a bronzed seal.

'Yes, of course.'

She handed him the tatty, damp note saying, 'I wondered if you could translate this for me.'

He removed his sunglasses and sat up, his stomach bulging and creasing into two large folds as he held the scrap of paper in front of him.

'Yes … so, it says… *"You have returned. I knew the island would call you back to where you belong."*'

'What?' Ella said, forgetting any manners. He repeated his translation. She was puzzled as to why the old woman would write such a thing.

'Thank you,' she eventually said, retrieving the note. She stared at it, as if the Greek characters would indicate how to make sense of the cryptic missive. Letters appeared to be following her around on the island too.

'Are you from Hydra?' he asked, leaning back on his elbows.

'No, from England. I mean, I was born here, but … thanks anyway. *Yiá sas.*'

She turned from him after saying goodbye and put the note in the front pocket of her shoulder bag. Sitting once more on a rock, she considered Zina's message. Why did she think Ella belonged on the island when the reality was she didn't want to come at all and had wanted to leave from the moment she'd arrived? But then, her feelings about Hydra were shifting … to what, though, she was unsure.

She looked at the sun as it began its slow descent towards the horizon, its beams beating hotter than ever as the day's temperature reached its late afternoon crescendo. It was nearing sunset. Almost time to face Georgia and to say goodbye to their mother.

* * *

On the harbour front, she waited awkwardly for the hotel boat to dock. When it did, Phoenix spotted her and ran over, flinging her arms around Ella.

'I feel like I haven't seen you for days. Where have you been? Are you OK?' she asked, almost frenzied in her questioning. Her grip was strong as she clung on, and Ella gently prised her away, taken aback by the sudden force of affection.

'I'm fine, just going through something,' she answered truthfully. Phoenix was too smart to be hoodwinked.

She nodded in sympathy.

'I'm here for you. I mean, if you ever want to chat.'

Unfortunately, she was the last person Ella could talk to. But she smiled and saw the sun reflected in Phoenix's warm brown eyes, tinging them almost pink with its diminishing rays.

Phoenix sighed audibly.

'I wish you and Mum wouldn't fight so much. I feel completely stuck in the middle. She's really upset, Auntie Ella. I know she loves you.'

Ella bit her tongue, measuring her response.

'Well, sometimes love isn't enough. I hope you never have to learn that the hard way, Phoenie. Come on, let's go and plonk your Granny in the sea.'

Phoenix giggled, which was like a song for Ella's soul. She was glad she'd inherited Ella's inappropriate sense of humour. Not desperate to behave correctly in public like Georgia. Except apparently, Georgia was capable of complete incorrectness, and Ella could hardly stand to look at her because of it. But she forced her eyes over to find her looking more tense than usual.

'Ready to say goodbye?' Ella said, fixing Georgia with

a look that she could choose to interpret several ways. She looked flustered and stressed, clearly afraid of what Ella would do and while she would never deliver on the threats she'd levied at her sister, Georgia didn't need to know that for now.

'Y-y-yes. The gentleman doing the ceremony is over there,' she spluttered. 'Shall I introduce you?'

Ella couldn't help but snort a laugh at her need to keep up appearances.

'Let's just get this done,' she said, stepping onto the boat and unsteadily clinging to the gunnels to stymie her fear. Ella preferred to be in the root of her phobia rather than near her sibling. All she needed to do was endure the next hour or so, return to the hotel, pack her things and find alternative accommodation in town.

The sunset was spectacular, and Ella was grateful for the loud hum of the boat engine, which prevented any small talk. Ella noticed Georgia was also wearing the necklace she'd bought, and she couldn't help shaking her head as her sister nervously fiddled with it before reaching into her oversized beach bag. She retrieved the wooden box containing their mother's ashes and a tear snaked down her cheek. Ella felt the communal pang of sympathy as the varying versions of motherhood on the boat united.

The sisters both knew the lengths a mother would go to, to protect their offspring. Ella had given up Phoenix to shield her from her pain because she couldn't provide for her emotionally or financially at the time, nor walk away from her studies. Ella's mum had supported and facilitated her decision with love and compassion. And Georgia had wanted a child more than anything and offered Phoenix a family. But their solution had ultimately severed their relationship.

Ella felt her chest become tight as her conflicted feelings

tumbled around. She felt the boat crest small waves and her panic began to claw at her. All she knew was that she couldn't continue with things as they were; it was too overwhelming. Hot tears began to flood from her eyes, and she covered her face with her hands, trying to hide her outpouring from the others. She needed her mother to guide her. The only time she'd required her counsel since having Phoenix adopted, and she wasn't there anymore. The sudden flood of grief took her by surprise as she saw Anna's face in her mind's eye. The look of unconditional love she'd given her, almost an understanding, as Ella had handed her baby over to Georgia, releasing her little one as her own from her arms forever. Her mother had held Ella as she'd sobbed like a small child for hours as Georgia and Oliver had left with her daughter, ready to give her the life she deserved.

She heard the engine cut as they reached their destination, far enough away from the port to legally permit their purpose. An arm coiled around Ella's shoulder, and she caught the scent of Georgia's expensive perfume.

'I'm sorry,' she whispered in her ear. 'I'm so, so sorry, Ella.'

Chapter 26

Georgia

Georgia couldn't stand for any conflict to blight the ceremony she'd waited a year for. And given how guilty she felt, the sight of Ella's face covered in tears was unbearable. Thankfully, Georgia's offering of an olive branch, in the form of a hug, seemed to have been received.

As proceedings commenced, Georgia's eyes traced the horizon, asking the surroundings to take good care of her mother. The moment had been so long in coming, she suddenly realised she wasn't prepared to say goodbye at all. Conclusion would edge closer with each handful of dust she consigned to the water. In a way it was liberating, and she wished she could let the secrets join her mother on the seabed.

But she couldn't live with her blemished conscience any longer. Looking to her sister again, she felt utterly mortified about her actions all those years ago. She'd only been a child, but still, she should have known better. It had been a stupid, split-second decision that she couldn't retract. At ten years old, she'd been old enough to know right from wrong, but it didn't stop her then and apparently, hadn't stopped her since.

Georgia took a deep breath to begin her reading – a poem by Keats. As the words bounced around on the page, rocked by the boat in the gentle swell, she wished she'd chosen something shorter, less stiff. Phoenix's hand on her arm gave the necessary succour to complete the final stanza. Then, Georgia turned to Ella.

'Your go,' she said, smiling her encouragement, but Ella faced away and spoke to the air, gripping the side of the boat.

'I read a quote by an explorer once, who said that an island was like a prison that makes you wish you could fly. Something like that, anyway. Mum, now you are free of this island; we all are. Soar with the birds, swim with the mermaids, glide with the fishes and send us your love in any way you can find.'

A small smile crept across Georgia's face, part relief that Ella had said something poetic, part humour as it was a very Ella thing to say. Analysing her words, she wondered whether Ella meant she wanted to leave Harrison along with Hydra for good.

'Phoenix, sweetheart,' Georgia said tenderly. 'Is there anything you'd like to say for Granny?'

She unfurled the piece of paper she was holding and started to sing.

'There's no life without end, love's measured by hate,

'The island tide will ebb and flow, the moon governing our fate.

'We say goodbye to love, cast to sea and air,

'You may be gone in body, but your spirit lives on there.

'So, swirl around sweet Hydra, dwell in this wondrous place,

'Be one with nature, man and gods, existing in your space,

'Protecting all your loved ones, shielding them from foes,

'You're more than just the island, you're where all water flows.'

Both sisters were transfixed by Phoenix's sweet, soaring voice. She became self-conscious after the last note, unsure of herself, but during the song she was lost in her own music.

'Phoenix, that was beautiful,' said Georgia, breathless with awe.

She shrugged modestly.

'Just something I wrote. It's not finished, but I wanted to sing it for Granny.'

'She would have loved it, Phoenie. Thank you,' Ella said, her bottom lip trembling.

They then each took a handful of ashes and scattered them carefully over the side of the boat. The wind had dropped away, and the sea was like a mirror. Georgia muttered a note of thanks to the elements. The three of them managed to smile at each other, briefly united in their grief and consumed with the finality of the moment. As the remainder of the ashes were set into the water, the waves gently swallowed them away.

Georgia watched, as Ella removed her matching necklace and balled the chain in her fist. The azure glass dangled from her hand as she held it outwards and she turned her head to lock eyes with Georgia as she let it drop. The gold chain glinted in the dying light as it descended in the crystal-clear water before it was lost in the darkness of the depths. There was no way Georgia could have misunderstood the gesture. Ella had bought her the gift as a token of peace, but then she had discovered Georgia's treachery in hiding Harrison's letters. Now the necklace, which had been a symbol of their sisterly truce, was meaningless. Georgia clutched hers where it hung around her neck, desperately trying to cling on to a piece of their relationship, even if it was only cheap costume jewellery.

Phoenix grabbed each of their hands and said, 'Please, both of you, Granny is at rest. Can you at least try to be friends?'

Georgia looked at Ella who wouldn't meet her eye. Despite sharing a tender moment and being united by Phoenix's song, the reality of what Georgia had done lingered. Forgiveness wasn't Ella's strong suit, and Georgia knew she didn't deserve it anyway. The silence lurked between them like an early morning sea mist until Phoenix broke the tension.

'Tell me what's happened between you. I can't endure another moment and I won't take sides either.'

Neither sister answered. Instead, Georgia nodded at the boatman who started the engine and turned them back towards the port. As the town grew, filling her blurred vision, a figure on the dock forced her to sit bolt upright from her slump. His size was unmistakable and, as they neared, his identity was confirmed. Georgia turned to catch Ella's attention, trying to convey her panic. Ella felt the shift in energy, looking to her sister and then to the harbour, her green eyes widening in fear. They both turned to Phoenix.

'What?' Phoenix asked, baffled by the pair of them. 'What's going on now?'

There was no response to her question – the truth was impossible to share – and Georgia refused to weave another lie. There also wasn't enough time to concoct a scheme to keep Phoenix away from Harrison. They were headed for a collision with the source of all their problems.

Chapter 27

Ella

As they moored alongside the harbour, Harrison moved towards the sea wall. Ella knew she had to try and prevent his meeting Phoenix, but it appeared unavoidable. It was now about damage control. She sprang out of the boat and sprinted up the steps.

It was still a novelty to see him despite how they'd parted this morning, with so much still left unsaid. She wanted to resist the compulsion to be in his orbit and have space from him to think clearly, but circumstances had once again conspired to thrust them together. She needed to divert his attention, quickly. Turning back towards the boat, she said to Georgia, 'I'll see you both back at the hotel. I won't be long.' She hoped Georgia understood she meant she should take Phoenix away immediately.

Harrison cut an imposing figure. His height seemed to even dwarf the water taxis from her vantage point, though it could have been a trick of the light as dusk was spreading rapidly across the island. As she reached him, he smiled in sympathy.

'Hey,' she said, suddenly unsure of herself.

'Hey, you. I wanted to see if it all went well. Or … as well as it can go. I didn't want you to be alone.'

His kindness overwhelmed her, and for a moment, the busy harbour preparing for night dissolved to a blur. She reached forward to find his hand as she absorbed his penetrating gaze. Then, his eyes left hers for a moment as he looked over her shoulder. His smile fell away.

'Shall I say hi to Georgia and explain to her how the post works?' he joked, but his face was stony. He was as angry as Ella that his letters had been withheld from her.

Ella turned and saw Georgia trying to herd Phoenix towards the hotel water shuttle. Unfortunately, her endeavours were unsuccessful.

'Who's that, El?' Harrison asked as the wind suddenly gusted around them. Ella dared not answer. She was rooted to the spot.

'No, wait!' Ella heard Georgia cry as Phoenix arrived beside Harrison and fixed Ella with an amused look. She held out her hand to him.

'I'm Phoenix Edmondson … Ella's niece. And you are?'

It was like watching a boxing bout in slow motion, except Ella felt the exchange of blows in the pit of her stomach, wincing in pain as they clasped hands in greeting, battered by Phoenix referring to herself as her niece. She noticed Georgia in her peripheral vision stop still nearby. She looked physically defeated as Harrison responded.

'Nice to meet you, Phoenix. Harrison Sutherland, an old friend of El's. A very old friend. We were at uni together.' He grinned at Ella; his white teeth beamed in the rising moonlight. Ella wasn't sure what expression she had on her face. Her mouth had dried, and she couldn't find enough moisture to swallow.

'You're him, aren't you? The guy from the station?' Phoenix said as she glanced to Ella for confirmation. When she didn't reply, Phoenix rounded on Harrison. 'I should give you a piece of my mind for what you did. You broke Ella's heart and left her alone with a … wait … sorry … Harrison Sutherland … the musician? As in, "Out of the Darkness" Harrison Sutherland…?'

Ella had no idea what Phoenix had been about to say, but her new line of questioning had dangerous potential.

He laughed modestly.

'Yeah, that's one of mine. And before you give me too much of a hard time – which I deserve – I actually wrote it for El.' Ella met his eye and she read the pain within him as he continued, speaking solely to her. 'But I'd rather be without that song than to have hurt you the way I did.' He reached for her hand and her fist nestled within his grasp, like she could hide within his palm.

'What?!' shrieked Phoenix. 'You never told me that song was about you, Auntie Ella!' She was incredulous. 'No wonder you were a bit weird after I sang it the other night.'

Harrison's head turned to Phoenix.

'You sing?'

Phoenix beamed, delighted to have found someone to talk to about music, a kindred spirit … though she had no idea just how kindred.

'I play the piano too, and write a bit – mainly jazz but, I mean, nothing like you, obviously,' she said.

'Jazz, eh? My favourite too. Creative talent runs in the family.' Harrison smiled. Ella knew he was referring to her photography, but he had no clue how right he was. It felt like she was on a torturer's rack being stretched, living an absolute torment seeing them together. Georgia had kept her distance throughout the exchange. Her skin was ashen and Ella had never seen her look more devastated. She suddenly felt immense pity for her sister in that second and their argument was momentarily forgotten. What was occurring had far more critical consequences. Ella dropped Harrison's hand and went to her sister.

'I'm so sorry, Georgia, I couldn't—'

She interrupted, hissing in a low voice, 'Get back there. You need to hear what's being said.'

'Why don't you?' Ella asked.

'Because I can't, Ella. I'm terrified I'll lose her to him. To you both. I don't know what to do. I need you to help me.'

Georgia had never asked for Ella's help before. She seemed to be teetering on the brink of something, a tumult of emotions crossing her face, and Ella worried she was about to faint again. Ella heard snapshots of Harrison and Phoenix conversing; jazz icons, musical terms. Their sweet faces pointed towards each other, the two people Ella held dearest in her heart; her precious loves. It was Ella's turn to protect Georgia but, above all, Phoenix.

'Mum, Harrison wants to hear me play,' Phoenix said. 'Are you coming? There's a piano bar around the harbour.' She paused for a moment and surveyed them both. The tension was once again palpable, but on this occasion, the sisters were united in their concern. 'You're both being odd. What's happened in the last few minutes to make you weird again?'

Georgia and Ella looked at each other. Ella knew she had to rescue this, rescue them all.

'Maybe you should do it another day, Phoenie. I'm sure we're all a bit tired after the ceremony,' she said.

'But … I want to play now. I might not get the chance again,' she insisted. Ella understood, but it was too dangerous and painful for her to witness more of Harrison and Phoenix's interaction. It was the life she could have had if he hadn't left,

205

if Georgia hadn't hidden his letters. They might have all been together on the island, just as she and Harrison had once dreamed of.

'I know, but I'm sure Harrison is very busy doing his own composing. You don't want to bother him.' Georgia's voice was tight and strained.

'It's no bother at all,' said Harrison, joining them. 'It's good to see you again, Georgia.'

'I'd like to be able to say the same,' she snapped. Ella caught Phoenix balking in embarrassment at her mother's words. She had never seen Georgia be rude to anyone apart from family.

Harrison laughed loudly.

'I see you haven't changed,' he said. Then he leant towards Phoenix, adding conspiratorially, 'She was never my biggest fan.'

'Well, despite the beautiful song you wrote for Auntie Ella, I have to agree. You did a terrible thing, abandoning her like that; quite unforgivable.'

Harrison winced.

'Wow, tough crowd. Well, the offer's there, Phoenix. They both know where I live.'

He smiled at Phoenix warmly then put his hand on Ella's shoulder. It was as if he was reaching inside her with his touch. She looked up to him, as Hydra surrendered to night.

'And *you* know where I am, if you need me,' he said quietly, and she felt his voice resonate like a ripple beneath her skin.

* * *

The boat ride to the hotel was quiet, with Phoenix in a huff, her eyes focused on her phone, Georgia reaching the highest point of terse silence, and Ella replaying the sight of her daughter with her father, together for the first time. The momentousness was almost too much to bear. Besides her own pain, she also felt sorry for Georgia. She was understandably terrified she was going to lose Phoenix, but Ella had promised the truth would never be discovered and she wouldn't renege on that.

In her room, Ella packed her belongings, shoving them into the rucksack. She couldn't stay in the hotel on Georgia's dime, not now. Although her initial rage had diminished, she needed to put some distance between them. Her laptop was open on the desk, and she couldn't help but scroll through old folders dating back years with scanned pictures from her college course before anything was digital. She found what she was looking for and double clicked the icon.

Harrison was shrouded in a plume of smoke, exhaling towards the sky, backlit by spring light. She'd taken his portrait the week they met and the cherry blossoms behind him almost undulated in the spring sunbeams. His beautiful profile was already etched upon her memory but now it was in black and white before her on the screen. She traced the outline of his long hair with her chipped fingernails, caressed the beard that masked his jawline. She began to cry, her grief for their wasted love was embedded in the marrow of her bones. As she drank in his features and bear-like frame, her tears were born of love and loss; for what they'd had, what he'd cast aside and for what had lived on, hovering in the island air. His long fingers, which were holding a joint, could fly across a piano with effortless dexterity; fingers that had gently caressed her skin last night, coaxing Ella to his own rhythm and song. They were two halves of a whole back then, and still were now. The warm brown eyes in the picture hid his pain and she felt sorry for her eighteen-year-old self; so desperate to fix him and save him. They had been right for each other, only they met at the wrong time. Their love was too big, its magnitude overpowering when it had saturated two such naïve hearts. As the years passed, they'd existed in a halfway house like a poem without a conclusion, a song without a rhyme. Harrison was her missing couplet. There hadn't been a place to put their love and pain, no safe space to bury it or cast it away. And now that old love had returned, filling up her heart once again.

Closing her computer she slipped it into her camera bag, then walked laden with her baggage towards Georgia's room. She longed to scatter the old versions of all their stories upon the island waters, just as they had their mother's ashes. Ella wasn't prepared to live another moment in between their chapters. She knew where she was headed and had always been destined to travel.

The Island

The ashes were welcomed into the water. Dust became the waves that caressed swirling sprites and sea serpents that dwelt in the deepest depths. Kindness co-existed with brutality above and below the surface. It was almost time for the island to reveal its final secrets.

Chapter 28

Georgia

Georgia needed to speak to someone but was too afraid to phone Oliver because what on earth could she say? That their worst fears were unfolding, and she was utterly powerless to stop them. She had nobody else to turn to. Being Phoenix's mother was everything and without her, what was left? They might not survive this storm and it could hammer the final nail into the coffin of their marriage. She felt destined to lose everything and almost resigned herself to the inescapable.

She filled a large tumbler with red wine and took a gulp. It burnt the back of her throat, but she continued taking sips, one followed by another, willing it to create a welcome numbness. Tears formed in her eyes as the tangy drink went straight to her head, and she slurred a cheers to the heavens in her mother's memory. The ceremony had been beautiful but more painful than she'd imagined, for so many reasons. The goodbye, Phoenix's haunting song, Ella discarding their relationship by sending the necklace to join their mother's ashes, and finally seeing Phoenix, Ella and Harrison together. It was too much. Georgia sobbed, her body racked with grief. She tore the necklace from her throat and discarded it, broken in pieces, on the sideboard.

Her tears were interrupted as her phone rang. It was her husband. She declined the call, returning to her misery.

Beautiful, sweet Phoenix, her little light in the gloom who had given Georgia hope and purpose when she'd been lost. But she had failed her daughter; she'd failed everyone. Her secrets had caught up with the present and she was afraid to set foot out of her room for fear of what would happen next. As she wallowed in her melancholy, a sudden realisation shot through her like a thunderbolt. Phoenix... Her name symbolised a beacon risen from the ashes of darkness. *That* song thundered through her mind like a freight train.

Out of the Darkness.

It was always about him. Harrison.

She longed to speak to Ella who held an understandable contempt for her. Georgia sighed. She agreed with her sibling, she hated herself too. She poured another generous measure, downed it, then refilled the glass again as pitch blackness wrapped its tentacles around Hydra, the moon casting a puddle of silver on the surface of the sea.

Her solo pity party was halted by the doorbell. Georgia tiptoed unsteadily to the peephole as the room swirled around her. It was Ella. She'd arrived just when Georgia needed her. She didn't look cross as she squinted through the peephole in the door, more agitated.

'Georgia, stop staring at me through the thing. I can see your shadow.'

She opened the door poised for a verbal battering, but Ella's face was ruddy from crying. She moved into the room. Her rucksack was slung over one shoulder, and she was holding her camera case. She deposited both on the sofa and turned around.

'Georgia, I...' Her voice cracked, and tears streamed down

her cheeks.

'You're leaving, aren't you? To go to *him*,' Georgia slurred, since Ella couldn't complete her sentence.

'I'm not here to talk about Harrison. I want to talk about us. I am trying, but I can't forgive you and I don't understand why you had to meddle. How do you expect us to come back from this? You took away my chance to have love, but more than that, those choices you made without permission or without my knowledge stopped me from being a mother. If I'd known he still loved me, things might have been different. I can't be here after what you've done, I'm going to stay in town.'

She sat down heavily on the sofa, sending the scatter cushions flying into unruly piles. One fell to the floor and Georgia was desperate to pick it up, plump it and put it back in its place. She resisted her compulsion. She wasn't sure what to say, but tried to appease her sister.

'Ella, I'm sorry. I know you don't think it, but I meant well. I was trying to protect you, though it hasn't worked. Obviously,' she added carefully. 'Please believe me, I did what I thought was best. You were so messed up after him and I didn't want you to go through any more pain. And you were pregnant. I was terrified for you and the baby. Your depression had taken hold and I didn't know what you were going to do next. There wasn't the right time to tell you and I wanted to save you from any more heartache. I'm honestly so sorry for hurting you.'

Ella laughed at her words.

'That's what *he* keeps saying and yet all of you keep on hurting me and you'll probably keep on doing it until I've learnt my lesson. But do you know what the worst part of today was?'

Georgia shook her head.

'It was seeing Harrison and Phoenix together; like a glimpse of what my life could have been. But you put a stop to that and now it's something I can never have. You slammed the brakes on my destiny, all because of what you did.'

Georgia found the courage to move closer, stumbling as she tripped over her own feet. Ella shot her a look of disgust. Georgia fell onto the sofa next to her, flopping a hand onto Ella's knee.

'I was selfish and so wrapped up in the lie, Ella. Yes, I wanted to shield you from any more pain but how could I have known how depressed you were going to get? His letters would have made it worse, or that's what I thought at the time. Then later, after the adoption, I didn't want Phoenix to be taken away. You gave me *my* only chance at being a mother. I'll probably lose her anyhow. I know you're going to take her.'

Ella turned to face her and grabbed Georgia's hands.

'No! You're being irrational, and for God's sake, stop drinking! We swore to protect her together. I don't like the untruth, but we need to stick to it. We have to. The alternative is too horrible. Imagine finding out your whole life was a lie. There's no way out now. I can't be here with you for another moment. I'm suffocating. We've done a terrible thing, the worst.'

Georgia felt her head swim and managed to stand to reach for the wine glass to drain it. This was the moment – if she dared. She could finally be cleansed, unburdened, free of the last piece of deceit. There was nothing more to be gained living in a falsehood, yet everything was at stake. But existing in perjury for a moment longer was unsustainable, and she was already wrecking everything around her, so she might as well finish the job. Georgia opened her mouth to confess.

'Actually, I have done worse. Ella, I need to tell you something. About me ... and I suppose Mum.'

Ella's green eyes bored into Georgia's blue depths from across the room.

'What about Mum?' she said suspiciously.

Nausea churned in Georgia's belly and the tang of red wine travelled up her throat, not quite reaching her mouth. She composed herself as much as she was able and prepared for honesty and Ella's wrath.

'When I was ten, we came to the island for the summer as usual.'

'Should I be worried about what you're about to say?' Ella asked.

'Please, just hear me out, no questions. You're just like Phoenix, bloody question after question. Just listen.'

Ella raised an eyebrow at her sharpness.

Georgia grabbed hold of the drinks cabinet for balance, her knuckles whitening.

'Just spit it out, Georgia.'

She poured another glass with a trembling hand and took a fortifying sip. She began to cry; the secret should be drifting upon the tide with her mother's remains. But it was too late, she had to finish what she'd started. It was the only way to truly be free.

'When we were little, I loved you so much. You were like my little dolly to play with. But a real-life toy, living, breathing, screaming. God, I remember how you screamed, you used to have these awful dreams – night terrors – all the time. I'd wake up to hear you screeching and Mum would hold you and sing to you until you went back to sleep, saying she'd never let anything harm you and that you were her "shining light". She never said any of those things to me.

'As the years went on, I started to envy you. I preferred it when it used to be just me and Mum, before you arrived here on Hydra, and spoiled everything.' She finished her wine and set it down with a bump on the side. 'Mum seemed to prefer you, always fussing around you, and I felt so left out. I was horribly jealous. *I* wanted to be her little girl, but no, you were her special one. I hated you for it. I was just plain old Georgia, nothing like you, all wild and interesting,' she spat, but forged onwards. 'So, one day, when she was out, she left me in charge and I … I took you out in her boat. The one in her garden with the herbs used to be moored in the harbour. It was just the two of us and we didn't go out far around the point. You were so excited at first, but then you started crying, asking to go home, and you wouldn't stop. I got so cross. I told Mum I'd been looking at the engine when I heard the splash, and you fell overboard. But that wasn't at all what happened. I suspect she knew deep down what I'd done, though we never spoke of it. I don't think she ever forgave me.'

Ella took a step backwards. Her eyes were wide in horror as her hand travelled to her chest, as if her heart might fall out of her body and she needed to keep it in place. Georgia poured another drink and took a further sip of courage.

'I'm so ashamed, Ella, and it's haunted me ever since. It's lucky I don't get to spend time with you often, because when I do, all I can see is you in the water, splashing around until you started to disappear. The image of you sinking, your hair all splayed out, helplessly hanging in the water below… It was like looking at you through glass. Your eyes went so wide, pleading with me to save you. It was then I realised what I'd done, but it was too late. I shouted for help, like I've never screamed before.' Georgia was struggling for breath, re-living

215

the awful scene in her mind. Her gaze had moved to the floor, unable to look her sister in the eye.

'I tried to reach you with my hand, but you were too far away and the life ring was tied up so tightly, I couldn't undo the knots. There was nothing I could do but watch and hope someone came to help. I was shaking and crying so much.' She slowly raised her gaze to Ella's, her breath shuddering in ragged snatches. 'When you asked me to adopt Phoenix, it was as though I could make amends for what I did.' She stepped towards her sister, but Ella backed away further. 'I'm so sorry, Ella, I was a stupid, spoilt, insecure child. I didn't mean it. I love you! I don't know what I would have done if you'd … you'd…

'It all happened so quickly. I sort of tripped a bit and bashed into you. You started to cry again, so I shoved you away hoping you'd fall into the sea and stop your noise. To shock you, I suppose, in the most unkind way. I wanted you to be quiet. That was when you fell into the water. Mum never used that boat again after the accident. That's what everyone called it on the island, an accident. Except it wasn't. It was deliberate. I pushed you in. I just wanted to make you go away…'

Chapter 29
Ella

Ella grabbed her things and bolted from the room, feeling smothered by her sister's presence.

She'd always known Georgia had emotional difficulties, with obsessive hot-headed compulsions, and a propensity for hysteria, but for a child to have wanted to kill her sibling ... that was a new height of disturbed. How could she expect any semblance of normal after this? Something had happened to them all on Hydra and Ella felt like she didn't know her sister anymore. If she ever truly did.

She summoned the water shuttle to take her to town and waited for it to arrive. Standing on the hotel pontoon, Ella gazed at the clear dark sky; millions of sparkling stars nestled within an inky blanket. Most of them weren't there anymore, they were just a trick of time. Everything about the island was a ruse filled with false promise.

Vasilis was on duty and it was good to see a friendly face. Yet again, she was forced to board a boat, though now the source of her fear had finally been revealed. Despite the fact she had no clear memory of the accident, the strange slices of recall that had started to appear since being back in Greece meant the incident was concealed within the recesses of her mind.

'*Kalispéra*,' she managed.

'Ella, *kalispéra*, but it's not a good evening for you it seems.'

She didn't know where to begin, but she knew she needed to find out more about what had happened to her. She stepped delicately on board, and as he set out to sea she turned to him.

'You said you knew me when I was little? So, you must know about the accident. I don't remember it.' She watched his reaction carefully. 'Tell me what you know, Vasílis. Please.'

He cut the engine and allowed the boat to drift just off the point where the windmill stood.

'You mean you have no idea?'

She shook her head. 'I get strange flashbacks – which until now I thought were just a weird echo of a dream – and I've been getting more of them these last few days.'

'I remember it, of course. You were pulled from the water barely alive by one of the fishermen who heard your sister's cries at sea. The church bells rang and everyone came to the dock. You were lying like a dead fish, limp on the side of the harbour. It was awful. The doctor arrived and tended to you. Then you suddenly came back to life. It was the most terrifying thing to see. Your mother was holding you and crying, and I remember all the villagers crossing themselves, weeping in fear for your life then suddenly celebrating because you had lived. But then, so clearly, I saw your sister standing like a statue. No expression on her face, just wringing her hands over and over. It struck me as strange that she was outside of the commotion and not by your side.'

Ella digested all she'd heard and tried to delve into the farthest parts of her memory, but nothing came. After a while, Ella nodded to Vasílis who started the engine once more, and motored towards the port. She let the engine noise fill her brain, her body absorbed the accustomed fear and she urged the waters to erase the words her sister had said.

I just wanted to make you go away.

Vasílis spoke only after they'd reached the safety of the harbour.

'My father helped your mother take the boat into her garden. She wanted it broken to be rid of the memory, but it is very bad luck to wreck a boat. One of the villagers, Zina, said so, and suggested that your mother keep it in the garden as a reminder of how precious life can be – to give it a new purpose. She helped your mother plant it with herbs.'

'I've met Zina. She wrote me a weird note saying I've returned home again or something like that.' Ella felt she was missing something she couldn't pinpoint. 'I wonder, when you're not working, whether you could come with me to visit her. I need a translator.'

He hesitated, almost reluctant to respond, but finally said, 'Of course. I have many shifts for the hotel, and in my father's store, but I will help you. Zina is somewhat strange – some say she is a witch, a white witch – but she is harmless. Though I would not delve too deeply if I were you.'

As he moored alongside the pontoon, Ella wondered if Vasílis was warning her about something. But her mind was consumed with retrieving her lost memory. She was unable to trust her sister's version of events and wanted to unearth her own truth. There was only one way to try and remember what had happened.

* * *

Harrison opened the door and automatically smiled. But it wasn't him she was there for. She strode into the house, dropping her rucksack and camera bag on the sofa as she passed, and breezed through the garden doors. The patio was floodlit, casting eerie shadows across the stonework.

Ella reached the battered boat at the bottom of the plot, depending upon it to yield her lost memory. No wonder Georgia invented a story about a monster to stop her from going near it, she was terrified Ella might remember. Another lie. She started to rake the earth in the boat's carcass, pulling out the herbs burrowed neatly within the dirt. She flung the discarded plants over her shoulder with no care for where they landed, and the air tinged with the heady combination of dill, thyme and oregano.

'El, what are you doing?' She could hear the incredulity in Harrison's voice, but she had no time to explain. Her tears mixed with the earth and she dug out a space in the bottom of the boat as though she was preparing the foundations to build something. But this was about dismantling the blockage in her brain. She pulled at the mud until her fingernails scraped on wood. Climbing in, she gripped the rotten gunnels with her eyes firmly closed.

'El, love. What's going on?' he asked again, but she didn't answer.

Willing herself backwards in time, she floated between then and now, ignoring the sound of his voice, pushing it away to prevent it grounding her in the present.

Suddenly her own cries echoed in her ears.

'Georgie, I want Mama … please, Georgie.' Her small voice pleaded with her sister, then the weeping dissolved, pulling her back into today.

Ella squeezed her eyes shut even harder, pressing her mind to travel to the past. Tears escaped as the scene began to play in her mind, arriving in small fragments of feelings, smells and shards of sound. The ozone wash of salty water, hot sun beating down on her arms. It seemed like they were miles out at sea, but she could still see the headland. She sank backwards into the memory ...

Georgia was at the stern with a creeping, cruel smile, then fury rapidly flushed her face.

'Shut up, stupid Els Bels. Shut up, shut up, shut up!' *Her anger built with a pinched expression. Ella felt the sobs rack her small body. She stared down at her yellow dress embroidered with blue forget-me-not flowers.*

Georgia stepped forward unsteadily. The boat rocked.

She lost her footing and fell onto the seat next to Ella at the bow. Her elbow jabbed at her ribs. Ella's cries resurfaced as she was pushed against the side; her tiny frame so light.

Hands pinched her shoulders, panic rose, shouting, a heartbeat thudded tremors of fear.

Ella cried harder.

Their faces were too close, and Ella shrunk backwards, quivering, suddenly terribly frightened.

'You've ruined everything for me. I hate you. I wish you were dead.'

Georgia's loud voice made her flinch.

Both scrabbled to stand.

Georgia suddenly lost her footing and crashed into Ella.

A sharpness shoved at her back, then she tumbled overboard, stranded in the air before crashing through a sun-tinted silver surface. The startling shock cold of water on her face, her clothes felt like lead, weighing her down.

Waves washed over her head as she thrashed around, unable to grip anything. It was like trying to capture clouds in her hands, there was nothing to hold on to. Ella hadn't learnt to swim yet.

Every word was devoured by seawater until her strength

began to dissolve. Her mouth was filled with salt. She didn't like the taste.

Then, a gentle peace descended as her body followed suit, submerging towards the dancing anemones on the sand below. The world as she knew it was tinged with a magical light. Sunbeams crossed her vision, transforming her new underwater land into a softer focus. As the darkness slowly took her downwards, Georgia's rippling face faded away above her until the island swallowed Ella whole.

* * *

Harrison folded a blanket around her shoulders as she cradled a mug of hot camomile tea. Her breath caught with each inhale as she attempted to still her shock. She was unsure where to begin or how to explain what she had relived. Ella discarded her tea on the coffee table and sank into his embrace, breathing him in as her face nestled into the crook of his neck.

'Harri, I need to get off this island. Please, take me away.'

Chapter 30

Ella

Wednesday

The next morning Ella was in a boat again, but this one was named after her. She was nervous to be on the water again so soon after re-living the 'accident', yet the fear was diminishing since unearthing the cause of her terror. But a phobic tightness remained in her chest.

Since being on Hydra, she had been relentlessly confronted with her past, the most painful elements of which had combined with her present. It sent her mind whirring into a spiral and she'd needed to escape.

Today was her thirty-eighth birthday.

Ella thought it odd Harrison hadn't remembered, since he never used to forget a date of significance, though in truth, she was grateful. She didn't want to be reminded of age, time or mortality more than she already had been.

Perched on the bow, she basked in the sun as Harrison steered Ella, the boat, over the waves towards Dokos, a tiny island across the water where he had a bolthole. She took photographs of the outcrop as they neared. Then, she turned and stole snapshots of him in the sharp morning light. He was watching the horizon and didn't notice.

Fatigue sat heavily in her bones. She had stayed up with Harrison until the sun rose, sharing all she'd learnt from her sister. Since the moment they'd arrived on Hydra, Georgia had done nothing but perpetrated unkindness upon Ella, punishment born from her own guilt, which manifested in jealous, unreasonable behaviour. Apparently, it had always been so, ever since they were children. But she was determined to break the pattern of her sister's control.

She'd eventually slept curled in Harrison's arms, scrunched up like a foetus, shrouded in his love. They still had so much to talk about, but the right time would present itself. For now, she trusted in the higher power she felt guiding her. Despite swapping one island for another, she felt freedom flood through her as Hydra became a fading mound in the distance. Though she wondered if she'd exchanged one dysfunctional scenario for another.

Harrison docked the boat beside a makeshift pontoon; a slab of plywood nailed to a pallet with a battered orange fender dangling into the lapping waves. He helped her step onto the shore, chivalrously offering his hand. A tiny white chapel stood like a square block on the hill. The shredded ends of a Greek flag attached to a flagpole fluttered in the breeze.

'Does anyone actually live here or are we casting away forever?' she asked, surveying the craggy landscape. It was peppered with sun-scorched bushes that must have been green once but were now faded, some blackened from the seasonal wildfires.

'Don't tempt me,' he replied, smiling. 'There's a handful of locals, but this is my sanctuary. When Hydra gets overrun with tourists, I escape to Dokos to think or find a bit of inspiration. I bought a house here after my first summer on

224

Hydra. When you and I came together that November, the main harbour was so quiet. I didn't realise how crazy it got during the season. Here, I found peace, I know you'll love it.' He unloaded the cool boxes, a duffel bag and some blankets from the boat. 'And when I say house, don't get excited. You'll see…' He laughed, handing her a bag. 'I used to come to Dokos and look back at Hydra, imagining what our life could have been like, the way we used to dream it. Romantic, but tragic. I know I'm a fool, El, always have been when it comes to us.' He ran his fingers through his hair. 'I'm sorry, love. Again.'

They'd hardly been on land for two minutes and had already started delving into the most painful of topics. Ella wasn't sure she could take much more deep diving into the past so soon after Georgia's revelation.

'Harri, please, can we not talk about back then or what could have been? My heart's too fragile, I'm exhausted. Later, please. Let's just be here, together, now.'

He smiled sadly.

'I know. But we have so much to catch up on.'

'We can still do that, just not the heavy stuff. I think it would finish me off,' she joked, though secretly she meant it.

They walked along laden with the bags he had packed, their footsteps on the shingle yielding pleasing crunches. Cresting a small hill, a lean-to came into view. Painted shutters in a faded olive green were fastened closed, almost camouflaged against the surrounding foliage. The local stone gleamed hues of brown and cream within the exterior walls. It was the most inviting place Ella had ever encountered. Much more her style than a luxury hotel. She placed the bags on the ground and raised her camera to capture the lonely hut, which had stood firm against the seasons; weathered, battered but still standing.

Harrison opened the door, and she stepped inside. The simple space was revealed as he cast open the window coverings and light flooded in. An uneven stone floor was deliciously cool underfoot and a welcome respite from outside. It was so beautifully basic, Ella had the overwhelming urge to ask him if she could stay there forever. A makeshift kitchen sat beneath one of the large picture windows with a glorious view of the sea beyond. This wasn't supposed to be a romantic cabin getaway; it was an escape from her sister and from reality. Yet she was on a remote island with the person she'd been hiding from for years. Or perhaps she'd been journeying towards him the whole time, in a perverse twist from the universe. Both islands, Hydra and Dokos, were urging her to face what she'd avoided for too long.

She unpacked the provisions on the countertop: soft drinks, beers, a bottle of wine and water, along with the ingredients for a salad, which she put in the fridge after switching it on. She lined up tins of fish, olives and a pot of olive oil on the side.

'I didn't know what you like to drink, so I brought everything except ouzo, although there might be some in a cupboard. I doubt it. I don't drink anymore,' Harrison said.

'If it's not too loaded a question, why did you stop drinking?' Ella asked, remembering how many pints he used to sink in their university days.

He laughed.

'I'm not sure any topic is off limits with us, El,' Harrison replied, taking a fishing rod from the wall where it hung beside an acoustic guitar above a keyboard on a stand. He picked up a plastic tackle box and stepped outside into the sunshine. Ella followed to hear his answer. 'I couldn't stand drunk people. That's the truth. Being in the music industry, exposed to every

226

vice you can think of, turned me off that stuff. I don't even smoke anymore. And now … well, now I need to keep a clear head.'

'For writing?' she asked. He didn't reply immediately and began to make a trace, taking a seat on a tree stump in the shade as he did so. She tied a handline since there was only one rod, expertly adding a weight and a silver lure concealing a hook. She had spent time photographing tribes beside the Amazon River and had learnt every kind of knot known to mankind as she'd fished with the indigenous children.

'Something like that,' he replied quietly. She felt a sad energy travel between them, and longed to grasp it in her fist and squash it. But if she'd learnt one thing from their past, it was that she couldn't save Harrison. Ella wouldn't repeat that mistake. Whatever he was unwilling to share, it wasn't for her to dig up, though she'd hoped over the years that if they ever reunited, he wouldn't keep anything from her again and let her in. He would open up when he was ready, but she needed complete honesty. It was an audacious thought given that she was withholding the biggest secret of all – their daughter.

She moved to sit beside him on another tree stump. He was struggling to tie a knot, his fingers unable to grasp the line, and when he did, he sent the loop the wrong way. His face scrunched in concentration as sweat formed on his brow. The air around them became thick and heavy. Ella hesitated, not wishing to patronise him, but she noticed his hands were shaking slightly.

'Do you need some help, Harri?'

His head snapped up and his eyes widened in surprise.

'El! I…' He looked towards the sea and breathed in and out several times, wiping his brow with his forearm. 'Yeah, sorry, can you give me a hand, love? I'm all fingers and thumbs here.'

She slowly took the fishing line and hooks from him.

'Are you feeling all right? We can go back to Hydra…'

'No, I'm fine. Just the heat getting to me.' He took off his shirt and balled it into his fist.

Ella deftly tied a knot and attached the hook to the trace as her eyes traced his torso.

'Then let's go and find the wind together and catch a fish!'

She took his hand and led him forward. Her palm fitted perfectly against his as they walked towards the water. Positioning themselves on a rock that jutted out into the sea, their lazily cast lines briefly broke the glistening surface. The peace was all-encompassing and for the first time since she'd returned to Greece, Ella felt settled. The breaths she took were pure and cleansing. She almost lamented the feeling of completeness from being next to him. It was disappointing her heart had returned to him so easily, but it was also like they'd never been apart. She wished that were true.

The silence united their energy as she enjoyed the closeness. Eventually, she spoke.

'It's funny, being with you again. It feels as though we've picked up where we stopped. Almost as if nothing's changed and nothing happened in between. Like putting on your favourite jumper or … Sorry.' She laughed and looked at him. His smile put a stopper in her babbling and his beautiful eyes caused her pulse to increase. Despite her wish to resist what she'd kept locked away, she was powerless to halt her feelings for him. It was an ancient love, older than their bodies and hearts.

'I wish I'd never been without you, but you wouldn't have wanted to be with who I was then. Maybe we needed to be apart to come back together again. I had to learn so much about myself. I wouldn't have been good enough for you if

I didn't work through my process.' He reeled in his line and cast it out again, the small metal piece attached to the end of his trace landed with a plop, causing ripples to disrupt the glassy surface.

Ella smiled, remembering her and Phoenix's mutual dislike of the word 'process'. But she didn't interrupt.

'You taught me what love was and it took me years of therapy to understand that I was unable to receive it from you or trust in it. I wasn't able to let you in. I tried to get it out in songs and while that worked for everyone else who heard them, I just couldn't believe it. I was writing the fantasy I wished we could have lived. Then I came to Hydra to continue our daydream, I s'pose, only without you. But, in a way, this island saved me. Wait, this isn't Hydra ... I mean the other island ... your mum's house ... and ... where is she...?'

Harrison looked down, frowning at the shoreline, then turned towards the hut behind them as if he were searching for something he couldn't find. Ella frowned as she wondered what he meant.

'Harri?' He met her eyes, and she rested her hand gently on his knee. 'We scattered her ashes yesterday.'

He looked at her and tilted his head.

'Yeah ... I know ... I just meant whereabouts in the sea. Hold that thought, let me get you a beer. And if you catch a fish, it's technically mine, 'cause I cast it.' He grinned. Ella watched him walk up the shingle beach, and saw him stop for a moment to look at the sky before moving towards the hut. It *was* oppressively hot, but he seemed confused, more so than from the heat. Georgia had passed out from the humidity, but she was probably overcome with all the lies she'd told. Ella pulled in her handline to guard the rod. She shuddered as she considered her sister, then the image of Phoenix and Harrison speaking about music together on the harbour floated across her mind. It was impossible to quantify what they'd lost from their lives. Though living in a land of 'what if' and 'if only' was where madness dwelt.

She suddenly longed to tell him about their daughter, but knew it would break every promise she'd ever made. Ella wasn't sure if Georgia still warranted her protection. Concealing Harrison's letters was bad enough, but to admit to wishing her dead as an innocent child was horrifying.

But Phoenix deserved to be shielded, so the secret must remain. Despite Ella's disgust at her sibling's behaviour, she couldn't help but feel some sympathy towards her. Georgia had never been adept at controlling her feelings. Yet just when she'd thought their dynamic couldn't become any more complex, it had. Ella could have done without knowing any of it. Ignorance was, indeed, bliss.

Harrison returned with a cold can for Ella who opened it. The hiss it made pierced the air as foam frothed over the lip.

'No bites yet,' she said, searching his face for a sign that he was OK. He sat beside her again, putting an arm around her.

'That's because you're staring at the sea instead of working the lure. What were you thinking about, love?'

Ella sighed.

'Oh, you know, how my sister tried to kill me, how you're living in my dead mother's house, why we've been put into each other's life again … nothing much.'

She laughed and Harrison drew her closer, kissing her temple. His skin smelled of sunshine and salt, and of him.

'I know it's not funny, but, God, El. I always thought Georgia was nuts, but this… I can't even get my head around it!'

Ella sank into him, leaning on his shoulder. If only it could just be the two of them, away from Hydra and on this island instead. It felt like the perfect way to spend her birthday, even though Harrison still hadn't mentioned it.

'At least Phoenix doesn't seem unhinged,' he continued, and Ella tensed under his touch. 'She's got great taste in music, I'd love to hear her play. Is she any good?'

Ella sat upright and took the rod from his hand, reeling in the line and wishing her stomach hadn't flipped to hear him say their daughter's name.

'She's incredible. But I don't think Georgia is going to let that happen. And no, Phoenie is nothing like my sister, thank God.'

'You should bring her up to the house, before you leave Hydra.'

The thought of having to go back to London suddenly gripped Ella's insides, a strange sensation when she'd thought of nothing but leaving since she'd arrived. She'd wanted to get away from the Hydra that had held such darkness for her, but now her feelings were changing; the island was an expert in seduction. She was thinking too much at once, but they'd only just found each other and there was little over a week left. Though he wasn't begging her to stay either. She leant the fishing rod against a rock beside the discarded other line.

'Don't think about it; I can hear your thoughts, El. You're not going home yet, and I don't want to let you go.'

He reached out and pushed her hair away from her face. She held her breath, her heart hammering as she leant towards him and his hand encased the back of her neck.

'I won't ever hurt you again, love. Please find a way to trust me, to trust in us,' he whispered as their lips brushed, their deep-rooted love for each other barely containable. She needed him again, longed to feel him love her, to know they were put together once more for a reason. She only hoped it wasn't another painful lesson. She took his face in her hands and stared at him, his expression of purest love was bliss and agony in equal measure.

'How do I know you won't leave me again, Harri?' she said, trying to mask her desire.

His hand held her wrist and moved it to his jaw.

'As long as there's a thought in my mind, and I have words to write, my heart is yours, love. And it always will be, my beautiful El.'

Tears cascaded down her cheeks and Ella began to sob.

'What is it?' he asked, gently wiping her face. Their gaze was unbreakable when they connected and Ella wanted to dive into his eyes and hide from the world.

'How can this work? You say the most beautiful things, but we can't live in some kind of fantasy just because we were once in love. I don't know if we're even compatible.'

He raised his eyebrows, his eyes sparkling with mischief.

'Not *that*, Harri, clearly we are in *that* way. You know what I mean. We don't know anything about each other now, today.'

He leant back on his hands and his lips curled in amusement.

'All right, catch-up crash course … we each get to ask something, and answer with the first thing that comes into our heads. And the only rule is we have to tell the truth.'

Ella smiled, amused by the pendulum they rode, which swung between unbridled passion and mischief, traversing pain and heartbreak.

'OK,' Ella replied, wiping her eyes. 'I'll start. First question … biggest disappointment?'

'Leaving you. What makes you happy?'

'Photography. No! Hearing Phoenix sing.' Ella's voice wavered slightly but she pressed on with speed. 'Favourite colour?'

'Blue. Favourite song?'

'Not yours, that's for sure,' she replied, laughing. '"Knocks Me Off My Feet", Stevie Wonder.'

Harrison nodded as he said, 'Great choice. Come on, faster. Your question, El.'

Ella sat cross-legged to face him, buoyed by the fun they were having.

'Favourite food?'

'Lamb chops. Jam or peanut butter?'

'Jam. Happiest moment?'

'Now. Black or white?'

'Black. Hot or cold?'

'Hot. Worst decision?'

'Giving our baby away.'

The Island

Secrecy and duplicitousness were unsustainable. But the gods used mortals as pawns for fun and their appetite for merriment wasn't yet satiated. There was no guarantee that good would prevail.
The island was watching and waiting.

Chapter 31
Georgia

'Dad, you will never, ever guess who I met today,' Phoenix said excitedly into her phone on loudspeaker beside her. Georgia had been avoiding Oliver and prepared herself for his reaction once Phoenix was out of earshot.

After lunch together on the balcony of her hotel suite, Georgia had demolished the remainder of the breadbasket, laden with sticky sweet Greek treats. Warm honey, heated by the sun's rays, dribbled onto her cream linen sundress and she didn't care a jot. She knew she was stress bingeing, but her nerves were in ragged pieces – she'd hardly slept a wink again last night. Georgia was surrendering to the fact that each secret she'd concealed over the years was being stripped from her grasp, like a snake shedding its peeling skin. Everything she'd tried to protect was being demolished, and she didn't know if she possessed the strength to fight anymore. She tuned back into Phoenix's phone conversation.

'Who did you meet, sweetheart?' Oliver asked.

'Harrison Sutherland! Can you actually believe it? *And* he used to go out with Auntie Ella *and* wrote "Out of the Darkness" for her. Isn't that wild? Of all the crap you guys tell me, this one interesting thing you leave out...' There was silence at the other end of the line, which was worse than the outburst of fury Georgia knew he was containing. '*And* he wants to hear me play. I could do the song I wrote for Granny. I've not quite finished it, but it's nearly there, you'll love it. I'll play it for you when we get home,' Phoenix chattered giddily.

Georgia heard Oliver breathing deeply.

'That's ... great, darling. I'm sure he's very busy though, don't go bothering him,' he replied, his voice laden with tension. Georgia knew the tone so well.

'Why does everyone keep saying that? First Mum, then Auntie Ella and now you. Harrison offered and I don't want to miss this chance. It could lead to other things.'

Georgia closed her eyes. Phoenix had no idea where it could lead.

'I know, darling, and that's very exciting for you, I'm sure,' Oliver replied. 'Could you pop your mother on a sec?'

'Fine,' she harrumphed, handing Georgia her mobile phone.

'Take me off speaker, please, Georgia,' Oliver said sternly, and she obliged, already tired, so very tired by a conversation that hadn't yet happened. Now Oliver could unleash his wrath. Not that she didn't care, she was simply sick of pretending that everything was fine between them. She took Pheonix's phone into the bedroom and closed the door.

'Go on, do your worst, get it all out,' Georgia said wearily. She had sent Oliver a message last night to let him know how the ceremony had gone, but had omitted to tell him about Harrison, and her confession about trying to kill her sister when they were children. His reaction to her concealing Harrison's letters was wounding enough. She had disappointed him, which was worse than his anger.

'I beg your pardon? What the hell has got into you?'

snapped Oliver and Georgia bristled at his tone. He wouldn't understand what she'd been trying to juggle on this trip and her resilience had evaporated.

'You haven't a clue what's been going on, not that you care. Perhaps if you'd made time to help me scatter my mother's ashes and shown *me* some respect for a change, none of this would have happened. But no, your precious work always comes first, ahead of me and Phoenix. This is not my fault!' For the first time since they'd married, she found herself standing up to her husband.

'Now I know why you've been avoiding my calls. It's downright reckless letting her meet *him*. How could you?'

'How could I?!' Georgia shrieked. 'I've been trying to keep Phoenix away from him and Ella as much as I can, but it was out of my hands. I will *not* take the blame for this, Oliver, I'm sick and tired of it all. We always knew it was possible she'd find out she wasn't ours and maybe it's for the best…'

'Keep your voice down, Georgia. You're getting a little frenetic and having one of your moments.'

'Don't you dare speak to me like that. I won't be called hysterical for pretending everything's perfect when it's the bloody opposite!'

'For God's sake, calm down and stop being so dramatic. You've only got another week to get through and when you get home things can go back to normal.'

'Normal?! What the hell is that, Oliver? You doing what you please while I sit at home bored out of my mind? No, not anymore. We need to talk when I get back.'

Oliver laughed unkindly.

'I should say so! I recommend you spend the rest of your time in Greece considering our future and how to navigate the mess you and that bloody sister of yours have created.'

'Oh, *that's* what you recommend is it?!' she couldn't help but laugh in exasperation. 'God, Oliver, I can't do this anymore,' she said as she abruptly finished the call, her last ounce of strength had expired. She flopped backwards onto her bed and stared at the ceiling. The mess wasn't just of her and Ella's making; they were all involved, including Oliver and Harrison. The innocent party was Phoenix, the only one among them who appeared to be capable of acting like an adult. She looked at Phoenix's phone in her clammy hand. The screen was still unlocked and the temptation was too great to resist. She opened her daughter's social media apps and scrolled through the private messages to check nothing untoward was being sent to or by her daughter. Then, she opened the internet browser. The landing page made her sit bolt upright. Phoenix had been looking at a genetic testing website and had placed an order for a DNA kit.

* * *

Phoenix had continued to badger Georgia about seeing Harrison again. Then she'd started on about visiting her grandmother's house. Georgia had resisted revealing both destinations were intrinsically linked, until she could no longer stand the inquisition and told Phoenix the facts. Phoenix then insisted they called in on Harrison, and Georgia had run out of reasons why they shouldn't. At least those she could say aloud.

'I get why he lives on Hydra. This island is so inspiring. And I've finished my song, Mum, for Granny. Being here … the words just came. I wish it was that easy all the time,' Phoenix said as they walked around the port towards the steps that led to the white house on the hill that their mother used to own.

Georgia's legs protested as they started the steep climb. Despite her fitness, the incline would challenge even an Olympic athlete, and the sun's heat was sweltering as it cast rays that danced across the small waves. The beams seemed to bounce onto the painted houses, which in turn reflected a brighter glimmer onto the water, illuminating her reluctant progress.

It's a vicious circle of unavoidable light, rather like the tangled web our family has woven, Georgia thought to herself as they continued to ascend.

'Is Auntie Ella going to celebrate her birthday with us today?' asked Phoenix.

'Oh God, I completely forgot,' replied Georgia in a panic. 'Phoenix, I honestly don't know where she is. She might be in the house with … him, or somewhere else. This is what she does. She takes off without any indication of where she'll be or for how long.'

'Well, we should at least try and find her,' said Phoenix. 'If she's at Harrison's place then maybe you two can sort out your troubles once and for all. That could be her birthday present from you.'

They rounded the narrow alleyway and took a breather on the corner, admiring the bird's-eye view of the port from their vantage point.

'It's so quiet, isn't it, Mum?' Phoenix remarked. 'Down there it's all noise, clanging and clopping, but it's so peaceful up here. I wish Granny was still here, and we could stay in the house together. Maybe one day I'll come here with my own children and make memories like you and Auntie Ella did.'

The thought of her own childhood and the hideous event

she'd confessed to her sister chilled Georgia to her core despite the high temperature. She smiled tightly, wondering whether to broach the subject of the genetic website she'd found on her phone. But then she'd be accused of snooping and she didn't want to rock any more boats. She shivered at her poor choice of mental analogy.

Seeing her mother's front door again felt significant, but knowing who now dwelt behind it muddied her sentimentality. She raised her hand to the painted blue surface and knocked quietly.

'Well, nobody's going to hear that!' Phoenix tutted as she stepped in front of Georgia to give four sharp raps. As the seconds passed; it became clear nobody was home. Georgia exhaled in relief, but it was only a temporary delay as Phoenix was determined to see both the house and the occupant. She didn't think she could stand to see the three of them together again – biological mother, father and daughter. On the harbour yesterday, it had been a glimpse of what life could have been for them all. A vignette which Georgia had played an integral role in preventing.

'We can come again another day,' she said.

'Or later. If she's in the harbour, I want to see Auntie Ella on her birthday. It's important.'

Georgia stopped walking and faced Phoenix.

'Why? There have been so many birthdays you haven't seen her for.'

'Because for once we can be with each other. I don't like to think of all the ones I've missed so far. It's about regrets, Mum, I just don't like them.'

Georgia circled her arm around Phoenix's shoulders as they walked down the steps.

'You're so sensitive, sweetheart. You don't keep things

locked up as much as your mother tries to.'

As soon as the words were out of her mouth, she wished she could take them back. She was talking about Ella. Phoenix's parentage had been dominating her thoughts so much that she'd almost resigned herself to confessing the truth and now had cryptically blurted it out. Or had she? She was spiralling and second guessing herself, and Phoenix was frowning.

'If I'm anything at all like you, then I'd have burst into tears and had a fainting fit ... Mum...' she added.

They stopped and faced each other in a narrow alleyway.

'You know you can ask me anything, don't you? Is something on your mind?' asked Georgia with trepidation.

Phoenix shrugged.

'Not really,' she replied, then turned and walked along the winding alleyways towards the heart of the island leaving Georgia to follow behind, afraid to take another step in case her worst fears were waiting for her at the end of the path.

Chapter 32

Georgia

Rounding the next lane, Phoenix and Georgia heard a clattering noise on stone accompanied by hushed chatter. Into view came an old lady accompanied by a man. She was hunched over her walking stick, which smacked against the cobbles with each laboured step.

'Vasílis!' shouted Phoenix as she almost galloped to his side, covering the distance in an instant.

Vasílis was carrying a small tray of plants and as Georgia nodded a greeting, she was struck by their perfume: dill, thyme and oregano. It was the familiar smell of Greek wild herbs that Mum had grown in her boat garden. It made her instantly nauseous, but she quickly recovered.

'*Yiá sas,* Vasílis.' Georgia said hello, suddenly struck at how attractive he was in the clear sunlight. 'How lovely to see you again after so long. Doing a spot of gardening?'

He shifted uncomfortably from one foot to the other, looking to the old woman then back to Georgia.

'*Yiá sas*, yes, something like that.'

Georgia waited for an introduction to the lady, but none was forthcoming, so she held out her hand.

'Hello, I'm Georgia. And this is Phoenix.'

The woman wasn't entirely upright and lifted her head to scrutinise Georgia properly. Phoenix was too tall to be in her eyeline. The old woman's kelp-coloured eyes narrowed, but she smiled at Georgia, returning her handshake. She spoke to Vasílis in rapid Greek. Not a single word was recognisable, so Georgia looked to Vasílis for translation.

'She says she is glad you are here and your sister has returned home to the island.'

Georgia was intrigued if not baffled.

'I don't understand… How does she know Ella?'

Vasílis looked awkward but recovered with a broad smile.

'She met Zina and helped her with some bags the other day. But where is Ella today?'

'We're hunting for her too,' said Phoenix. 'If you run into her, do tell her we're looking for her. And if you see Harrison Sutherland, could you let him know I need to speak to him as well? You've got my number.'

Phoenix crouched to clasp the woman's hand, entering her eyeline. The woman muttered a prayer, then crossed herself before stepping forward to clasp Pheonix's face, tilting it downwards. Zina reached the top of Phoenix's chestnut curls and seemed to pretend to spit in her hair with what sounded like a '*Ftou ftou ftou*'.

Phoenix looked puzzled and sought out Vasílis for an explanation.

'It is for good luck, a superstition to ward off bad demons. She believes there are many here on the island.'

Vasílis offered the woman his arm, and they moved slowly in the opposite direction bidding them goodbye.

'Well, that was random,' said Phoenix, watching Zina shuffling away with Vasílis dutifully guiding her.

'Very,' said Georgia. 'Now what? No sign of my sister or

… her friend. What do you fancy doing?'

'Why are you so down on Harrison? If they're meant to be together, then you may need to get used to him being around.'

Georgia couldn't think of anything worse and chose not to answer. They silently zigzagged through side alleyways until they came to a square that was dominated by a taverna. Huge olive trees seemed to grow out of the paving and the wooden pergola was covered in low hanging lilac wisteria.

'Wow! This is the Leonard Cohen place that Ella told me about. Apparently, he did his first performance here before he was famous,' said Phoenix as she took a seat. 'Let's have snacks, I'm starving, I need to soak up the poetry in the air.'

'Lovely,' was all Georgia could muster.

Diners were feasting merrily as waiters carried huge trays on their shoulders laden with delicious smelling plates. Despite the jovial atmosphere, Georgia knew she was about to be bombarded with questions and found herself wishing for Ella's presence to distract Phoenix's attention.

'So…' Georgia said after she'd ordered a tiny jug of wine for Phoenix and her to share along with a bottle of water. 'Your college offers will arrive soon …' The thought squeezed at Georgia's insides. When Phoenix left home, the only significant role she would be left with was wife and she doubted her ability and desire to play that part anymore.

Phoenix poured herself a glass of rosé and sipped thoughtfully, her eyes not leaving Georgia's.

'I don't want to talk about that. I'd actually like to ask you some questions, and I'd appreciate some honesty.'

Georgia sat back in her chair, hoping Phoenix's chosen topics wouldn't back her into a corner. But she suspected they would. Still, she was determined not to lie, and prayed she could stick to that resolution.

'Let's order your food first,' she said, playing for time. Phoenix rolled her eyes as Georgia picked up a menu, choosing courgette fritters, tzatziki, and a couple of fish dishes.

'Right, now you've ordered,' began Phoenix. 'I have several things I'd like to discuss, and I won't be fobbed off any longer.'

'Check your tone, young lady. Show your mother some respect.'

Phoenix raised an eyebrow, leaning forward on the table.

'Are you though?'

Georgia felt her pulse picking up pace.

'Come on, darling, let's try and have a fun day without any drama,' said Georgia, pouring herself a splash of wine.

'I'm sorry, I'm not letting you palm me off anymore. You might think you're all so smart with your whispered conversations and meaningful looks. You and Ella do it all the time, in between your incessant squabbling. You vie for my attention and you're so jealous when the light doesn't shine on you. And you both treat me like a child, thinking I won't notice. But the problem is, I'm not a kid, and I can see quite clearly what's been going on. I sit back and watch you so called grown-ups with all your smoke screens, secrets and lies. I haven't got to the bottom of them all yet, but rest assured I will.'

'Phoenix, please...' started Georgia, but she faltered. She hadn't decided what she wanted to say.

A waiter arrived with a small plate of *gávros marinátos* – marinated anchovies – the *kolokithokeftédes* – courgette fritters – and creamy garlic tzatziki. Georgia smiled politely as he gave them each an empty plate, then she fished the napkin-wrapped cutlery from the bread basket. Phoenix served herself helpings of everything while Georgia made a slow show of unfurling her knife and fork from the paper serviette.

'Right, where were we?' said Phoenix. 'Oh yes, question one. Is Ella my auntie?'

Georgia picked up her water with a trembling hand. She accidentally breathed in as she swallowed and started to cough. Her eyes streamed with tears and Phoenix jumped up to pat her back.

Georgia dismissed the help and Phoenix's brown eyes flashed with irritation as she re-took her seat.

'Have you finished deflecting? I brought you here so you can't have a meltdown and escape the truth this time, you have to keep up appearances in public like you always do. Or try to. But I am begging you to be honest.' She leant forward in earnest. 'I deserve to know. Is Ella my auntie?'

'No,' replied Georgia in a small voice as she felt the fight leave her body. She'd been herded towards a dead end in a labyrinth, chased by monsters of the past with no respite, no hero to save her nor any hope of return. She would deal with the consequences regarding Oliver another time. Phoenix might feel like the greatest island detective that ever lived, but she could also be contributing to the end of their marriage. But that wasn't her burden to shoulder.

'Is Dad ... Oliver ... my father?'

Georgia's heart was hurting so much, she could hardly stand to say the words. She wriggled in her seat and opened her mouth to answer, but her chin wobbled, and her tears began. Not from choking on water but from the spectacular unveiling of all their family's secrets in the beautiful taverna. The smell of wisteria would forever be linked in her mind with the moment she finally told the truth.

The waiter arrived with the remainder of their order just

then, placing the plates on the table with a flourish.

'*Kalí órexi!*' he said, wishing them a good meal, but Georgia's appetite for food and the idea of ever returning again to Hydra had deserted her. Phoenix continued to stare with her piercing eyes, which burnt almost golden in the dappled sunlight. Georgia took a steeling breath, reaching across the table for Phoenix's hand.

'Before I answer your question, know that we have loved you since the second you were born, and we will always be your parents. If you want us, that is.' She took another sip from her glass before returning her hand to Phoenix's. She wasn't ducking or hiding from what must be told.

Phoenix's eyes began to fill, which hurt Georgia's heart more than being forced to confess. A gust of wind swirled around them, lifting the edges of the tablecloths, and a scattering of purple petals dropped from the overhanging blooms like unwanted confetti. 'But in answer to your question, no … Oliver isn't your biological father. And I'm so very sorry, my darling, that we never told you the truth, that I...' Georgia's voice finally cracked as she yielded to the litany of lies that led her back to this wretched island. 'I... am not your birth mother.' She felt the weight of carrying the last pieces of deceit shift from her shoulders as she completed her circle of truth. Though she knew the fallout would be immense, it felt liberating to finally be entirely honest. 'You may have already filled in the blanks, and I am desperately sorry if you feel misled or lied to. And of course, you'll feel that way. As I've said to you before, there are things you do as adults to protect those you love, though you didn't deserve to be fed a pack of untruths. But we had no other option at the time. Not me. And not your natural mother.'

Phoenix's gaze dropped to her plate as she pushed around her food before returning her penetrating stare to look at Georgia.

'Ella,' said Phoenix.

Georgia nodded and closed her eyes in submission.

'Yes, Ella.'

The Island

As the seabirds rode the invisible thermal currents overhead, so all mortals were drawn towards their destiny, no matter how painful the voyage or unclear the path. The women would find their rightful place in the world eventually. With or without each other.

Chapter 33
Ella

Ella and Harrison had been staring at each other in silence for what seemed like aeons. She hardly dared to breathe, let alone speak. Perhaps she'd imagined telling him she gave their baby away, and he was still waiting for her to share what her worst decision was in their absurd question and answer marathon. But from the look on his face, she knew she'd let her precious truth out into the air.

'I don't know if I'm dreaming or if you just said what I think you did,' he said, his eyes not leaving hers, seeking answers.

'It's just a silly game. We should swim, it's so hot.' She needed to think quickly. Having seen him with Phoenix must be nagging at her subliminally, urging her to make that illusion a reality. Now it was too late to take it back and all she wanted to do was escape and hide within the island waters.

She undressed to her bikini and waded into the sea. The cooler shallows were a welcome change from the scorching temperature and the heat of their conversation. She dived beneath the surface and swam underwater for as long as she could. Harrison followed her. She could see his strong arms pulling his defined body swiftly through the current. The closer he came, the nearer she was to telling him about Phoenix.

The sea wasn't deep, but she was out of her depth with Harrison and with the subject matter. She kept her body concealed within the shallow water, as though she could veil herself and the truth.

'El! Stop running away,' he shouted.

She laughed nervously. They'd both been guilty of running away from each other, though he won the prize for the most dramatic and devastating exit.

'I'm only swimming, nobody is running.'

'Just stop, please,' he said as he reached her. His height allowed him to cover a greater distance in a shorter amount of time. As he stood in the water up to his waist her eyes traced the hairs on his chest downwards and desire vibrated inside her once again. He smoothed his wet hair backwards before extending his hand to her, encouraging her to stand. She took it and her shoulders left the safety of the sea as the waves lapped around her ribs.

'El, you need to tell me. You can't just say something and pretend you didn't. We ... we have a child?' he said, desperately searching for confirmation of her words.

She looked at the cloudless sky, at a loss as to how to explain. Their love had started waist deep in a river and now they were back in the water again but this time it might signal their ending.

'You won't be able to forgive me, Harri.'

His eyes creased with a raw tenderness.

'Just like you can't forgive me, El? We're too old to play these games. But you need to explain what you said ... about our baby. You owe me that.'

She shivered; he was right. Her long wet hair chilled her back as the breeze rose again and her eyes drifted to the shore.

'We made our baby on Hydra. I didn't know it then, but when you left me at the station, I knew I was pregnant. I wanted to tell you that day but I was so afraid because it wasn't in our plan. Nothing made sense to me after you got on the train. I still wanted you … but our daughter—'

'We had a girl?' His eyes widened in excitement, which further crushed her.

Ella saw his body was trembling. He would be wondering what she had always imagined: what kind of parents would they have been. But they would never find out.

'Yes, we had a girl,' she said quietly as a sudden gust of wind whistled around them. Her skin rippled with goose bumps. 'I was in a very bad place after you left and throughout my pregnancy, as dark as I ever thought possible. I didn't want to live anymore. Georgia and Oliver sent me to get help.'

He put his hands on her shoulders and pulled her close. Her silent tears created a flow of warmth on his chest. The saltwater made her eyes sting, but it was nothing compared to the ache inside her heart and her barren belly where Phoenix once grew. Being on the island had coaxed her emotions to the surface and she surrendered to letting them roam free. With Harrison, there was little point trying to hide what had lived in her soul for so long.

She pulled away from him.

'Harri…' She prepared herself to share the worst part. 'I had our baby adopted after she was born.' His face fell, and she knew she'd mended and re-broken his heart within the space of a minute. 'I'm so sorry. I gave her away. I had to.'

His body visibly tensed; he was angry. He had every right to be.

'It was the best thing to do for her. I was so young, I didn't feel like I had a choice.' He took a step back. She felt her feet sinking into the sand where she was stranded in mid-water. 'I was desperately unhappy and felt so alone. She reminded me of everything I'd lost. The way you left, with no means of contacting you ... the rejection was too much given what I was willing to sacrifice – I was going to give up my studies for you. I became determined never to do that again, not even for her.' Ella's voice dropped, barely audible above the wind, the shame of her selfish, heartbreaking decision echoed around the bay. 'She was so like you; she had your beautiful eyes. I'm so sorry.'

His brown eyes darkened and misted with tears.

'You should have told me, found a way to let me know.' His voice was steely. 'It could have changed everything for us. Our whole world.'

'But I didn't know where you were. You left before giving me the address, remember? And what would you have done? Come back to be a pity parent when you'd already chosen to be apart from me even when I was willing to forfeit my life's plan for you? You would have run even further away, and you know it. If you'd accepted me and our baby back then, it would have broken us, we would have resented each other for giving up our ambition just to live some fantasy, romantic version of us.' She didn't want to be angry, and in her heart she knew they wouldn't have been any good for Phoenix. Not then, perhaps not even today. 'She was placed with a family who couldn't have children. She is loved. It was the best of the very worst situation.'

'Where is she now?'

His voice was like ice and it chilled Ella further. She hesitated, not wishing to be dishonest, but the whole truth still wasn't an option.

'She isn't eighteen yet, so she probably doesn't know she is adopted. She might one day. I'm sorry, Harri. I really am.

We can't be her parents, no matter what happens with you and me.' She'd said enough. The expression on his face was excruciating, and she felt his wound deep within her.

He started to wade back towards the shore then turned to face her again.

'You had no right to do that without me.' He moved away through the water, the ripples he made clawing at her skin. It was as if the sea was made of pinpricks, every swell that bounced against her body hurt as she was left in his wake, alone in the island tide.

* * *

The afternoon succumbed to evening as the shadows lengthened over Dokos island. Hydra twinkled in the distance like a sparkling reminder of their crushed dream. Ella longed to escape into the most remote location she could and lose herself in her work. It's what she did when life became too much and in that second, she felt completely overpowered.

Harrison had made a fire and was playing his guitar beside it. He hadn't touched the mezze she'd made. The light from the flames kissed his face, making his tanned skin glow. Ella stared at him, but he wouldn't meet her gaze. She watched a tumult of emotions cross his face; anger from the tension in his jaw, then devastation in the form of tears that slid from his eyes, which had turned the colour of pure-spun gold in the blazing campfire. He was composing, stopping to replay a phrase until a song began to build and take shape. Even without lyrics it was beautiful, haunting and terribly sad. He was marking yet another episode of their doomed love within a song.

Eventually he discarded his guitar against the tree stump where he'd been sitting and went for a walk. She let him have his space. As he left, she saw the flames catch his tears again. They shone in the spreading darkness. Cicadas struck up their own music to replace his composition and the stars peeked through their dark velvet curtain. She was alone with all the decisions she'd made that had led her once again to be without those she loved. Moving to sit beside the fire for warmth, she poked the dying embers with a stick then idly strummed her fingers across the guitar strings. The burning wood smouldered white hot as she stared into the ashes, willing some kind of hope to rise from it.

After a while, the crunch of feet on shingle signalled Harrison's return. His tall silhouette was slowly illuminated by the diminishing flames as he neared. He joined her, sinking onto the other seat, exhaling heavily.

'I owe you a final apology, El,' he began.

She waited for him to continue, her heart frozen in anticipation.

He didn't look at her, speaking only to the fire. 'If I hadn't left you, we could be here living our dream with our little girl.' His voice cracked and Ella hated the fact she couldn't tell him that they'd already had a small glimpse of that life on the harbour with Phoenix. 'I have to take responsibility for the events that followed my leaving. The blame isn't yours alone to shoulder. I'm devastated about not being a parent and the fact there's now a young woman out there who has no idea I exist.' He nodded in the direction of Hydra but he couldn't know that was precisely where their daughter was.

Ella bit her tongue.

'The incredible love she was made from was so powerful. But you made that decision about her future for us and for her, and you need to let me struggle with it. I can't imagine what you went through, bad enough to have given her away. I'm the reason that happened, because of the pain I caused you, and

255

the fact I couldn't let you throw away your education to be with me. In one way I'm glad I did that, because of everything you've achieved, but this… I need to come to terms with it and forgive you for what you did. But more so, I have to find a way to forgive myself.' He still only spoke to the fire that had now all but died.

She was desperate to meet his eyes, to reconnect with their strength of feeling.

His hurt circled in the air, encasing them in the history of their tragic love. 'I'm sorry, El. I won't keep apologising, nor take the blame for everything, but this I concede. We don't have our daughter and we're not her parents because I got on that train without saying goodbye and giving you a way to contact me. We are both being punished for what I did. And always will be. Georgia has her part to play in keeping us separate, but it's possible we would have made each other unhappy and blamed one another for everything that was wrong, and our child would have suffered – trying to be grown-ups when we were anything but… El, I don't know how we move beyond this. I wonder if we aren't good for each other and should think about leaving the past where it is. Maybe we aren't meant to be together in this life…'

She'd dreamed of the moment he found out about their child, but re-considering their future wasn't an outcome she'd imagined. He was being rational, but his line of thinking seemed to suggest that whatever it was between them, was over. There weren't enough hours left to unpick then re-stitch the loose threads of their wounded story back together. They both felt it as the thought vibrated in the air.

'I wish things could have been different, Harri, I really do. But we're here now. We've been put together again at this time for a reason. I wish I knew why.' She crouched in front of him, and he lifted his eyes to meet hers. She held both his hands in hers. 'I love you. For so long, I wished I didn't feel like that, denied that I did, but I'm glad I do. Your knowing about our baby makes me happy, regardless of what happened with her and what happens now. I could never have kept it from you if we'd tried to make this work. Please know how sorry I am. I can't change it – I wish I could, but I can't.'

He managed to smile, and his thumb caressed her cheek as he leant his forehead to meet hers.

'El, I love you too. And I never stopped either. But I don't know where we go from here apart from tomorrow, we'll return to Hydra. But tonight … this is our island and it's just you and me. I don't want to think anymore, it's too much.'

* * *

That night, Harrison made love to Ella in a way she had never experienced. She felt as though she had turned into air, water and earth, like they belonged inside one another, never to be parted. But it was as though they were saying goodbye. Every touch of his hands, mouth and body was heightened, as if somebody had turned up the volume of their love to an excruciating level. With the sharpest clarity and most focused lens yet, she felt every movement echo within the depths of her soul. She chose to yield to their destiny, rather than predict where their course would take them, either together or apart. Ultimately, she trusted the universe and the island that had united them. If not now, it would eventually – one day – be their time.

Chapter 34

Ella

As Hydra loomed ahead, Harrison encouraged Ella to take the wheel of the boat. There was scarcely enough wind to allow the gently billowing mainsail to catch as they silently glided back to port. Steering the boat allowed her to confront fear head on. The gentle pace of the vessel with Harrison's arms folded around her coaxed a feeling of calm forth that replaced her usual terror at being afloat.

Harrison had shown such compassion for the mental state she'd been in after he left all those years ago that Ella felt she should seek similar grace in relation to her sister. Besides, it was the start of a new year for her, following her birthday yesterday, albeit uncelebrated. She was determined to change the narrative, especially when it came to both Harrison and Georgia. Her sister had done a reckless spur of the moment thing in that boat and hadn't fully understood the consequences. She had only been a child whose temper had exploded unchecked for a split second. Yes, Georgia was overtly emotional and dangerously insecure, but she wasn't innately cruel, and Ella knew deep down that her sibling had

258

never truly wished her dead. Georgia should have known better but her emotions had overruled sense – something Ella was guilty of too.

Being on Dokos had offered a new perspective, despite the heaviness of what it might mean for her and Harrison.

Since returning to Greece, Ella was being urged not only to find understanding and forgiveness for those who had wronged her, but also to admit her own part in making decisions with far-reaching consequences. Giving away Phoenix wasn't the only choice she'd had at the time, but it was the one she'd made. Whether Harrison was able to forgive her for having their daughter adopted, she had no way to influence. But she could forgive herself. It had turned out for the best then and now. She could also absolve Georgia's hot-headed childhood mistake and pardon her for withholding Harrison's letters. She'd only been trying to protect Ella in the vulnerable state she'd been in at the time, even if her motives weren't entirely altruistic. But she had empathy for her sister. The pain of losing Phoenix was something Ella understood only too well because she had already lived it.

In Hydra harbour, Harrison tied the stern ropes around the bollards on the dock to moor the boat. Ella stood behind him and wrapped her arms tightly around his waist. Throngs of people moved around them, but she barely noticed; there was only him. She felt his body expand with a deep breath.

'You're not making this easy, El,' he said, his voice lacking the usual warmth. He'd held her all night in his arms, though she hadn't slept much. She'd wanted to savour the feeling in case it was their last time.

'None of this is easy, Harri,' she said into his back, pressing her face into his T-shirt to inhale his scent, the smell of love. He turned and cupped her face, tilting it up to look at him.

His head was framed by the midday sky. The colour of lapis, it seemed bluer than it had ever been. The world had become a vibrant collision of technicolour. Usually, she found such sensory overloads too much to absorb, which was why she focused on a single subject through her camera. Now, she yearned to be annihilated by the thousand colours of Greece.

'Now what...' he said, as his knuckles brushed her cheek.

'Now... I don't know. I guess I should find somewhere to stay.'

He held his hands behind his head and looked upwards to the cliffs before his arms returned to her shoulders.

'I don't want to be away from you,' he said with such longing.

He had the same compulsion she felt to be together. She took his hand.

'Come on then. Backgammon at The Pirate. Maybe we let the gods decide what happens next on the roll of a dice. If you throw a six, we talk some more and make a decision. Or if someone throws a five ... we pretend for a bit longer.'

He slung his arm around her.

'Yeah, I don't think we should be in charge of any more life-changing decisions. We've messed up every important one so far. Fate brought us back together, so it can decide what's next.'

They found a seat outside in the shade and Harrison went in search of *távli*. Ella had got the taste for the game over the years on Hydra, claiming it was part of her Greek birthright, and they used to play for hours at university. Harrison almost always won, which was vexing. As she waited for him to return with the board and an ouzo for her, she looked around at the port. The bustle and busyness, the familiar faces and characters she knew of old were like a warm embrace. It was as though her darkest experiences on the island were being erased with each moment spent with Harrison. Her pain was hers to own, but it also belonged to them. Perhaps they could heal each other even though they had previously torn each other to shreds. If they weren't destined to be together in this life, then perhaps the next time around might be kinder.

Harrison opened the board, its hinges creaking as it was spread on the table. She took a sip of her cloudy ouzo, the ice clunking as she raised her glass. Harrison hadn't started to set up his side of the game but she added her pieces and waited for him to place his. He stared blankly at the coloured stripes on the brown and black background, frowning.

'Harri...' Ella said. 'Do you want me to do yours?' Something felt wrong with him again, like on Dokos. He raised his head to face her, and his pupils were large in his soft brown eyes, his expression vacant. They knew each other's eyes so well, but she hadn't seen this expression before. It was like looking at a stranger.

'Harri...?' she repeated.

His eyes suddenly flashed with warmth and creased, exposing the laughter lines she had grown to love.

'Sorry, love. I was a million miles away.' He deftly arranged the counters in their rightful places and picked up the dice. 'Highest number starts. We know what a five or six means, but I hope you're ready for a beating.'

Ella knew in her heart something wasn't right but began the game. She threw a one and he a five. They both smiled at his throw, hoping that chance would turn into favour. The roll of the dice allowed pretence for a little longer as they'd agreed before on the pontoon, avoiding reality until it inevitably confronted them again. Hope swelled in her heart and she closed her hand over his.

'I do forgive you, Harri, for everything that's happened. I

have to, otherwise we'll never find a future, if we're meant to have one, that is. I don't know whether being back here on the island with you is right for either of us.'

He turned his palm to face hers and clasped her hand.

'Nothing else matters but you, El. I'm sorry I did this to us, but I forgive you too. The problem is, I need to forgive myself. And I don't know if I can.'

He was more grown-up than she ever had been over the years. She escaped her demons through the lens, whereas he confronted his with therapy and by writing it into songs. Her treatment when she was pregnant had delved far enough into her troubles to coax her away from the depths of depression, but there was still so much work she had to do on herself.

'You can tell me anything, you know that, Harri.'

He looked at her and hesitated before saying, 'You know everything you need to know in this moment.'

He grinned as he threw the dice, but for once, the smile didn't quite reach his eyes.

* * *

Harrison had won three times and they'd ordered several plates of food to accompany their competition.

Ella recalled how easy it was on Hydra to while away a day simply people watching or chatting to islanders. There was always a casual conversation to observe or have and someone to greet. She pointed out the animal handlers that she recalled from her youth, their facial hair larger and more elaborate, and some walking with the languid gait of age. It was comforting to know some aspects of the island remained unchanged. They talked about how Hydra had altered since they came together in November 1997, and Ella felt them slip into an easy rhythm. Their foundation of familiarity

262

was a gateway to adult understanding, though she still had the occasional rush of nervousness, just like she'd had at the beginning of their relationship. They chatted and laughed with effortless ease, and it was thrillingly strange to see Harrison being greeted by locals she already knew from years gone by, like another part of their past was fusing together.

They walked around the harbour hand-in-hand to another bar to leave the memory of Ella's poor gaming performance behind and enjoy the last of the afternoon's sunshine. Neither wanted to return to his house yet, the place where judgement and decision lived. There they'd have to discuss whether she stayed elsewhere or not.

'This isn't about me moving in with you for the rest of my trip – and we don't have to decide now – but would you indulge me so I can cook just once more in my mum's old kitchen?' Ella asked with no ulterior motive other than to bask in the happier times connected to her mother.

'You know I want you with me, and I'd love that.' His expression was tender, and she felt his need to be with her from across the table. He suddenly laughed. 'At least you learnt to cook. I seem to remember all we ate at uni was instant mashed potato, pasta, or those awful crispy breaded pancake things.'

'Well, people change, Harri. You'll see,' she said, laughing as she bent to kiss him on the lips. 'Won't be a moment. I'm going for supplies.'

Even though they had many more weighted conversations ahead, she felt lighter as she walked towards the store. There was a nugget of joy to be found in one more evening of entertaining the fantasy of being together. Whether their fractured history and old love was sufficient to sustain a future, she had no idea, but it was enough to grasp on to for now.

She headed for Vasílis' father's shop. There, she selected ingredients to make a classic Greek salad, inhaling the scent of the beef tomato skins as she chose each fruit. She planned to cook lightly fried *kolokithákia* – courgette sticks sliced so thinly they'd resemble skinny fries – along with roasting an assortment of vegetables in the oven with fresh herbs, lemon and capers. Classic, simple but exquisite Greek food with the freshest produce kissed by island sunshine.

'Ella!' she heard her name from across the store.

'Hey Vasílis!' she said. 'Are you helping your dad out?'

'Oh yes,' he replied, laughing. 'There is no escaping a shift at the shop, not when *Babás* owns it! You seem happier than when I last saw you.'

Ella was grateful for his honest account of the accident. He'd helped slot a few of the missing pieces into place as she'd digested the horror of what her sister had done. Or had tried to do.

'I *am* happier. Listen, I wondered if you're working tomorrow? I want to visit Zina and I really, really need your translation skills.'

'I'm not sure what help I can be. Oh! Happy birthday for yesterday,' he said, then seemed to regret mentioning it.

'How did you know it was my birthday?' she asked, bewildered at how he could possibly have marked the date in his memory when Harrison had forgotten.

'I saw your sister and I … uh … I think your niece must have mentioned it.' He smiled, but Ella didn't believe him. Though what cause would he have to lie?

'Thanks, but the birthday is done!' she said. 'Anyway, how about eleven at Zina's tomorrow?'

He put his hands in his pockets and looked at the floor before answering her. He seemed unsure, whereas he had been anything but when they'd had that drink together that ended platonically, much to Phoenix's disappointment and Ella's relief.

'Sure. I'll help you. See you there tomorrow.'

* * *

Ella swung her shopping bags as she walked back to the port. As she neared the bar at the far side of the harbour, she expected to see Harrison still at their table. But their drinks had been cleared away and it was empty. Her pulse started to thud.

No, no, no, she thought to herself. *He wouldn't run out on me again.*

She closed in on their seats and looked around at the other tables. Most had emptied, which was unusual for that time of day, and there was no sign of him. She hated the fact she automatically feared the worst of their past was repeating itself. Then, as she heard the sound of a piano, relief flooded through her. Her favourite song she'd told him about on Dokos was being played and she knew instinctively it was him. It was a slowed down version with beautiful additional jazz embellishments, showcasing Harrison's exceptional skill. The way he played was unmistakable. She could almost feel his fingers on her skin, recognising the way they caressed the keys.

She turned to the entrance of the bar. The lights glowed from within, and she couldn't see at first where the piano was, there were so many people inside. Then, it was as if her heart was struck by a thunderbolt. The sweetest sound took the melody line, delicious husky tones with astonishing but effortless vocal runs. As Ella made her way further into the bar, the crowd parted to reveal what thrilled and terrified her in equal measure.

At the end of the room was Phoenix, singing her heart out. And beside her was Harrison.

Chapter 35

Georgia

Georgia was hiking to the monastery at the top of the mountain in the middle of the island.

She paused to take in the spectacular view, though the trek hadn't been her greatest idea; the late afternoon sun was beating down fiercer than ever. Georgia hadn't applied enough sunscreen, she wasn't covered up and her flip-flops were not fit for purpose. She wasn't her usual prepared self. In fact, she wasn't herself at all. She felt free but also empty. There were no more secrets left.

As she sat beneath a large tree, her eyes scanned the distant coast of the Greek mainland then stared at the island spread out below. The whole of Hydra appeared to be blurred, a collection of small geometric shapes with occasional splashes of colour. Her perspective had changed. She felt like a goddess looking down on her kingdom, invincible and liberated. Even the thought of informing Oliver of the latest in their family drama didn't faze her. There would be consequences, but she felt strangely unconcerned. She had declined all his calls since she'd hung up on him and hadn't listened to any of his voicemails. There was little she could do to influence circumstances now and she'd learnt from Ella to trust in the way things were meant to be.

After their conversation in the taverna, Phoenix had wanted to be alone. Georgia's heart had sunk as she'd watched her daughter elegantly walk away. How long she'd suspected that Ella was her birth mother, she had no clue, but she hadn't treated Georgia any differently, which was of some comfort. Phoenix's ability to accept revelations was the opposite of how Georgia would have reacted. She wished Ella had a phone so she could tip her off about what Phoenix now knew. She had no means of warning her. Harrison being uncontactable was one of the things Ella had been devastated by, but her sister was just as bad, deliberately living out of reach.

Now, at last, Ella could have her perfect family: Harrison and Phoenix. Whereas Georgia might have lost every single one of them along with her husband.

She typed out a message to Phoenix beneath the shady canopy.

My darling Phoenix. You will always be my little girl and I will always be your mother. I cannot begin to tell you the torment Ella and I have lived with hiding the truth all these years. You are an incredible young woman and more adept at being an adult than any of us. But when you are ready, please can I explain what happened? From the first moment I held you in my arms, I loved you as if I'd carried you myself for all those months. And Ella loves you so fiercely, though it may not feel like it at the moment. She didn't reject you, and please don't punish her for the difficult choice she made. She was unable to cope at the time. You saved me, Phoenix, and you have no idea of the burden you carried on your tiny shoulders back then. I didn't think I would be able to have a child, and then you appeared like a bright light in a world that had become

so dark for us all. I loved you the second you opened your
eyes, and I will continue to love you until I close mine for the
last time. Whether you can forgive me, I don't know. But I
will love you as I've always done. Your father – Oliver, that is
– and I adore you and are so very proud to be your parents.
I love you, Phoenix, and you will always be my light in the
darkness.

As she'd sent it, she'd realised just how apt Harrison's
love song was. He'd spoken of a love illuminating the dark,
which for him was Ella. For Georgia, it was Phoenix. And
she suspected it would be the case for the three of them when
they slotted together in their new family unit. But there was
no place for her in that. They'd all be better off without her
in their world, and they likely wouldn't even notice she was
gone. Perhaps Harrison's song was a prophecy.

She was ashamed by her first impression of him all those
years ago because it was informed by her snobbery, judging
his class and intelligence from his rough accent. At that first
meeting, she could hardly stand to admit to herself she found
him as thrilling as Ella had. He represented a different, exciting
and impulsive world compared to her predictable property
developer of a husband with perfectly received pronunciation.

Georgia had lost track of time as she'd sat on the floor
beneath the canopy of the tree, ants crawling up her legs,
which she could no longer be bothered to brush away.
Nothing mattered to her the way it used to. She wanted
passion, love and raw emotion that wasn't an over-reaction to
her losing control. What time she had wasted trying to master
everything around her, only to spiral when things didn't go
to plan. It was a dawning of new truth and honesty, a time
to reconnect with who she was, having finally confronted the

murkiest parts of her being. She had misplaced her identity and wasn't sure if she liked who existed under her crafted layers of illusion. She was an empty shell.

As she eased herself upright, she began to trudge back down towards the port, not knowing what she'd find there. Her life had changed unequivocally forever. She'd thought laying her mother to rest would close a chapter in her life, but instead it had heralded a new beginning with its own finality brought forth by her repeated deception. She longed to scream aloud at her growing despair if it wouldn't disturb the monks from their meditation.

Walking past the mules and ponies on the front, she stopped to pet one. It grunted its appreciation and nodded its head. Its ears felt like velvet and as she caressed the animal, she knew she needed to escape herself and start anew. A compulsion overtook her; she needed to be in the water to wash away her sins like a baptism. She passed a crowded bar at the end of the harbour, catching a waft of beautiful piano music as she went, and rounded the headland.

There was nobody in sight, the sunbathers having finished their tanning for the day, and the sea was empty. She longed to feel the waves around her body. The strenuous walk had soaked her clothes with sweat and as she removed her T-shirt and stripped to her underwear, she didn't care who could see her. Climbing down the rusty metal steps, she gasped as the cool water lapped her thighs. She took another rung before flinging herself backwards into the salty sea. Her head was submerged briefly as she stroked away from the diving platform. In that moment she wanted to escape her life, the island and everyone on it.

As she floated, held in the tide's embrace, she closed her eyes. Tears trickled down her face, but still she smiled. She was terribly happy in her unhappiness, wishing for all the hurt to end. The pain and heartache, secrets and lies ... she wanted it all to be over. Water filled her ears and the only sound she could hear was the blood pumping around her body, her heartbeat gently tapping her lifeblood. She wished for complete and ultimate silence.

Chapter 36

Ella

Ella felt like she was outside of her body, unable to remove her eyes from Phoenix who was in full flow singing beside Harrison.

When she reached the end of the song, the crowd burst into rapturous applause, but Harrison didn't stop playing.

The back of his head made Ella want to run towards him, inhale the nape of his neck where two lines in his skin crossed over to make an 'X' and whisper, *'You are playing piano for our little girl.'*

But she was glued to the spot, unable to summon her own voice. They didn't know she was watching. She felt like she was in a dream, a picture she'd painted of a far-off fairyland she'd hardly deigned to imagine. It was inevitable those chords would come, the iconic opening to 'Out of the Darkness' reverberated around the bar and those gathered roared in anticipation. Someone started singing too early, interrupting the introduction and provoking laughter. But Ella's face remained still, watching the cast of players in her tragic love story. There could be no happy resolution without further disarray being inflicted on those she cherished. It was almost impossible to watch in its absurdity, yet powerfully compelling.

Phoenix began to sing again, and her voice cut through the masses, slicing through all other noise. Ella took a moment to marvel at the astonishing composition Harrison had created from their misery. It had been her musical nemesis once, but now she permitted herself to hear it in its beauty, and she found it more exquisite than ever. She didn't want it to end.

Suddenly, in the middle of the chorus, Harrison stopped playing, but the crowd and Phoenix continued to sing. His hand reached for the top of the piano, and he hung his head. Ella took a step forward, unsure what to do. Phoenix looked to him and a frown crossed her face, but she kept singing.

Ella saw Harrison tilt his head up towards Phoenix. She witnessed a look linger in the space between them, but she couldn't decipher their silent exchange. Phoenix carefully moved his hand away and held it before sitting beside him on the piano stool, all the while continuing to sing. Harrison moved to accommodate her, and Phoenix's hands began to play the chords, joining the song where her voice was. It was seamless, but something had occurred amid the verses, and Ella felt a shiver of unease travel through each vertebra of her spine. She moved to the corner of the bar and the throngs filled the space she'd vacated. She stood on tiptoe and saw Harrison staring at Phoenix. Ella reached for him with her mind and heart, folding her energy around him. He sensed it immediately and turned his head to meet her eyes. He held her gaze and she felt the reason for his reaction in her core, their unspoken ability to communicate across the years narrowed to the few metres that now separated them. Her heart swelled with more compassion than she could ever imagine as the song reached its pinnacle. She whispered aloud, 'I'm sorry.'

It was an apology to him, to her nineteen-year-old self and to their Phoenix. When the end of the song came, Harrison turned to Phoenix and put his hand on her shoulder, leaning in to say a few words. They both looked over to her before turning back to each other. She watched them converse but still she couldn't move. Harrison eventually broke away and Ella watched him approach, desperate to fold into him. But as he arrived in front of her, his fists were clenched at his sides, and she felt the reason for his angst in her heart.

'Love, you need to tell me the truth. Is she … is Phoenix…?' He was unable to finish his sentence but Ella already knew what he was asking.

'She doesn't know, Harri. Please, not here, not now. She has no idea.'

He looked back to Phoenix who was receiving compliments for her performance, though she occasionally glanced uneasily over at them. He raised his eyebrows.

'I wouldn't be so sure.'

Ella's body tensed with the urge to flee. She had a sudden and complete understanding as to why Harrison had tried to escape undetected at the train station. The idea of facing something that would tear your heart apart… Of course you'd avoid it. It was what she felt in that moment and she longed to sprint out of the door and seek refuge in a concealed alleyway. Harrison's jaw was fixed, and he gave her a look that sang betrayal without a tune. He turned and walked out of the bar without a goodbye. She didn't know if he would ever come back.

Her eyes stayed on the empty doorway, then Phoenix appeared in her view. Ella found a smile from somewhere, pushing down her anguish to blend with the sickening somersaults in her stomach.

'Phoenie, that was just … more than words. You are … you are something else.'

Phoenix smiled, hesitating briefly before she quickly recovered to say, 'And you, apparently, are my mother.'

* * *

The waiter delivered two Metaxas in heavy based crystal glasses to the table outside the bar. It wasn't the ideal place to attempt conversation as Phoenix's many new fans sought her out for photos or discussions about music.

Ella supped her Greek brandy and waited for Phoenix's attention to return. It was inevitable that the truth had risen to the surface even though it had been buried so deep, but how on earth did she know? And Harrison had worked it out too. Ella felt nauseous, wishing for Georgia to appear armed with the necessary social etiquette to navigate the irresolvable.

One very keen fan was wittering on to Phoenix about how she wanted to be a singer and requesting tips, before she asked gushingly, 'And how do you know Harrison Sutherland? He's written, like, all of my favourite songs ever!'

Phoenix turned to Ella.

'An excellent question. One I'd also like to know the answer to. Ella, remind me, how do I know Harrison Sutherland?'

Ella squirmed at Phoenix's loaded request and the Harrison fan looked incredibly confused.

'He's an old friend of the family,' Ella finally managed.

Phoenix shot Ella a look before recovering her composure and said, 'There you have it, the official line – he's an old family friend.'

The girl looked baffled but bid them goodbye and headed

off armed with a selfie and a story to tell her friends.

Ella watched warily as Phoenix downed her brandy and sucked in her breath at the scorch of the acrid liquid. She reached into her bag and produced a pack of cigarettes. Ella looked on in horror as she lit one and leant back into her chair, exhaling into the twilight.

'Are you going to tell me off, Mother dearest?' she said, indicating her cigarette. 'Bit late for that, though, isn't it?'

Ella took a deep breath. Evidently, she was being punished. She only hoped that Georgia wouldn't blame Ella for Phoenix's smoking if she didn't know already. Another secret to grapple with but not a priority for now.

'I deserve your anger, Phoenie, but, please, not your unkindness. I will tell you anything you need to know.'

She took another drag and Ella was desperate to rip it from her fingers and stub it out beneath her foot. She waited as Phoenix's eyes strayed towards the cliff above them, to the house with the two olive trees.

'Where would you begin if you were me? If your whole life had been invented and everything you thought you knew was in fact quite different. What would *your* first question be?'

Ella could feel her body shrink within the agony. It was almost as bad as handing Phoenix to Georgia as a newborn… No, nothing could surpass that brand of pain, not even Harrison abandoning her. Though all those heartaches were interconnected.

Phoenix filled her silence.

'I don't know how I didn't see it before. We're so alike, and not just in colouring. Though I'm about ten feet taller. Clearly I get that from him … my father…' She almost spat the words and her bottom lip began to quiver, yet she pressed on. 'Mum, I mean Georgia, and I have nothing in common, but why would I believe anyone else could possibly be my mother? No child decides their family are all liars or questions what they've been brought up to believe. Your mum is your mum, and your dad is your dad – there's no reason to think otherwise. And yet, as I got older, you kept your distance more and more, never available to see me, only sending random emails and occasionally popping up as a voice at the end of the phone. It made me wonder why you always avoided me. And your relationship with Mum … Georgia … whoever she is… The constant squabbling was inexplicable, far beyond sibling stuff. I started to think, and really look at you all, my so-called family. And then we came to this island, and the mist started to clear. All the clues only confirmed what I'd suspected. Mum – Georgia – having secret conversations about you and your baby on the phone with Dad … Oliver … fuck! I don't know what to call anyone anymore.' She rubbed her eyes with her fists, a ringlet singed as her cigarette brushed it. 'But what I cannot fathom is why you gave me away, why you didn't want me. How could you?'

Ella inhaled, wincing at her directness. Hearing Phoenix dismantle the lie in a minute was like being stabbed repeatedly with a thousand blades. There was only one option: to tell the truth and answer her queries with complete honesty.

'Phoenie, I—'she began, but Phoenix interrupted.

'Don't call me that. It's bullshit.'

'OK,' Ella continued carefully. 'I wasn't well at the time … because of everything that happened with him, with Harrison.'

Ella scoffed a bitter laugh.

'My father?'

Ella nodded.

'Yes. But it is as much my fault as his – more so, in fact – so don't blame him. Please hear me, I was desperate, depressed.

I was only a bit older than you are. Can you imagine being responsible enough and financially able to raise a kid right now? Actually, don't answer that because you're way more mature than I was and probably ever will be. But being a mother to you would have meant leaving my uni course. You haven't started yours yet, but if you had to give it up when it had hardly started, would you? I love my job – a job I got because of that degree – and you feel that way about music. If I chose you, I couldn't finish my course, if I chose uni, I had to give you up. There was no other way. Would you sacrifice your dreams and career for motherhood and a man...?'

'I can't answer that question in a million years with honesty or without bias. So, continue...' Phoenix said. Ella was floored by her measure.

'Also, and it pains me to say it – and it is no reflection on you – but my mental state was such that I couldn't be near the memory of him, let alone be with you, this perfect little creature we'd created. I wanted to die, I was that depressed, I couldn't shift the sadness that took hold of me when he left. I doubted who I was, and I was lost; completely broken by everything that was happening. I had an impossible choice to make that would hurt me horribly whichever decision I made. And I chose the most painful route.'

Phoenix shook her head in disbelief.

'I can't ever imagine you being like that. But God, Ella, wanting to end your life over a man is so sad. You're better than that, surely. I suppose you wanted to kill me too.'

'No!' Ella shouted. 'No! You were what stopped me. If you've never experienced the very worst depression, it's hard to explain. I'm not making excuses but I couldn't see any possible way out of it to make everyone happy. And I know it's hard to understand, but what I had with Harri

... Harrison ... was so intense and then it was gone. I'd lost myself and couldn't remember who I was without him when he disappeared. I know who I am now. Love from someone else doesn't define you. But I was so young and so desperately afraid that my life was going to end before I'd got it going, I didn't feel like I had any other option. And Georgia, she wanted a child more than anything and couldn't have one. Allowing her to adopt you was a way I could keep you near and love you from a distance and I do, I love you so much.' Ella's voice choked and she felt the years of regret and punishment strangling her, but she pushed through. 'It wasn't supposed to come out like this. I'm sure we would have all told you one day, but it was never meant to happen here on this island.' Ella finished her drink and signalled to a waiter for another. 'I'm desperately sorry you're in the middle of the mess we've all made, you didn't deserve to find out this way.' Ella's voice began to waver again. 'I never wanted to hurt you, but I've managed to hurt us all. Harrison has worked it out too.'

Phoenix sat back in her chair and breathed out heavily, smiling sadly.

'I saw it, the moment he did. It was when I was singing. He gave me this funny look and then he went blank, like he didn't know where he was. It was only a few seconds, but he stopped playing like he couldn't remember where his hands were supposed to go. We have the same eyes, don't we...?'

Ella nodded.

'It was like looking in a mirror.'

'Phoenie ... Phoenix. I'm sorry. I don't know what else I can say other than I've always loved you. But Georgia and Oliver are your parents. They've done more for you than Harrison and I ever could. We just took care of the biology. Nothing has to change as far as they're concerned.'

'But everything has changed!' Her voice was tight and high, so alien a sound when her natural tones were so husky. Probably from her secret smoking habit, Ella thought.

'I know.' Ella reached for her hand, a gesture Phoenix rejected. 'I need to speak to your … my sister about how we all handle this together. We all just want what's best for you. But try to remember, everyone loves you. You are so, so loved.'

Phoenix finished her cigarette and stubbed it repeatedly in the ashtray, snuffing it out as hard as she could.

'What about Harrison? Does he care I'm his?'

Ella sighed.

'I know he does. But he only found out yesterday that we'd had a child together. I didn't say it was you, so he's probably processing.'

'Everyone and their stupid process. I hate processing,' said Phoenix, managing a small smile.

Ella laughed in relief at the glimpse of their usual exchanges. It gave her a glimmer of hope.

'Me too.'

Phoenix looked at her and rested her chin on her hand. She shook her head slightly.

'It kind of makes things different but also … not really. You know, when I was little I sometimes wished you were my mum. I'd make up stories for my friends telling them how my "real" mum was taking pictures all around the world. You were so cool, living this amazing life, though it makes sense now, why you never hung around for too long.' She lit up another cigarette and Ella resisted the urge to chide. 'I'm sorry for you, that you went through so much. It must have been a lot to give me away.' She reached to briefly squeeze Ella's hand. 'Are there more of us, any other surprise brothers and sisters on Hydra?'

Ella shook her head, amused by Phoenix's tone. It was preferable to that of a few minutes ago.

'Just you. Your birth was rather dramatic – it was quite the first performance – and I needed surgery afterwards, which they said would make it almost impossible for me to have any more. You were my one and only chance. I fucked that up royally, didn't I?'

'Sorry I busted your body,' said Phoenix.

'Sorry I busted your life,' replied Ella as they smiled at one another. Sharing the same sense of humour had permitted them to navigate the first of no doubt many conversations on the difficult topic of their relationship.

'Do you want to come up?' asked Ella, indicating Harrison's place with her head. 'I don't know if he's there, or if he'll ever speak to me again, but...'

'What, and play happy families while you cook for us all?' Phoenix nodded at the bags of shopping filled with wilting vegetables. 'Not sure I'm quite ready for that yet.'

'I know you can't reach me because I'm an idiot without a phone, but you know where I am if you need me, no matter what time of day. I'll be somewhere in the harbour if not at your granny's old house.' Ella didn't know where she was going; the feeling of freedom that had thrilled and sustained her life deserted her in that moment and she suddenly craved a place to belong. 'I'm sorry, Phoenie. Believe me, I've never been sorrier.'

Phoenix stood and stepped towards Ella as she rose from her seat.

'I'll be fine. I just need to have a good long think. I'll speak to you later. Ella ... Mum ... Ella...' She shook her head and sighed, as her voice faltered, pinching at Ella's heart. 'I don't know who anyone is anymore.'

She was unsure whether to hug her or keep her distance, but Phoenix saved her by offering her arms and stepping into Ella's space. The two women held each other with the knowledge of who they were to each other for the very first time; as mother and daughter. An embrace had never felt so pure and painfully beautiful.

The Island

*Biology was a fact, but nurture could be just as powerful.
The bonds formed with those unconnected by flesh were
often stronger, more meaningful, a family chosen, not
forced upon us by circumstance. Blood may be thicker than
a hundred droplets of water, but the sea could suckle the life
from a thousand mortals and yet still need to feed on.
Its thirst was unquenchable.*

Chapter 37

Georgia

Georgia was uncertain how long she'd floated around for, but the sky above her had deepened in colour to a balayage of royal blue and navy. Exposed to the elements, she was almost delirious encased within the island waters. There was a faint humming, like there was a bee inside her head. It made her giggle. Perhaps she was finally unhinging for the last time. She didn't see the speedboat in the distance heading towards her.

A kind of madness had taken hold. She didn't care what happened anymore, she had lost it all. Oliver and Phoenix could merrily exist without her, she was quite sure. And so could Ella. As the gravity of the hell she'd unleashed upon their lives descended, she started to sing Harrison's song, her own fevered voice sounding thick and strange between her ears.

The waves around her seemed to increase in size, the rhythm of the sea shifting, and she enjoyed the danger of the current nudging her around. The unseen forces of Hydra's waters concealed what lurked beneath and she yielded to the tide.

She heard her name like it was being bellowed from the muffled centre of a cloud, and it removed her attention from her tuneless voice strangling Harrison's lyrics. Perhaps it was the island calling to her, or a sea demon or nymph. She giggled once more, but again and again, a deep booming voice shouted her name. Then it was replaced by the earlier buzzing, which was growing in volume.

She wasn't alone in the water.

Something suddenly grabbed her leg and she yelped. She lifted her head but the movement sent her face underwater. She tried to right herself, but the grip tugged at her shin dragging her along. She coughed and spluttered as she surfaced, kicking at whatever was now wrapped around her ankle. She couldn't work out where the noise was coming from as she tried to survey the undulating horizon. Georgia gasped as she saw a speedboat closing in on her. Rendered incapable of movement, she watched in horror as the pointed triangular nose of the boat continued its progress. It seemed to be happening in slow motion.

'Stop!' someone cried. Georgia's confusion cleared as she turned and saw Harrison in the water beside her, waving one arm above his head and pulling at her leg with the other. Georgia tried to scream but no noise came, only a mouthful of the salty sea. Her body couldn't organise itself to swim as the vessel continued at full throttle towards them.

We'll be killed, she thought, as a strange calm flooded through her, and she resigned herself to her fate. *This is my punishment for all I've done.*

'Georgia! For God's sake, move,' Harrison yelled. She was jolted into action by his plea and tried to swim sideways, his grip having released her. But she couldn't make headway as her panic began to rise and the size of the waves increased, the wind whipping at the sea like a serpent's tongue. She knew they were barely visible above the peaks and the boat was closing, Harrison still desperately trying to attract the skipper's attention.

But it persisted, cutting through the sea like a steel blade until – at what seemed like the last minute – the driver spotted them. The boat's engine dropped to a lower pitch and swerved, almost toppling over broadside, but it couldn't avoid Harrison.

He had summoned his remaining strength to shove Georgia from its path, and instead put himself in its way. He held out his hand in an attempt at protection as the boat careered towards him and Georgia shrieked in terror as the boat struck him with a thumping crunch. His roar of pain was like a lion screaming in excruciating agony as he clutched his arm. The noise bounced off the island's rocks and cliffs and returned in a wall of sound, filling Georgia's body with horror. Then his eyes rolled up into his head and he disappeared beneath the waves.

Georgia was treading water, whimpering in shock, but adrenaline suddenly surged within her and she dived downwards into the murky gloom. The darkening skies had turned the sub-marine world into a sinister shadowland.

She saw Harrison's silhouette and pulled him towards her, but he was too heavy for her to manage. She kicked and kicked as hard as she could, desperate to take a breath but she couldn't let him go. She wouldn't. The pressure behind her eyes was almost unbearable as her body demanded breath, but she was not going to be responsible for keeping Harrison and her sister apart a second time. She had orchestrated it deliberately before, but now she conjured strength for Ella's sake and for Phoenix's, calling on a power she didn't know she possessed to protect the family she had ripped apart with her lies.

A cluster of bubbles shot downwards beside her as a figure appeared, making her start. With the help of another pair of hands, they managed to haul Harrison to the surface. As they broke through the waterline, Georgia saw it was Vasílis who had aided the rescue. She gasped as the welcome air entered her body, but Harrison's eyes were still closed. They swam with him to the rocks. Thankfully, the tide had turned and was cresting them quickly to the shore.

'*Voítheia!* Help!' Vasílis shouted towards the pathway above the makeshift dive platform. There were several people who had witnessed the dangerous collision and Georgia heard a woman say in English that she knew first aid. Church bells rang, sounding the alarm, and word would spread speedily around the island. The woman tried to bring Harrison around as Georgia began to convulse from the shock and the cold, hugging her arms across herself. Her underwear had turned transparent, but she was focused only on the fact that she might be responsible for Harrison's death. Someone put a jumper around her shoulders, but her eyes didn't leave his body where it was splayed on the ground. The rock he was lying on looked like a mortuary slab.

His right arm was bent at a hideous angle and his fingers pointed in every direction. That side must have taken the brunt of the collision. What if he couldn't play the piano again? Her mind drifted back to the accident when Ella had been laid out on the harbour, the sound of the bells pricking at her memory. She'd stood stony faced then and watched helplessly, just as she was doing now. As Harrison was attended to, the burden of blame hung like a noose around her neck waiting to be tightened. Her eyes met Vasílis' and she felt the weight of fate lingering heavily in the air like a humid smog. The silence stretched; seconds seemed like

286

minutes and minutes became an age. Suddenly Harrison choked. Then his eyes flashed open and he spewed water. Hands swiftly manoeuvred him onto his side and he coughed until his lungs wheezed and he had no more water left to purge. He groaned in pain as he tried to lift his arm and his eyes started to roll again. Georgia rushed to his side, taking care not to touch his injured limb.

'Harrison! Thank God you're alive.'

He struggled to focus and blinked heavily before rasping, 'Either that, or I'm in hell because you're here...' He tried to laugh but recoiled with pain as his eyes travelled to his arm. He surveyed the distortion, and he tried to reach for it, but the English woman put her hand on his good shoulder.

'Don't,' she said. 'I think it's dislocated and broken. We'll get you to the hospital in a moment. Try to stay as still as you can.'

Harrison lay back on the ground and grimaced. Georgia breathed a sigh of relief now she knew he would live, and then the shock coursed through her, and she couldn't keep still. She managed to find her clothes and tried to dress herself, but her hands wouldn't stop shaking. Vasílis appeared beside her.

'I saw he saved you. I am sorry, Georgia, it was my fault. I did not see you in the water.'

She managed to slip on her sundress before facing him.

'Accidents happen, Vasílis. And yes, he saved me, but you also saved him. We're all in each other's debt forever.' Her teeth chattered as shock made her arms jerk around, but she still managed to locate her decorum. 'But ... but ... thank you. Are *you* OK?'

He nodded, but Georgia could see he was also suffering from exposure to the elements and the thought of what could have happened. As her mind whirred through all the versions of how the afternoon could have turned out, she realised there was little point in dwelling on what might have been or what could still happen. The most important thing was now.

The clarity was like a shaft of sunlight through a darkening thundercloud.

Harrison was alive to pursue whatever he wanted with Ella, and if Phoenix wanted to explore a relationship with her biological parents, then Georgia would have to embrace it. She felt like she'd paid her penance, though she hoped Ella didn't think this was an attempt on her part to extinguish another family member.

* * *

At the small island hospital, the on-duty doctor confirmed Harrison had indeed broken his wrist and arm, dislocated his shoulder and broken his fingers. Thankfully the breaks were clean despite his arm's mangled appearance.

Georgia bubbled with frustration that she had no way to reach Ella. She felt helpless in the crisis, unable to let her know what had happened. If Ella heard whispers around the town, she would be frantic with worry, and Georgia yearned to protect her sister from that stress.

Damn her for not having a phone.

After painfully putting everything back into their respective sockets, Harrison had a lengthy plaster cast, several splints, a sling and a sizeable supply of very strong painkillers. He had sustained no long-term damage and the doctor had said he was unconscious for only seconds, having fainted from the pain, though to Georgia it had felt much longer. Georgia had arranged a generous donation to the medical facility, which was part of a charity; it felt like the only helpful thing she could do. She was incredibly grateful that, as bad as

Harrison's injuries were, it could have been much worse. They both could have been killed.

Once he'd been discharged, Georgia walked with him up the hill to his house using the torch on her phone to light the way. He'd refused to stay in the hospital overnight despite medical advice to the contrary, and had balked at her suggestion of taking a pony home.

'I'm not done for yet, at least my legs work,' he'd managed, still wincing in pain.

As they slowly reached the final lane leading to his home, he stopped to gather his strength.

'Georgia…' he started, cradling his poorly shoulder with his other hand, his brow glistening with sweat.

'Please, let me go first, if I may,' she interrupted. 'I want to thank you for saving me and I'm sorry you got hurt in the process. It seems to have been a bit of a theme of late. All the good intentions in the world and you still get smacked in the face. Or on the arm in this instance.'

'I know about Phoenix,' he said breathlessly as they faced each other in the narrow alleyway. The lights of the port below glimmered as the breeze whistled through the streets, bringing with it truth and the hope of resolution. 'Ella told me we'd had a child that she had adopted. I s'pose I put the pieces together. Phoenix's talent, her eyes … the fact she looks just like me… It was pretty obvious once I knew.'

Georgia laughed.

'Like father, like daughter. Phoenix worked it out too. I'm quite sure she's also joined the dots and knows about you. How else could she explain her musical gifts? They don't come from me, that's for sure.' Her smile betrayed an innate sadness she found impossible to hide.

He leant against a stone wall, and grinned.

'Yeah, I heard your rendition of "Out of the Darkness" while you were floating away into the path of a speedboat. A bit pitchy.'

Georgia pretended to be horrified and found a true smile at last.

'Look, Georgia, I know we've never been the best of friends, but because of Phoenix… I do plan on being in her life. If that's what she wants, and if it's all right with you and Oliver.'

Georgia had expected him to say this at some stage.

'And what about my sister, the one you abandoned at a train station?' she asked.

'You mean the sister you tried to drown?'

'Oh sod off, Harrison. It was an idiotic, split-second decision. I was a stupid kid unable to control my emotions and apparently I haven't evolved that much since. But I'm trying to do better. I've regretted that day every second of my life and wish I could undo it. You of all people surely know what regret feels like.'

He watched her carefully and his brown eyes softened.

'Maybe you and I aren't so different after all. We've both made the worst choices. I can't say I'm delighted you ambushed my letters but we'll never know how things could have turned out and it's a waste of time to imagine what could have been. How about we try and keep the peace from now on … for all of us. I'd shake your hand but I'm slightly incapacitated.'

'Not sure how Ella will feel about that. We haven't spoken since I told her the truth about the boat incident when we were kids. And I haven't seen her since Phoenix worked it all out.'

'Well … I haven't spoken to her about Phoenix either. No time like the present. You coming? Safety in numbers …

because somehow you and I are on the same side.'

He started up the incline ahead but Georgia stayed where she was for a moment, suddenly exhausted. Her body ached like she'd run a marathon, but she forced herself onwards. As she trudged up the hill, she mentally braced for an onslaught from Ella about the letters, the accident, Phoenix, and now for having put Harrison in danger. Georgia was sure that even a saint couldn't find the necessary forgiveness for her catalogue of errors. She only hoped this was the last grave mistake she'd make.

Chapter 38
Ella

It was late, well beyond dinner time, and Ella was drumming her fingers on the countertop. The sound filled Harrison's empty house now the incessant church bell clanging had thankfully ceased. The metallic ringing had felt like it was teasing her with the continuation of island life when hers was hanging in the balance.

She'd sliced the courgettes into skinny sticks and lightly floured them ready to fry. The other vegetables were coated in oil and herbs in a roasting tin ready to bake. But she was alone. Phoenix and Harrison had left her, both walked away, and she had no way of reaching either of them. Because *she* was unreachable. This must be what it feels like to love her, she thought, and the frustration burnt. Past conversations with men who had become infatuated darted through her mind, their lack of understanding at why she refused to commit or at least stay in touch. Attachments were rejected because she wanted no binds, nothing to tether her to the spot. It was all suddenly so clear. She'd deliberately evaded love in a bid to escape the person she used to be – the one who'd wanted to give up her career for a man and then brokenheartedly gave up her child. She hadn't been running from Harrison or Phoenix, she'd been running from herself.

After the revelation at the bar, she hadn't expected Harrison to return to the house quickly, but she'd hoped he'd at least come back for supper so they could talk everything through. His house was unlocked, as was usual on Hydra, but as she'd stepped inside, she'd felt wrong being there without him. An unsettled feeling had formed in the pit of her stomach, and her energy felt off-centre.

It was strange to be standing in this kitchen again and she found herself looking for her mother, reaching back into her memories...

'Georgia, wash your hands before we eat, please, sweetheart,' Anna said.

'No! I don't want to. I haven't got mucky hands. Els Bells has; she was digging in the garden like a dirty dog. Look! Tell her off first.'

'Georgia, please, my sweet angel, off you go and wash your hands. And Ella, my little shining light, please come down from that tree,' she shouted into the garden. 'Time to eat!'

Ella was at the top of the olive tree and could see her mother through the window. Even from there Georgia's shrieks were unavoidable. She watched the mules clop their way towards their stables in a line, tethered to one another. It was her favourite evening ritual on the island, watching as the animals obediently hoofed their way towards their rest. Usually, she and Georgia would imitate the funny noises the handlers made. But not that evening, teenage Georgia was in one of her moods.

Ella retrieved the camera hanging around her neck. It had been her tenth birthday present and she hadn't put it down since opening it. She took a photograph. The foreground was olive leaves, and the background was the bustle of the *harbour, diminished and blurred like it had had no effect on nature. She suddenly became aware of the bough vibrating and she looked down to see Georgia angrily shaking the trunk. Below, her sister was littered with displaced leaves and pollen, showered in a potpourri of her own making, and Ella giggled. Georgia's flushed face pinched, incensed by the sound of Ella's laughter, and so she reluctantly climbed downwards to prevent her older sister throwing an angry fit.*

Georgia had been gently scolded by their mother and Ella had watched on as Anna had calmed Georgia's rage with soothing, loving tones, explaining that shaking the tree could have put her sister in danger.

Mum had been such a tolerant voice of reason in their lives. Armed with practical advice, able to talk Georgia out of her tantrums and happy to permit Ella to be who she was – no constraints or rules, simply free. Perhaps it would have been better for Ella to have had a stricter upbringing. She might have formed a better sense of judgement. But all of those choices she'd made had led her back to her birthplace, to this house on Hydra.

She heard the front door open, and she rushed into the hallway but stopped still as she found Georgia there, her hair frizzy and unkempt. She was even more shocked to see Harrison by Georgia's side, his arm in a sling. His skin looked shiny and grey.

'Harri, what on earth happened?' Ella shrieked. 'Georgia?'

Georgia's eyes were tracing the walls and furnishings and Ella realised she hadn't been there since before their mother had died. But her focus pressingly moved back to Harrison. How had he come to be injured? Ella put her fingertips lightly onto his plaster cast and looked at him, questioning him with her eyes.

'Bit of a run-in with a boat. I'm all right, but there won't be any piano for a bit.'

Ella rounded on Georgia for an explanation, wondering how she was involved, but saw her eyes were filled with tears. She paused her queries and stepped over to her sister.

'Hey. Are you OK?'

Georgia sniffled a little.

'Just a bit overwhelmed being in the house again. It's as though she's going to walk through the door any moment, it feels … like she's still here.' A tear escaped from her blue eyes. 'Sorry.' She wiped her eyes, trying to gather herself to continue. 'It's been another drama-filled Hydra day.' She nodded at Harrison. 'He saved my life. Which you probably don't think I deserve.' She paused again to wipe away more tears that had streaked down her cheeks.

Ella took her hand as she continued.

'And now Phoenix knows everything. I told her what she already knew deep down … about you and Harrison being her parents. I haven't spoken to Oliver. It's the last thing I want to do. I'm in a bit of a state, really. I'm sorry, Ella, believe me, I am. About everything.'

Ella pulled Georgia into her arms to stop her gabbling, and to give herself a moment to digest that she could have lost both Georgia and Harrison today. She held her sister tightly.

'We'll sort it out. Together. We're family.'

Harrison's voice broke them apart.

'You know, Georgia actually saved *my* life. She pulled me out of the sea,' he said.

Ella's eyes widened as she stepped out of Georgia's arms.

'What? Would someone please fill me in?' She looked at the state of them both and changed tack. 'Though maybe not now, you both look terrible. Wine…? Food…? I've prepped dinner.'

Harrison smiled, then his deep belly laugh filled the space with warmth.

'Trying to feed us in a crisis, El? It's like you've lived here all your life. Georgia, will you stay?'

'Would you mind if I step out and call Phoenix to let her know where I am? In case she's worried about what she might have heard.'

He nodded and indicated the study just off the lounge. Georgia closed the door behind her as Ella turned to Harrison.

'Harri, what on earth happened? I could have lost you, again.' She gently cupped his cheek. She wanted to be closer. The idea of losing him after only having just found each other again was too much to contemplate. 'I don't want to be without you, I can't be. I love you too much to let go. Please find a way to forgive not just me, but us – the old you and me. We didn't know what we were doing or what would happen all these years later. How could we?'

He clasped her hand to his cheek and closed his eyes.

'Everything can change with a roll of the dice, love. We've learnt that in the best and worst way and I'm sure there's more left to learn. I love you too, but—'

'Why is there always a but? Please don't. Why won't you let me love you, Harri?' She didn't mean to raise her voice but couldn't help it.

He went to speak, but Georgia awkwardly re-entered the living room, clearing her throat to warn them.

'Um … so sorry to interrupt… Phoenix is in the town but she won't say where. I might try to find her.'

'She'll turn up. Why don't you go and have a lie-down? You look shattered,' said Ella.

Georgia looked uneasily at Harrison.

'I don't want to intrude.'

'You're not,' he said warmly. 'You're welcome to stay. You know where the rooms are.'

Georgia smiled weakly, nodding acceptance of his offer and looking relieved for a place to lay her head. She clomped wearily up the stairs.

In the kitchen Ella poured herself a glass of red wine after settling Harrison on the sofa. She made a small plate of bread and cheese and some water so he could take another painkiller. She knew he was hurting, but true to form, he didn't give voice to his pain. She put his glass, the food and her drink on the coffee table and sat beside him, taking care not to jog his arm as she crossed her legs to face him.

'You were saying before...? But what?'

He stared ahead, not meeting her eyes and shook his head.

'I don't know, love. I can't ask you to give up your life to be with me. I couldn't let you do it before and I'd never ask you to do that now. It would be unfair. There's nothing on this island for you. Understand that I love you and want us to be together, more than anything, but I can't inflict my world on you.'

'What do you mean by your "world"? Hydra? It was mine before it was yours; I was born here,' she said, her anger flickering. She didn't comprehend why, after a near-death experience, he wasn't throwing caution to the wind and grasping the second or even third chance they'd been given.

He sighed, fixing her with the eyes she adored.

'We haven't unpicked our past yet and now we have a child together. One who is a stranger to me. She is beautiful, magnificent ... and...' His voice cracked, which halted his sentence.

'And what? What could possibly be so bad that you won't allow me in? Why do you keep doing this, Harri?'

He leant forward and with difficulty tried to tear off a piece of bread. Ella tried to assist him.

'I can do it,' he growled. 'Leave it.'

'I'm only trying to help. I don't understand why you're being like this.'

Her eyes pricked with tears as he sighed again before raising his head. Their gazes linked once more and love surged forward. She reached for his leg and silently pleaded with him to open up, to show her he had changed, that he could share his true self and his honest thoughts, not like before. His eyes washed with tears.

'I can't do this, El, I'm not well.'

'Then rest, Harri. We can talk in the morning.

'No, not the accident.' He reached for her face and ran his thumb across her bottom lip. 'One day I will look at you and I won't know who you are.'

Ella frowned, trying to work out what he meant without any grasp of what he was saying. He leant forward and brushed his lips against hers, sucking in his breath as he did so. The movement must have hurt his shoulder. A tear tracked down his cheek and she wiped it away with her fingertips, watching the droplet transfer to her skin. She wanted to cradle his teardrop, cherish every part of him he was willing to give her.

'It's inevitable, love. I will sit at a piano, and I won't know how to play. Your face won't mean anything, and I'll need to be reminded of who you are every single day. Phoenix won't even be a memory because I have none of her to lean on. That's how it works, the recent memories go first as the present starts to disappear. I will become someone you'll resent. If I can't play the piano or look at you each morning with the love I have for you in my heart, there is nothing. I will be pointless. Just an empty shell with nobody left inside to find. I will let you down and be the worst kind of stranger. I can't put you through that. Or Phoenix.'

Ella's mind raced through their time together on the island. His fumbling hands unable to tie a knot, the vacant stares, forgetting chords in his own song, the question about her mother's whereabouts after telling him she was dead, not remembering her birthday... She closed her eyes as she felt her heart crack, reopening wounds that were barely beginning to heal.

'Harri,' she whispered. She folded her arms around him, and he rested his head on her chest while she stroked and kissed his hair. They stayed like that for some time, wrapping their bodies together as she digested what she'd heard and arrived at the devastating realisation of his illness without the official term being given life. She heard his breathing deepen and slow and she held him as he slept. Ella made her decision then, listening to her heart and her own voice for the first time since they'd parted. She knew she couldn't save or rescue him, as she'd never been able to, but she could ensure their love was the last he would know. They had wasted too much time separately and now, more than ever, they needed to make up for the years they'd squandered. When they were first together she used to whisper to him not to leave her, but that night, she whispered as he dozed, 'I won't ever leave you, my sweet Harri. My love. I'm here.'

* * *

Harrison was woken by a throbbing pain in his arm and shoulder and Ella insisted on putting him to bed with more medication. She sat beside him, helping him to settle.

'You don't have to do this, love. I can manage.'

'I want to care for you, I...' She burst into tears, suddenly unable to control the flow of emotion and grief that was racing through her bloodstream, her expression contorted from the agony of their circumstance.

'See? That's the face I want to avoid. It's already hurting you and it will only get worse. Why would I do that to someone I love more than I want to live?'

Ella wiped her face on the bedsheets.

'Don't say that, Harri. Just tell me what you know. How long has it been going on? What's the diagnosis? I need to understand.'

'So you can make a decision?' he asked.

'No! So I know what I'm dealing with. What *we're* dealing with. There isn't anything in the world that can stop me loving you. I only hoped you'd learnt that by now.'

He smiled and adjusted himself on the pillows that propped him up as he took a sobering breath.

'Four years ago, I noticed I was forgetting bits of music. Pieces I knew better than my own face, that I'd played since I was small. And I felt anxious all the time. I didn't want to go out because I became afraid that I'd forget something important and embarrass myself. It's a small island and a lot of people know me here. And I was scared – what if I offended someone because I didn't recognise them? So, I became a bit of a hermit, I s'pose. It hit home a bit more when I was here on my own. I was playing the extra verse I wrote for you in "Out of the Darkness" one day – and believe me, I know that song inside out – but I couldn't remember the chorus. A chorus that almost everyone in the world knows was gone from my head. I sat staring at the keys and nothing came. I stayed there until the sun set, and it still didn't arrive. I knew I had to speak to someone, something wasn't right. I was so scared, but

300

not knowing was the worst part. My dad had it. I'd already behaved like him, treating you the way I did, so it would be a fitting punishment for me to get it too. Anyway, I saw this consultant in Athens, and he diagnosed me with what they call "young early onset". I have to see him every two weeks to get an IV for a drug that delays memory loss. It's unusual but not unheard of for people under sixty-five to get...' He took a breath before continuing. '...To get dementia.'

He'd said the word, giving it energy, letting it coast upon the island air. It was real.

Ella chewed the insides of her cheeks to prevent any more tears. It was horrifying and deeply unjust that someone so creative and talented would slowly lose his gift. Fade into nothingness, retreating into darkness when he had so much to give not just to her, but to the world.

They sat in silence and stared at each other. She'd never felt closer to him or experienced a more powerful feeling of love, aside from looking at Phoenix as a newborn. It seemed her destiny was to have all she loved taken away from her. Hydra appeared to have become an emblem for all she had lost and yet still would lose.

'You can leave. I wouldn't blame you, love,' he said. 'You don't owe me anything.'

'I am going nowhere,' she said stoically. 'I choose you today, tomorrow and every single day. Even when you look at me and have no idea who I am, I will still choose you. And you get to learn who I am all over again, you lucky thing. It'll be like our first time every day, our own adventure.'

A smile tried to creep across his face but failed.

'You know it will be nothing like that, El.'

'I don't care. I have you now. I do, don't I?'

He managed a small laugh.

301

'For what it's worth,' he said, looking down at his immobile arm and shoulder.

'Oh, I don't know. Most of you still works,' she joked, then her voice became serious. 'I don't want to miss a moment of you, of us, Harri.' He made her stomach somersault as his eyes twinkled with their inimitable mischief.

She would cling on to the way he looked at her that night forever. Their conclusion was written when they had barely re-begun. Because for that day, and as many more as they were granted, she would love him as much and as hard as it was possible to love another. It had already been foretold; their whole love affair was predetermined, unable to exist without excruciating pain to make it feel worthwhile. Love and pain, life and death ... they were all interlinked for Ella and Harrison.

Their twin flame was burning bright again, and she would keep that fire alight for as long as she had Harrison in her heart.

Chapter 39

Ella

With her sister and Harrison both asleep, Ella crept downstairs, careful not to disturb them. It was an odd notion to know Georgia was sleeping in what was her old bedroom and equally strange for Ella to be with Harrison in what had been her mother's room, where they'd slept the last time they came to the island and unknowingly created Phoenix. Though Harrison had redecorated throughout and the furniture was new, he'd left what had been Ella's original bedroom untouched by paint.

Ella couldn't help but smile at her strange, dysfunctional family. Somehow, despite all the lies, deceit and terrible behaviour, she loved Georgia and resolved to find forgiveness to forge onwards with her sibling. It's what her sister needed from her, and Ella was past hiding her feelings by burying them away. She would always be grateful to her for rescuing Harrison and to him for saving her too. How ironic. Georgia had once done her best to destroy their relationship, but now, through the intervention of fate, she'd facilitated its survival.

And Georgia had finally told Phoenix about where she came from after all these years. It was as surprising as it was shocking. But time was precious, and she wasn't willing to let a moment pass without letting her loved ones know what they meant to her. The era of pretending was over.

Ella sat in the garden nursing the red wine she hadn't managed to drink earlier. She heard the church bells chime their last for the night. Her eyes drifted to the wooden boat. The piles of earth and herbs she had dug up had been tidied and replaced with what looked like fresh plants. She allowed the evening version of Hydra to wash through her as spices drifted on the wind and the remnants of supper smells in the air pulled at her appetite. She hadn't eaten, nor had the others; the urge to fuel their bodies had deserted them all.

As the cicadas replaced the sound of the bells, she asked her mother for guidance; to furnish her with enough strength for the future. And that, she hoped, included Phoenix. She hadn't surfaced yet, but Ella knew instinctively she would. Hydra had given them all another possibility of love. How many people were given such grace? She prayed to the island that they would be granted many years, but however much time they had, she would fill it with memories while they could still be held.

She heard footsteps treading the steps to the house from the side-gate and turned in the direction of the sound.

'Hello?' she asked the darkness.

'It's me,' came Phoenix's husky voice. She rounded the corner of the house and stepped onto the patio.

'Hey,' said Ella warily, unsure what mood she would be in after their earlier conversation. Ella had no further desire for consternation given what she'd learnt about Harrison that evening.

'Hey yourself. What on earth has been going on? I heard in the village what happened.'

Gossip here spread faster than a wildfire.

'Well, everyone's fine, thankfully. Georgia is asleep upstairs. So is Harrison. Tell me what you've heard, because I know very little.'

'Here? Mum and … I mean Georgia and Dad … I mean Harrison,' she said, sitting with an exasperated sigh. 'I'm not going to get the hang of this, am I? Thanks for being the most complicated people ever!'

Ella smiled at her assessment.

'Nothing to get the hang of, Phoenie. Just a bunch of misfits who are your family. We all belong to each other. Does it matter how?'

Phoenix reached for Ella's glass and took a sip.

'I guess not.' She sat back in her chair. 'So, let me get this straight. My auntie is really my mum and the woman I *thought* was my mother is in actual fact my auntie who is asleep upstairs where my father, a famous Grammy award-winning songwriter, is also snoozing. All together in my dead grandmother's house. How am I doing so far…?'

They both laughed, although a palpable sadness lurked beneath the surface, despite Phoenix's humour.

'Pretty accurate, I'd say. We've really messed it all up, haven't we, Phoenie? The rest of us, not you.'

Phoenix raised her eyebrows and crossed her legs, scraping her long hair into a ponytail with an elastic from her wrist.

'Yes and no. Yes, because you all lied to me and thought me too stupid to work it out, and no, because I've got two lots of parents who I am assured all rather love me.'

Ella's heart sprang awake.

'Yes, you do have that. So much love, more than you may need or ask for, but it's yours if you want it.' She shouldn't speak for Harrison but she knew that his capacity for love when he permitted it was immense and she felt in her bones

305

that he loved Phoenix already, even though they'd only met briefly. Sharing music together would have sped up that bond and would continue to do so for as long as he could play. The clock that would always be ticking for them was something else Phoenix needed to know, but it wasn't her news to tell. Harrison would have to be prepared to share it. Phoenix broke through her thoughts, lighting up a cigarette.

'Well, it is timely to suddenly acquire double parents. It means a lot more presents for one thing. And with my eighteenth coming up…' she joked. 'But I have one last question, for now,' said Phoenix.

'If it's "should I give up smoking?", then the answer is yes!' Ella said.

'It wasn't actually, although it's along the same lines,' Phoenix replied. 'It was: Which mother do I listen to when I'm being told off?'

She smirked and then Ella reached forward and snatched the cigarette from her hand.

'Whichever one believes they're right at the time,' Ella said, grinning, stubbing it out underfoot.

* * *

Ella showed Phoenix to what was her old bedroom. A flood of memories rushed to greet her as she opened the door. The pale lilac walls remained the same, along with the original wooden floor, scraped and dented with age.

Showing Phoenix into the room was like stepping into a time capsule.

'I want to see if something is still here…' Ella said, moving the bed away from the wall to reveal a scrap of wallpaper that was lifted at the corner. She'd peeled it away when she was twelve years old to scribble on the wall with a pen after a particularly turbulent exchange with Georgia.

The bed clunked and scraped the floor as it moved.

'Shhh! You'll wake everyone,' Phoenix said.

Ella lay face down across the bed and raised the edge of wallpaper, finding her scrawl.

I hate my sister and I hate Hydra! had been crossed out and replaced by *Hydra = love. Georgia is my best friend, but I won't ever tell her!*

'See? Mad indecision and secrets have always lived here,' Ella said, turning to Phoenix who peered over her shoulder. 'I used to change my mind like the wind about Hydra and Georgia. This island has a special kind of magic and you either loathe it or love it. It's not the kind of place you can be indifferent about.'

Phoenix sat on the bed beside her.

'And how do you feel about it now?' she asked tentatively.

Ella sat upright and looked to her hands as her mind travelled next door to Harrison.

'Well, it's where you were made and it's where I was born, so we both have that connection ... and it's given me love ... you... It's given me a lot to think about...'

Phoenix laughed. 'You can say that again!'

Ella smiled at Phoenix and reached to push a stray curl behind her ear.

'It never leaves you; it stays forever.'

Phoenix looked at the floor.

'I'm glad I know. About everything. And I hope we can spend more time together now it's all out in the open. When I didn't see you for ages, I was so sad. Being with you is like sitting in the sun and then you'd leave and I'd suddenly be in the shade, cold and uncomfortable, and all I could think about was being warm again.'

Ella's chest tightened. Phoenix had such a way with words, just like Harrison.

'I'm sorrier than you will ever understand but my giving you up gave you an incredible childhood. I could never have done that for you. Georgia provided everything I was unable to. Emotionally and materially. You were everything to her and always will be. I'd forgotten at the time how to love, and even though I loved you so much, I was spent. It wouldn't have ended well.'

Phoenix nodded in understanding.

'I know. I get sad and dark too sometimes, lost in my own thoughts. But I'm grateful to Mum and Dad, they did give me everything. I can't imagine having a baby at my age, having to give up my plans. And I know it's not your fault, you were sick, and coming to terms with it all. I'm only sad we missed out on so much.'

Phoenix suddenly looked small and child-like. Ella felt the weight of her choices bearing down, but she knew it had all been for the best, despite the inelegant web of untruths they'd all spun.

'Well, that's the thing with time. Sometimes – though very rarely – we get to make up for the bit we've lost. I don't know how any of this will work, Phoenie. But... I'm going to stay here with Harrison. He needs me and I need him. So, now you'll know where I am at all times.'

Phoenix looked confused.

'Tell me you aren't giving up work for love. You nearly did it for him once, and now you're going to again...?'

Ella smiled.

'No, my little feminist, I'm not abandoning work completely, but this is where I belong. I feel it in my bones. I was destined to come back here, and I don't want to be without him. He is the only man I've ever loved, and I get to do it all over again. Our future isn't as long this time, but while we have one, I'd be crazy to let it go. I can't. We're meant to be together. The only thing I'm giving up is geography and that means nothing because I've never settled anywhere. This is where I belong, Phoenie.'

'If you're happy, then I'm happy. Please promise me the second you're not, you'll tell me. You've had so much sadness and you've been alone for so long; you deserve only lovely things.'

Ella shook her head at Phoenix's wisdom and maturity. She was a surprise each day and put the supposed real adults in her life to shame.

'That's not your burden to carry, sweetheart. And this island is as much your home as it is mine. You can come as often as you like.'

'I'd love that. And I can get to know you and Harrison, together … maybe I'll write a song about it.'

'Please! Nobody else write another bloody song about my woes, I beg you!'

Phoenix threw her head back and muffled her laughter with her hand.

'It's more romantic than tragic, if you think about it.'

Ella tried to smile but couldn't, because it *was* tragic. Instead, she pulled Phoenix into her arms as her mind travelled to Harrison's diagnosis. Their romance would have another heartbreaking ending and there was nothing anyone could do to halt the passage of time and what it would inevitably bring. There, on Hydra, where she'd said hello to love again, she would eventually say goodbye to it forever.

Chapter 40

Georgia

Friday

Georgia opened her bleary eyes, confused by the different ceiling before her body fused with her mind. She was in Mum's old house. She turned over and burrowed beneath the sheet, a tear pooling on the pillow. She missed her mother, and longed to hear her tuneless humming from downstairs before shouting, '*Breakfast, girls!*'

Then she and Ella would race downstairs to see who could get there first. Georgia always won, but she suspected Ella let her.

She'd slept heavily; every muscle in her body hurt. Yesterday had been utterly horrifying and she dreaded to think what might have happened to her if Harrison hadn't intervened. Phoenix would have been motherless ... although she had Ella now. Perhaps Oliver would have been relieved. She still hadn't spoken to him and had well and truly defied her therapist's instructions of daily phone conversations. It might be able to wait until they got home, though she didn't feel like putting anything off that could be done now. If he wanted to give up on them when he learnt the truth of what she'd hidden, then it was best she knew sooner rather than later. She reached into her bag for her phone and saw three missed calls from him, but more surprisingly, she saw that it was after nine. She'd never been one to languish in bed before.

*   *   *

As she stepped out of the shower, the sound of Phoenix's singing voice floated upstairs, wrapping around her. She was playing the song she'd composed on the island. How she came to be at the house, Georgia didn't know, but suddenly felt nervous about bearing witness to Ella and Harrison together with Phoenix now they all knew their relationship to one another. Despite her automatic insecurity and feeling of rejection, she knew they had every right to know the truth. They'd been kept separate for too long, partly at her own doing. She fixed a brave smile and went downstairs.

She waited until Phoenix finished singing before she burst into applause, making every head turn in her direction.

'It's even better the second time around, Phoenix! Morning, everyone,' said Georgia, forcing cheer as she looked at Harrison who was sitting in a chair beside the piano. He looked shattered. *He must be in so much pain,* she thought as the pang of guilt tugged at her. 'How does your shoulder feel?'

'Like I've been hit by a boat.' He smiled, and Georgia was relieved he didn't appear to blame her. Not for that at least. 'Help yourself to coffee or tea, whatever you need. I'm not a very good host.' He gestured to his sling.

'I'll get it,' said Phoenix, standing from the piano stool. 'It sounds like you both had a lucky escape yesterday. I don't know what I'd do without you, Mum.' She threw her arms around Georgia and the embrace sent waves of love darting around her body. She still called her 'Mum'. She let Phoenix take her to the kitchen where there was a pot of coffee on the go.

'I'm so proud of you, Phoenix, not just for your obvious talent, which you now know comes from Harrison, but also for the way you seem to be dealing with all of this.'

Phoenix smiled, decanting hot drinks for them both.

'Well, I had a pretty amazing role model bringing me up. You're still my mum, nothing's changed, although it's a lot to get my head around. I got your text.'

Georgia held her breath.

'Imagine if that was the last thing I had from you, if you'd been killed yesterday. It would have been the biggest comfort to know how much you loved me. So, we need to make each other feel like that all the time from now on. All of us.' She handed Georgia a cup of black coffee.

She couldn't speak or reply to Phoenix, she felt too emotional to trust her voice. She managed a nod and a small smile.

'I hope it's OK with you, but I'm going to hang out here with Harrison and do some writing. He has some ideas about my song. You don't mind, do you?'

'Not at all,' said Georgia, slightly too quickly, which Phoenix caught.

She raised her eyebrows.

'Honestly, Phoenix, I'll be fine. We've all got lots to navigate but it's for the best this way.'

'Have you spoken to Dad?' she asked.

Georgia took a sip of scalding coffee and shook her head, ashamed to still be hiding something, even if it was only a short delay before the whole truth was revealed to her husband.

'I'd like to talk to him with you; both of us should do it

together,' said Phoenix seriously. 'When we get home, though. I'm not sure it's a phone call conversation. I've chatted to him on and off, but didn't get into specifics. He asked about you… but I didn't say much really.'

Georgia smiled, relieved to have an ally in their strange new world. She kissed Phoenix's cheek.

'Who on earth gave you such wisdom?'

Phoenix looked at her with her beautiful dark eyes.

'You did. You taught me better than anyone could have. I love you and don't you ever think that you can be replaced. You can't and you won't be.'

* * *

After breakfast, Ella and Georgia went to meet Vasílis at Zina's house. It was time they needed together as much as Phoenix wanted to spend a few hours with Harrison. There was still tension between them, but it had receded to mere discomfort rather than the unbearable strain they'd existed within for as long as Georgia could remember.

'How are you doing this morning?' Ella asked. 'Phoenix seems good, but are you?'

They meandered at a gentle pace, taking the track along the cliffs before they dropped down to the pharmacy to collect a prescription for Harrison.

'Yes, remarkably, I am. It'll take a while, but I have faith we can be a proper family, no matter how tricky we've made it for ourselves.'

Ella laughed.

'Show me one family that isn't complicated. Everyone has their skeletons and secrets, ours just all came out at once. We don't do anything by halves!'

'Apparently not!' replied Georgia. 'I'm sorry for my

massive meltdown about the thing when we were kids. I was a bit tipsy, and I just couldn't hold it in anymore.'

'A bit!? Georgia, you were wrecked. Look, I've had a bit of time to think about it and if I thought you actually wanted to kill me, I wouldn't be standing here. Given how perfectly you like everything to go, if you'd really meant it, you'd have made sure I was done for. It's not my favourite feeling knowing you hated me that much, but it wasn't actually the worst thing you did. You knew how I felt about Harri and you deliberately kept us apart. Rather like the Elgin Marbles being separated from their rightful home in the Parthenon, it's wrong and inexplicable. But not even you, my determined sister, could put permanent brakes on me and him. It's weirdly worked out the way it was supposed to, as much as it has hurt us all to get to this point. Let's not mention it again. We don't seem to do very well with boats, our lot. And there's no escaping them here, so we all just need to be more careful.'

Ella linked arms with Georgia as they walked in step along the cobbled side alleys, into the shadows and out again into the blazing sun. Georgia embraced the feeling of the Greek sunshine on her pallid skin.

'Tell me again why we're going to see Zina? I ran into her with Vasílis by Harrison's place. They had a load of herbs like the ones in Mum's boat.' Georgia suddenly found it difficult to swallow. 'Is it still there? I haven't looked. I couldn't face it.'

Ella frowned.

'Yes, the boat of doom is still there, but I ripped out the herbs the other night. But I think Harri has replanted them. When did you see Zina?'

'On your birthday. Happy belated birthday by the way, for what it's worth.'

'Funnily enough, I didn't feel much like celebrating this

314

year.' Ella paused and considered her strange connection with the old woman they were visiting. 'Zina is a bit random. Good vibes though, and definitely one of a kind.'

'Why do you want to see her again?' Georgia asked. 'Of all the things going on, surely this isn't high up the list.'

'She gave me this and it struck a bit of a chord.' She handed Georgia the scrunched-up note and translated it. 'It's like I was meant to come back to the island, not just for Mum, but for me. I feel like I *do* belong here, but I can't explain it. Especially when it was the last place I ever wanted to set foot again. Something's changed.'

They neared Zina's dark brown door.

'No wonder you're intrigued. She sounds as much of a hippie as you are. Kindred spirits perhaps.'

'Open mind, Georgia, open mind,' said Ella.

They pressed their backs to the wall as a string of ponies clopped past, laden with crates of vegetables. The wrangler leading their chain made the familiar noises they remembered from childhood, communicating with his beasts. He drummed his lips together so they vibrated, followed by an '*ich, ich*'. The animals understood and fell into single file as the pathway narrowed, more orderly than before. Both sisters instinctively looked at each other and repeated the noises, making each other giggle just like they used to. It was a small glimpse of the place Georgia hoped they might be able to return to when their healing journey was complete.

Ella raised her fist to knock and the mahogany door opened a moment later. Vasílis stood in the doorway.

'*Kaliméra*, good morning, Georgia and Ella. *Kaló mína*! It is what we say for the first of the month. Please come in.'

He walked back into the house as if he lived there and the sisters exchanged a puzzled look. They followed him through the hallway, the shrine on the mantel glittering with candles beside a photograph of a man. The pungent scent of incense filled the small corridor, along with the remnants of burnt sage. *This was a witches' house indeed*, Georgia thought, then something pricked at her memory, but she could neither place nor find it.

In the kitchen, Georgia looked around at the basic set-up as the former interior designer in her stirred, longing to gut-renovate it, opening the space into the adjoining room. She'd recommend painting the dark cabinetry in a lighter oatmeal shade and would gladly re-arrange the mis-matched china into a more ordered display. But she wasn't here as a decorating consultant. She wasn't sure why she was here at all.

Zina was sitting at the kitchen table, clutching her hands. Her hooded eyes lifted to greet them, and she smiled. A photograph of a woman was propped up against the pepper grinder.

'*Kaliméra, kaliméra*,' she said, then she spoke so rapidly Georgia was clueless as to what she'd said, given that her Greek language understanding expired at 'good morning'.

Ella moved to the woman and clasped her hands in hers and greeted her in much better Greek than Georgia had ever bothered to learn. But her sister was a frequent traveller and well versed in having to adapt to the customs and languages of a foreign place. Whereas Georgia only hopped from one luxury resort to another, something she'd like to rectify. Ella's love for authenticity had sparked her imagination. Ella fished out the note from her bag and put it on the table in front of Zina.

'What did Zina say, Vasílis? I didn't understand a word...' asked Georgia.

Ella joined her in looking to their voluntary translator for clarity. He stuffed his hands in his pockets and shuffled a little as Zina said, '*Nai, nai, Vasílis*' – which Georgia knew was 'yes, yes' – encouraging him.

They all looked towards him and waited. He took a deep breath and said, 'She says she is sorry she did not get to wish her granddaughter *chrónia polá*. Happy Birthday.'

'Oh, that's such a shame,' said Georgia. 'Does she live on the island?'

Vasílis translated and the woman roared with laughter.

'*Óchi, allá éheis epistrépsi, to nisì se éfere spìti. Eìse esì, agápi mou.*'

She pointed her gnarled fingers towards Ella as Vasílis repeated what she'd said in English.

'She says "You have returned; the island brought you home. It is you, my love."' Vasílis looked to the sisters' confused expression before speaking again.

'Her granddaughter … she is talking about you, Ella.'

Chapter 41

Ella

'But … I…' Ella couldn't find the words to respond as she sank into the chair beside Zina. Her knees felt weak. 'How am I…? I really don't understand.'

Georgia and Ella asked Vasílis for a further explanation. He also took a chair at the kitchen table and Georgia followed suit. Ella's gaze drifted to the photograph. She recognised the woman's picture from the shrine in the hallway she'd seen last week when she accompanied Zina home. Now, it was the kitchen table centrepiece.

'There is a complex tale to tell, and I only know some of it, so you must be patient while I translate. Zina's words are very important for me to be able to tell you the full story.' The old woman nodded, somehow understanding what he was saying.

'But how do you know about it?' asked Georgia.

'It was a great family secret. And I used to know her,' he replied, indicating the woman in the picture before hanging his head.

'Well, we all know about family secrets,' Georgia said wryly, looking at her sister.

'*Used* to know her?' asked Ella, ignoring her sister as her eyes flicked over the photograph again.

'Yes,' he said. 'Used to.'

Zina rose from her chair and fetched a pot of coffee then a plate of biscuits. She slowly returned to the countertop to collect cups. It was painstaking to watch her move, and Ella tried to fill in the considerable number of blanks within the silence in her head but was at a loss as to what she'd meant.

The island has brought you home.

Again, the sentiment from the note had been repeated. There was a creeping sensation in Ella's gut she didn't want to second guess.

Vasílis asked the old woman to explain and start at the beginning. She picked up the photograph of the woman and kissed it, then propped it back up on the table again. Vasílis would interpret her words as she went along. Ella and Georgia were transfixed, looking to Zina and then to Vasílis for translation. It was like being a spectator in a tennis match of words.

'Many years ago, *my* daughter in the picture here, came to Hydra from the mainland. She was in trouble, in the old-fashioned sense if you understand. Our family, our culture is very traditional. You young people would not know what this is like. But back then, in those days, and sometimes even now, to have a child born out of wedlock is seen as shameful. It was not an option to keep this child in our family, as much as it pained us all.' Zina took a slug of coffee then broke a biscuit in two. The scent of vanilla danced around the kitchen on the gentle island breeze. She took a deep breath, and continued, Vasílis translating every word.

'So, she came home to the island to be with me where nobody would know of her condition. She was confined to the house, permitted only to walk in our garden, I couldn't allow anyone to suspect. It was a very hot summer and June

319

was intolerable; fires raged on the mainland but didn't reach us here, thankfully. One day, the front door was open to let in what air there was, and she stepped outside, unbeknown to me, to go for a walk. When I think of it, I wish she had stayed on Hydra in the first place instead of leaving for Athens for her studies. The island would have protected her from the consequences of bad choices, but she left, so determined to commit to her education, she let nothing stop her. This is what happens when you ignore the voices on the wind who wish to guide you.' She paused again and offered the plate laden with biscuits to her guests, her hand shaking from its weight. Georgia and Ella both politely took one and put it beside their coffee cups, waiting for Zina to continue.

'She was almost at her time and should not have left the house, but she did. Again, another questionable choice, but it turned into a blessing. She began to have her contractions in one of the streets not far from here. They had come on so quickly. A woman found her pressed against a wall heaving and panting, dripping with sweat. She was brought back to this house moments from giving birth. That woman who came to our rescue was your mother, Anna.' She briefly paused to let Vasílis catch up and nodded at Georgia. 'My daughter brought her baby into the world in this very kitchen with the help of your mother's magical hands.'

Zina stood and walked to the garden door and stepped into the sunshine. She continued to speak as if only to the elements, but Vasílis heard every word and translated for her captive audience.

'As she gave birth, a beam of sunlight shone through these doors. It was the island marking its own, to say that wherever the child would go in the world, she would always come home to step into Hydra's light, where she belonged.'

Zina turned back to the room and shuffled slowly back to her seat. The prolonged wait stretched for what seemed like a day. Ella knew Georgia was bursting with as many questions as she was. But something told her to allow Zina to conclude in her own time.

'The baby would have brought shame on my family so I tried not to love her ahead of the fact. But she was so peaceful, so perfect. I have never experienced such feeling for a tiny soul before, but our destiny was already selected.'

Georgia suddenly began to weep, and Ella shot her a look to be quiet. She didn't understand why Georgia was crying. What had she gleaned from the tale that Ella hadn't, apart from emotion at their mother helping the poor woman? Her midwifery experience had come in handy, but Ella was yet to understand the point of the tale.

'Please, Vasílis, tell her to carry on. What happened next?' Ella said in urgency, longing to have an ending to this cryptic story.

'We could not keep her, the baby. This had been discussed as there was no father in the picture to assume his responsibilities, though I am not sure we were prepared for the heartbreak after having seen her. We were to take her to an orphanage on the mainland and pray she was adopted by someone that would love and care for her. The idea of giving her to strangers was terrible but it was the only option for us.'

Ella and Georgia turned to each other with innate understanding. They had experienced the same with Phoenix and although the discovery of her true parentage remained an endless maze to traverse, at least she was with loved ones and not untraceable nobodies. Zina carried on and seemed to pick up on their train of thought.

'But then it was not our only choice anymore. An opportunity presented itself. My daughter asked if Anna would consider keeping her baby. It made sense as she had been present for the birth and essentially brought her into the world, only not from her own body. We could falsely register the birth under Anna's name and get a signatory from the clinic to confirm it was hers. My sister worked as an administrator at the hospital, which is why my daughter came to Hydra for the birth – here we had access to discreet medical support. But the way it happened, it was like it was taken from our hands, guided by another power. Suddenly, there was a clear way to know that our beautiful little light would be cared for. It was wrong for the right reasons, illegal to falsify such documents, but we could work around the laws to ensure our baby would be safe.'

As Zina had regaled her family's history, her eyes had mainly fixed on Ella's, but suddenly she turned to Georgia, and Vasílis mirrored Zina as he translated for her again.

'You were here, during the birth, playing with my ornaments in the other room. I sat with you while my daughter laboured with her child. You had lined up my figurines in a row and were chattering away. You were so small, but you had rearranged all the cabinet china and cushions into colour order. I remember thinking, this little girl needs a sister to care for. And this is precisely what happened, as though the gods heard me. We named the baby for the sunbeam that blessed her as she came into the world. Ella. In Greek, the name can mean the dawn or light. You are home, Ella *mou*, my Ella. You are home on Hydra once again. It has brought you back into its light and into my life by the grace of God and Anna's blessed hands.'

As Vasílis finished translating, Ella's mind raced, retracing what she'd heard while staring into the wise gaze of the woman who claimed to be her grandmother. Zina's dark green eyes glimmered and Ella recognised aspects of her own reflection – the shape and the secret whispers of past times floated in the ether. But she didn't know where to begin. The island that she'd hoped would be gone from her life had dug so far under her surface, it had now become her skin.

Georgia gasped and covered her mouth, and Ella instinctively knew she was about to fire an onslaught of queries. She allowed it, though, only because her own mind hadn't landed on a question she wished to begin with.

'And where do you fit in to all this, Vasílis?' asked Georgia.

He looked to his hands on the wooden table.

'Because Ella's mother was my father's step-sister. We are cousins, Ella.'

Ella had a moment of silent, temporary horror. She'd almost considered exploring their attraction, but, as it had transpired, they only had a friendly connection. Family energy. But that was the least of her worries. Ella stared at the plate of biscuits, her mind skirting through a myriad of questions. But still Georgia couldn't contain her curiosity.

'So, on Ella's birthday, when I saw you by our mother's old house—'

Vasílis smiled and interrupted. 'Yes, every year on Ella's birthday, Zina plants herbs in the boat that nearly took her grandchild's life. Your life,' he said as he turned to Ella. She felt Georgia shrink into her chair at the mention of the accident. 'The man who lives there now is very gracious and always leaves the side gate unlocked for Zina. He doesn't understand why we go there each June but thinks it simply a quirk of this island. He is very good with Zina and occasionally plays her music on the piano, which she enjoys. It is now a custom we share each year, although this year sadly he was not there on the day.'

Ella looked to Georgia as their family tree wrapped its branches outwards, entwining their past with their present.

'The man who lives in that house now, Harrison, is the father of … Ella's daughter. Zina's great-granddaughter. She is called Phoenix,' Georgia said, and she shared a look with Ella, signalling she was trying to find peace by calling Phoenix 'Ella's daughter'. The truth on this island kept coming, like a tsunami of emotion, and Ella wasn't sure how much more she could endure. As panic threatened to grip her throat, she considered the parallels of her and Phoenix's circumstances: both children yielded to adoption for the better life they would have.

Finally, after some time, she found her opening question with a small broken voice.

'Zina, what was my mother's name?'

'Elena,' replied Zina, somehow understanding Ella's question.

Vasílis added, 'It means bright, shining light.'

Just like Ella's own name. As she sat back in her chair, her mind drifted to Phoenix: the hope that had come from her and Harrison's bleakest of endings.

Out of the darkness, you will be the light.

Chapter 42
Ella

It was like a piece of a puzzle that she didn't know was missing had slotted into place. Ella had felt so different to Georgia and Anna growing up, within what she'd thought was her family. And those instincts had been confirmed with Zina's story of her hidden past.

It made sense, but she felt misled and duped, having spent her life trying to fit into a place where she did not. She should have been raised on Hydra among her blood family, the island where she truly belonged. As soon as the thought occurred to her, she acknowledged that she had done to Phoenix as Elena had done to her – though Phoenix had been raised by relatives... But no, she hadn't! Because Ella and Georgia were related only in name. They shared no genes, no similarities. Did this explain Georgia's innate resentment manifesting in the incident in the boat as children? Georgia had known Ella was a cuckoo and impulsively acted upon it, trying to nudge her out of the nest for good. Her mother – Anna – had done everything she could to ensure her comfort as a child, calling Ella her 'shining light', and it now made sense why, after hearing the story in the simple Greek kitchen.

She wished Harrison was with her, but she braved the

question she already knew the answer to as she picked up the photograph of her biological mother.

'Is Elena dead, Zina?' she asked both the photograph and her grandmother.

Her gaze left the picture briefly to see Zina's eyes cloud and she nodded sadly. It needed no translation. Ella looked at Elena's high cheekbones in the picture, which she recognised from Phoenix's face, and sought out her own features. She found them along with the identical chestnut curls and green eyes. How she wished to have photographed her beautiful mother, but she wasn't afforded the opportunity. She momentarily resented Anna for never telling her, but then said a silent thank you, which replaced any stirring anger. If it weren't for Anna's bravery, she could have ended up in an orphanage, trafficked or stuck in a system that wouldn't release her from its grip. She had been saved by circumstance, just as Phoenix had.

'Vasílis, would you ask Zina if I could come another time? I'd like her to meet Phoenix properly and I might have lots of questions. You don't have to be here, I can always use Phoenix's phone to translate.' Ella felt the weight of exhaustion press down on her body and longed to climb beneath Harrison's arm, to curl into a ball as this new information settled into her blood. Her blue and white Greek blood.

Vasílis nodded and spoke briefly to Zina who nodded concurrence and replied in rapid Greek.

'She says you must come for lunch tomorrow at one. She would love to cook for you and also you should bring the man who plays the piano. Zina is very fond of him.'

Ella smiled at the affection they shared for Harrison. She embraced Zina warmly, then saw Georgia looking a little dejected and said, 'Can my sister come too?' asked Ella, putting her hand in Georgia's whose eyes flooded with tears. Zina understood and agreed. Ella leant over to Georgia and whispered, 'Hey waterworks! You'll always be my sister. Don't you dare forget it.'

* * *

Each lost in their own thoughts, Ella and Georgia walked together down to the port. Away from the hubbub of the harbour, the side streets were so quiet, like on the clifftops. There was the occasional sound of mules' hooves, but the constant hum of tourists was absent. Birdsong, heat and a gentle breeze was all that accompanied them.

Georgia was the first to speak.

'Penny for them...'

Ella shrugged her shoulders.

'I don't know where to start, Georgia. And how do I tell Phoenix? She's been through enough and now has this to deal with.' She didn't mention Harrison's diagnosis; Phoenix deserved to know first and Ella was determined to do things in the right order from now on. 'Maybe it'll hit me later, but after the barrage of drama on this island, the more that arrives, the less dramatic it seems. Even though what we've just heard unpicks my entire family tree. But, like Phoenix, I feel like it makes sense.'

Georgia smiled.

'Weirdly, me too. I mean, it explains a lot. It's kind of amazing what Mum did. The system out here can be a bit loose. I researched overseas adoption when I hadn't got pregnant in the first two years of trying, and the Greek system historically used to be pretty vague. You could make a verbal agreement with adoptive parents, with no involvement from

327

the authorities, and just give your baby away. Or present at a clinic with a newborn, having agreed the adoption, and claim them as yours – as long as you got signed paperwork from someone medical, that's all you used to need. The laws have changed a bit but still, there are loopholes. Mum must have been so worried someone would find out she forged documents to get you. But blood or no blood, I guess we have that in common; we're all good at keeping secrets. Until we came back to Hydra that is.'

They walked onwards in silence until the wall of sound of the harbour wrapped them in its noise. They both stopped in front of the church entrance and looked up to Harrison's house. Ella's mind galloped through a thousand memories from her past and visions of how life could have been – should have been – if fate hadn't intervened.

The sisters looked at each other for a moment before their eyes returned to the cliffside.

'You're going to stay, aren't you? On the island,' Georgia said, not looking at her sister.

Ella took her hand and held it tightly, still gazing at the house she hoped to make a home.

'Yes, I am. I've loved him my whole adult life and this island has always haunted me. I thought it was for sinister reasons, but it seems it's where I'm destined to be.'

They stood in silence for a while before Georgia spoke.

'I wonder how Phoenix got on with Harrison today.'

Ella laughed.

'They've probably written a whole album by now.'

'Quite likely. She'll have loved chatting quavers and couplets with someone who understands.'

'Wow! Your musical knowledge is astonishing, sis!' Georgia laughed at Ella's kindly intended jibe. 'So, you didn't respond to my staying on Hydra. Are you going to be polite, Georgia, or be honest?'

Georgia couldn't help the sigh that escaped her lips as they ascended the steep hill towards the house, still hand in hand.

'I'm being protective. I don't want you to be hurt, by him or by anything. You barely recovered before and if it happened again, I'd be afraid of losing you. That feeling has been too familiar since we got here and I want you in my life, in Phoenix's. Please, Ella, this time guard your heart.'

They stopped to take a breather before the final sloping flight of steps.

'I have spent every moment since giving Phoenix up protecting myself from being hurt. And yet all I've achieved is distance from the people who only wanted to love me. I accused Harri of not opening his heart to me all those years ago, but I've inflicted that upon everyone I loved – you, Phoenie and Mum. My eyes are wide open now, and I know what I'm getting into, Georgia. I love him. I can't explain it any better than that. We're meant to be together, and I knew we would be, I just didn't know when or how. I hope we have a long and happy time with each other, like you and Oliver.'

Georgia shook her head sadly.

'I wouldn't be too sure about that. He'll hit the roof when he hears about what's been going on here, and the fact is that I'm not even related by blood to the little girl we raised. That's the saddest thing about all of this.'

Ella placed her hands on Georgia's shoulders.

'Hey, you are part of me and Phoenix and we're all still family whatever's happened. And I get double families like Phoenix has two lots of parents,' she said as Georgia eventually nodded in agreement, and they started to walk again. 'Are things with you and Oliver all right?' asked Ella.

'We're fine, of course,' she started. 'Actually, that's a lie. If I'm really honest, I'm not sure I love him anymore. And the feeling, I fear, is mutual. We're just pretending, living yet another lie. It's what you're supposed to do, isn't it? Keep up appearances and muddle through and hope for the best even when it's not what you thought it would be. The truth is, we haven't had sex for years, our couple's therapy isn't making a difference and I'm only useful to him to host dinner parties and impress his clients. He always does the right thing by everyone else but forgets about me. I'm sick of the pretence, Ella. I can't do it anymore. He never wanted me to carry on working when we got married; he resented it even before Phoenix so it was deeply convenient for him that I gave up my job to look after her. He then did everything to discourage me from pursuing my career again after she started school. By then it all seemed a bit late anyway, and I felt too old, too out of touch with everything. So, I focused on raising Phoenix instead of working – and look how that turned out. I've got very little to show for my life.'

'That's not true,' said Ella, trying to reassure her sister. They reached the house and sat down together on the front step, like they used to as teenagers.

'Isn't it?' replied Georgia. 'Phoenix is leaving for college in September. Divorce? Maybe. And then I'm alone, a forty-three-year-old spinster. Who'd want me?'

'Don't be silly. You're beautiful, Georgia,' Ella said, but Georgia shook her head in disagreement.

'I'm not and I'm impossible to live with.' She pressed her fingers to her temples. 'It's all gone to pot since we arrived on Hydra, hasn't it? Though, if I'm frank, it's been a mess for a long time. Everything just came to a head here, all at once. Quite efficient really, if you think about it. Just how I'd do it if I'd ever wished such hell to rain down on us.' She tried to laugh but made a small squeak instead.

Ella put her hand on Georgia's knee. She'd had no idea things were this bad for her sister, but she wasn't exactly a regular presence in her life, so how would she know if nobody told her the truth?

'I'm so sorry, I didn't know. I've not been there for you, have I? Maybe this is our chance to change, you and me.'

Georgia lifted her head, turning her tear-stained face towards Ella who continued.

'I can't stand the idea of you being miserable, feeling unloved, not desired. What can I do to help you fix this?'

'Just be my sister.'

'Always.'

Ella smiled and offered her little finger in promise which Georgia accepted. They held each other, garnering strength from their bond and the island air that swirled around them. As they parted, soft piano notes floated towards them from within the house.

'Come on, sis, no doubt it's concert time. Let's see what those musicians have been up to while my whole life was turned upside down. Also, I don't know about you, but I need to eat.'

'Then get cooking, Ella! I'm absolutely starving.'

Ella looked at her in surprise. Georgia admitting she was hungry for once was an incredible change.

'Just so you know, that was the very last time you get to boss me around. But yes, let's eat and drink and find a way to mend our funny little family. Together.'

The Island

The waves that lapped the outcrop began to calm as the wind stealthily retreated. The air relaxed, exhaling in relief; the tension contained within the rocks dissolved into sand and the whole island shifted its shape, undetected by mortals. But the gods felt it.

The storm that had brewed relentlessly began to yield to the beginning of a new tranquillity.

Tempests would always come, often when least expected, but that day, the sun shone brightly, making the light crisper than the first breath of dawn. The sea sparkled the deepest blue yet, waiting to welcome the sunset into its watery embrace. A contagious peace rippled around the cove. Conflict was born of surrender to truth; war rose from false harmony.

How destiny would unfurl, only the island knew.

Chapter 43

Georgia

Ella looked perfectly at home in the kitchen as she made dinner. Georgia couldn't help but feel like an intruder, but she shook off her discomfort and contributed by making a beautiful tablescape of wild flowers and, fittingly, olive branches. She wanted to add fresh herbs and stood nervously in front of the boat at the bottom of the garden, asking for forgiveness. She felt as though she found it with each frond of dill and stem of rosemary she harvested. Unearthing some candles from a kitchen cupboard, she placed them on saucers dotted around the patio table, ready to light when it was time to serve.

Phoenix was working her way through her entire jazz repertoire at the piano, while Harrison schooled from his chair. She received his tuition gladly. They had such a bond already, and Georgia experienced a pang of sorrow as she felt Phoenix slowly slipping through her fingers. Ella arrived at her side with a large glass of red.

'Get that down your neck and stop worrying. I've still got to tell them both about Zina.'

Georgia took a large gulp and Ella followed suit with her own drink.

'I ought to get back to the hotel tonight. I mean, Phoenix can stay with you if she wants, of course, but I need my things around me. You know what I'm like.'

'Well, I know it's not my house, but I'm sure you're welcome to stay here. Not just tonight but longer. We've only got a few days left and I don't want you to go yet.'

Georgia leant her head on Ella's shoulder as they listened to Phoenix play.

'I can't stay longer. We've got to get Phoenix ready for college in September wherever she ends up going. And here ... it's yours. It's where you belong. With Harrison.' She didn't expect Ella to help with the college preparations. In fact, she wanted those last moments with Phoenix as her little girl, to complete that part of parenthood. 'I think you should tell Phoenix about your Greek family alone. Go in the garden, just the two of you. It's important. She's had a lot to deal with and an audience might stress her out.'

Phoenix finished her piece with a flourish and they both applauded. She turned around on the piano stool and beamed at them.

'An audience doesn't seem to upset her at all,' whispered Ella to Georgia.

'You know what I mean,' said Georgia, still clapping enthusiastically.

'You guys...' Phoenix pretended to be coy, but like Ella, she was confident in her skin. She knew her gifts and was so self-assured it made Georgia's chest swell with pride. She knew she had done a wonderful job bringing her up. But now, that chapter was closing. Phoenix would leave to take her first step towards adulthood. And Georgia didn't know what life held for her anymore, without a daughter under her roof.

Ella went over to Harrison and kissed him. Georgia

couldn't help but gawp at their obvious mutual passion as his hand snaked around her neck, pulling her closer. They'd been like that from the moment she met them as a couple, and that spark hadn't diminished with time. She felt embarrassed to be watching and sad for the closeness she and Oliver had lost.

Thankfully, Phoenix broke the awkwardness.

'Please, try and control yourselves, you two. God, where's the wine?' She walked into the kitchen and poured herself a glass, asking Georgia permission first with her eyes. Georgia observed how well Phoenix fitted into the house, like she'd always been there. She also belonged on the island. After all, it was in her blood. Glass in hand, Phoenix slung her other arm around Georgia's shoulder and they watched Ella and Harrison giggling and whispering to each other.

'Phoenix, I'm going back to the hotel after supper. But stay here, don't let me stop your time with your … parents.'

'Nope, I'm coming with you. And I will say this for the last time, it changes nothing between us, OK? You're my mum and always will be.'

Georgia smiled at Phoenix, heartened that all was not lost.

'I wrote a song for you today with Harrison. I'll play it for you before we go.'

'Then I'm going to need a bigger glass,' joked Georgia, enjoying the carefree exchange between them, such a contrast to the tension that had blighted their time on the island. 'I think Ella might want to chat with you outside.'

'OK,' Phoenix shrugged and took her drink into the garden where Ella was now sitting.

Georgia looked to Harrison, unsure how to approach him. Despite their recent lighter accord, their history weighed heavily.

'Georgia, would you mind getting me some water? I need

to take my pills. That girl of yours is relentless and I missed a couple of painkillers. I think I've heard every jazz song ever written.' He laughed, but Georgia could see he was in pain. She was glad of the task. Taking a glass to him she perched tentatively on the piano stool, glancing occasionally to Phoenix and Ella outside. Her hands went to the keys but made no sound.

'Give us a tune, then,' Harrison said with a warm smile.

'I would have thought you'd had your fill for the day. Besides, I can hardly manage "Chopsticks", so you're out of luck. Phoenix gets all her talent from you.'

She raised her eyes to him, and he looked at her with a genuine empathy before saying, 'This can't be easy, Georgia. But nobody is going to replace you. Ella and I are just a strange added bonus for Phoenix for as long as we've all got left together.'

Georgia frowned.

'Why, where are you off to?' Her heart began to beat faster, hoping he wasn't confiding a secret she couldn't keep. Especially if it would hurt Ella or Phoenix. She looked to them in the garden again, their heads bowed together with the seriousness of their discussion.

Harrison laughed.

'I have no intention of leaving your sister. I wouldn't make the same mistake twice. Georgia, I love her. I need you to believe that and support Ella's choice because we are going to be together whether you approve or not. I'm going nowhere. Not in the way you think, at least.' He swallowed his pills with a gulp of water and adjusted his sling.

'Harrison, of course I support you. Anyone can see how happy you make Ella. But please, just spit it out, whatever it is you're trying to say.'

336

'Ella knows, and I told Phoenix today so you might as well be next. I have a diagnosis that means at some point in the future, and I don't know when…' His voice choked, and he took a breath to steel himself. 'I have the beginnings of a kind of dementia. It's very early, but it's happening. I forget things and sometimes it's like searching for a memory or a name through fog. It goes away for a bit now and again, but it will always come back. And eventually it will get worse. I want to get to know Phoenix as much as I can, before … before I don't know who anyone is anymore.'

Georgia couldn't feel her tongue. It was stuck to the roof of her mouth from the outrageous injustice of it all. After so long, Ella and Harrison had been reunited with the cruellest caveat: an expiry date looming somewhere in their future. She gently touched his forearm.

'I don't know what to say.'

He shrugged one shoulder.

'There's not much to say apart from you and I ought to put our differences aside and try to be friends. Those two will need you in the future.'

Georgia clasped her hands in her lap, attempting to stop emotion overtaking her as tears swam in her eyes. But they weren't hers to cry. It was incomprehensible that someone as talented as Harrison would one day sit at a piano and not know what to do. And poor Ella, headed once more towards heartbreak, though at least this time she knew it would be her destination.

Georgia's fingers lifted to trace the black and white keys again as she considered what the future looked like for her family. Despite not being related by blood, it didn't matter. She loved Ella and Phoenix fiercely and would rearrange the rocks around the island if she thought it would shield them.

She turned her head to Harrison.

'I will do anything you ask. If I can help you in any way, you only have to shout, call, send up a smoke signal ... anything. I'm here for you all.'

'Thank you, that means a lot coming from you, Georgia. I don't want the past to come between us. Any of us. And I know how to get hold of you. I've got your address, haven't I?'

Georgia smiled and accepted his barb about the letters she'd prevented reaching their intended recipient.

'That's the last jibe you're allowed, Harrison. I'm not saying I don't deserve it, but I was trying to protect the people I love. If we're to go forward as a family, then we need to put what's happened, if not behind us, then at least to the side.'

'Well, lucky for you, one day I won't remember any of it, and you can tell me a brand-new version of our story and I'll have no choice but to believe you.' His good humour shone through despite the heartache it surely must be disguising.

'You see, that's what's different about this trip to Hydra. It's put a stop to all the lies. And if you don't recall what a terrible sort of sister-in-law I am, then I will gladly remind you when the time comes. And you can hate me all over again.'

'Well, isn't that something to look forward to!' Harrison said, standing with difficulty and a groan. Once up, he grinned. 'Come here, Georgia. Bygones and new starts, yeah?'

She nodded and stepped into his embrace – taking care not to hurt his shoulder – firmly locking their differences away and allowing their chequered past to dissolve into the warm Greek air.

* * *

Ella had cooked the most incredible supper. It was Greek simplicity at its best: moussaka served with a beetroot and rocket salad.

This is absolute heaven, thought Georgia, as she scraped her dish clean having devoured every sliver. Their newly blended family had fallen into a surprisingly easy rhythm over their hearty meal in the balmy evening outside, and any tension had receded like a mist tumbling down a mountain side only to evaporate when it reached the sea. It was a glimpse of her future if she and Oliver parted ways, and suddenly it didn't feel so frightening. She still belonged to Phoenix and her sister; she wasn't alone.

Ella had shared today's discovery of her own parentage with Harrison in front of them all. While she did so, Georgia sat quietly admiring her emotional openness and measure. Ella had included her in the retelling of their visit to Zina's and she was grateful to be a part of it. Harrison was sympathetic, kissing the top of Ella's hand tenderly. It was fascinating to watch their love ebb and flow like a tide around the table. She reflected on Ella and Phoenix, who shared such similar origins. Both displaced at birth from their biological mothers, both creative and beautiful. And they each belonged on this rocky outcrop nestled in the Aegean that had haunted Georgia's dreams.

Ultimately, the island had set her free. And for that she was grateful.

The only outstanding question was whether her relationship with Oliver would survive. But that was outside her control, and Georgia was shocked to find she trusted in the universe to steer her on the right course. Their trip to Greece had changed everything for the worst and for the better.

She helped Ella clear the table and began to make her excuses to leave.

'Hang on a sec. Before we go, can I play you the song I

wrote – well *we* actually wrote – today?' said Phoenix.

'Of course, darling. I'd love to hear it,' replied Georgia as everyone moved into the lounge and sat around the piano.

'It's called "Mother". For you,' she said to Georgia, who gulped in anticipation.

Phoenix began to play and seemed to sing more beautifully than Georgia had ever thought possible.

'*Sunlight fades behind the clouds as rain begins to fall,*

'*Hearts will crumble with the roll of dice, fate can change it all,*

'*Although you didn't carry me, we'll always have each other,*

'*I'll love you when it all goes dark, my light, you are my mother.*'

As Phoenix continued to sing her exquisite composition, Georgia's heart swelled with an overpowering love, but also with grief. Their relationship would never be the same when they left Hydra.

As she reached the final verse, Phoenix suddenly stopped playing, overcome with emotion.

'Anyway, you get the gist.' Phoenix sniffled and looked around the room. 'I'm not usually a crier, but this is all a lot to process – even though I hate that word. Remind me again whose idea it was to come to this island?'

Georgia sheepishly raised her hand and said, 'In fairness, it was actually my mum who made us all come here.'

Phoenix shrugged.

'Maybe she wanted us all to find out. Would have been way more helpful to have told us before she died... But as we can't raise the dead to answer our questions, best to get it all out while we can. So, if anyone else has something they'd like to share...?'

Harrison laughed deeply and loudly, the sound filling the space. He fixed his warm brown eyes on Georgia. 'She has magic in that voice and she can really write. All those piano lessons seriously paid off.'

Georgia found herself blushing.

'I didn't really do anything; she had the gift to start with. That's your doing, Harrison.'

'Team effort, then,' he said, and Georgia beamed at him. She caught Ella's surprised look.

'Yes, Ella, we're friends now.' She paused briefly and softened her tone. 'Harrison told me about his illness and I'm determined to help you all and be here as much as I can.'

Ella stepped forward and said quietly out of the others' earshot, 'Put your own oxygen mask on before you rescue someone else, Georgia. Promise me you'll do that. Not for me, Phoenix, or any of us ... but for you. Please, for the first time in years, focus on what's right for you, sis.'

Chapter 44

Ella

As she climbed into bed beside Harrison, Ella felt content because, for the first time in her life, she had somewhere she wanted to stay. Not just next to him, but on Hydra. They were moths drawn to their twin flame, damaged by the disease of destiny but still surviving.

'Phoenix is incredible,' he said as she lay her head on his chest, taking care to avoid his injured arm. 'I can't believe we get to have her in our lives. Pretending she wasn't your own, El, for all those years must have been horrendous.'

She lifted her chin and looked up at him.

'Yes and no. You've seen her eyes, they're yours. Every time I looked at her, I fell in love with her even deeper, and with you all over again. It was torture. But look at who she has become. If we're honest, neither of us would have been any good for her. We were too young. We took everything precious for granted. And we were selfish, obsessed with going out into the world and making our mark, which is exactly what you should be doing when you're eighteen. I have to make peace with that. Despite all the heartache, it played out the best way it was supposed to, for all of us. We'll never get that time back, but we can do better with however long we've got left.'

Harrison pulled her closer.

'You're extraordinary. I would have gone mad in your situation. But it's led us here, to your island, together. And our daughter is here with us.'

Ella couldn't help the broadest of grins crossing her face.

'It's our island, Harri.' She traced his profile with her fingertips, drinking in every part of him. 'I won't be without you ever again.'

He sighed.

'You can't say that, love. My body will exist, but you know the day will come when I wake up and I don't know you anymore.'

She put her hand on his heart and said, 'But you will know me in here.'

He placed his hand over hers and closed it into a fist.

'You will always have my heart, my first and final love. No more chances; this is it. Me and you.'

They talked into the early hours about Zina and her family's story. There were still several gaps in the information she possessed – about how and when her biological mother had died and who she was. But when the time was right, the missing pieces would fall into place.

* * *

Saturday

The morning church bells woke her as they marked the start of the day. She was curled up into a tiny ball, her head still on Harrison's torso. She rubbed her eyes and watched him sleep for a while, drinking him in, just as she had done all those years ago in that same room in the winter when, unbeknown to them, they'd created Phoenix. The sound of his deep voice made her jump.

'You've successfully stared me awake,' he said as a smile crossed his lips, his eyes still closed. 'You should know what I look like by now.'

'I was just checking,' she said, sitting up and stretching her arms above her head.

'For what?' he asked, opening his brown eyes.

'That we're really here.'

He leant over to his dresser and took a painkiller.

'I promise we are. How are you feeling about seeing Zina again today?'

Ella considered her Greek relative as she stood to open the balcony doors off the bedroom.

'I feel weirdly fine about it, like having confirmation of something I've always felt deep down. Of course, I'm sad that my birth mother is dead, and I'll never know her. And Zina ... well, there's a bit of a language barrier so it'll be hard.'

'You'd better find a Greek language class and bond with your *yiayiá* then – that's "Gran" in Greek, if you didn't know. But El, you don't have to stay on the island out of pity for me.' He propped himself up on his working arm. 'You need to know what you're getting into. I don't mean to start the day this way, but you need to be certain. You can leave with Georgia and Phoenix and, if it's what you decide, I respect that, I won't love you any less.'

Ella allowed the rising sunbeams to light her face, hearkening back to the island sun that she'd learnt had kissed her when she entered the world. Turning from the window to look at him, the rush of love in her body was too much to stand without reaching for the source of her desire. She moved to the bed, climbing astride him. His need to be intimate immediately mirrored her own.

'Harri, I want you and us and our future,' she said in between kisses. 'Even if it's only a year, a week or a day, it's worth it. We've lost too much to lose each other again.'

She lifted her hips and guided him into her body, loving him as deeply as she could with all she had to give. The morning air cooled the layer of sweat on her skin, making her body acutely alert to every sensation, and Ella was determined to absorb every part of Harrison while they still had time. She needed to feel him within her, wrapped around her, to consume him physically as much as she could. She'd lived too long without him and as he re-took the space that had lain in wait for him for years, it felt like they were both finally home. It didn't matter where in the world they were, they belonged together. They'd been drawn back to their own fire, succumbing to whatever fate held for them. Two halves of the same whole, they completed one another. His eyes didn't leave hers as they climbed towards pleasure, and Harrison's hand reached for her heart as Ella's reached for his. They were joined inside and out, and their love would outlast their bodies, their flame burning like an echo on the island for an eternity.

* * *

Harrison and Ella met the shuttle boat as it moored in the harbour. Georgia and Phoenix disembarked, bringing with them hugs and kisses. Ella trusted the path they had all taken to reach this point, though she wished it hadn't taken near death and endless bickering to find their version of harmony.

She was grateful to have support as they began to walk to Zina's. Phoenix and Harrison quickly engaged in a discussion about song writing, arguing who was the greatest lyricist that had ever lived, and Ella observed silently as they discovered their relationship's natural rhythm.

'Peas in a pod,' remarked Georgia as she watched them conversing ahead. She was holding a bunch of flowers and a box of baklava she'd bought from the hotel gift shop. Ella hadn't thought to bring a gift and she wished she had Georgia's elegance. Sometimes.

'Phoenix will find out soon if she's got any offers for college. I'm a nervous wreck!' added Georgia.

Ella's pulse picked up pace.

'God, poor Phoenie, I remember that feeling, like your whole life depended on it. At least she has a distraction with Zina and Harri.'

Georgia managed a tight smile.

'Ella, are you quite certain you want me with you? This is your family, not mine. I don't want to intrude.'

Ella stopped walking.

'Don't make me repeat myself. You *are* my family, more so, in fact, than anyone else. Yes, I bloody well want you with me. But hand over the flowers so I can pretend they're from me. I'm already a rubbish granddaughter.'

'Are *you* bossing *me* around now? My, you have changed on this island.'

They continued to weave along the side streets, and through the alley littered with the oversized cacti in pots where Ella had first met Zina and helped her with her bags. She took photographs of the towering plants, the midday sun casting elongated spikey shadows on the whitewashed stone walls. It was like seeing everything for the first time. Ella saw Georgia watching her capture the beautiful light. Today felt overwhelming, but through the narrow lens of her camera, a calm was restored, and she hummed appreciation as she appraised her shots. Georgia looked like she had something to say, but Ella pre-empted her speech.

'Before you say it, no, I'm not giving up work. But I can be selective about what I do. I can sell my flat in London or let it out, and I've got savings and the money from Mum's house too. I'm not cut out to be a kept woman...'

'Like me, you mean?' said Georgia.

'I don't think I said that – that's your stuff, not mine, sis. You know I'm not one for convention, but I'm not going to stop my career to play house, not completely anyway. I just want to enjoy the novelty of putting down roots. I thought you'd be pleased.'

'I am,' insisted Georgia. 'I just don't want you to lose yourself in all this. Your incredible free life and mad treks across the world are what make you, you.'

'No, Georgia, that's what I *do*. That's the difference. I'm not defined by a job, or by whatever society reckons I should or shouldn't have done. You should stop caring about what people think.'

Georgia looked up at the orange bell tower and Ella covertly took her portrait. Her pale skin was now lightly tanned, freckles peppered the bridge of her nose, and her features were relaxed, less tight. A weight had been shed. If Georgia could see the photographs Ella had taken on their overnight stop in Athens compared to this one, she wouldn't recognise herself. Greece suited Georgia. It had not only lifted the burden of secrets, but also the binds that tied her to convention and duty. Those shackles were the source of her unhappiness – the endless need to do what was 'right'. *It must be exhausting to be her,* she thought.

'Come on, you two!' shouted Phoenix from up ahead, and Ella moved her lens towards her. Cast in sunlight, Harrison and Phoenix stood side by side, looking over their shoulders to face her. She caught the moment before they realised she was taking their picture. She knew it was one she would always hold in her heart. Her daughter standing beside Harrison, her father, on the day Ella took her to meet a newly discovered blood relative. As she looked at the digital display, she zoomed in on their faces. Their identical eyes formed the same shape as they smiled, and their height made the alleyway seem so narrow and small.

'Go up and join them, Georgia,' said Ella.

The three of them posed together in the technicolour surroundings; bright pink bougainvillaea tumbling over a wall behind them, merging with a second plant, which boasted zinging scarlet flowers. An unlikely combination, but they went together beautifully, colliding in an unusual yet complementary fashion. The sentiment could be applied to both the foliage and her family.

Chapter 45

Ella

July

Ella knocked confidently on Zina's door, despite the nerves buzzing around her tummy. A hum of murmuring chatter and music came from within, and the scent of grilled lamb spoke directly to her stomach like a guitar player was strumming her hunger. Vasílis opened the door.

'*Yiá sas*! We have much to celebrate, and you are all welcome.' He kissed Ella on both cheeks, and she introduced him to everyone, even though he already knew them. Vasílis didn't know it was to save Harrison's blushes in case he didn't remember. She would always have to be mindful of his condition and whether it was a good day for him or not.

The shrine with its flickering scented offerings was in the hallway, the photograph of Elena, Ella's birth mother, was back in its place since she last saw it on the kitchen table yesterday. She paused beside it and Harrison placed a hand on her shoulder as Phoenix peered at the picture.

'Is that her?' she asked.

Ella nodded, unsure what to feel about it. How could she

form any attachment to a dead stranger? She would never know this woman; although the thought caused a quiet, regretful sadness, she still had Zina and Phoenix – both a product of her family's genes. She would know her mother through the surviving bloodline.

Inside the house, there was an unexpected crowd of people who had spilled out into the garden. The smell of charring meat filled every room and there was an infectious atmosphere of celebration with no obvious occasion. Ella took Harrison's hand and Vasílis guided them to seek out Zina. Passing the kitchen table, which had been pushed against the wall, Ella saw there was an incredible amount of food piled high. Traditional bouzouki music was playing from a battered stereo on the countertop and Georgia humbly placed her offering of baklava where she could find a spot among the elaborate home-made buffet.

In the garden, beneath a large pomegranate tree, Zina was sitting in a chair, the matriarch of the family presiding over her guests. It was surprising how far the back yard stretched, given the narrow alley the house was nestled within.

'These are all your cousins one way or another,' said Vasílis, gesturing to the gathering as Ella gawped at the astonishing amount of people crammed around the patio and into the garden. 'Not all of them know the story of your mother, but they know you are somehow a relative. We are used to large, extended families and it's a good excuse for a party.'

Zina spotted them approaching and beamed a satisfied grin. Ella couldn't help but return the smile. It was unlikely she would find any answers to her questions today, given it wasn't the intimate lunch she had been expecting, but it could wait for another time. Ella greeted Zina, pressing the flowers into her hands, which she placed on her lap. She gestured to Phoenix who crouched down beside the chair. Zina brought a hand to Phoenix's cheek in a gesture so familiar to Ella and to Harrison. They turned to look at each other, sharing the special moment as their daughter formally met her great-grandmother. Zina's beady eyes drifted towards Harrison, and she nodded, smiling broadly, miming a piano, which made him laugh. She said something to him in Greek, and he looked to Vasílis for help.

'She says, the piano man will make my family happy with his music and his heart if he can make it open. Does that make sense? Sorry, I don't know if I translated it correctly.'

Harrison nodded.

'It makes perfect sense, Vasílis.' Harrison blew Zina a kiss and she giggled, blushing a little. He then put an arm around Georgia and brought her into the group. 'Can you translate this for me? Remind her this is Georgia, Ella's sister.'

'Adoptive sister, yes?' asked Vasílis.

'Ella's sister,' repeated Harrison seriously.

Vasílis carried out the request and Zina's eyes lit up and she nodded. She patted the chair next to her and invited Georgia to sit, chattering away as she sank into the chair.

Vasílis interpreted.

'Zina says, "You are part of my family also. Your mother, Anna, saved us all and you, Georgia, are given a special place in my heart. If it weren't for the care that runs through your blood, we would not be here today. You will always have a place at my table. You are one of the island's people."'

Ella watched Georgia's emotions flash across her face, moved by the gesture of inclusion. It was affirmation that they still belonged to one another, no matter what had transpired, and that they all had a bond with Hydra that could never be severed. It was the kind of place that pulled you back into its bosom like a magnet, compelling you to return over and over until you couldn't bear to leave.

'Now, you all must eat!' said Vasílis as Zina nodded, gesturing to the barbecue that was billowing smoke up into the clear blue sky. Ella didn't need asking twice; she led Harrison towards the mouth-watering food, leaving Georgia with Phoenix and Zina.

After accepting offers of skewered vegetables and various grilled meats fresh from the charcoal, Ella carried their plates over to a cluster of beanbags at the far end of the garden. Harrison sat down with some difficulty, given his height and sling, which made sinking to the ground a challenge.

'Could you have found somewhere more awkward to sit? It's all right for you, you're tiny.' He smiled as she handed him a fork and balanced the plate on his thigh.

'Do you want me to feed you?' she said, half joking.

'Not here,' he replied, his eyes sparkling with desire. 'Later.'

She leant forward to kiss him, enjoying the taste of sunshine on his lips. His flavour and scent was unique to him and it spoke to her heart, as if his perfume had been created just for her.

'Are you doing OK, El?' he asked as he returned to his lunch.

'I am. I feel good – better than that, in fact. I get to discover a whole part of my life that I didn't know about. I feel like I'm excavating my own history. It's exciting in so many ways. Of course, I'm sad I never got to meet Elena, but what Mum did for her and for me was selfless, risky and completely made of love.'

'Also highly illegal,' said Harrison, picking at a piece of lemon-marinated chicken. Ella had already eaten some. It had a dark, charred coating but was deliciously soft and tender inside.

'I know. She was such a rule follower like Georgia. She compromised her profession as a midwife forging those documents, and I respect what it would have taken for her to do that. But in a way, Georgia did the same for me with Phoenix, although she legally adopted her. I have nothing but admiration for them both. The idea that I or Phoenix could have ended up with a stranger or stuck in an orphanage is horrible, and it so nearly could have happened if it weren't for Anna and Georgia. Like mother, like daughter.' She smiled, her eyes drifting towards her sister.

Georgia must have sensed Ella's stare and she turned, catching her eye. She moved towards them from the shelter of a large tree and picked up Ella's camera. She took a photo of Harrison and Ella. 'Why don't I take a picture of you, Phoenix and Zina? Three generations together. Finally united on Hydra,' she said.

'Are you sure?' asked Ella, rising to her feet. She noted that the subtle, passive jives were gone from their relationship. They had broken their destructive pattern with honesty.

'Of course. I can't say it'll be as good as your pics, but I'll give it a go.' Georgia ushered Ella across the lawn towards Zina.

As she stood between her daughter and grandmother, Ella took her own picture with her heart, committing the moment to memory. She didn't want her sister nor Phoenix to leave Hydra, but she knew in her bones they would be back. They'd be drawn by the lure of the waves that kissed the shore, and the healing sunlight on the magical rocks in the ocean that belonged to them. It was their island and always would be.

***

On the way back from Zina's, Ella stopped at the mini-market for food. The amount of bags she'd filled meant a pony needed to be called to transport it up the steep hill to Harrison's house. As they waited outside the store, Phoenix suddenly walked away from the group, glued to her phone, scrolling frantically on the screen.

'Oh God, she's heard about one of the colleges,' said Georgia in a tight voice, grabbing Ella. She began audibly muttering prayers to the sky and Ella put a hand on her arm.

'Prayers are too late, sis. She'll end up where she's meant to.' But Ella felt incredibly tense. She didn't know how she'd comfort Phoenix if the news was bad. She'd never had to do such critical parenting before, and she also didn't wish to tread on Georgia's toes. It would be a precarious tightrope of tact going forward.

After what seemed like an age, Phoenix turned to face them all. She walked to Harrison and showed him her phone, saying, 'What do you think...?'

Ella looked at Georgia but neither of them dared to take a breath or speak until they knew what they were dealing with. Harrison frowned before allowing a grin to spread across his face. He kissed Phoenix on the side of her head and hugged her with his available arm.

'What does your gut tell you?' he asked.

Phoenix jumped up and down and twirled in excitement.

'Then that's where you're headed. Congratulations, Phoenix. For what it's worth, I'm so proud of you, not that I have any right to be, but—'

Phoenix interrupted him. 'You have every right to be. If it weren't for you, I wouldn't have any musical talent; nobody else can hold a tune in this family. Don't ever ask any of them to sing! So, yes, you may be proud of me!'

'You should call your dad, Phoenix,' Harrison said gravely.

Georgia cleared her throat loudly, waving comically.

'Would someone care to fill me in? Fill us in, please…? Standing over here in the dark…'

Phoenix almost galloped over.

'I got in! Well, subject to my grades being what they've asked for…'

'*Where!?*' Ella and Georgia shouted at the same time.

'I've only heard about one so far, but it's the one I wanted. Mums, I'm off to the Royal Academy. I can't believe it.'

The three of them danced around in a circle, squealing with elation. It was the first time Phoenix had called Ella 'Mum', perfectly including Georgia too. They stopped when they heard a loud click and saw that Harrison had taken a picture with his phone.

'That is a moment I want to remember forever. Now, Phoenix, please call Oliver, he deserves to know your incredible news.'

'OK, Dad,' she replied wearily at being nagged, and wandered off with her phone. Harrison took a step back, like someone had punched him in the chest.

'Did she just … did she call me…' He couldn't finish his sentence and he clutched his heart like he was afraid it would stop. Ella looked to Georgia to check if she was upset, but instead she beamed as she watched Harrison experience his first taste of being a parent.

Georgia moved to him.

'I never thought you were such a softie, Harrison, given previous form. Welcome to parenthood. Oh, and get used to the tears – they don't stop coming.'

Harrison managed to gather himself.

'You have made all of this possible, Georgia. Which seems unlikely – given previous form,' he echoed her response from seconds before. 'But the truth is, I think you're more amazing than all of us put together.'

Georgia blushed scarlet before recovering.

'Well maybe as a thank you, you could write a song all about me!'

'I think Phoenix has done that better than I ever could,' he replied, reminding her of Phoenix's composition.

They travelled up the hill to Harrison's house, with the pony behind them laden with groceries, drumming their passage with its hooves. Harrison whispered words of love in Ella's ear as they walked side by side, his arm slung around her shoulders. They fitted perfectly, like two halves of the same mould. There was no clunky rhythm or awkward jarring of body parts. It was easy, and Ella couldn't think of anywhere she wanted to be more than in his embrace on Hydra.

Her initial reaction to Georgia first mooting the idea of Hydra months ago to scatter their mother's ashes suddenly struck her as amusing. She'd avoided the island for as long as she could, yet now her whole family was together in her birthplace, stepping into the light with truth rather than dwelling beneath the cloak of darkness in deceit. She didn't want anything to spoil her elation and she clung on to the happiness she felt. She knew she would need it during the inevitable difficulties to come, when the person who would give her the most joyful memories became only a memory himself.

*   *   *

'Cheers, *Yiá mas!*' said Phoenix as they all raised their glasses after finishing their dinner at Harrison's house. 'This has been the most memorable trip for the very wrong and the very right reasons. And I'm toasting myself. So, if you could all repeat carefully after me... Hooray. For. Phoenix!'

Everyone couldn't help but agree and they dutifully repeated her words, laughing and marvelling at the extraordinary young woman at the table, and clinking their drinks to congratulate her on her college offer. She'd united them all and would be the glue that held them together as they repaired. There were only a handful of days left together for now, and Ella didn't want it to end. They were all setting out on new and unexpected journeys of their own, but in tandem.

Phoenix helped Ella clear the table and piled the dirty dishes in the kitchen beside the butler sink before running the tap to mask her question from the others.

'Harrison's going to be all right, isn't he? I mean, if I come back in August, he'll still know who I am?'

'Oh, Phoenie, of course he will. It won't happen that quickly. Not for a long while, I'm sure. But we don't know for certain. He's undergoing treatment to delay the memory loss, but we need to take each day as it comes.'

Phoenix nodded sadly before saying in a wavering voice, 'I've only just found him, I don't want to lose him.'

Ella couldn't help but agree. They shared the same sentiment about Harrison, a different love but an identical spirit. She didn't want any more sadness to blight their moments together.

'Well, here's the good news, Phoenic. I'm getting a phone, so you can speak to me whenever you want, and I'll keep you updated with how he is. At least if things get tricky in the future, it won't come as a terrible shock.'

'I think I've had a lifetime of those this holiday. We all have,' Phoenix replied.

'Listen,' started Ella, 'I need to speak to Georgia about it first, but you can always live in my flat in Camden, if you want a place that's yours. It's not far from your college and my sister can redecorate the whole thing, in beige if she likes! I just want to help. It's time I made a contribution.'

Phoenix squirted washing up liquid under the hot water and watched the bubbles foam and rise.

'You have doubled the size of my family in less than a fortnight. I'd say that's a pretty great contribution.'

Epilogue
Georgia

Saturday, one week later.

Georgia waved frantically from the ferry window. It was hard to know if it was the dirty glass coated in salt spray or her tears that made it hard to see.

Ella and Harrison returned their own frenzied waves from the harbour in front of the museum. They then started to walk to the edge of the headland where the naval statue presided over the sea. Georgia's blurry vision tracked their progress, watching them wrapped around each other.

'Don't cry, Mum. We'll be back soon. Together.'

Phoenix took Georgia's hand as she sat back into her seat and closed her eyes. Georgia was buoyed by the fact she still was a thought in Phoenix's future, especially in relation to Hydra.

'Ella will be fine, won't she?' Georgia wasn't really asking Phoenix; she was asking the island.

The boat engine started with a growl as the mechanical pitch rose, summoning action from the vessel, and the ferry rocked from side to side. It was as though Hydra had answered her through the waves.

'She has love and is loved just as much – if not more – in return. I reckon she'll be better than fine,' replied Phoenix. 'But what about you?'

'Amazingly, I feel great,' answered Georgia with complete honesty. 'I actually am, though I'm quite pleased to be leaving Hydra for a bit.'

Phoenix opened her eyes and looked at her.

'No, I meant do you have love? An all-consuming, "don't want to fall asleep because I love them too much" kind of love?'

Georgia breathed in and out.

'Yes, Phoenix, I do. I have you.'

The only loose end yet to be tied up was Oliver and her marriage. She had to find faith that she had been led a merry dance by Hydra for good reason. As she watched, the island became a distant line on the horizon before it eventually disappeared from view.

'Only time will tell,' she whispered to herself.

Epilogue
Phoenix

August, one month later

Grown-ups were the exact opposite of what they should be sometimes. *They make life ridiculously complicated for themselves,* Phoenix thought.

She packed the first of three suitcases ready to move into Ella's flat in Camden. A fourth smaller bag held clothes for her journey to Hydra tomorrow ahead of starting at music college at the end of September. A whole month with Ella and Harrison stretched ahead and she was so excited about it. She would turn eighteen on the island, which felt like a new dawn for her and her newly drawn family. Phoenix looked at the stunning black and white photograph of Zina that Ella had taken before any of them knew who she was. A moment before everything changed. Ella had had it framed and gave it to Phoenix, along with enough photographs from their trip to fill the album she'd bought on the island. She put them on top of her bags.

Phoenix had made a vow to herself and to Hydra as she'd stood in the garden of Harrison's house before leaving in July: she would never lie to someone she loved, even if the truth was hard to deliver. When you lied, someone inevitably ended up hurt, and what was hidden always found a way to rise up, making everyone a victim in matters of the heart. She'd witnessed and felt that too keenly of late.

Her life could have been so different had Ella brought her up. But then she wouldn't have had Georgia as her mother. And if she was truly frank, she wouldn't have changed it for the world. She'd had a loving family and a privileged upbringing that allowed her to pursue her musical talent. But it could have turned out so much worse when she'd learnt the truth about them all. Love was sacred and should never be taken for granted. She'd decided that *Sacred Love* would be the title of the album that she was going to record with Harrison. It would include her composition for Georgia – called 'Mother' – and 'The Island Love Song', the piece she'd written for her granny to scatter her ashes on the water.

Upon reflection, Phoenix had always known she shared a deeper connection with Ella. Something hidden within her had told her that her auntie was so much more, though her younger self thought it a fantasy, nothing more than a childhood obsession. It was why Phoenix had immersed herself in dedication for music; it was her only way of making sense of her conflicting and confusing world. Ella had done the same with her photography, and their unfiltered and divergent way of understanding their surroundings set them apart and ultimately bonded them. Their perceived strength they shared also hid a fragility that could, sometimes, become overwhelming. She knew her thoughts were far more complex than Georgia and Oliver had ever known. They'd also underestimated Phoenix's capacity for observing and over-hearing snatched conversations and whispers.

For all her insight, when the truth had eventually been revealed, she couldn't help but feel displaced and ungrounded, which was worse than the deception that had fuelled those feelings. But after being back in London for a few weeks, she was comforted by the knowledge that one part of her complicated family was happy out on Hydra.

As for the other...

Before they'd left she'd also asked the island to guide Georgia, to seek out satisfaction for herself. She gave her all to everyone she met, but forgot to give to herself. Whether she'd manage it or not, only time would tell.

Epilogue
Ella

Sunlight streamed through the open windows. The surprising part of living in Greece was the unexpected sunshine in the depths of winter. But she didn't resent her sleep being broken by the novelty of Hydra's golden beams.

The early morning clarity was stunning, like nowhere else on earth. The air was clear and clean without cars on the island – save for the rubbish truck that careered around corners sending the native cats fleeing each day. The rolling mounds within the cliff formations, the characters on the front and the ever-changing sea photographed like nowhere she'd ever visited.

She wrapped a woollen blanket around her shoulders to ward off the early chill and stood in front of the open windows. On the floor beside her was a suitcase for her work trip to Italy tomorrow. Harrison was coming with her and even though she'd miss Hydra, they'd be back in a week. The island sparkled quietly in the watery sunshine, its colours muted compared to the glorious vibrancy of summer technicolour. Time seemed to have accelerated since she'd moved there and Phoenix's month-long visit in August was not nearly enough. It had been a nerve-racking joy having her to themselves before Georgia arrived for a week to celebrate Phoenix's eighteenth birthday. The bond between Harrison and Phoenix was built rapidly as they had so much in common. It had been like watching identical spirits dance around each other with words and music, writing together and creating a magic that was theirs alone.

Georgia had returned again with Phoenix for a wonderful island Christmas – their first in their new family incarnation, and it was beautiful. Her new Greek family and cousins welcomed them all into their lives and they had celebrated with party after party, marking every moment, creating precious memories that would endure beyond any heartbreak ahead.

Georgia was changed, more so than any of them. Ella and Harrison were navigating the novelty of each other while being thrust into parenthood, whereas Georgia was well practised at that role.

What she was unfamiliar with was the challenge of single life.

As she'd predicted, Oliver's temper had erupted. No matter how hard Phoenix reassured him that she understood and accepted the circumstances that had led to them keeping her parentage a secret, Oliver still blamed Georgia with a simmering resentment for unmasking what they'd agreed to keep hidden. He said she wasn't the person he'd married anymore, that she'd duped him by withholding who she actually was. He couldn't see past her past.

Their break-up was a huge shame after their decades of marriage, but Ella had always thought him a bit of an uptight prissy prig and Georgia would benefit from learning who she was all over again without him.

She much preferred the new Georgia, who flirted outrageously with Vasílis, and she positively encouraged their liaison. She'd made new friends and started her own business. Georgia was finally living her own life. When she next came back to the island with Phoenix for Greek Easter, Ella was determined to matchmake, or at the very least facilitate a fling for her sister.

Ella lay down on the bed, facing a sleeping Harrison. The thrill of their new now hadn't diminished; it had increased. His eyes blinked open, and he looked at her. She absorbed his beautiful brown eyes, searching them for which Harrison they'd bring into that day. She sought out a flicker of acknowledgement, but he stayed still for what felt like an eternity. Ella did not dare to breathe. Their history began to replay through her mind, slowly at first but with increasing pace:

The river in Guildford.

The train station.

Harrison behind the door of her mother's old house.

Harrison kissing her for the first time on Hydra.

Harrison refilling the space in her body as he'd made love to her again.

Telling Harrison about their baby.

His hands on the piano.

Harrison realising Phoenix was their daughter.

She waited as he stared, their gazes circling, reaching, searching for one another. Her pulse seemed to pause as the world hung in precarious balance. It was barely detectable, but she felt her eyes widen a fraction as she waited. Finally, his eyes creased at the edges, and he smiled. Pulling her towards him, he kissed her with a passion that seemed to grow each day. How many years they had left of their love, neither of them could know. The gift of time was a luxury they didn't possess, but they could bask in every second, trying to catch up on the years they'd forsaken, making up for them with each brush of their lips. Ella breathed him in, taking photographs with her mind, body and heart, cherishing each second. As she returned his kiss, she whispered a prayer to the island:

'Don't take him from me. Let me have my love, Hydra. Please, give us the time we need.'

She was about to alter their lives in the most unexpected and welcome way. All the moments they'd lost with Phoenix, they could win back, not only with her, but with the miracle treasure growing inside her. Their baby would arrive at the beginning of autumn. Yet another shaft of light to keep the darkness at bay. She only hoped Harrison would remain with her, present and able to bear witness. But that was up to fate. It was out of her hands.

Harrison pulled back, his honeyed eyes shining brightly as their hearts tangled together.

'Morning, love.' He cupped her cheek with his hand, running his thumb over her soft olive skin. He breathed out and they stared at each other with the unconditional elation of requited love, the greatest power there was. It would outlive any island rockface that succumbed to the waves' erosion, transcending all powers of mortal understanding. They had made another joy born of their love on Hydra, re-fuelling their flame to blaze more strongly than ever.

'Morning you,' she replied, mirroring his gesture. His hand travelled to hers, clutching her close as he inhaled the crisp island morning. 'I have you for another day, my Harri.'

He smiled and reached for her again.

'I have you for another day, my beautiful El.'

The air vibrated with a magical energy as sunbeams pierced

the glass, dousing their bodies with the island light, as if it were claiming them. Ella pushed Harrison's hand down to feel the small swell of her belly. The child growing in her body was created from a great love, grown from the echoes of their history that lived within the ancient cliffs surrounding Hydra. Reuniting was their destiny. Whether they'd have months or decades together, only time would tell. But their twin flame would always glow brightly on the island and would burn yet for a thousand ages to come.

Acknowledgements

This book amongst many things is a celebration of every possible version of parenthood. There is no such thing as a perfect family nor textbook way to be a mother or father, but it is an exploration of nature and nurture. It was, in a way, inspired by the displacement and division of so many families in the history of Greece through conflict, which sadly remains present throughout so many parts of the world. I also want to thank those who shared with me their beautiful experiences of adopting or being adopted.

My story is dedicated to Greece and the people of the country that I love with my heart and soul! The warm welcome my novels have received in the place where I've set them has been overwhelming and humbling. In summer 2023 when I was writing this novel, my debut – *One Last Letter from Greece* – was published in the Greek language by Pedio Books. If you've read it, you'll know that the beautiful seaside corner of Methoni where it is set is called 'heaven on earth' in the book. And it truly is! The Friends of Methoni Castle and various educational establishments throughout Messenia held an event to honour my debut – to say I shed a few tears would be a considerable understatement! It was like living a dream and I will remember that night always. To have such a response to my love and passion for Greece from its residents is more than I could ever have imagined.

I want to thank my 'Methoni family' including Nikos and Eglé at Ulysses Hotel for spreading the word, Antonis and the wonderful team supporting and preserving Methoni Castle, my soul sister Katérina, Liza for your incredible translation skills, Debbie and friends for driving from Mount Olympus armed with delicious olive oil to say hello, Maria at the Anemele bookshop and all the readers who came along to celebrate my first novel, Methoni style! To Christina, Sofia, Yiula, Mina, Vasílis, Angelos, Athina, to name a few of my overseas family, and to the Hydra Pirate Bar gang – the inimitable Wendy, dear Zeus and Fiona and all the cats, especially one-eyed Jack! I love you all and miss that beautiful island – it changed my life and I'm coming back soon!

My foreign publishers, Pedio, Insel Verlag, Muza, Grada, Eksmo, Forlarget Zara and the super talented translators, thank you all.

I continue to be astounded by the support of **you** – the reader! Thank you for buying this story and for the lovely messages I am lucky enough to receive about my writing. To the wonderful book bloggers, bookstagrammers and reviewers, you have no idea how much your encouragement means, and this authoring lark would be ever so lonely without you all. The booksellers – your enthusiasm and passion shine through and it will never get old seeing my novel on a shelf or in a shop window.

Kate Burke, my other twin flame. Thank you for being such an amazing friend and agent and to the team at Blake Friedmann for flogging my stories around the world – thank you and please keep on doing it!

Team Avon... every single one of you believed in me from the get-go and I want to say a huge thank you to you all for continuing to bring my books into the world. Every one of you have such passion, so thank you all. Also, my fabulous editor Sarah Bauer, Helen Huthwaite for steering the ship with elegance and ease, the comms and marketing team, the brilliant sales gang and Rella – thank you for smiling sweetly when I practise the less savoury elements of my Greek vocab on you! Thank you Anna Nightingale and Vasiliki Machaira for Greek-checking and adding the beautiful accents!

My dearest family and fabulous friends, your belief in me and support keeps me going as I juggle this new world – I am grateful for your forgiveness when you don't hear from me enough or I'm late with cards because I'm in a writing rabbit hole! My darling Mum, I think of you every day and endeavour to make you proud with the words I write. TC, my first ever reader! Your patience, pep talks and expert eyes help me immeasurably; your love and care spurs me on every day and I literally and literarily wouldn't be here without you. Thank you to my friends who candidly shared their experience of the twin flame phenomena. And coincidentally after finishing this book, I unearthed that twin flames have their roots in Greek mythology too. Fascinating! Thank you, Dad, for your endless support and the Moss and Grumett family for all the inspo! Jamie – I promise you're in the next book! And last but by no means least, Harrison and Georgia, our fabulous niece and nephew. Georgia you are nothing like your fictional namesake (thank God!) and you are one of my favourite people on the planet. You inspired in some way every female character I wrote – with your many questions (Phoenix) and your feral early years and creative flair and untethered approach you take to your life (Ella) – I adore you and never change. And real-life Harrison, I know you will have every success in music because you are quite brilliant, and we are so proud of you. I fear our little band we formed to amuse our family, Slinky Blanket, will be dust in the wake of your incredible future ahead. You two give me joy and thank you for inspiring me. And well done Nicholas and Katie for making two exceptional human beings!

And finally, some things are destined to be together like Harrison and Ella, and should never have been parted; like the Elgin Marbles (Parthenon Sculptures to use their correct name) and the Parthenon. I hope they can be reunited one day soon ... At the time of writing at the end of 2023, they were still inexplicably being kept apart and not returned to their home in Greece.